ALSO BY DENNIS BOCK

The Ash Garden

Olympia

THE COMMUNIST'S DAUGHTER

THE COMMUNIST'S
DAUGHTER

A NOVEL

DENNIS BOCK

ALFRED A. KNOPF   NEW YORK   2007

THIS IS A BORZOI BOOK
PUBLISHED BY ALFRED A. KNOPF

Originally published in Canada as a Phyllis Bruce Book,
by HarperCollins Publishers Ltd., Toronto, in 2006.

Grateful acknowledgment is made to Alfred A. Knopf, a division of Random
House, Inc., for permission to reprint excerpts from "Sunday Morning" and
"Thirteen Ways of Looking at a Blackbird" from *The Collected Poems of Wallace
Stevens*. Copyright © 1923 and renewed 1951 by Wallace Stevens. Reprinted by
permission of Alfred A. Knopf, a division of Random House, Inc.

Library of Congress Cataloging-in-Publication Data
Bock, Dennis.

The communist's daughter / Dennis Bock. — 1st American ed.
p. cm.

ISBN 1-4000-4462-6 (hardcover)
1. Bethune, Norman—Fiction. 2. Sino-Japanese Conflict, 1937–1945—Fiction.
I. Title.

PR9199.3.B559C66 2007
813'.54—dc22   2006047384

Manufactured in the United States of America
First United States Edition

For my magnificent sons, Adam and Oliver

The enclosed manuscript was found at Huang-shih K'ou, Hopei Province. It was likely written in the Chin-ch'a-chi Border Region, north China, sometime between May 1938 and November 1939. Included among its 448 pages were numerous medical illustrations, a telegram, a newspaper clipping, a personal letter and drawings.

Each member of the committee will be asked to provide recommendations regarding suitability for translation and wide distribution throughout the territories of the Border Regions.

Recommendations will be considered and incorporated into the final report made by this Office.

Major Lu Ting-yi,
Director of the Propaganda Department
   of the Central Committee of the Chinese
   Communist Party, Yan'an, Shensi Province

ENVELOPE ONE

It is my hope that your understanding will win out against any mistrust or anger you may harbour against me when you finally read this. It is so easy to feel anger, and Lord knows I deserve a good dose of it. But I am trying, and you will see I have been trying for quite some time. I also hope that you will read this many years from now, when you are grown, at a time when this story will be long past. With an adult's eyes it is more likely that you will see this letter for what it is, and know the regret and tenderness I feel as I compose this history for you. Of course, I know I have no control over any of this, yet still I hope. The dead must relinquish so much.

Heaven forbid these pages return to you without me, but allowing for such a possibility I give you my word absolutely that I will recount my life as faithfully as I recall it, nothing added, nothing lost.

Will I be dead? That is certainly the way things seem to go around here, but it is not my intention to go off and die any time soon. You may also take some consolation in knowing that we Bethunes are fighters, first and foremost, and never go down without a mighty struggle. For a man nearing fifty I have got a good bit of life left in me.

The reality is that you have missed every word of the story I will tell, and I cannot change that fact. When such a small miracle as you awaited, I chose to look elsewhere for purpose. I chose to leave you behind, and that is the sadness in my life. I feel there is no adequate apology a father can offer his child for something like that, but it is my hope to tell you a little about the world as it was before you came into it, and about the terrible forces that pulled me away from you once you finally did. And to tell you why I came to this faraway country. One's journey through life is fraught with contradictions and compromises. I see that now, and perhaps one day you will see it too.

There is a boy here in north China with me named Ho. You would like him. The plain truth is that nothing would get done around here without him. He is my vigilant sentry, my water boy, my trusted valet, my cook, my barber. He is the one who provides me with everything I need. When he saw the state of this typewriter ribbon (I had been using the old Remington portable to write up a number of medical reports) he dipped it in some oil he found dripping from the belly of a wounded generator hidden behind the hospital (which was, not so long ago, a Buddhist temple), and lo, by nightfall, it was set for another ten or fifteen pages. It has since become part of his morning ritual.

The reason I mention this so early on is that whatever it is that he puts into this customized ink of his reminds me of a perfume I once purchased for your mother in Madrid, before the war in China came to take me away. A whiff of lavender and mint that is my own Proustian delight. As I work, these keys release small shock waves of that perfume into the air, making this letter—for brief periods at least—an almost pleasant walk down memory lane. I imagine these additives, whatever they are, are meant only to suppress the oil's natural foul composition, and perhaps to deepen the colour of the imprint of these letters. It works surprisingly well, I must say. Every morning I find the Remington stripped of its ribbon, and every morning Ho comes to me with my breakfast of millet or steamed rice and tea, his hands stained the same colour as these pages.

*   *   *

I do not have much idle time here, but what little there is I spend trying to make some sense of the fates that have shaped me into the man
I am. I'll admit to finding this quite a task. I often think about your
mother and see now that she was not so unlike my own mother, how
they shared a common desire to improve the world they lived in. I also
think about who you will be when you finally read this. I like to imagine the glow of understanding that will light up your face as you move
deeper into the history of your father's people and your own miraculous beginning. And I like to imagine that I will soon be home to see
you, that peace will descend upon us, that there will be no need for
these writings other than to help recall the vicious events that took
place before this war made things right.

My first memory is of my mother stepping out of a baker's shop,
me in one arm, a bag of cinnamon buns in the other. I was four years
old. It was looking to be a fine day, as I had earned one of those buns
for my good behaviour that morning. I was stuffing it into my mouth,
nestled there in the cradle of my mother's arm, when she suddenly
turned on her heel and swung her shopping bag at a man who was
entering the shop just as we were leaving. The man fell—he must have
been old, certainly caught unawares—and as my mother stood over
him I munched away happily, thinking this was some sort of pan-
tomime enacted for my amusement. The baker came out from behind
his counter and stepped into the game. His apron was white. He was a
large man and wore a pleated hat. I remember thinking that it looked
like a mushroom. More, I said, and the baker with the mushroom hat
raised the man by the collar and threw him out the door.

This early memory, though I include it here, is not typical of your
grandmother, for she was, in faith and in deed, a woman devoted to
the Lord and to the improvement of His world. She was a warm and
loving mother, gentle as a lamb, but a fighter, too, who wouldn't turn
the other cheek when confronted by the ugliness of disrespectful men.
It was your grandmother who taught me and my brother and sister
that things could be made better by virtue of regular Bible study and a

calm spiritual persistence, and that our highest calling was to commit ourselves to the betterment of our small corner of the world. This was a first lesson in life and one I carry with me to this day, greying sinner that I am. She instilled within me the impulse to make the most of what I had been given. We are all given talents, she would say. Each of us to our own abilities.

Every Sunday in the parlour, she told us one of Jesus's parables. I remember my mother's soft hand on my head as she read through Matthew. The Parable of the Talents has stayed with me. You might know it. One man hoards his gifts while others bring them out into the world to gain strength and knowledge. Her hand lifted from my head and gently touched the open Bible.

"And what does this mean?" she asked softly.

"That it is God's will for us to make the most of what we're given," I said.

"Yes, and that what you're given belongs not to you, Norman, but to the Lord, who has favoured us all with a special gift, each of us in our own way. You are now the keeper of these talents, Norman, and you have many of them. You must not bury your gifts but share them with others."

I told your mother about these Bible lessons, more than forty years after the fact. I told your mother that I had taken my Presbyterian upbringing very seriously. That I saw life as a series of lessons, of morally correct or incorrect choices. That the decision to lead a good life was yours. I still feel it in me, I told her, even now. She sat on a stool before me. We were in Madrid. The war there was on then, and still is.

"Turn your shoulder toward me, please," I said. I thought of myself as something of a weekend painter, if that's the right expression. It was a quiet night at the Hotel Santander.

Your mother said, "Yes, I know that about you, Norman. I can see how you are."

"Move the shoulder a little more, please."

She said, "There's no other place I'd rather be than here, at this very moment, with you."

I was silent for a moment, then said, "I don't know if I'll ever get your skin right. You're like a snowflake. You're the whitest thing I've ever seen."

"I am your Swedish princess." She shifted the blanket on her shoulder and tossed her hair. She spoke English very well. "Did you ever believe you'd find someone here? In the middle of this stupid war?"

"No, I did not," I said.

And she said, "Does being happy diminish your sense of purpose, Norman?"

And I said, "I've always had purpose. What I never had was peace."

I have thought about that conversation often, and I can still say with confidence that the look your mother gave me on that night told me she would never expect to hear another truth so full of sadness as that one, not as long as she lived.

Today was a difficult day and it is late now. I need sleep very badly. We've had little water, and in this heat that's something to worry about. Most mornings Ho replenishes my cistern. I hear him pass my door just after first light on his way down to the river. Sometimes he's singing to himself. When he came back empty-handed this morning I knew something was wrong. Last night we heard the fighting up near Chin-kang K'u, a village in the clouds. Ho found the stream running a deep red. When I went out to see for myself, I watched the limpid pink water slipping over the felt-green rocks like a cool summer lemonade. An hour later, a second stain came, lighter still, from the executions that followed.

Sepsis, starvation and tuberculosis are the three main killers here, after the Japanese. How desperate this place is, how wrenching its agonies. I wish you could understand, and somehow at the same time I hope you never will. But I am glad for the silence of writing. This is my one respite, though it is difficult to find the time. Today I operated on seven wounded, two of whom were no older than seventeen. Another 126 are yet to be seen to. The odds are overwhelming. I am alone here but for two under-trained assistants, both too recent to medicine to be of any real help. General conditions in Shansi Province are ghastly. We have few supplies. Without complaint the wounded lie dying in their ragged and filthy uniforms. In the heat of the day they are covered by flies and lice and dust, sweating away the last of their strength, and in the cold of these mountain nights, without blankets or fire, they live moment to moment in shivering agony for lack of morphine or nitrous oxide. The small houses of this village offer scant comfort. There are no windowpanes and there is not enough fuel for fires. This landscape is almost barren of trees but for a few willows at the bottom of a steep valley to the east, practically impassable from here. I am afraid for these men, perhaps more so than they are for themselves. I have never seen a breed of men as tough as these peasants of north China.

It seems to me that religion figured out long ago that the central tenets of belief must be embodied within a single entity. Let one man bear the burden of perfection and suffering. Since arriving to China from Spain I have come to the conclusion that the absence of a leader in the Spanish War amounts to a grave danger that might possibly doom that struggle to failure. That is not the case here, I can say with some authority, and I will try to help you understand why. This is one thing these men do have, an embodiment of their ideals. Perhaps the new Spanish Christ has risen since I left Madrid, and with all my heart I hope that is the case.

The first thing that struck me about your mother was the paleness of her skin. I don't think I ever did get it right in that painting. Her beauty demanded a greater talent than I was able to muster. Her eyes were hazel and streaked with gold, for one. I have never seen anything like it. One day you will see it in her portrait. It's like trying to hide a lit candle under a bushel; the light escapes through the cracks no matter what. Her hair was blond, cut just above the shoulder, and parted at the side. Her bangs curled from right to left, as if rebelling against those conservative Catholic hairstyles that had become all too common in Madrid. Her nose was long and delicate and sat perfectly above a wide half-smile that only barely concealed a wry pout, which, the beauty that she was, never failed to pull my attention from whatever was happening around us.

Well, journalists from England, Norway and America had started coming around to see about the blood-transfusion work that we were doing in Spain. The clinic was attracting a fair bit of attention, I can say without presuming too much. Even a film producer came with the idea of making a documentary, which I did in fact agree to. One January afternoon, in walked the English journalist Frank Pitcairn. He'd come to conduct interviews for the story he was going to write about me. At first I thought your mother was his assistant, perhaps an interpreter.

She smiled and said with her distinctive Swedish accent, "This is all very impressive, Doctor Bethune."

She wore a short leather coat—a flyer's jacket, I think it was, the type with a high fur collar—and dark slacks. She carried herself with remarkable confidence.

"And you are?" I said.

"Kajsa von Rothman," she said, extending her hand. We were foreigners. We did not touch cheeks the way the Spanish did.

Only a few weeks before, a fifteen-room flat at number 36 Príncipe de Vergara Street, Madrid, had been given over to my transfusion unit by the Ministry of War. Before then it had been occupied by a German diplomat named Koll. Of course, he'd gone running with the rest of the Fascists once Madrid declared itself with the Republic. I remember the portrait of himself he left hanging on the wall between the French doors overlooking the street—left there, I can only guess, in some final gesture of defiance or megalomania, or a bit of both. It was a sad reminder that this address had once been a hotbed of attachés, emissaries, dignitaries—Fascists come to enjoy its lush surroundings while discussing the glories of totalitarianism. Brandy and cigars in the library—consisting of some eight thousand volumes, mostly German—furnished with Aubusson carpets and gold brocade curtains. It must have been a fine time while it lasted.

Within days of occupying the abandoned consulate we opened our doors to the public. It was a remarkable turnout. I am obliged to report here that the Spanish put these Chinese peasants to shame in that regard. When I arrived in north China, little more than a year later, the locals were terrified by the very thought of a blood donation. In Madrid, though, young mothers, old ladies and even children formed a line that reached down the block, well past the cinema, at the time running an inspiring government propaganda film whose name has not stayed with me. The old Prussian's liquor cabinets were now stocked with medical equipment and canned food stuffs. We produced our serums and improved our instruments in a small room where the diplomat had once kept his stiff shirts and top hats.

As I walked the journalist and this elegant associate of his through the rooms of the clinic, I explained the process of transfusing, storing and transporting blood. I showed them the stations where we worked and provided statistics, details and a few simple medical anecdotes he might find useful for his *Daily Worker* article. I introduced the staff, among them the Castilian doctor Antonio Calebras, a talented man, though consumed by an odd inferiority he overcompensated for through a haughty impatience with foreigners and their near-universal inability to master the language that came to him so effortlessly. It always seemed to me that he felt we were crashing his war. I attempted to avoid him most days, but often this proved impossible. We regarded one another with a fair bit of contempt, I should think. He offered the two visitors a limp hand, the very portrait of the noble Iberian. I believe Kajsa's Spanish surprised him. The way it held his attention was unusual, though I suspect her beauty may have had something to do with that. He was a little man with black, slicked-back hair. In fact he looked a bit like photographs of the Andalusian poet

García Lorca. Appearances being shallow, however, Dr. Calebras certainly did not possess the great artist's sense of poetic fraternity and political idealism.

"Do you have an average travel time," the woman asked, "based on your trips up to the Guadarrama Pass?" I now presumed your mother was another journalist, asking a question like that.

They called for a second interview the following morning, and after some persuading I agreed. It was mid-evening when I arrived at the Cervecería Alemana. It was my first break in eighteen hours. I could have worked another eighteen and still left things unfinished. Kajsa was standing at the bar with Pitcairn and leafing through a Spanish newspaper. She was more beautiful than she had seemed the day before. She wore the same jacket but different trousers, I think. She pushed her thick bangs back over the top of her head, folded her newspaper under her arm and greeted me with a handshake. Pitcairn slapped my back and thanked me for making time for him.

They began by having me describe my day, which had begun with a visit to half a dozen basement hospitals. Then came meetings with officials from the Ministry of War regarding supplies, I said, that were rarely available. I had performed three surgeries that day as well, and spent three hours on blood collection and storage.

When I finished speaking I turned to Kajsa. "You're with the *Daily Worker*, I take it?"

"Oh, I tried my hand at writing when I was a student," she said. "I've got more sense in my head now."

"Good sense and ideals," I said, "don't often go hand in hand."

She said she was with the Mujeres Libres, the Free Women of Spain. This was an organization of anarchist women that helped get prostitutes off the streets. They pulled them up from their misery and found them honourable work in the textile industry or in the city orphanages. The bombing raids made sure there were always lots of motherless children for the reformed ladies of the night to take care of. "From a life of hell to a life of helping," she said. She'd been studying in London but left university when she saw how pointless it was when compared with the real issue. When I asked what she considered this to be, she said, without a pause, "Nihilism. A passion for destruction."

"I see you have read Turgenev," I said.

"Would you both please stop?" Pitcairn said. "We're not dead yet. So let's forget about gloom and doom and the class struggle, shall we? I'm a bit done with the revolution for tonight."

Soon after exiting the café we found a long, narrow street lined with bars and anaemic plane trees that barely reached past the first balcony of the adjacent buildings. This was Huertas Street. I think your mother called it "charming," or something along those lines, and it was. In a tavern called Casa Alberto I drank my first glass of absinthe. It was green and turned milky white when the water was added. I didn't like it much. "Go on," she said. Its taste and effects seemed terrifically overrated. I drank another, impatiently. Your mother, who wasn't a drinker, told me to send it back when I said it tasted more like formaldehyde than liquor, but it wasn't that bad and I drank it anyway.

All the bars were busy. It was close to midnight. I was feeling the alcohol by now. The street seemed to be moving in slow motion. Groups of people were singing, chanting in deep, low voices, marching up and down the street like lumbering elephants. It seemed an entire neighbourhood of drunkenness. The smell of black tobacco was on everyone's clothing. I remember a blanket of smoke hanging over the street. Some of the bars were reserved for quiet old men who played dominoes and listened to radio reports of the war and watched the young people through the windows. Heads turned when we walked in. I was not as young as the rest of the crowd but not so old, either. No one said anything to us. I was used to that by then. In these bars nobody liked seeing a new face. It was understandable, your mother said, even healthy, to be suspicious of strangers in times like these.

13

* * *

This evening Ho passed before my door, propped open to permit the breeze, and stopped. He may have seen my foot protruding from behind this desk, hunched over as I was and thinking about where to go with this story. I rolled another sheet into the Remington. Off he walked to the sound of my clacking.

I remember rumours were an ongoing source of debate and discussion. They became something of a fascination and a pastime, I think. For some months it was said that the French would not buckle under British pressure to reverse their promise of military aid, and that the Americans would enter the war within six months. People spoke of Mussolini with ridicule and of Hitler with fear and of the devilish Moors with such a grinding racial hatred that I myself began to feel it. Up at the front, during the lulls in fighting, the urge to talk grew, and spies were a frequent topic. Emilio Mola, the Fascist general, spearheading four columns of soldiers at Madrid's southeastern flank, had proclaimed that a fifth column of sympathizers was said to be waiting quietly, patiently, in the heart of the capital. Soon this was considered fact, though nothing was known for certain.

Entering the world of gossip and rumour was a common rite of passage that greatly relieved the tedium. At the front there was only waiting and fighting and talking. Women and prostitutes also figured in these conversations, until some remark unwittingly reminded the men of the rapes they'd seen or had themselves committed. Then the jocularity was sucked out of the air as if fire had suddenly stolen oxygen from their lungs, and they would return to their silent stares and memories as the war again became real. Most days, recollections of my own experiences many years before, in Belgium during the Great War, came to me. I never spoke of them, not to your mother and not to these young men. Stories of another war to end all wars would do no one any good. Your mother knew enough to guess what I'd seen before coming to Spain.

I have been thinking about the night your mother and I spent in a bomb shelter. It was our first night together, and a very strange night, indeed. I'm sure she would tell you the same. I can close my eyes and still smell the dankness in the air, and feel the closeness of those arched brick passageways we moved through under the city. Most of us spent a fair bit of time in cellars and basements in Madrid, but this night was unusual and I think you should know about it.

Frank Pitcairn had led us into a bar called Los Gabrieles, where colourful mosaic advertisements for brandies and biscuits and sherries covered the walls. It was probably close to one o'clock in the morning when the loud, high whine of an air-raid siren came through the door and all conversations stopped. People made for the basement. Your mother seemed oddly calm, I thought. Could she be so used to this, already? I carried my drink outside and watched the streets being vacated as people ran for the safety of doorways. She followed casually behind. I did not hear the planes, but when the explosions began, the last of the drinkers and the staff quickly headed below for shelter. Your mother and I followed and walked through a long hallway, past the washrooms and down a narrow, dimly lit set of stairs. The air grew thin and dank as we descended the steps, and the thud of the exploding bombs grew muted.

Upon entering this basement I saw quickly enough that it was unlike any other shelter I had seen in Madrid, or anywhere else for that matter. It was a magnificent labyrinth, an intricate series of rooms linked by a main tunnel that branched off into smaller, darker tunnels that ran even farther beneath the city. Rooms waited at the end of four of the tunnels, each one representing, in miniature, a stage of a bull-fight. Like the bar upstairs, they were decorated with ceramic tiles, depicting scenes that took up an entire wall. The mosaic of the first room we entered was that of a vestiary. On one wall the tile showed the bullfighter's brightly decorated suit of lights, gold with red sequins along the arms and legs. The room was crowded with customers from upstairs, people still holding their drinks. We found the main tunnel again and walked through the dank air to the chapel, where the matador pauses for a word with his Maker before entering the ring. The scene was well lit by the open window portrayed in the mosaic, and visible in its frame was a bright day, with the Virgin Mary hovering in the centre. Radiance emanated from her outstretched hands. The ceramic also showed a desk, on which sat a Bible propped up against a stack of books, an unlit candle, notepaper and a fountain pen. This room, too, was full of people. We exited and continued down along the main tunnel.

We entered a circular room constructed to represent the main bull-ring, the *plaza de toros*. It was less than ten paces across and also near capacity. The tiles showed stands filled with people facing us, creating the perception that we ourselves were the main attraction and not some hapless bull and matador. The bombs falling outside, perhaps ten blocks away, sounded as dull thuds over our heads. The room shook with the force of the distant explosions. Tiles scattered on the dirt floor had been shaken loose by previous bombardments—or this one, it's impossible to say.

Frank had found a seat and sat with his back to the wall, talking quietly with an old man. Your mother and I continued along the main tunnel to the fourth and last room.

She said, "This would be absurd if it wasn't so terrifying."

Absurd moments in Madrid, there are plenty of those to choose from, and I shouldn't be so surprised. I suppose that is the nature of war. I remember my first encounter with the absurd very well. It was on my first morning in Madrid, in early November of 1936, a few months before I met your mother. I recall taking my breakfast at the hotel cafeteria on the Gran Vía, Madrid's principal east–west thoroughfare, only a few doors up from a bar called the Museo Chicote. I knew very few people in the city at the time and had brought with me nothing but my few items of luggage, a small amount of cash in the form of American Express orders and safe-conduct papers issued to me by the Spanish Embassy in Paris. I had begun walking east along the Gran Vía when an annoying little creature approached from behind and grabbed me by the elbow. Of course, I had no idea what this man was trying to tell me. He spoke very fast and I didn't understand any Spanish. I was just then indicating to him the impasse, shaking my head and gently but firmly pulling away, when his free hand casually slipped under his coat. He patted something there and raised an eye. It was a gesture he might have picked up at the movie house just down the road.

Having no option but to take his lead I followed him the few steps back to my hotel, where he rang the service bell and waited for the lady to appear at her desk. She was, I know now, a typical *patrona* of the type you find all over that country—efficient and powerful in the small world of her clean hallways and uncomfortable, tubular pillows, loud, talkative and helpful. She helped me understand the gist of the man's complaint. It seemed he was connected in some form to the security apparatus of the Republican government, and that he'd heard me, while conversing with another hotel guest, say "Fascist." He had not liked how I'd spoken the word. Perhaps had I spat it in disgust he might have waived his suspicions and bought me a brandy. It's no secret, of course, that small men tend to puff themselves up, but I was to learn just how much they can do so when acting on behalf of powerful organizations and, moreover, carrying a sidearm. As I was thinking this, the other reasons for his stopping me came out, and at first I could only believe that the proprietress had translated incorrectly. He had not liked the fact that I was well dressed and wore a moustache. Fascists, I've since learned, wear Abercrombie & Fitch and sport trimmed facial hair, not Socialists or Communists or Marxists. This was beyond ludicrous, but, reading an unmistakable excitability in the man, I chose the cautious route. I had the lady explain that I had just arrived to the country, as my papers would indicate, supported the Republican cause, and would soon be donning the appropriate clothing. I did not, however, mention what I had planned for my moustache.

I watched his enthusiasm wane slightly when the landlady produced my passport from her desk drawer. With his permission I retrieved my safe-conduct papers from my breast pocket. He studied both documents, overly carefully, I thought, guessing that he was not much more than an illiterate thug looking for something to keep him occupied before lunch. He returned the documents, nodded slightly and, with a tinge of regret in his eyes, told the landlady I was free to go. I supposed that was the end of it. I took the lift to my room to splash some water on my face and shake off this ridiculous scare. It was an inconvenience more than anything else, but also a reminder that certain aspects of security were not to be taken for granted in a city ringed by Fascists and said to be brimming with spies.

Not five minutes later, as I was preparing to resume my day, a knock sounded at the door. Here stood another man, dressed in a black leather coat—very impressive and fit, quite handsome, and bearing a briefcase. With him were five guards, each armed with a carbine. This man, too, demanded to see my documents. Apparently his colleague had scampered down the road to get some help. One of the guards, instructed to descend for the passport, returned a moment later. The man in the leather coat sat down on the bed, briefcase on his lap, and began flipping through its pages. Two guards stood barring the door. I heard others in the hallway, their voices striking a chord of boredom, and the man on my bed looked up and shook his head, as if annoyed by their banal conversation. While a suspect, and perhaps a spy, I still might understand the superior regrets of an important man obliged to spend a whole war in the company of bumpkins. But this handsome, haughty police officer wasn't having such a good day, either, and seemed just as let down as his predecessor had been. My status was unimpeachable. He stood up, organized his minions with a short bark, and finally I was left in peace. For a few minutes I watched from the window, hoping to see them leave, but saw nothing but a busy street teeming with mules and military vehicles and pedestrians.

Then another knock at the door. This time a friendly face greeted me. Henning Sorensen was a Canadian associate of mine with whom I would soon travel (I did not know this yet) up to Paris and London in search of a car and various instruments, gadgets and chemicals we would need to get our clinic up and running. He had been in Spain for a number of weeks, preparing the groundwork, and spoke a bit of Spanish. Shortly before departing for Europe I'd been entrusted with a letter from his sweetheart back in Montreal, and after explaining my encounter with the secret police, I retrieved it from my luggage and handed it to him. Just then the man with the briefcase swooped through the door, accompanied by his bored, grunting men. Greatly enjoying his line of work, he snatched the letter out of Sorensen's hand while his guards aimed their rifles directly at us. Greedily, he ripped the letter open, clearly believing he'd smashed a ring of Fascist plotters until he read, "My dearest darling . . ." With that there was nothing left for him but a quiet retreat.

It was a ridiculous episode, but again, a reminder. Sorensen and I watched them leave the building, walk up Gran Vía and disappear into the crowd of vehicles and mules. We descended to the street not long after, looking to soothe our nerves with a drink at the Museo Chicote, though not before I changed my clothes and shaved off my moustache.

I remember the tunnel growing narrower and deeper. The things we remember! Your mother's hand brushed against mine. I remember that so well. I felt like a schoolboy! What did I do? I pretended not to notice, of course. I did not move my hand but stretched my fingers out in case her touch might come again. A moment later we entered a small infirmary that was not as crowded as the other rooms had been, situated at the confused and narrow end of the tunnel. It was the end of our journey, and the bullfighter's. The mosaic of this last room represented an operating theatre. Well, I said, at last something I understand. Perhaps the fallen bullfighter had already been gored and was now being carried down to the infirmary, for three doctors and a nurse stood at the ready, all looking very concerned, as well as a solemn-looking priest with long, thin El Greco hands and an old, grey face. The portraits were beautifully rendered and close to life-sized. The artist had required nine tiles to depict the surgeon's rib-spreaders, laid out on the table beside a stethoscope and various cutting instruments. Their smocks were still shiny white.

This last room was the dimmest of the four, with only one electric light hanging from the stuccoed ceiling. The air was stale and damp. Two unoccupied stools sat in front of the mural. The three people in the room were sitting against the opposite wall, looking at the medical scene, and now us, while sipping from the glasses they had brought with them from the bar. They were Spanish. I gestured to the stools, and one man nodded and shrugged. We sat down and listened to the not-so-distant bombs pounding through the walls. After a few minutes Kajsa stood and said, "Take my hand."

I did, and rose to my feet, saying, "I think we're at the end of the line here."

She led me out of the room and into a smaller side tunnel. We moved down it perhaps ten feet, crouching, and stopped in front of a chair on which sat a wooden crate full of empty bottles. This alcove had, I supposed, been used for storage.

She moved the crate and chair, then pulled open the small door hidden behind. "What about this? Where do you think this goes?"

"A trap door leading down from the bar?"

"Well . . ." she said, but without finishing her thought she slipped inside.

I lit a match, stepped in after her and looked down a steep set of narrow stairs.

It's difficult to understand the impulse that told me to follow your mother like that, but I did. I suppose I already felt drawn to her, though I was trying to resist it. As I've said, it was a very unusual night. We walked, slightly hunched, down the stairs and along a cramped passageway for twenty or thirty paces before another explosive thud shook us. We journeyed deeper under the city. I struck match after match and walked slowly so as not to extinguish the flame. Occasionally, out of the dark appeared a crate or box or shovel or a bundle of clothing. It was difficult to guess from such objects who came down here, when they last had or why. There was no one in sight. We shouted out but heard no one answer.

We found no rooms off the tunnel, as there had been in the basement of the bar. It was just a narrow passageway, bricked in a low arch like a wine cellar. The path must have curved gently, for we'd entered it, I was almost certain, in a westward direction and now, if I had any sense of orientation left, were heading east toward the Retiro Park and the Prado Museum. It was difficult to tell since we couldn't see farther than a few feet in front of us. As we walked, the walls of brick around us grew silent. The bombs had stopped falling.

"I think it's this way," she said.

"Why? This might go on for miles."

"We just follow the wall," she said. "It'll lead us out somewhere."

We walked for some time, and then I struck the last match. We were walking side by side and I looked at her face in the dim light. The dying flame disappeared into my fingertips, and a perfect dark surrounded us. We heard only our quiet breathing and footfalls. When she lit a cigarette lighter, we saw a large door, pushed it open, went down another series of stairs hewn from the rock and entered a large, frescoed room with dozens of niches carved into the walls at different heights. Each one, not much more than a small ledge, held a funeral urn.

Kajsa let the light die. "Listen," she said.

The silence and darkness were total. We waited a minute or two, listening for vibrations coming down from the streets above. The flame flicked on again and we passed under a low overhang and through another short tunnel into a second frescoed room, also devoted to the ashes of the dead. But each of these urns, instead of resting in a niche, had been afforded its own small vestibule with a bench in front. People construct the strangest shrines to honour their dead. I remember thinking that. A cross on a hill. A pyramid. The hushed reverence for the dead spirals out of control to establish these odd fabrications of rock and clay. There is something beautiful in that. But also something very, very lonely.

I am beginning to understand that Ho is a very odd boy. I never required thanks after I took him on, only discipline. That he seems as aloof as a cat is fine with me. He is a beautiful child, his dark-gold skin not yet hardened into the tawny hide of these mountain dwellers. The future awaits. He does not limp or scowl or weep at night, at least that I know. May his dreams carry him off through the dark.

There are worse places for dreams, I suppose. I imagine myself at his age, caught in this vile nightmare. How would I have stood up to the test? It is not a thought I like to contemplate. These children are amazingly tough and have earned my silent reverence. What did my father use to say? Children are the heritage of the Lord.

While I am thinking about it I will tell you about another encounter you might rightly call absurd. It was on a warm, overcast day in April of that same year, 1937, just over a year ago, though in memory it belongs to a different century. I was walking toward the Gran Vía in good spirits. The unit by then was collecting and distributing between one-half and three-quarters of a gallon of blood per day, and, on average, performing three transfusions in either Madrid or the hills north of the city. I had left the clinic before the usual hour, giving myself an extra few minutes to pick out a gift for your mother. What I had planned for that afternoon, beyond the purchase, was a brief short-wave radio address. The demands on my time were enormous then, but the address would be transmitted to North America and therefore be well worth the effort. It was, of course, an exercise relating to the war. I had been approached by the Spanish government, through the Ministry of War, and had agreed to their request.

We'd returned only the day before from the front lines near Guadalajara, forty miles northeast, where we had photographed bridges, roads and various other points of interest as regards communications. This trip alone would give me ample fodder for my radio address. But so would Madrid, I remember thinking. I could talk about the indiscriminate bombing of its neighbourhoods and the wanton killing of innocent women and children. It was known that the Fascist bombs falling over Madrid carried, as well as high explosives, hundreds of rounds of ammunition, much like the French 75 mm shells of the Great War, in order to inflict as many civilian casualties as possible. Too many times I had seen the angelic, blood-spattered faces of children. Too many times had their small, crushed bodies been placed before me on my operating tables.

I would say this was no longer war as we had once known it to be. The Fascist war was directed at the women and children of this great society. If you were once neutral, believing this an isolated struggle between two abstractions, the carnage *demanded* that you think again. Ours was a struggle against a murderous machine that would not stop killing until the machine itself was destroyed. I remember how your mother's thinking had begun to influence my own. This was a fight against nihilism, I would say, a fight for the very existence of hope. The machine was run by the mad dictators Hitler and Mussolini and Franco. Never before in history had the nations of the world had so much at stake. Never before had these nations been so united against such bloodthirsty fanaticism.

Apart from a single patrol plane flying over the city that afternoon, the atmosphere was calm and relaxed. Buses ran, the cafés were busy, the streets alive with workers on their way home for the afternoon siesta. The street I walked along, Valverde Street, was relatively quiet. The clock at the top of the Telefónica building, which had just come into view, read one-thirty. Up there, beside the clock, two men stood with a 20 mm AA Oerlikon gun, waiting for the next group of Heinkels or the big Italian Capronis to power in from the south. For a moment the war might have been a thousand miles off. The smell of cooking meat and olive oil and wood and coal-burning fires filled the air. Seeing and smelling this I realized I hadn't eaten that day, and, wondering if I might steal ten minutes out of my schedule, I saw the green door of a restaurant, with *El Escondido* stencilled over the big plate-glass window, open directly across from me. A man staggered out, bleeding from a cut above his eye and supported by two others dressed in black leather jackets. Another man followed. These three looked to be of the same ilk as those who had harassed me on my first day here—overeager, bored, stupid brutes.

Of course, it was quite possible that the man they'd apprehended was of legitimate political interest; yet it was just as likely, elaborating from my own experience, that he had failed to sneer deeply enough, or spit in disgust, when speaking of Fascism, or that an acquaintance with some axe to grind had denounced him as a member of the Fifth Column. When they put him in the car idling at the curb, they were careful to push his head down gently, almost gingerly, under the rim of the open door. It was an oddly caring gesture. I looked into the man's eyes as his head went under. Then all the doors closed and the car started off down the street, stopped briefly for traffic, turned left and was gone.

A half block up along the Gran Vía I found the perfume shop that had been recommended to me. I made my purchase quickly enough, scented with lavender and mint, and was again on my way. Another ten minutes of walking brought me to the address I was looking for, an old building adjacent to a small dirt square and a crater hole covered over in planking. There was a hardware store and a small café at street level. I followed the stairs up to the third floor and knocked at number 3D. The door was opened by a thin, pale young man who looked terribly deprived of sleep, with large dark circles under his eyes. He introduced himself as Paco, then led me down a long hallway to a large room, where I met the producer of the radio program. Jorge looked to be in his mid-thirties, and he asked me how I was, if I'd had any trouble finding the place, then offered me a glass of wine. It was their lunchtime, he said, and would I join them? He produced a loaf of bread and a wheel of cheese from under a desk. His English was precise but very accented. His reading skills, he explained, were superior to his conversational ones. "We have time to eat something," he said, and gestured at the control panel behind him. "I will explain this later. Please sit."

He cut pieces of cheese from the wheel and laid them out on a plate. He did this very delicately and rapidly. His thin fingers shook only slightly and he moved them quickly so I wouldn't notice that he no longer had fingernails. They'd been bitten down to nothing. I had seen this many times in Madrid. His voice was smooth and clear, and after dividing the cheese he pulled a large red sausage from a bag under his desk, then slid the sausage and knife over the desk. His colleague joined us, and we tore the stick of bread into three pieces. I was very hungry, I told them, and would have eaten something on Valverde Street but for the commotion I'd witnessed at the restaurant, the man being taken away.

"Do you think they were police?" I asked. "They put him in a car and drove him off."

"Yes. Probably."

"What do they do to these men?"

He put a finger-gun to his temple and pulled the trigger.

"He didn't look like a spy."

"Tell me," he said, "what does a spy look like?"

"But what if he's a cook or a dishwasher, just any man?"

"Then he has a big problem. But if he has nothing to hide, a release will be granted—unless they shoot him before they understand their mistake."

When we finished eating we turned our attention to the business at hand. I spoke my address into the radio-microphone. It went well, though my hands shook as I read from my notes. Afterwards Jorge thanked me, and assured me I shouldn't worry so much about innocent men getting into trouble. Naturally, there would always be casualties of this sort. Still, walking home, I couldn't help but wonder about the man I'd seen being ushered into the car, the hand tucking him in so gently. The restaurant on Valverde Street was quiet now. Only a few old men were there. It all looked very normal.

I remember digging in the dirt as a boy. I suppose that's not so unusual. Girls skip rope, boys get themselves dirty any way they can. So there I was, digging a hole and putting a cat down there and covering it up with a sheet of wood. This old tom was more trusting than your average cat and didn't seem to mind. I put him in, slid the plywood over his head and heard a few meows, but that was it. The hole was a foot or so deep. On such a hot day he might even have enjoyed the coolness. There was room enough for a cat twice his size to circle around, roll over and have a nice nap. A few minutes later I pulled the wood away and bent down to haul him up into the sunlight. The look he gave me made me feel very stupid, the typical cat look laden with boredom. He was through doing me favours. Then he lifted up his tail, showing me his hindquarters, and sauntered off.

Well, today I remembered that episode because the tunnel your mother and I got trapped in has been winding through my dreams these last few nights. I am thinking about it now, and what strikes me is how long we were down there and how different everything seemed to me. Of course, I found out exactly how long and how different when it was all over, but just then it was difficult to tell. I remember thinking there was no such thing as time down there, and no such person as Norman Bethune. It was a strange feeling. We walked for what seemed hours, these odd thoughts circling round in my head and doubling back again. Being underground can play tricks on your perceptions. I have never been fond of it. Being underground strikes me as very unnatural. We walked forever, it seemed. Your mother and I didn't talk much. I suppose we were a bit too outside ourselves for words. We passed through doors and small rooms of no description, mostly empty except for discarded construction tools and gardening implements, shovels and pickaxes and so on, and then I began to wonder if it was possible to die down here in this maze of darkness with this beautiful stranger. Could these tunnels loop back upon themselves? Had that necropolis represented more than the memory of the dead?

We felt the walls and on we walked, using the flame only when we became unsure of our footing or when we found another door.

Your mother reached for my hand in the dark. I couldn't help smiling. The world was ending and here I was, smiling because a pretty girl was holding my hand. The Lord's mysterious ways, as my mother would say. I felt the walls with the other hand, reading them as I read the inside of an open chest or abdomen. Now we were inside the entrails, and here I was smiling. I said, "Light, please," and your mother lit up the cup of her hand, and then the lighter failed and the darkness grew deeper. I stopped. "Try again," I said, but that was the end of our seeing. Neither of us let go of the other's hand from that point on, and my smile fell away. After twenty paces I tripped over a shovel, almost bringing her down with me. Ten paces farther, I tripped over a bag of sand. We rounded a corner, then another, and finally stumbled onto more stairs, at the top of which was a storage room with a vertical sliver of light showing in the corner of a door at the far end. When I pushed the door open, dimly lit stairs and a handrail led us up to where the grey morning flashed before us. We had walked under the city to the Retiro Park, a distance of some ten or twelve blocks.

We stood in the early-morning light blinking at the Crystal Palace, a great glass structure set near the west end of the grounds and empty but for the light filtering through its panes. No one else was present. The park was ours. In the heart of the city, volunteers and Civil Defence teams were looking for survivors and extracting the dead from heaps of rubble. But we saw only ginkgo and birch and plane trees, benches and sky, tree sparrows and chickadees and white wagtails watching us from their branches. Behind us, encompassing the door we had emerged from, was a large rock garden on the edge of a small, mist-covered pond in front of the palace. The ducks floating on its calm surface were still sleeping, heads tucked under their wings. After the tunnels, the air was fresh. We saw no planes, no wisps of smoke from the bombings. The sky was quiet. Testing the door, we pushed through and stood there in the Crystal Palace and toasted with imaginary champagne an imaginary end of the war. It is something I thought you should know, and something to think about, that the first night I spent with your mother was under a burning city.

This morning I was awakened by the sound of shuffling outside my hut. The boots making most of it belonged to five Japanese prisoners as ragged and hungry and young as the Chinese escorting them past my door. It is hard to imagine such men committing themselves to this wicked enterprise without being grossly coerced and manipulated. I cannot explain it, how people and nations rise up in the name of evil. I can tell you for certain, though, that these Japanese boys come not from the wealthy families of the generals and robber-barons they fight for here but from the unemployed and working classes they've been tricked into fighting against. On both sides, it is a sad waste of youth.

I have been thinking lately how to express my thoughts, not simply my needs, to Ho. I'm sure he is a clever boy in his own language. Jean Ewen—the nurse here (before she left)—told me only that he had family in Yan'an and enjoyed reciting the poems of Liu Bang of the

Han Dynasty. It goes without saying that I'm unfamiliar with Han Dynasty poetry, so at least in my eyes, this marks this youngster as special. The things we don't know perhaps impress us more than they should. Be that as it may, his practical abilities are what make the difference. With a straight razor, for example. On Sunday mornings the young poet sits me down and applies a steaming towel to my face with the strict authority of a Turkish barber. A smoother shave I have never known. Without a word he flutters about my head like a pigeon on a statue, efficiently hacking off a week's worth of grey whiskers. In all this time—nine months and counting—I am relieved to report that he has never drawn blood, not so much as a nick or scratch. It is difficult now, tonight, as I exhaust this ribbon of its voice, to imagine a time when my beard could do without his clever, wordless razor.

It occurs to me, before we proceed any further, that you might be interested to know something of the Bethune history. Let me assure you that it is not my intention to speak harshly of anyone in this family, least of all your paternal grandfather. But let me say also that fairness and truth shall reign, that is my promise to you. He was, in the end, only a man; and, as such, his decent character and natural goodness waged a silent war with the anger he carried within him. Over time that war spread, as does this present war in China, to consume the life and thoughts of his older son, your absent father.

My mother and father were introduced in 1883 in Hawaii—that flowery paradise so unlike these sparse mountains—by the charismatic preacher of a church that had wrenched her all the way from Plymouth to do its Christian work, namely, to bring salvation to the heathens. Apparently it did not take my father, a traveller in search of business opportunities, long to see the light as well. A coconut might have fallen from a nearby tree, or perhaps a bird sang hidden somewhere in its palm fronds, a sign to a young man looking to change his fortunes. We can only imagine.

I am told that my father, Malcolm Nicolson Bethune, a Canadian, timidly shook the hand of the evangelical English missionary Elizabeth Ann Goodwin in that paradise on earth, by then an Eden in decline, an island of lost promise. That he took her hand, made her his, and that together they sailed for Canada.

But did my dear mother know what she was getting into? Knowing her as only a son can, now an adult older and wiser than the innocent evangelist she was then, and bracketed by my own failures in love that we'll get to later, I can only answer that no, she did not. It is true that her tutelage only strengthened my father's sanctimony. He was a machine waiting to be tooled, to be sure. But did she know to what extent he would embrace this new salvation? My mother, I believe, lived to regret it.

Once married and back home, in the village of Gravenhurst, Ontario, he became minister of the Knox Presbyterian Church at number 315 Muskoka Road, though in the years to come we would move constantly. This is where your father comes into the picture. A village known as the sawdust city, Gravenhurst smelled of amputated trees and manure. But its greatest promise, this new job, was my father's rock-solid guarantee of a lifetime of rectitude. He was respected, as were all men of the cloth in his day, and both feared and hated by all but the most forgiving of souls.

His father before him—whose profession and name, Henry Norman Bethune, I proudly share—was, in 1850 in Toronto, a founding member of the Trinity College Medical School, a good man and a disappointed father. I never heard that truth spoken openly and neither will you, but at the age of seven I saw in his eyes, as his fingers delicately picked at the tired sheets, the regret of a defeated man. After he died they tied his jaw shut with a red handkerchief and took him away: my first experience of death. His secret grief soon became my silent companion. And your grandfather, my dad, was free to do as he pleased, now that the only authority on this earth greater than his had been silenced forever.

My father was a sedentary, slow-moving man. We lived in a quiet house. I recall the nature of his fierce concentration, which the whole house was taught to respect, and those moments when he would emerge from his study and stare off into space. It always seemed to me that he was plotting some exquisite *coup de grâce* against all the unbelievers surrounding him. He was a strong man, both of body and spirit, though as I recall his only two forms of physical exercise—the first powered by a steady stride, the second by those unaccountably gnarled fists—were his twice daily walks to church and the vigorous thrashings he doled out to his children.

I was carefree before the troubles between me and my father began. We were well loved and warm and fed, my siblings and I, and in this silence I now thank my mother and father for basic comforts that in those days we all took for granted. I can say we benefited from the favours that came to the family of a respected man of God. I suppose you might even argue that God has not failed me in that sense. In fact, I'll admit that I enjoyed time spent with my father. So you see, it was not all fire and brimstone. I took pride in his strength and the respect he commanded in town and enjoyed the family histories he regaled us with as we gathered by the kitchen fire on a cold winter's night. He was at times a warm man, and he held us close in his big arms as he told stories of the world he'd seen before crossing over to the Lord—of Hawaii and the prairies of Canada, the Maritime provinces and other places he'd been to and ultimately renounced for the small world we now inhabited. The Lord was All and All was the Lord, he would say, Amen. What a grand spectacle and delight was Creation. You will see it one day, God willing, he would say. Our mother looked on, a contented woman at those times, I'm sure, busying herself with needle and thread or reading Shakespeare and Ibsen and Saint Teresa. These were fine moments, and to this day I cherish their memory.

My mother, a woman of great imagination, never failed to encourage the natural curiosity that was brewing deep down inside me. She left books on my bedside table and two or three days later would sit with me and listen patiently as I described the adventures of Tom Sawyer or Jim Hawkins or White Fang. Evenings, when the house was quiet, you would find her reading at the kitchen table over a cup of tea, as I was in my bedroom, the covers pulled to my chin. We were both very bookish then. I still remember the magic spell a volume from her evangelical days cast over me, a large, musty old thing that told the story of a Catholic missionary's travels through Mongolia. She hadn't said a word about it, but one evening I found it under my pillow. There was no telling what my father would have thought of all those Catholics and Buddhists traipsing through the clouds together; it was best not to invite scrutiny. She was eager, I think, to have me pick up where she left off. The world of the mind, of travel, of good works. The great world awaited me, as it had awaited her in her day, in all its glory and sin, before motherhood overcame her.

ENVELOPE TWO

I should tell you that my scientific nature began to manifest itself at an early age. I wonder if we will have that in common, this interest in the workings of the natural world. For my tenth birthday I was given a jackknife, so I suppose my parents had me figured out by then. My experiments with this handy tool were in the beginning barely a step ahead of the frog hunting and ant burning of my peers. But one day, early the following summer, the single most important idea of my young life leapt out at me from the bony cavity of a battered and eyeless gull—at first glance no different from any other dead animal, yet my interest in it would fire the opening salvo in the war between father and son.

We were living in Owen Sound then, a small community northwest of Toronto that clings for life to the southern tip of Georgian Bay. It was lovely and wild, the bay, changing from day to day, hour to hour, its rocky edge a rich playground of delight and discovery for a boy my age. It seemed to me possessed by rebellious spirits I couldn't help but identify with. I felt its moods, I believed, and it felt mine. Such was my fanciful imagination. In any case, it was a sunny afternoon, with only a spot of cloud hanging in the east. The bird was nestled snugly in an open tomb of cracked shale and warped driftwood and pulsating with maggots. I recall the feeling that overcame me, even now as I write, so many years later—the feeling of something turning inside me, some new and unusual consciousness. I cannot say what it was in this animal that coaxed such trembling from my fingertips, such pure excitement. Perhaps overnight I had turned the right age to finally appreciate the breadth of my world and its unsubtle avian tragedies. Whatever the reason, it was as if a thunderbolt had struck me between the eyes. I realized in an instant that I was completely alone in the world, and that all that my father had taught us about the Good Book and angels and the Resurrection was lies.

After hacking at it with my jackknife, I decided not to bury the bird behind the cedar woodpile, pray for it or utter a child's fairy tale of last rites, as I usually did. No, I left it right where I'd found it and visited it day after day, watching it wither before my eyes. I didn't study the bird's inner workings but instead focused on its descent into nothingness. It was a remarkable experience, for my curiosity burned with the meaning of life itself.

Every day the gull grew smaller and the maggots grew fatter and more numerous, and then it was the maggots' turn to die. One day, it stood to reason, my turn would come. Before the next rainstorm the bird was no more than a hollow shack of bones and feathers. For so long my quiet neighbourhood, including that rocky shoreline, had been ruled by my father's silent God; and now, suddenly, it was not. I fail to describe adequately the force such a revelation had on my young mind. Perhaps one day you will have such a moment yourself and understand what I am talking about.

One early evening, at the end of a glorious summer's day, the dinner bell rang. As we took our seats at the kitchen table, I felt somehow that my life was about to change, that poor bird doubtless having prepared me for the impending confrontation. My father's sharp hands formed a spire in front of his face. His moustache back then was as bushy as a raccoon's tail. "Let us pray," he said, and we did.

O Divine Master, grant that I may not so much
seek to be consoled as to console,
not so much to be understood as to understand,
not so much to be loved as to love;
for it is in giving that we receive,
it is in pardoning that we are pardoned,
it is in dying that we awake to eternal life.

He then asked God to bless our food, and continued with a brief prayer for each of us, speaking our names in the tired crescendo I knew so well from his sermons. The secret I held—the second, really, the first being that look in my dying grandfather's eyes—had practically throbbed against the bones in my skinny chest as we spoke the words of Saint Francis of Assisi. We prayed along with my father—myself, mother, brother and sister—and when we finished we offered a humble Amen, then set to eating our chicken and green beans and potatoes—a meal I remember so clearly—in silent gratitude.

I don't pretend to blame him for the violence that followed. My impertinence and love of words often outran my deference and good sense in those days, and this is something I have trouble with from time to time even now. Clearing my throat, I put down my fork and knife and stood. "Father, say a farmer's son has no taste for his father's rutabagas—what then?" My family looked up from their plates.

"Well, then, he eats carrots," said my sister, Janet, rather sensibly.

"Norman, sit down, please," my father said.

Vexed, I refused. "Nor carrots! What if he doesn't like carrots either!"

What I was trying to say—and eventually did—was that one was not required to love vegetables simply because one's father earned his living farming the fields, and though a boy's father was the minister of the church in a certain small town, he himself might be right in considering Jesus less real than a rutabaga or carrot.

My heart racing, I glowed with defiance and pride. My father's face turned pale as a sheet, then flashed bright red. His eyes narrowed. He rose like thunder from the head of the table, slammed a fist down against it—upsetting the plates and glasses—and seized my right ear in his other spade-like hand. The rest of me followed out the door and was soon sprawled upon the ground. It was a hot evening. The squirrels chattering in the overhead branches fell silent. My mother stood in the doorway, young Malcolm and Janet under either arm. None moved to help me but I could not blame them, either then or now. This was my battle.

Well, he was too angry to do anything but push my face into the ground and hold it there, grinding. It wasn't much of a fight, and I won't hide the fact that I began to cry. He lowered his mouth to my ear—this deaf one, the left—and I could feel his hot breath on my skin. I suspect it was here he saw himself for what he had become, a brute, a bully, a man who would smite a child, and he began sobbing. "Children are the heritage of the Lord," I heard him say as he collapsed over me. My mother rushed forward and lifted him off, then took me in her arms and wept and begged for mercy for her injured family. She held me, and together we wept like saplings snapped in a storm.

The little things you remember—sometimes it amazes me. Today Ho walked past my door with a crate of empty bottles of some sort or other, and that sound got me to thinking about Spain. This was how we got blood up to the front, after we packed the bottles in ice in the back of the Ford. I don't think I ever consciously listened to that sound at the time, but now I can remember it so clearly. After the first few trips we found ice was more reliable than the Electrolux refrigeration units I'd brought down from London. Sometimes we would stop the Ford on the way up the Guadarrama Pass, which separates the provinces of Madrid and Segovia, and there, just shy of the summit, cool the bottles in one of the streams that ran down the south face of the sierra, while we waded barefoot under the bony pines.

After thinking about it for some time I have decided that in war, the lucky man is one who has something of a serene resignation regarding his fate. It is not whether he lives or dies but that he knows he has no choice in the matter that makes the difference. That should make things a great deal easier. I'm certainly not saying I don't care one way or the other, only that death out here is too random to think otherwise. I don't want to scare you, or myself. I fully intend to keep my head down. But I suppose I am resigned, as much as is possible. You see it in the eyes of the partisans here. I think they know, each of them, that the end of the day belongs to chance. I am aware of that resignation in their eyes, since I see it every day; it is so very close to an absence, I think, that I often find myself looking again to see if I'm understanding it quite right. Well, the truth is that a man prepares himself for death up here, and the faster he does it the better off he is. That's all well and good, at least when you're surrounded by people who are out to kill you, but the nihilism your mother spoke of had claimed a part of all of us in Spain in a way it does not in China. One does not hear of suicide in China, nor is there much drunkenness. I can't say why we feel differently about it here, and perhaps this is only my own bias showing through.

In Spain I saw many men fail to find the resignation I'm talking about. You saw it when a man took his own life so that another was denied the pleasure of doing it for him. I think alcohol also helped, though it did not stop you from getting killed. I knew that well enough from my time in the Great War. Regarding matters of life and death, some men wore a strange nobility and patience, which others characterized as madness or ignorance. Some died with the fervour of the righteous. Others sought their death with a blind fury. Some didn't care either way, and those were the fortunate ones. Very few mentioned a wish to speak of God or other spiritual matters, and none asked for last communion as this was frowned upon mightily. The common expression of the time was I s——t on God or I s——t on the Virgin or I s——t in the Milk of the Virgin. I was shocked by the blasphemy at first, but in times like those you get used to so many things so very quickly.

Fewer men died after we got the clinic up and running in Madrid, a consolation I try to remember, but we were only a small group. The ones we were not able to get to lay awake and lucid as they watched their own blood spill into the earth and soak it with curious indifference and puddle deep, as if a storm of black rain had passed unseen over their heads. Many of them lay murmuring with their faces to the ground and their thoughts consumed by the furious negotiating of the dying, which on occasion you heard coming across the fields: O That I May Live One Day More, O That I Do Not Die. But this negotiation rarely prevailed, and the earth grew darker and the negotiating more frenzied. Then gradually it grew fainter, and soon there was little thinking and no negotiating, just the quiet calm of resignation as thunder and chaos pealed through the sky. Sometimes a gentle hand came out of nowhere, really, to close the eyes of the dead. When this hand failed to appear the eyes were left open to stare blankly upon the streaked ground, and some men were carried to me in this fashion, confused with those wounded but still alive.

The strange slowness of the fighting continued through February and March of 1937. We were a besieged city. The fighting at the western edge of the capital continued and we went to it almost every day. If a man fell to the earth to escape a raking of fire he might choose to close with his thumbs the sightless eyes of the fallen man beside him, if he himself believed this simple kindness might come in line with his own private negotiations with fate, this respect for the dead as payment in lieu of one's own death. But in fact there were very few men who still believed the dead could be abused or desecrated any further, and so the many who had yet to die fought on, mindless of the bodies piling up on the landscape, and instead turned their thoughts to survival, not salvation. I did not blame them one bit.

Wars never go hungry. There were always new men coming to this one—Americans, Poles, Czechs, Germans, Italians, Canadians, Britons, Dutch, each man committed to defending the legally elected government of the Spanish Republic. The war attracted the intellectuals of the world, of all classes and professions. Foreign professors fought shoulder to shoulder with local farmers. In village squares throughout the country men gathered to collect a rifle and armband and listen to an oration by a town leader, or perhaps a radio address, and organized themselves into units, and all the while believed their numbers and weapons and brotherhood were sufficient. They were moved forward singing and hopeful to meet with their brothers, whom they would assist and from whom they would inherit the worst of the fighting, and the capital would quickly enough hear of their gallantry and from tavern to tavern up and down the land their names might spread. One evening it would slip under a creaking old door back home and alert a sister or mother or father, pride and overwhelming gratitude filling the house like the arrival of a new baby, neighbours hearing of how well the boy had done in the fighting. Such thoughts were harboured in many a chest as men sat in trenches only two hundred yards distant from those who would kill each and every one of them if they should be so lucky.

It is late. In under four hours I will be back in the operating theatre and I will now try to sleep. But let me leave you with this thought: I wonder if, in time of war, anything can be as vivid as the imagination, anything so clear and riveting as a man's thoughts at the moment he draws his last breath. It has sharpened my own, I can say that, even through this exhaustion. I saw it over and over again in Spain—not those thoughts, no, but the men those thoughts inhabit or haunt. The imagination journeys longest when the body is tense with fear, when someone unseen lies in wait. It dreams of a moonlit dance and melancholy loves and gathers meaning and significance where before there was none. A spontaneous word, a wisp of hair—in normal life a moment gone almost before it was fully noticed. Yet only a short drive north, scattered over miles of front line and dead-dog gullies and scrub deserts of sharp mountainous terrain, the silent dreams of men took wing. It is in the silence hanging over the land that you find what is worth fighting for. Sainthoods are here for the taking.

Early July. The sound of insects fills the sky. China seemed a lovely country today, and so, too, on this night. We had a beautiful afternoon and early evening, and the darkness now chatters with an abundance of life that remains hidden until dark falls and then, all of a sudden, surprises you with its forceful insistence. I'm watching the faintest streak of orange-red sunset retreat beyond the eastern face of the Wu-t'ai Mountains. It is a spectacular drama—the light crawls back over miles of rock in the space of time it takes me to write this sentence. From here it's half the length of my forefinger, yet it holds within its embers the light of millions of years. That will give you a sense of the size of this country and the small place we occupy in it.

We have moved shop to General Nieh's headquarters in Wutaishan. General Nieh is the Divisional Commander of the Communist Eighth Route Army, one of the key military forces in this war against the Japanese. Conditions are generally better here than up in Shensi, where we spent some miserable weeks this past winter. General Nieh is a fine man and spares no effort in securing what medical supplies and funding he is able to for me and my assistants. I still have great concerns regarding the lack of trained medical staff. I have been sending letters back home, hoping to raise awareness, because we need all the attention we can get. Today I finished an article for *The Manchester Guardian*. Ho will send it tomorrow. With its proceeds I intend to reduce for the Chinese the burden of keeping me on, though I claim no more rations than anyone else. How I would like to pay my way! Every cent counts.

We are presently camped at the edge of a small stream whose name Mr. Tung, my translator, told me, but I've forgotten it. I find its splashing calming after these last few terrible days. I have dark circles under my eyes and am no more than skin and bone. I am told to rest more. Of course I should. This is because my nerves are showing. God help these people! The Chinese are too polite and obedient to say anything to me. They are a deferential race in the extreme but all so incredibly devoted to our work that it pains me when I'm short with them and bully them perhaps a little more than is necessary. Each man and woman pulls his or her own weight and then some. I should be grateful for that. Yet I push and push and push. It's uplifting and gratifying to see how much they give, but often I am too forceful and too angry. Nerves and exhaustion and a short temper by nature, I suppose, and these late nights with you, though you're scarcely to blame for that! Well, this trickling stream helps. Anyway, we are hunkered down here with time enough, it seems, to return to the story I want to tell you.

Why *am* I writing? I'm so very busy, and I ask myself this question night after night. I ask it now. I know it is not to spout political slogans for you or to claim idealistic affiliations. None of those may make any sense to you by the time you read this. They're just words, after all, and I'm aware that words change or lose their meaning. What do you think, for example, when I write the words "justice" and "society" and "democracy"? They are often used these days, and so they should be. But will they mean anything to you twenty or forty years on? Probably not, and maybe that's for the better. Maybe there will no longer be any need of them. Maybe we will have accomplished what we set out to do. When my dear old mother raised me we had no such words. She said only, Do unto him, Norman, as you would have him do unto you. You see how complicated this has become?

I remember thinking this on a particular day in Montreal. I had just returned home from a full night and day at Sacre-Coeur Hospital. Not long out of my marriage, I passed before the hallway mirror and glimpsed a tired and conflicted man. I was taken with the desire to examine my heart. Do unto him, I thought. The odd thing was that I didn't know what it was I was in need of. I saw traces of my wife, Frances, wherever I looked. A portrait of her I had painted during our days in Detroit. A novel I had read aloud to her years before. An old

Eaton's chair, worn, comfortable and entirely out of place. I found blame and regret in each of these, but no connection to myself. Soon, too exhausted to continue, I switched on the shortwave radio hoping to catch the opera from London and thus calm myself before bed. Do unto him, I thought, as you would have him do unto you. This seemed to me a baffling riddle.

But the signal did not come clear. I picked up the crackling transmitter, shifted it, shook it, held it upside-down. I practically stood on my head to get a proper sound out of that rickety old box. In fact I put myself into all sorts of contortions trying to coax the signal but still nothing came through, just a crackling, hissing blur. Do unto him, I thought. Finally I leaned out the window, hoping this might help, and it was then that I heard through the background noise the terrible news of war in Spain.

Tonight I am thinking about your mother and that morning she and I emerged from those tunnels. It was almost as if the war had ended for me, as if the world *had* changed, for the better, as well as something inside me. Soon, when I could manage, between surgeries in various neighbourhoods and trenches and running the administrative affairs at the clinic, we began sharing our nights together in hotel rooms not far from where those bombs had first driven us underground.

We stayed at the Hotel Santander, a fourth-floor pension with a lift that sank noticeably when you stepped into it, then creaked and popped as the cables over your head dragged you up through the building's sour old innards. The pension smelled of the woodsmoke that rose from the chimneys in the neighbourhood, of bleach, of the lentils brewing in the family kitchen down the hall where a radio played most of the day behind a beaded curtain. It smelled of hand-rolled cigarettes, of oil paints and turpentine and of coffee brought up from the bar downstairs.

In the morning we would walk east on Huertas or on Cervantes Street to the Plaza Cánovas del Castillo, where we'd part with a discreet touch. Smiling, I'd walk past sandbagged fountains, uprooted cobblestones, blown-out buildings. I was a man in love. I remember your mother's scent following me as I joined the bustle along the Paseo del Prado and then slipped into the quiet Retiro Park to walk past its shimmering, steaming ponds, among its trees and morning strollers, thinking what a gift the world was to those who chose to see, and up I walked to the Crystal Palace and Vergara Street on the other side of the park, where the clinic and its empty bottles and cold syringes awaited me.

Early in March your mother had taken the paints and brushes and canvas from one of the studios at the Prado where the restorers had worked before the war began. That month the fighting at the western fringes of the city went on without stop, but the city itself often fell quiet and we could almost pretend the war never was. On nights such as those she sat in the chair by the window overlooking the street and allowed me to resume my work on her portrait. She said the restorers had abandoned their work after the first bomb punched a hole through the roof of the seventeenth-century Italian Room. "No one else is using them," she said. "So I thought, 'Happy Birthday, Norman.'"

I dragged my thumb over the bristles and said, "Forty-eight years old."

They were excellent brushes. I hadn't held a paintbrush since coming over to Europe.

"What about this?" she said, pulling the blanket from the bed and draping it over her shoulders. It was past midnight.

"I like it."

The blanket slipped to reveal a perfect white shoulder.

"You'd rather stick to saving lives?" she said.

"I prefer the artist's life."

She waited before saying, "Wrong war, then."

I found a piece of charcoal in the tin of paints and used it to begin sketching. "In what war was the painting any better than this?"

"There must have been one. The Napoleonic, maybe."

"Goya liked that one. Shoulder, please."

She adjusted the blanket.

"This lighting's too romantic," I said. "Too many shadows. Turn your head a little. A little to the left."

"We can't have people thinking you're a romantic, can we?"

"I would certainly be ruined."

"So would I," she said.

The war always came back soon enough. You'd almost have forgotten it, then the sound of planes would come over the city. Usually it was difficult to tell how many. We got a better sense when the bombs started falling. You'd hear them out there, even if they were falling up in the north end near the Estrecho metro stop.

"Three or four," she said the first night I took her up with me.

"More than that," I said.

Then she said, "I'll bet that's Cuatro Caminos."

"I'll take you to a shelter. Then I'll go up there."

"I want to see it."

"It's nothing to see," I said.

When she insisted, we left the hotel and walked to Sol and flagged down a truck carrying eight or ten boys from one of the Socialist youth groups. This is a memory that troubles me still. They circled around, waiting for a raid, then went up there with picks and shovels and buckets and dug people out of the rubble. I told them I was a doctor. They gave us a hand up. The driver took Alcalá Street to Recoletos and turned on Raimundo. It was a fifteen-minute drive. The city was dark, no lights whatsoever, and felt abandoned, dark and quiet but for the far-off pounding in a distant neighbourhood. We drove in silence. There were very few vehicles on the roads.

Continuing up Raimundo Street we saw a glowing mist rising over a horizon of squat buildings. It became a leaping mass of flames a little way up Bravo Murillo. The planes were gone now but had set a dozen buildings afire. There was only the sound of the fires and gas explosions and the confusion of people crying and screaming. Teams were already going through the wreckage. The boys we'd ridden with started clearing rubble with their pickaxes and shovels. When they pulled away part of a wall of a music store they found a small girl pinned under a piano and bookshelf and rough wood beams. She was not conscious. A man came and claimed her as his daughter, calling her name again and again. The flames from the burning buildings glowed off the piano top like a candelabra. The man finally permitted us to move his daughter to the aid station two blocks up Bravo Murillo, where she died just before first light.

By then the fires were under control. The rest of the wounded had been taken to hospitals around the city. I would see them later in the day as I made my rounds. I often visited ten or twelve hospitals per day. On a side street up Bravo Murillo I saw Kajsa sitting on the curb beside an old woman. I walked down and waited just out of earshot. The old woman was rolling rosary beads between her fingers. They would be worn to nothing before the end of the war. The morning light filtered through the blue smoke of the smouldering fires. The whole neighbourhood seemed shrouded in the deep blue light of an old forest.

I waited for your mother to finish comforting the woman, then we walked back to the centre of town. Away from there, the city was back to normal. Cafés rolled open their shutters, jewellers and fruit-sellers swept their storefront sidewalks. Automobiles and military vehicles drove through the streets without urgency. The sky was clean and pure again. You wouldn't have known there was a war on for a thousand miles in any direction.

That is what it was like to live in a besieged city. The war flew in upon us from the front lines and from the Nationalist airfields to the south, most often at night, but also first thing, or at midday, or at the hour of the siesta or the afternoon stroll. Sometimes it was predictable. Three or four days running the same three planes came overhead, the Italian Capronis, each marked with its identification number under the left wing. They cut the sky in perfect thirds. These were men of ritual. Other times seemed to bring no pattern to the brutality. After a stretch of quiet days the bombs always fell again.

Kajsa found more paint. No one would miss it, she said. Occasionally she went down to the Prado to pick up the new announcement posters from the printing presses in one of the basements there. She was always going, always busy. During the day she worked with the prostitutes in the same Madrid neighbourhoods that we went to at night when the planes came. I thought you might like to know that she gave of herself in this world.

One day the room smelled of figs that she'd bought on the steps of the San Miguel market from a little old man, she said, "who subsists on bread and water. He probably eats scraps gathered up from abandoned market stalls. Maybe a few of his own figs. And he's made happy with a couple of extra centimos."

"Do you deny him that?" I asked. Your mother seemed troubled, and I couldn't understand why.

No, she did not. In fact she'd emptied her purse into his hand.

He shook his head, she told me. "No, no. Not that much. Only three of these," he said, picking out the coins, "only this."

When she insisted he grew angry. He began to shout, "I am no beggar! The pretty American believes I am a beggar!" Every beautiful foreigner in Madrid was thought to be an American.

She told me this as I sat on the bed eating the old man's figs. It was something that troubled your mother more than I was able to understand at the time.

"Spanish pride," she concluded.

How would he have seen her, that old man, I wondered, this beautiful "American" in the midst of all that chaos? He would not have seen condescension in her, or pity. That was not possible. Your mother was a generous soul. She stopped people in the street. She asked questions. The smile she wore, and her soft brown eyes, perfect comprehension, would have revealed that this woman's proffered gift was a simple, pure, muted gesture. I cannot imagine otherwise.

"I suppose you could be his daughter," I said. "He would not take alms from his daughter. That would make him weak."

The figs sat in their paper cone on the night table. In the street below we could hear the neighbourhood beginning its ritual evening stroll.

"The street's filling up. Do you want to go down for a walk?"

"I don't even remember why I'm here," she said.

I rolled a cigarette and lit it. "I don't believe that." It was a cool evening. I opened the ceiling-high double windows. The crowds streamed by below. "You know more about it than I do."

"Maybe I'm just worn down," she said.

"I think that's it."

"I'm dizzy a lot. Spells."

"Headaches?"

"No," she said.

I checked her. I knelt down before her and looked into her eyes. They were not so different from those I looked into a hundred times a day.

"Exhaustion," I said. "Stress. Tell me if it gets worse."

That night we were awakened in the dark by the sound of a single rifle shot, not very far off. Perhaps a block up the street. We lay together, silently, listening, waiting for the night's emptiness to return. I wasn't able to sleep after that and I just kept waiting, but there was no second shot. I rose from the bed and sat in the dark beside the half-finished portrait near the window. I rolled a pinch of tobacco into the small yellow paper and smoked and looked down at the street below, waiting for someone to pass. She didn't speak but watched me watch the empty street. I wondered what had made her say that, about her not remembering why she'd come. She couldn't mean it. You know why you're here, I thought, but I didn't say that.

Instead I began to talk about my life.

Your mother said nothing, asked nothing. She lay staring up at the ceiling. When I stopped talking I sat and listened to her breathing and studied her eyes and the lonely silhouette of her body curled under the blanket. It was cold in the room. I didn't need her to explain.

I slipped back into the bed and felt her hands. The morning brought its first pale shadows to the window and the room began to expand and take shape, and the magic of the world was swallowed up by the light of morning.

What was it that I felt with your mother in our small room at the Hotel Santander? What did I begin to feel? Again and again we'd awaken together deep in the night. It was as if we had become other people and re-entered the world at a different angle, a perfect tilt that helped correct for the terrors we both knew. We became, each for the first time in our lives, ourselves. One night, after weeks of this, your mother surprised me.

She said, "Sometimes I am afraid to sleep."

"I'm afraid of more than that," I said.

"Death?" she said.

"I am not afraid of dying. That will be easier than the part that comes before it."

She watched me. "I said 'death,' not 'dying.' "

"No," I said.

The blanket moved slightly. Cigarette smoke rose silently in the dark. I sat without moving.

"I am afraid that I'm more than I can be. More than I'm able to be. Alone with you I am no longer the man I'm supposed to be."

"You're much more than that."

"No, I'm like a little boy, an insecure snot-nosed brat. I'm scared senseless."

"A little boy who will grow up to be a great man."

"He doesn't know that yet. The boy is still afraid of his father's thrashings. Displeasing those around him. Of *failing*. And it's only you who reminds him of this. You remind him that he must make himself new every morning."

She sat upright and placed her bare feet on the floor. She reached over and took the lit cigarette from my fingers. She looked at it, then inhaled. She leaned forward, I thought to kiss me, but instead she brought the cigarette close to my skin. She held it there, embracing me. I felt the ember hovering above my neck.

"Are you afraid now?"

"No."

"This is real," she whispered. "Are you afraid now?"

"No."

She sat back on the bed. "Of course not." She raised the ember to her own neck. "But you are afraid for others. See? You flinched. Is it as a doctor that you're afraid for me? Or as a man?"

"It's the same thing," I said.

"Just like the boy and the man are one and the same." She nodded. "This is who you are. That's what I know about you."

High summer. The fighting in these hills continues. Our lack of supplies is perhaps our greatest gift to the Japanese. That and the shortage of properly trained medical staff. I have begun producing surgical drawings here in my free time. (What free time is that? I should ask myself.) "Surgical Fixation of Complex Femur Fractures" is my latest. We're getting a lot of these, you see. One drawing is worth ten demonstrations, and in a place like this, where language is a complicating barrier, it's a shame I didn't begin using these drawings much sooner. Presently I shall start in on "Surgical Fixation of Bilateral Lower Leg Fractures." I have found it difficult to avoid smudging the drawings and must take greater care. It helps to draw with a cloth between the forearm and paper. We shall see how that goes.

* * *

I have mentioned the fact that we saw a fair number of journalists at the clinic. Well, the filmmakers Kline and Karpathi were among them, though they weren't exactly journalists but, I suppose, propagandists. They proposed making a documentary about the clinic that could be used to raise money. One afternoon I made time for them. They told me they wanted to employ a strategy of contrasts, that they wanted something beautiful and uplifting, something that would bring the message home to people who knew little or nothing about the struggle over there. They needed my help, they said, because I was representative of the sort of international solidarity that was required. Once it was done, someone would take the film around North America, raising awareness and donations. They wanted a roller coaster of emotions, they said. A beautiful landscape. An orphaned child sifting through rubble. Some shocking contrast. A collage of images that would mould a political aesthetic and present an undeniable truth regarding the oppressors, Good and Evil, Us and Them. Nothing chronological, nothing like a "News of the World" trailer at the front end of a Clark Gable picture. They thought that beginning with an image of a painting by the great Goya might position the film correctly, allowing one fine moment of beauty and horror to stand for all that is noble and depraved in man.

That was what they talked to me about that afternoon: the struggle for man's dignity in the face of death. And then the reversal: a painting flipped on its side as it was walked out of the Prado, then a victim carried on a stretcher from a bombed building. It didn't take much to convince me. Karpathi followed us around Madrid and up into the hills for more than three weeks. Synchronous sound shooting proved too difficult, but the music and commentary could be added later.

* * *

One morning your mother sat leafing through a month-old issue of *LIFE* magazine. She looked over her shoulder at where I was straightening my jacket in the mirror, preparing to leave. "Will you take me with you?" she said.

This was a week or so after the bombing raid on Cuatro Caminos. I looked at her reflection. "To sit in a car all day long?"

I'd told her the night before that Sorensen and I would be driving out that day to the Guadalajara front to take a look at some roads and bridges and deliver ten pint bottles of preserved blood.

She said, "I am suffocating in this city."

"It's not such a good idea. It's dangerous."

She turned back to her magazine. I thought that was the end of it.

"What about your work?"

"It will not miss me today," she said.

I crossed to the window, raised the blind and watched the street below. She seemed uninterested now. This part of the city had largely escaped the bombing runs of the past months. The Italian fliers had concentrated their efforts on the working-class neighbourhoods. Here, near the heart of the banking centre, they'd been more careful, though bombs still flew out of the sky with frightening randomness. You couldn't walk far in any direction without coming across towering heaps of rubble, but along San Jerónimo Street the buildings stood untouched. A bright winter sun shone down over the canyon of dirty white and beige buildings. The street below was busy.

Under an hour later, near ten o'clock, we collected Sorensen and Calebras at the clinic. They each gave me a puzzled look when they saw Kajsa. Though Sorensen said nothing, I knew he was annoyed. In France that November I had put my foot down regarding Moran Scott, a friend of Hazen Sise, our driver and utility man, who'd wanted to cross the border back into Spain with us. This lady friend of his had wanted to come along. I'd let Sise and Scott know that we were not a taxi service, fact one. And fact two: I was not willing to assume the responsibility of delivering a civilian through hostile territory. In any case, his reservations about Kajsa's presence were of no concern to me.

Dr. Calebras was another matter. As we prepared to leave, he'd been looking over his shoulder, waiting for Kajsa to step away. "Doctor," he said, finally.

Sorensen came over to translate. "He thinks you're taking liberties not entitled to you. He thinks the woman should stay. She doesn't belong on such a trip. He says she's a liability."

"Tell him I have taken his protest under consideration. Tell him we leave in five minutes. With or without him."

Neither he nor Sorensen spoke as we loaded the vehicle with supplies: a lunch of bread, cheese and omelettes prepared for us by our cook, Maria, a lady from the neighbourhood; the Leica IIIa, given to the unit by the Syndicate of Spanish Photographers; three tin boxes of medical supplies; and the pint bottles of blood, packed in a wire basket and ice. Finally, nearing eleven o'clock, we set out. Alcalá de Henares is just forty miles east of Madrid and we arrived in under an hour, then recorded the state of the roads and bridges leading into town.

Kajsa and I waited near the car while Sorensen walked upriver to get a photograph of the eastern side of the bridge. Calebras sat in the back seat, beside the packed blood. It was a cold day, bright, with few clouds in the sharp sky. The river was shallow at this point, only a foot or two at its deepest, but the bank was so broad and muddy that it would prove next to impossible to cross in our vehicle if the bridge were to suffer damage. We watched him walk upstream along the bank. I turned to my notebook and jotted down the travel time from Madrid. This information would prove critical for future operations along the front line. I hollered over to Sorensen that he should get the bridge from the west, as well. He walked downriver and another twenty-five yards beyond the bridge, took the shot, then started back, found a path and came up onto the road.

"We don't need this, Beth," he said. "I think you should talk to Calebras."

I smiled, then rapped the hood with my knuckles. "Leave it alone. Get in."

We drove through Alcalá de Henares, stopping to assess the condition of the bridge leading out to the Guadalajara road. On the open road we made good time, averaging sixty miles per hour. Calebras sat in the back silently watching the view, bouncing with the packed blood. The road was still in excellent shape. It was paved, very unlike the irregular Burgos road, but there were plenty of bumps he could feel back there. Kajsa looked splendid sitting between me and Sorensen. Sorensen was a very serious man at the wheel and didn't once take his eyes off the road. The Leica sat on the dash. The flat landscape rolled by. Some stone outbuildings, not much more than shacks, could be seen now and again, but very little else on these lovely, unbroken plains. A Spanish farmer did not live on or own the land he farmed but arrived to it as a factory worker might. He worked it but received no profit from it, only subsistence, and in effect was an indentured slave. You could drive for hours through groves of olive or corn or wheat fields and see not a single farmhouse, only stone fences or outbuildings where someone kept his tools. This was a system as old as time.

Fifty miles north, the Guadarrama range was capped by late-winter snows. Soon we came upon a slow-moving convoy of gasoline trucks, supply wagons and carts pulled by automobiles and donkeys. Sorensen was forced to drive on the shoulder of the road. Shortly after that we saw a long line of transport trucks loaded with Republican soldiers, their bayonets fixed, staring off to those same, unchanging mountains. A significant mobilization seemed to be in progress. I counted fifteen personnel transports, and each one cheered us as we sped past. Blow the horn, I told Sorensen, let them know we're here. As we passed we heard various languages as the International Brigades called to us. Their shouts grew more enthusiastic when Kajsa leaned over my lap and out the window. I held her by the belt. When we heard German, and saw these men's helmets, I knew they were the shock troops of the Thaelmann Battalion, Socialists, Communists and anarchists who'd escaped their own country to fight against Fascism here in Spain. The men waved and thrust their weapons in the air and hollered and blew kisses at Kajsa.

"How wonderful!" she cried, tucking her head back in the compartment, the rapturous curl in her bangs leaping in the wind. "Oh, those boys are marvellous, aren't they? Each and every one of them. It's impossible to lose. Say it, Calebras, your country can't lose when all the world is here! Germans, Poles, Yugoslavs!"

"Even a Swede!" I said.

He nodded and smiled thinly at her with an evident disgust that I couldn't understand. Minutes later there appeared a large cloud of dust on the horizon. This was the reason for the troops' enthusiasm and confidence. As we approached from behind we saw the column, still unsure as to what it was we were witnessing, and the first of a long line of tanks came into view. We felt the ground rumbling beneath our car and the air filled with the roar and smell of diesel engines. They were Soviet T-26s. That is a very impressive machine to see right before your eyes, I can tell you, and a very terrible one, too. We sped past, honking. Kajsa took up the Leica from the dashboard, leaned out the window, waving, and then started snapping. She cheered and hollered into the din and we drove on, knowing nothing of how this moment had changed our lives forever.

Today I performed a double amputation. A land mine took this boy's legs out from under him. He may have been twenty years old. Unfortunately not such a rare occurrence in these parts. But today I considered what an obscenely apt metaphor a minefield is, and by that I mean its ability to surge up from the unknown to grab hold and twist. Isn't this so much the case of our past, our hidden lives? Well, not always hidden, sometimes simply discarded or forgotten. This poor boy, his legs blown apart, and me above him looking over my white mask to see an inkling of the hidden banalities in my own life. Perhaps I'm just too tired. Surely he needed no such lessons in the metaphysics of life. An honest man has no discarded memories, none worth dredging up. Metaphors are gratuitous out here, of that I'm sure. I was ashamed. I took from him what was left of his legs, turned away and began with the next boy. There were six more, just like him, waiting.

This has got me to thinking of a number of failures in my life. By which I mean my own failures that have affected people I've known.

The need to make good use of myself in the world first came under fire when I was eighteen years old. That may still be young enough to appeal to the inexperience of youth as some sort of defence for my actions, but I know that's no excuse and will therefore show you due respect and not use it here.

It was the winter I was taken on as a schoolteacher in northern Ontario, and through this posting I met someone I will do my best to tell you about. Through him you will see why I might fairly characterize this entire episode as a failure, one that started small, in that schoolhouse north of Toronto, and ended in tragedy on a dark battlefield in Belgium. You will see why it keeps coming back to me, and why it's something I need to tell you. It is something a man does not forget.

This happened in the small town of Edgely, during the bitter January of 1908 or 1909. The youthful minds I found waiting for me there seemed as harsh and ignorant as that cruel weather. From the very beginning I was thwarted, vexed, deceived, chuckled at, abused, ignored, tried, hounded, belittled and tested. Until one morning I awoke from my slumber. I remember the day with particular clarity. I'd just begun a class on prime numbers when I was greeted with a series of spitballs. I turned quickly. A buckle of laughter rose from the back row. These were restless children, I knew, but here a line had been crossed. I felt the laughter spread forward until the whole room—that is to say the entire schoolhouse—was wetting itself with laughter (pardon the expression). I stood stricken, dumbfounded and burning with anger. When I asked who was responsible there was, of course, no response. I asked a second time. The laughter retreated like an ocean tide to the back rows and there it stalled. "Hands on desks now," I ordered, then slowly walked down the aisle examining each boy, his hands and funereal smirk. As I approached the back of the class, where the laughter had both started and ended, a foot caught me. Up and over I went, tumbling to the boards. Another howl of laughter rained down over me. Cursing now, I rose to my feet and with great eagerness pulled up the guilty boy, or who I thought was the most likely culprit, by the collar. I very nearly lifted him out of his shoes as I held him against the back wall of the classroom. His eyes suggested that I had gained his undivided attention. Three times his head hit the wall and three times his yellowy eyes rolled over like broken egg yolks. I would surely have continued, for my anger felt quite intoxicating, but something came over me—common sense, most likely.

Before I was able to release the boy from my grip I felt a punch on the side of my head. Another boy was on me. I turned to face a big farm lad named Jimmy, a sullen and angry boy I'd never much liked to begin with. Without a word I laid him out with a single punch. He fell like a sack of potatoes, and silence descended over his classmates. Stepping over him, I returned to my desk and sat ramrod straight, staring down the young cretins like a regent awaiting signs of full-out rebellion. Soon the boy came to, whimpering somewhat. He moved his jaw with a hand, testing it as he returned to his seat. When the hour struck I rose silently and walked out the door, convinced that this was the end of my teaching career.

That evening I was restive. I lived with an old woman who had difficulty remembering my name, but her head for figures was fine and she never failed to remind me how much I owed her from week to week. I lay in my hard bed late into the night and wondered what the following day held in store. I had no fear of the law for I knew this community frowned upon its Constable Ryan. He was a sad drunk, they said, and kept his nose out of their business as best he could, as long as they didn't come between him and his favourite taverns. It was not the law I was concerned about.

I shaved that morning, and though it was doubtful I needed to, that is what I did. I suppose I was shoring myself up. I probably made threatening faces in the mirror, but I remember staring at myself and wondering what my face would look like cut and smashed and what hints of regret it might bear should my body be laid out on a slab awaiting identification by my parents, and what their reaction would be beyond the sorrow felt by my mother and the pity and shame felt by my father. Would I be a good-looking cadaver? I wondered. A strange thought—though it has crossed my mind a number of times since.

My heart racing, I left my landlady sitting silently in her rocking chair and marched down the single street of that village, prepared to meet whatever awaited me. I unlocked the schoolhouse—being as much custodian as headmaster, principal and teacher—and arranged my textbooks, then began pacing nervously up and down the class-room.

To my surprise, the morning proceeded without incident. I sensed no rebellion whatsoever. The boys were well behaved, better than I had ever seen them. It seemed that yesterday's confrontation was precisely what was needed to settle them down a good deal, so I thought we might make some genuine progress. We concentrated on mathe-matics, then reading and history in the second and third hours, and when geography came we began with a lesson on western Europe. Only four of the twenty were able to locate that continent on the map for me. This ignorance suggested a sad state of affairs indeed. But the manner in which these boys wore their ignorance that morning was almost endearing, for they were humbled and by no means proud of their lack of knowledge. I could hardly blame them for their rowdy behaviour in a school that had managed to teach them so little.

I dismissed the boys for lunch on a positive note, liberating them a few minutes early as a reward for their co-operation. I worried that I'd misjudged their cruelty and thought badly of myself for doing so.

They were a fine lot, I concluded, and the day was looking up. I returned to my lodging for a meal of barley and beet soup and three slices of dark rye and started back to my schoolhouse before half past noon.

The mood there was very much changed, with boys swarming and snickering in the schoolyard. I felt their energy from a hundred yards and slowed my pace, unable to construct a strategy to help the situation. As I stepped through the main gate the crowd of boys parted and before me stood a large man, much larger than any student and taller than me by half a head. I knew this man to look at from the village but did not know his name. He stepped forward to meet me. Too young to be the father of a student, he perhaps was a brother of the boy I'd knocked down.

"Bethune," he said, "you need some of that thrashing you like to dole out to these helpless boys."

"I give back only what's given out."

"Well then, I've come to return what's yours."

He hit me with a fair punch to the left side of my head. I saw it coming but was still too bewildered to react. It was not possible that I should find myself standing in a schoolyard on the point of entering into a fistfight; this was not what any teacher expects, though I believed it soon enough. My vision turned white and my ears rang for a quick moment with the force of another blow. I staggered but stayed upright. When the lights cleared and my ears stopped ringing I was able to hear whoops of joy coming from the crowd that had gathered around. My students were overjoyed by the promise of my defeat.

All this happened quickly. I should hope you never see such a fight, but imagine if you can a man—a boy barely yet a man—strong enough, back straight, fists forward. In a fight like that instinct counts, but experience means the difference between standing and falling. After that second punch I regained myself and the shouts of joy became calls of encouragement for my opponent. I soon learned his name was Robert. Kill him, Robert, the boys shouted, make him sorry he done that to poor Jimmy, and so on. We began in earnest then, weaving and bobbing in and out. One of us threw a good punch now and then. We were circling a fair bit, looking for the invitation of a dropped fist or a missed step. It was snowing lightly and a beautiful light was shining down, and a surprising calmness came over me—akin to the elation I'd felt the day I understood myself to be alone in a Godless world, that the world was mine to make. Within a minute or two it was snowing heavily, but I finished the matter so splendidly that the new-fallen snow had not yet made a noticeable accumulation on the snow already trampled in the yard or on the slate roof of the schoolhouse and the caps of the watching boys. Their cries of encouragement were silenced when it became clear in whose favour the fight was turning. He was a large lad but in the end that did not help him. I laid him out as I had laid out his brother the day before. Serves you right, I thought. There I stood, a trace of blood on my split lip, taunting him, "Get up, you, get up, you, I'll finish you, you miserable s——t."

He was finished but I wanted more: I am ashamed to say it, but it's true. I felt the surprise in the crowd's silence when I finally stopped demanding he rise to his feet, and an overwhelming pleasure, a sort of delirium, at my victory. At the same time I was overcome with shame. Is this what my idealism had turned into, the desire to stomp a man? I was the one who had finally taught the thug a lesson, the oafish brother of the boy who'd tripped me up, and by the looks of it this was something new in this town. I was not a teacher standing there now but the town bully, an enforcer, warrior and constable all in one. I was drunk with satisfaction and I was red with shame. I knew his nose was broken, I'd heard the crack. The cold air had delivered the resounding snap for the whole school to hear. It was as if the frozen branch of the greatest tree in the county had buckled under the weight of wet snow.

✳   ✳   ✳

Earlier this evening I had a free moment. I carried my chair outside and watched this village from the doorway of the old ramshackle hut they've put me in and sat there like some old man waiting for his time to come. There was a chill in the air, which has become sharper in the hours since. (Thank goodness the heat has broken!) I leaned my chair back against the door frame and breathed in the smells of China. A man enjoying his peace. But for the chaos around me, that's what you might have thought, that the world had for a moment fallen still, and what a lovely thought that is. When all one has ever dreamed of accomplishing is set out before him, like a series of paintings or poems ready for cataloguing, there to speak for him once he is gone. Is that what a great artist would feel? I long to settle into the weary comfort of age. There I was, biding my time. For a moment I felt truly at ease.

I will tell you flat out that I myself was not a model student and so should not be so hard on those poor boys of Edgely. My dear mother, bless her heart, would take this opportunity to remind me that we are each granted our own particular skills and abilities and talents, some of us for book study, some for ploughing, some for healing the sick. When I gained entrance to the university the following year I was reminded of that fact once again. I have not forgotten it since, despite my failures by the cartload. I have always been a bit impatient, a bit impertinent, a bit hot-headed. The only crime would lie in the denial of this truth. In the lecture hall I was inattentive, openly rebellious, bored and short-tempered.

I left the university for a time, only to return again, and during the winter of my second year the Great War began. I was twenty-four years old. I recall that day with deep sorrow, though at the time I didn't know enough to see through the smoke screen of patriotic pride and glory. Within a week of the announcement, the halls and classrooms at the university were abuzz with talk of driving the Kaiser back into his hole. Oh, it was heady stuff for a boy looking to make himself into a man. We all went in for it. It was not difficult to leave the university behind. I had not excelled, and the European war offered an excuse for all of us to abandon that cloistered world and begin the great adventure of life. I signed up and for the first weeks of my enlisting was proudly occupied with the task of saving humanity from itself. Soon my enthusiasm was replaced by tedium and a longing for the comforts of home. I had never seen so many uniforms and so many people thinking identical thoughts. The army is like that. It is sure to reveal your individuality, if you have any, and stamp it out as quickly as possible. What had begun, in the spirit of good fun and adventure, at the university and in the streets of Toronto and every other Canadian town and city—and continued at Valcartier, where I enlisted, and aboard the SS *Cassandra* to England, where we would endure months of training—became a grinding routine of drills and grub and close quarters. Already the romance of war was wearing thin.

Only fools and thugs enjoyed this life. You can probably imagine. Our patriotism was orchestrated and came in waves, soon competing with a nostalgic yearning for a good home-cooked meal. Unbelievable casualty numbers circulated among us, rumours purporting wildly unrealistic sums of the dead. Ten thousand in one day, thirty thousand the next. We were officially warned to disregard such slanders, you can imagine why. Propaganda was manufactured by the Hun and directed toward King and Country, we were told. But even still you began to fear that this was indeed a war and not an adventure, though we were insulated from it by razor wire and soapbox speeches and optimistic newspaper articles regarding the outcome.

While I was at Fort Pitt, in the south of England, thousands of Canadian boys came through. Only a mild feeling of curiosity and nostalgia grew within me when I saw the boy, now a man, I had beaten in the schoolyard four or five years earlier.

"Hello, Robert," I said. He looked at me without a glimmer of recognition. I smiled and faked a left jab and still he had no idea.

"Bugger off," he said.

"How long have you been here?" I asked.

"Thirty-nine days," he said.

"Maybe we were on the same ship over, the *Cassandra*?"

"That's the one," he said. "Stinking s——t bucket."

"It'll get worse, don't worry about that," I said.

"Maybe it will," he said.

That evening at mess, I sat two men down from him and ate my supper without drawing attention to myself. I watched him. He ate with his head hanging over his plate, a horse feeding at a trough. He had no interest in the men around him. He ignored their taunts and rough jokes. But all around us were boys committed like him to their silence in the hope that it would speed their time there and maintain the peace of mind they'd brought over with them. He was determined, eating with fear and concentration. He would fill his belly and sleep and complete whatever duties he was assigned. He was a farmer allotted a single furrow and would not stray outside its narrow rut, I could tell. I was intrigued by this connection to home. I had no free time, not even for letters to my family. My concentration was fiercely set on the adventure ahead.

The presence of Robert Pearce was strangely comforting to me, though. He was a link back to something I knew, and though we'd fought, he was the one who had helped me establish myself in that town. It was through him that I had become the sheriff and the bully and the enforcer with a higher purpose. Something had happened that afternoon, something exceptional in my life, by equal measures shameful and ennobling, something beyond the bullying that I felt still. I wanted to know what that was. I studied him over the following days and weeks. But his sad eyes told me something had changed in him since we'd stood face to face.

I didn't know if it was his being there that pulled him low, or if my knocking him down years before had reduced the bully he once had been to a meek and soft man, lonely for his people and his town and the simple tasks he'd grown used to over his short life. He was maybe twenty-four, my age. He caused no trouble. He marched in a straight line like the rest of us, performed his physical exercises and his rifle work proficiently and not a whit better than was expected. It was as though he was always thinking of something else, and for the weeks I watched him I believed it was the miserable town of Edgely he was dreaming about, caught up in his idyllic boyhood.

The early morning of the day we sailed for Belgium I told him who I was. He smiled softly and said, "It was a fair fight so I don't hold nothing against you." We sat for a moment in silence as the ferry pulled out from the docks. The rumble rattled our bones. The lumps of porridge gurgled in our guts. A low murmur of voices filled the hollows of the ship.

"What are you thinking?" I said.

"I'm thinking I'll die over there."

"We all might," I said. "But there's no knowing."

"I know it," he said.

I said, "Keep your head down, Robert. That's all you can do."

The Channel whipped up, and the crossing took close to two hours.

"This is a sign," he said. " 'Turn back,' it's saying."

"I don't think so, Robert, it's just weather."

We went above deck and watched England recede through the hundreds of Jacob's ladders that descended from above in gleaming columns. Though the farm lad Robert was full of dread, I felt a sense of history fill my heart and hold me in the good favour of my ancestors. I'd never been so close to war before but had heard all my father's stories of links by blood to the noble past. I knew of the Highland Scot named Angus of Combust, the Jacobite who fell in the battle of Culloden in 1745 and then dragged his wounded body to safety and, through toil and the grace of God, was able to make his way to the Isle of Skye, where he met and married Christina Campbell of the Isle of Harris who bore him a son, my great-great-grandfather John. This man, John Bethune, arrived to North Carolina as a result of the Clearances. There, as a chaplain, he fought with the Royal Highland Immigrants to put down the American rebellion, and then, with the Royal 84th Regiment, he helped defend the Citadel of Quebec against the American invaders in the winter of 1775–76. From these histories and others, I took no small measure of pride and strength in knowing I was of fighting stock, and fight I would when the time came. You see how little I knew then? How flush with romantic dreams I was! This Bethune blood had on many occasions been spilled in earlier times, and if my blood were destined to stain the soil of France and Belgium this year or the next, so be it, I thought, it would run again in the veins of future generations of great-nephews and their sons. But I did not say this. I simply said, "Robert, it's just weather."

I knew what he meant to say, though, and wasn't inclined to look down on him for his anxiety and sadness. He was a man connected to his fear. It was the simple truth. In some ways he was more truthful about the matter than I was. I would never call that cowardice, not then and especially not now. He had every right to fear the coming days. Europe was already a graveyard. He had no ancestry or lineage to warm his breast. He had only a plot in Ontario to look forward to, nothing more than hay and beans and superstitious, nonsensical ideas of poetic weather.

I wished for his sake that suddenly a great fish would leap from the water or a sunny sign would break through the clouds, but the sea was chopped by winds alone and the sky grew only darker as the lovely columns of light streaming down were choked off by great fists of cloud. When we landed at Flanders we organized ourselves and then began filing down the gangplanks loaded down with our packs. The clouds at once disgorged sheets of rain over the Channel behind us and Belgium before us, nothing but rain and more rain. Poor Robert took no heart in what he saw waiting, and later I thought he somehow had known what was coming.

It was as cold as England, and maybe as cold as northern Ontario, where the trees were white with snow now, and suddenly we were much closer to the war.

If you had been unable to imagine the fighting thoroughly enough before coming over, you saw it in the country once you arrived. The landscape was a torn carcass stretched before us like nothing I'd ever seen. Limbs hung from tree branches. Barbed wire stitched across open wounds in the earth. An arm reached out from the mud like a pathetic shrub.

I remember on our left flank we had the French 87th Territorial and the 45th Algerian Division. On our right we had the Brits. They looked as if they'd suffered ordeals a thousand times worse than our basic training. There were already ghosts in their eyes. It was quiet the first night I arrived, though, and I had occasion to pretend the worst was over. I was racked with fear and excitement, quietly hunched in a ball in an underground bunker with forty or fifty men. Its dirt walls were supported by thick lumber. A cloaked man brushed past me, looked down, and my eyes met his. It was as if he couldn't see me, not with those haunted eyes. But he *had* seen something he would never forget, I thought. Perhaps now he saw only cadavers in the uniforms around him. He had seen and smelled the unimaginable, and it would not let him go. The eyes offered a story but it was a coded, silent mystery I could make no sense of. He scurried off in the dark. To help me pass the hours that first night I recalled my father's stories of France in her glory days and our family's life there before they migrated to Scotland. On that cold first night in Belgium, the family legends provided a curious mixture of strength of purpose and impermanence. On the transport ship over, I had been buoyed by thoughts of genealogy as destiny, but as the black night deepened these family histories no longer held me in such thrall. I felt more akin to Robert the farmer than to any distant nobility.

It is late September. We have arrived without incident to the base of the Wu-t'ai Mountains at Sung-yen K'ou. How many villages have I slept in since arriving, how many abandoned huts have hosted my restless sleep? I am told this area of Shansi Province holds some significant religious aura. You will not be surprised that I cannot myself attest to its spiritual power, but I can tell you that it is a remarkably beautiful place. There are Buddhist temples on every hill and cliff here, it seems. I suppose I can imagine some god smiling down upon this landscape in some previous century. But be that as it may, the Eighth Route Army can use as many solid structures as they can find, and these temples of stone and mortar were built to serve the most eternal of spirits.

We have found a hospital here in thorough disarray but are whipping it into shape. I take it you know by now that in north China "hospital" signifies nothing more than a ramshackle and incomplete assortment of medical supplies and poorly trained doctors gathered together under the nearest roof. This is what we have here, of course. I have taken to giving daily lectures on sanitation and other basics as well as tending to the wounded. I expect to stay here through the month before moving on. Twenty men of my training here would still not be enough. I have been provided a hut not far from the hospital, and Ho is hard at work turning it into something that resembles a home. He's even found a desk for the Remington. More than I can ask, really, considering.

The truth is that Robert Pearce was just one man among the mass of brown-uniformed men moving through snaking gorges cut into the mud and earth. I sought him out and spent time with him when I could. We met at chow on the narrow stretch between the trenches and the Regimental Aid Station. He was not a man given to words, though his eyes told me he was thinking all the time. He had impressed me with his gracious acceptance of defeat, so I tried to engage him. He was a familiar face, I suppose. Initially that is what drew me to him. I took pity on him, too, as perhaps he did on me. He was as lost as the rest of us and maybe more so, but he made no secret of it.

"I can't say I'm having a good time here, Beth," he said one day, when I saw him standing off by himself.

We all went by nicknames. Beth was the one I answered to.

"Farmer," I said, "it's not what they told us to expect, is it?"

"I believe you like it here, Beth. You're that type. It's not a world I care for."

"I like it here less than you," I said. "Do you read the Bible?" He shook his head. "Good," I said. "What do you think about?"

"I think about home. I think about trees. Here it's only mud."

"Trees," I said.

"Climbing. Sitting under. Building with. Pissing against. Blooming. Falling. Colourful leaves. Trees in all their shapes and uses. I dream of a roof of leaves over my head."

Three days later, in the evening, the Germans released poison gas from their positions. It crawled toward us like slow-moving green worms, hugging every pore of earth, cowardly in its advance. Heavier than the air we breathed, it sought low ground and was pushed forward by obliging winds.

The Algerians and Moroccans got the worst of it. When they rose in choking desperation from the gas, the artillery began—a tactic no one had seen before. If they stayed low, the poison got them; if they ran, the shells or bullets did. It was a brilliant and merciless attack. Equipped with respirators, the enemy walked among the dead and blind and breathless as an army of exterminators. This was like nothing we knew. Our communications were down but news spread along the line for miles that the Hun had changed the rules of war. Runners brought word that we were to contain the salient at all costs, despite this new weapon.

We were ordered to prepare a counter-attack. As dark fell, fifteen hundred men collected in a nearby field. It was a grim sea of mud-splattered faces. These men would move against the enemy in eight waves. We would follow behind, the members of my Field Ambulance Unit, tending to the fallen, then carrying them back to safety. It was a night of terrible anticipation. Silence was the rule, and in this silent gloom each man attempted to master his fear in his own way, and accept his coming death. Just before midnight the whistle blew and the first wave went over, then the next and the next, like a pulsing, raging heartbeat running down to its last, until No Man's Land was overrun by the living and the dead.

We began our work then, searching in teams of six in the darkness and listening for calls, groans or weeping, the organic noises of the fallen. It was not possible to run in mud as deep as that, and the shells and screaming and gunfire deafened anyone who tried, leaving him disoriented and useless to those whom he had come out in search of. Sometimes you stumbled over one of your men even before you knew what he was, not just a stump. That first night we went out more times than I could count. It was by far the dirtiest day my life had yet seen. All night long I saw things I had never imagined possible. In the ghostly green lightning of bursting shells men glowed and flickered as their flesh dropped away from them in pieces. Those men you could not help and their screams faded as the burning grew brighter.

I listened for the cries of the living, not the dying. These led down into dark holes, like a string pulling you by the guts to your own death, in hopes that you might load a man on a stretcher, all six of you committed to this one simple, near-impossible task. It felt nothing less than superhuman. Back and forth we trudged, often more than an hour for every man. We worked like machines in the mud with no time to think or feel pity. There were occasions of nausea at the sight of exploded bodies. Again and again the night lit up with cannon and flares to illuminate the sight of one of our men doubled over retching. We moved forward, avoiding a single building in the distance that was said to house a machine-gun nest. We'd advanced and taken the forward trench of the enemy with bayonet and hand-to-hand fighting, and following the capture of that ditch we stretcher-bearers descended into the pure dark to find what we could. We ignored the enemy's pleas to staunch the flow of their wounds. There was much leg- and boot-work on the dying. This was how we'd been taught to dislodge a stuck bayonet—the full force of the body, foot against shoulder to pull mightily if the blade had wedged into the chest plate or single rib. If it was stuck deep into the spinal column there was no hope for the boy, and sometimes a man came out of nowhere, without a word, and helped him die quickly, but I was not forced to do so, not yet, though I had already heard the necessity for it in inhuman groans closer to death than to life.

Through the night the fighting continued, horror upon horror. The Germans counter-attacked, having previously buttressed their forward lines with reinforcements. Waves of them came at us, and in our turn we advanced against them, and my comrades and I picked over the deep fields for the wounded who awaited us. A disembodied voice was always imploring from the darkness beyond, but too often a search party was denied permission if the position was too exposed. And so the night proceeded. Our spotters informed us as to the approximate position of a man located through sightings or his cries, then off we went like spelunkers down a dark cave.

Just days into it, we were as experienced as the French Colonials to our left and the British to our right. Distant explosions and sniper fire never let up during the lulls in fighting. Catching a moment's rest, I leaned against a wall of earth and timber and conjured thoughts of the sacrifices and the ancient battlefields of my forebears. It was my desperate attempt to find heroism in my blood. But by now I knew that it was all—the gallantry, the romance, the glory—a great deception.

On the seventh day we consolidated our line with the help of British reinforcements who'd arrived at the small town of St. Julien. The day broke sunny and clear. It was a great relief to feel the natural warmth on my face, but a dread, too, as the enemy's spirit would be similarly improved. Waiting for instructions to move, we played cards, wrote letters, thought about home. I wrote to my family reporting that I was alive and well, the war was proceeding apace and with luck I should be home before the end of summer. Belgium was not what I had imagined and neither was the human spirit, in fact, more noble than anything I had ever known. The common man here—the farmers and bricklayers and factory workers so in abundance along the front— possessed such dignity in these least of humane conditions that I felt honoured to be associated with them. It was horrible to witness the true horrors of war, but we all were committed to the certain victory ahead and in good spirits, our morale undaunted.

I felt obliged to include these lies for the sake of my mother and sister, whose worry preoccupied me as much as my own fate in those days. I attempted to keep my letters optimistic and descriptive in nature, highlighting my daily rituals and observations, along with a telling anecdote, such as the time one of the boys, named Bud MacFarlane, had stood a stretcher on its hand-grips and danced a waltz under a full moon. There were twenty men in the Number Two Field Ambulance, myself included—numbers enough to find characters of Bud's sort. I wrote home about some of those boys, and about a soft-spoken lad named Robert I'd met over here from my teaching days, explaining that he had no greater ambition than to return to his people back home, find a wife and raise children. As I wrote this I felt a momentary desire to claim those plain desires as my own, suspecting that my mother would find peace in such wholesome simplicity, given my perilous situation, but knowing, too, that fabricating such sentimental nonsense would do no one any good in the long run.

The Regimental Aid Station was located only three miles behind the front line. When not writing letters, we spent our time preparing for an assault, either offensive or from the enemy, organizing and stocking and making sure all was in order, from generators and surgical equipment to operating tables. Idle time was best filled with labour, an occupied mind finding fewer opportunities to dwell on the madness around us.

In fact, the solemn anticipation felt among the men before they jumped the bags and until the stretcher-bearers came forth to fetch the wounded was, in its way, less terrifying than the idle waiting. In those last moments the mind races and the body, powered by adrenalin and fear, becomes a coiled spring. Just moments behind the forward rush, the stretcher-bearers poured from the trenches into the fighting to collect the wounded and hurry them back to the Aid Post, where the surgeons worked on the boys who needed it most while many others waited. We returned again and again to No Man's Land to bring back those who could be stabilized then loaded onto horse-drawn carts and transported by lorry or tram to the Field Ambulance, where they were further cared for and eventually shipped in the space of a day or two to the clearing hospitals near the French ports, or maybe as far away as Merry Old England, if they were lucky enough to find themselves wounded out of the war.

As I say, I attempted to maintain an optimistic tone in these letters regarding my own situation, on occasion hinting at the fear and anxiety and harsh conditions, hoping that the censors would not interfere; but for the most part I wrote of my longings for home and study and the company of my family and the north woods. These letters gave me great respite and were a forum for my dreams to run free, a release from the tedium and filth and death all around me. As if from a well I drew memories of camping and fishing trips and clear air and even the confines of Edgely, Ontario, where I'd learned a thing or two about the strength of will and learning to fight with your fists. I always signed my letters "Yours with love," and those I received with such anticipation began in my mother's hand "Our dear son" or my father's "Dear Norman." Those words alone often provoked tears and I felt an impossible distance separate me from my family. It was like reading a book from a century past, with every paragraph registering the irrecoverable years and miles. Upon opening a letter, I sometimes found a man hiding behind his cloth. "Dear Norman," he would write, "It will do you good to remember the Lord's words in times like these. Every day I pray for your safe return:

Thou shalt not be afraid for the terror by night;
nor for the arrow that flieth by day;
Nor for the pestilence that walketh in darkness;
nor for the destruction that wasteth at noonday.

And with a definitive Amen, your grandfather would hurriedly sign off like a man late for his own sermon.

Of course, I preferred your grandmother's letters, filled with news of my brother, Malcolm, and sister, Janet, and of the precocious children in her Sunday School class and talk of neighbours and their pride that I was here in the fight as all good boys must be. Some letters I saved while others were lost in the chaos of those days. I remember clearly one in which your grandmother wrote that they were pinning white feathers onto the lapels of able-bodied men back home. "A league of women who make it their business to meddle," she said, and went on to describe rallies in Toronto. Though my mother was no warmonger—nor was my father, certainly—their letters were predictably patriotic. Such thinking had become almost like breathing, I supposed. I did not think badly of this, only saddened on occasion that people should have such strong opinions of things which they knew so little about. Here we saw the fighting through a different lens. We did not see "war" but only a few hundred yards of nothing, beyond which were men who wanted to kill us. It was nothing like this present war in China, since we had no ideals other than to avoid death.

In an attempt to entertain ourselves, we sometimes read aloud our letters from home—the funny or pleasant bits, in any case. When I read my mother's account of the women and their white feathers, a young French literature major from the University of Toronto made a smart remark about those old biddies taking after the decadent scatologist Rabelais and employing their white feathers in a more useful manner.

The same day I saw Robert, who'd been sent to the Aid Station after cutting his hand while sharpening a bayonet. I wrapped him up, it was not serious, and sat talking with him afterwards. He seemed peaceful and said, "Does this mean I'm going home?"

"It's not up to me, Farmer," I said, "but it's not likely. You have to be hurt worse than that."

He nodded. "That's all right, Beth. I feel it. I'm going home soon. Look at this stretch of weather."

"Good things to come," I said.

"I got a letter the other day. It was from my brother, the one you walloped in school that time. He can't wait to come over and fight the Kaiser with me. He's just turned eighteen and my mother can't keep him from coming no more. Jimmy's not a violent boy, and I don't think he'd like it here. I have a letter for him in my breast pocket that I'll send tomorrow. I'm asking him to wait on the enlisting, and promise I'll be back soon. I told him I can feel it coming."

The fighting started again the following day. It never went away but levelled off with constant ongoing skirmishes. There was always the crack of rifle fire or an exploding shell in the distance, but these seemed like waves from a distant shore. On April 29 it came as a tidal wave.

The attack began that morning at eleven o'clock. The inevitable counter-attack followed, and shortly after that we went over. Each man that day took an average of two hours for the mere three hundred yards we had to travel. The mud was often past our knees. We were still going out at sunset, and the sky had a purple tinge to it when we went up for our last man, just then spotted by one of the snipers. He was lying wedged against a post, tangled in barbed wire, on a slight rise in the terrain. We followed the ears of a boy named McGraw, from Calgary, Alberta, who claimed he could hear the Kaiser sneeze in Berlin on a quiet day. It took close to an hour to locate and approach the man. The closer we came the more sure I was that he was dead and this dangerous attempt would end in futility, but from twenty yards off we saw the lump flinch. An arm wiggled, almost waving us on. "It's Farmer, I think," one of the boys said. We came closer, and it was Robert.

It was a wonder a sniper had failed to get him in such an exposed position. Maybe the gentle rise in the land had obscured him, or from the opposite angle the enemy was unable to notice the twitching that became more evident as we approached, or they were just too tired to care. Maybe they thought to let him die out there, slowly. Then I heard the whistle of a shell. McGraw called us down right then and we jumped and the shell exploded. I realized that Robert was the lure, the bait. We'd been drawn out, I remember thinking. This was the end of us. As the dirt settled I waited. The debris cleared, and I waited still. I didn't dare to call out to my friends. Crawling on my knees, chest to the ground, I found my party dead. I tested each man for signs of life but they were all gone, each one of them. I lay motionless and cried and asked God why I had survived. I spoke to God, for the last time in my life, and He did not speak back.

Then I heard a single moan. I lay flat on my stomach without moving. It seemed I waited a century. I shifted my head ever so slightly and saw Robert, removed from the fence post now—likely by the force of the mortar blast—and sprawling flat on the ground. I saw him, or what I thought was him. He was a lump of clothing staring up to the sky. I waited. I watched him. The sun behind him sank below the horizon. The sky turned a lovely pink and yellow and slowly the blues and purples dropped from the centre directly above, spreading downward slowly to the horizon like running paint washing out the colours from the sunset, and then I was alone in the night surrounded by the dead and a handful of stars.

I listened to Robert's moans. In the new dark I saw him roll his head toward me, and his eyes opened. They were small white things. I crawled toward him carrying a canteen, an aid kit and my sidearm. "Robert," I said, "it's me, Beth. Stop your groaning, they'll hear you." I examined him and found a large piece of wood piercing his left thigh. His cheek was hanging open like a second set of lips. He was missing his left ear. He was a terrible sight. I told him to shut his mouth. "I'll get you back," I said, "you can survive this. But you have to shut up.

They're not far off, and they can shoot with their ears as well as their eyes."

I remember thinking it best to leave the leg as it was. I wrapped his thigh tight with a tourniquet to staunch the flow, though it seemed already to have ebbed. In the dark I hefted him up onto my shoulders and began walking. I managed perhaps ten or fifteen feet before we fell into a crater. I lay silent, trying to catch my breath, and watched the darkness above us. Our round view of the universe looked peaceful and still. I was very tired now. It was like looking up from the bottom of a well, darkness on all sides giving way to a dark sky specked with lights. It looked like a hat full of stars above us, flowers in a lady's bonnet. A sharp chill draped itself like a shawl over my shoulders. I heard potshots and cannon fire but it felt far removed from our situation, as harmless as distant thunder.

I whispered, "It's like a spring evening back home, Robert."

He moaned, a sound deep and throaty, almost echo-like. I didn't understand what caused it but then I realized that the hole in his face functioned as a second mouth and he was trying to speak as if with two voices. There was nothing I could do but keep him company in his suffering. I had no medicines to induce unconsciousness. "When you get back," I said softly, "you'll tell that brother of yours that a German hits from behind, like a woman."

He moaned again. After a minute he tried to speak but nothing comprehensible came out, only a strange murmuring through his teeth and that doubled sound as it passed through his destroyed cheek. He gave up and fell silent again. Soon I dozed. When I awoke it was full dark. The stars have closed their eyes, I thought, and now I am blind. I reached over and tapped Robert, who stirred and grunted. "It's time to start again," I whispered. His head fell forward, so I tapped him again harder.

I pulled up to the ridge of the crater and left him slightly below, protected, while I peeked out. I saw nothing, just blackness spotted by distant fires far behind the enemy's lines, or maybe they were our lines, I couldn't be sure. I slipped back into the crater, took hold of Robert and dragged him moaning up into the night. "Shut up," I said, then gripped him by the crotch and arm and stood, turning slowly in a circle to get the lay of the land. I believed I noticed the gentle incline pointing toward home and so I started. "Robert, if you know something I don't, feel free to tell me now," I said. "Because we're knee deep in s——t now, Robert." I stopped to adjust my grip, then continued. "Robert," I said, "I'll be honest with you, Robert Pearce. I wish we were standing in that schoolyard. I'd take a bleeding lip over this any day."

After a time I put him down again. I remember feeling that my legs could go no farther. I looked in all directions, again turning in a slow circle. I saw no distinguishing features, nothing on this landscape to direct me. There were no fires now, just complete blackness. I rested as long as I thought it was safe, then picked him up again. I continued in the direction I believed we'd been walking now half the night. My feet sank into the mud and each step felt like the Devil himself was grabbing hold of my foot down there. God had not answered and now Satan would, his fiery hands reaching up to grip my ankle as I struggled to raise it again.

And this with a man on my shoulders. I walked on with my burden, my friend. Suddenly the earth would open before us and down we would slide to the bottom of a bomb crater. I would catch my breath and then climb up again to the edge, hoping it was the proper side to come up on, and pull him up over the lip of mud so we could forge deeper into the night.

I hoped for a single star to break through the cloud cover, but none did. "Don't worry," I said quietly, trudging along, "and do you know why, Farmer?" I heard that raspy, echoing breathing through mouth and cheek. "There's no need to worry because we're brothers and this night will end once and for all, and we'll come out on the right side. We're brothers, after all. Not because we think alike, you and I—we couldn't be more different—and it's not because we have a common enemy who wants to see us dead, but because together we're being tested and we have no one to look to or depend on, just ourselves. We're brothers because my life is in your hands and yours is in mine, because on this night we'll find out what we have in store for us. I can say I've never been in a situation like this, Farmer, this is rock bottom as far as I'm concerned. We only have each other, and what we find out here in this wasteland will make us as close to holy as we're ever likely to get, and holy I wish to be, although you don't look to the Bible in times like these. But that doesn't change the fact that out here in this muddy, starless night, not knowing which way to go, we'll be made either holy or dead, and I much prefer the former, Robert, so just hang on. It's just as well you can't hear me because I don't know what I'm saying, but I'll keep talking anyway." His breathing rose and fell gently against the back of my neck. "Farmer, this will be a story one day. A story to tell your little brother."

The tourniquet on the upper portion of his left thigh was still tight. "You were right, that weather did mean something. I think it means you'll be out of this war in no time. This is the story of how you got out of the war. Beth carries you to safety. Won't that make a grand story? You might even beat that letter in your pocket home. You'll be having breakfast one morning with your little brother when that letter comes knocking and you'll take it from the postman's hand and think of poor me still stuck here thinking of you." I rolled him off my shoulders and sat.

I waited. I dreamed the world was full of light. Bright blue stars streaked across the sky. When I opened my eyes I saw this was not a dream. A flare had been sent up. For a few seconds I sat in full daylight in a vast ocean of mud and mounds of churned earth and the tangled bodies of men. I did not move. I watched the flare sink in the sky, and the sky slowly returned to its sombre grey, then the indifferent dark returned. We were alone in our private sea of darkness.

Just as the green glow of dying ember-tip was extinguished and I was attempting to lift Robert, I heard the crack of a German Mauser—distinct and not difficult to distinguish from a Lee-Enfield. I knew this before I felt the bullet penetrate my leg. I collapsed and thought, Thank you. Thank you for pointing me home. I gripped the leg while keeping my sights aimed in the direction opposite the one I knew the bullet had come from, for behind me was the Mauser and ahead of me was home and what I now had to do was tie off my leg below the knee without losing sight of that hole in the darkness. It pointed a straight line away from the Mauser. Assume the life of the bullet, I told myself, and continue in the direction it was travelling. I sat down, rolled Robert off, removed the tourniquet soaked with his blood and wrapped my leg. Go, I told myself, follow the bullet. The world glowed again. It was not the light of flares or bombs or fire. The night glowed ecstatically.

Maybe I've told you too much. I am sorry. It was not my aim to burden you with difficult tales of my life. But I'm beginning to think that's exactly where the truth lies. You take strength where you can find it, whether from the dark or the light. Those were terrible times. But they did not belong only to me. If you are to know anything about me, you will understand that. I have acted with fine intentions and failed miserably. I have given the best of myself and found that it wasn't enough. I have wished for my father's strength. I have envied his ability to pray for those things he himself could not provide or achieve, and have envied his God-like patience when it came to waiting for an answer. I have envied his faith, in the face of the horrors I've seen. Tomorrow, another day. Higher into the hills.

I was shipped to Southampton, England, like so many wounded out of the war, and then on to the Cambridge Military Hospital. It was there I learned to walk again. There I mastered, for the second time in my life, the baby step. And there, three days into my convalescence, it was confirmed for me that both Robert and God had been left for dead in that wasteland. It is not pleasant to dwell on this dark time, and if I'm correct in saying that the difficult tales of my life will bring forth some hard truth, you can be sure there will be a fair measure of it here.

In total I spent eleven weeks at the hospital. With great pain I waited from one day to the next for some sign. For the darkness to lift. I was wheeled about in a chair, but the windows were set high in the walls and poorly designed for viewing from that position, so I sat in the grey shadows waiting like a crippled child for his father to come and take him in his arms. Near the end of my third week I rose with a great teeth-grinding effort. Aided by a cane I managed briefly to teeter on my legs and peer down into the garden, and slowly, in ever-widening arcs as the weeks passed, I began to explore the wide polished hallways and stairwells, the lounges and cafeterias. Into my sixth week I investigated the carved granite front steps leading back into the world, and when I was ready I journeyed down to the bright lawns and their gentle slopes to the riverbed.

Standing at this window I watched the elms and the ginkgoes display their new blossoms on the grounds below, and the river grew fat and brown with the spring rains and carried away the buds of willows. I attempted to compose a letter to Robert's family but was not successful. Every afternoon I took my spot at the window and put pen to paper, yet nothing came. Both God and Robert were dead, and words, too, were dead for me. Birds came down from their branches to pick in the grass and fluttered up and off at the approach of a cheerily dressed nurse strolling with a patient on her arm. I observed the world while trying to write the correct letter, though all I could think about was that night I'd left Robert out there to die. In the dark I closed my ears to the panicked calls that issued from the nightmares of sleeping soldiers. What did they see? How I tried to dodge that question as I lay waiting for light to break through the darkness.

I watched the hushed frenzy that marked the arrival of a new man, or the ordered regimen of nurses going about their business. I visited other floors, and sometimes a nurse sent me away; others merely regarded me with a look of irritation, and some did not regard me at all. There were many young nurses whose responsibilities had been accelerated prematurely as a result of pressing need, whereas the doctors seemed too old, many having come out of retirement; but the hospital was always calm and efficient, and I was cared for with a high degree of professionalism and attention.

It is difficult to live for months in the dark without once seeing the face of an angel. Wait long enough, dream long enough, and she will come. What finally appeared to me was not an Angel of God but an angel for a young boy turned man, still young enough to hold such silly dreams but old enough to feel the crushing solitude of the place that housed him.

Such an angel came to me in the form of Agnes McGinnis, a quiet, intelligent girl from the hand-loom weaving village of Little Goven, near Glasgow. This was many years ago—you must permit me a wide berth here—but these memories of her, the lilt in the voice I can still hear in my head, suggest a lighter heart than I have attested to. Perhaps I was even younger than I knew. She was only one of many who tended to us in that ward, but she was the one I most remember, the one who raised my spirits. In practical terms, she was very good at blanket-bathing and wound-dressing. Her patients hardly noticed her going about her work. In not so practical terms, she was too fast for my liking. From the moment she snipped off the old dressing, cleaned my leg and applied the new bandage, the process rarely lasted more than two minutes. Often I simply closed my eyes. Other times we exchanged snippets of conversation. We struck up a friendship. I told her what I could of myself and my family. After I mentioned the Scots blood in my veins, she came to me every afternoon with a new story of her village—Crazy Pete, the story of the talking ducks, the day Jimmy Quinn fell down the well. She painted such a fine picture of the place that I decided to go there with her and stay a lifetime. I listened eagerly. Her eyes hinted at a future I could only long for.

As she snipped my bandages, she told me she spent her one day off a week in London, an hour and a half distant, where she liked to sit for hours in the great cavernous silence of the British Museum. She preferred Ancient Egypt above all else. She admired its gods and goddesses, each with an assigned place in the world. She went with a girlfriend, a nurse in the opposite wing to mine. They saved for the train and ate sandwiches as they watched the countryside roll by. They complained to each other about the matron, Simpson, who managed to torment all the nurses equally. I squirmed and moaned as she talked, hoping to slow her down. Her fingers raced across my leg. To keep her by my bedside longer I asked if she had a favourite part of London. Had she ever seen the Tate Gallery? Did she know Soho Square? One day, not expecting any sort of considered answer, I asked if she had any favourite god or goddess. This question seemed to catch her. It was as if she'd been thinking this over for some time. Her fingers stopped their work. She said she didn't have one, not really, but I could see her thinking. "Well," she said, "if you'd have me choose, it'd likely be Nephthys, not that I'd like to be her."

"Well, why's that?"

"I'm just being truthful, I suppose. That's what all the nurses would say, and the doctors too, if you asked them, if they had any idea of that sort of thing. Nephthys, you see, is the friend of the dead."

"But I'm not dead yet," I said, smiling. She finished quickly, without saying more, and went on to her next patient. She did not come back to me for some days, and when she did I asked if I'd upset her. She laughed off the suggestion and asked what I thought about the food, wasn't it approaching criminal?

Although I still could not be sure what had thrown her so badly that day, our private communications resumed, and no one knew that we grew closer, though I suspected some of the other men in the ward might have guessed what was going on between us despite Matron Simpson's admonitions to avoid fraternizing with the patients. For a few days after this disclosure, there was a lull in our conversations as she wrapped my leg. I knew she'd been shaken by her own words.

Despite her change in mood, I looked forward to her visits and pre-pared questions in advance. But I did not question her on the gods any further.

On a Tuesday she wheeled my chair down to the river, which by early June had been reduced to a shallow brook strung with waving ribbons of algae. The willows were in full bloom now. It was a beauti-ful English day. She sat on the grass beside the chair. We watched the clouds don their costumes and strip them clear again. First we saw a dragon, then a tiger, then a cat, then a sheep. The inventions were swift and effortless as the mile-high currents turned the shapes inside out.

"What will you do after the war?" she asked.

"I will do my best to forget about it, I think."

She said, "I will get very drunk and stay drunk for a week."

"That isn't very ladylike."

"But isn't it a wonderful idea?"

"I have a week's furlough coming up," I said. "I'm staying at the Union Jack in London."

"I could show you my museum."

Two weeks later, in London, she called for me at the club at half past three on the Saturday as planned. I was pleased and full of expec-tation. We enjoyed a short stroll around Green Park. My leg not yet entirely healed, I still walked with a limp and a cane. I wore my wound stripe, as I was obliged to do. Civilians nodded with grave admiration when they saw me. After an hour I took no more notice.

We hired a horse cab and rode between neighbourhoods. It was a wonderful escape from the hospital. We saw signs of the war—a bombed building from one of the German zeppelin raids, torn up cobble. Uniformed men were everywhere. When my eyes met another soldier's, one of us would always turn away too quickly. Was my dis-comfort as clear to him as his was to me? The outside world was a pleasant reminder of another life. We would remain there as long as possible. I had heard the stories of men from the Field Hospital vomit-ing or turning violent at the scent of a lady's perfume after months of living in the stench of blood and sewage, knocking down a well-heeled gentleman for spouting off about the war. But I felt nothing as desperate as this, only the sadness of my loss and the sharp grinding in my damaged leg.

We took a second cab to Great Russell Street and walked slowly through the museum. We stopped often to sit as my leg could carry me only a quarter of an hour at a stretch. We passed from room to room. It was lovely to leave our century, and humbling to know these great civilizations were gone—that the eyes and hands and minds were dead, and their secrets along with them.

Agnes pointed out Nephthys for me. She was drawn into a stone tablet, surrounded by lifeless bodies.

Agnes said, "You know, I don't feel right about what I said, it just seemed tasteless and insensitive, among all those injured men. I say things like that, stupid things. I feel quite ashamed of myself."

"If that's the worst of your sins you'll be okay."

Later in the afternoon, we walked over to Tottenham Court Road, where we decided to drink a pint of beer and found a dim pub. Its hard planks creaked as we walked across the floor. Weary and worn, the place smelled of old men with a faint whiff of lavatory. We took a table. A group sat at the bar drinking, exchanging sudden rough exclamations between their long silences. These usually had something to do with the war. The devils, one man said. Godless heathens. The usual sort of cursing, I will spare you. I drank two pints to the half Agnes drank. I wanted a third and was ready to ask for it but I sensed she wanted to leave. One of the men in particular was getting agitated. He said there was a wickedness attacking the heart of the British Army, a moral degeneracy that threatened to undermine morale. The pacifists and the homosexuals were proof enough that an invasion of home soil had begun and it went as high as the Foreign Office. One of the Kaiser's plots as sure as the Hun's a devil in uniform, he said. But on this subject the others were mute. He seemed a man they didn't want to bother with.

Just as I was thinking this, one of his colleagues, a large fellow, said, "Now, William, drink up and go home. Better yet, go home straight away. You shouldn't need reminding it's our boys dying for us over there." He placed his pint glass, emptied, on the bar before him.

William sipped his bitter, apparently debating his position. He finally said, "You shut your hole, I'll speak my mind if I care to."

"All right, William, all right."

"You'll not talk down to me." He shoved away his pint.

"You'd best be going home now," the bigger man said. "Or why don't you go off to war, brave William, and show us the man you are." The others, their heads hung low till now, looked up and smiled.

William glowered at him but held his tongue. He seemed to realize the man he was provoking was a good head taller and fifty pounds heavier, for he said nothing. Likely he knew he'd been made a fool of, and his only hope was to formulate some way of saving face. A sour black fog had enveloped him. I sat back in my chair waiting for a second round of insults and taunts, then looked over at Agnes. She was gazing out the small window, focused on something far off. William held himself stock-still. He didn't say anything more, simply stared at the other man.

"I'd like to leave now," Agnes said.

"All right," I said. "We'll go."

We hired a cab over to Victoria Station and waited for the Cambridge train, due to depart just after six o'clock. We watched the pigeons and the lottery sellers and the uniformed men.

"He was a drunken fool."

"Yes, he was," I said.

My leg had begun to hurt and I wanted another drink. I knew the leg would feel wooden in the morning. I was glad she was leaving. The excitement of being with her was gone. I had nothing to say and felt drained. I wanted to be alone. I walked her to her platform, where we shook hands and I helped her board the train. Then I walked back to the club.

I have thought about that day off and on over the years, and what strikes me most, I think, is the profound sadness I felt when I understood that this kindly girl could do nothing for me, despite her goodness and patience, and knew for the first time that something in my heart had been changed forever.

ENVELOPE THREE

A nother lovely day. It has been a fine autumn here in Shansi, the air crisp and clean. Almost a month has passed since I wrote last. Please forgive me. I might say the war has detained me, which is true enough. I might plead exhaustion, which also is true. Conditions here provide few natural breaks for a man intent on looking back on his life thoroughly, as this letter is prompting me to do. Yet I will admit now that time, or its lack, is only half the problem.

The story itself, I suppose, is the other half. We've now come upon a difficult chapter in my life, and I have been hoping to avoid it. I have been circling, let's say, gathering strength. Bravery I seem to possess in abundance. Courage is something quite different.

Where, then, to begin?

The Bentley Park Hotel in December of last year.

My stay in New York coincided with some journalism that had brought Frank Pitcairn from England to New York City. I had recently finished touring with the documentary film on the unit, leaving it up in Montreal before coming down to New York to prepare for this China expedition. I tracked him down at the Bentley, wanting to thank him for the piece he'd written for the *Daily Worker*. I also wanted to take the opportunity to invite him to write a piece on our coming adventure. It was to that end that I would offer to buy him dinner and fill him with drinks and details about the cause in China.

When I finally got hold of him, though, he seemed distracted. It had been months since we'd spoken. He was evasive for no reason I could understand and told me his stay in the city would be short. This was not a good time, he said. He'd already overextended himself and was working under a deadline. Yet I persisted. At length I was able to pin him down for later that night, promising a casual bite and drink, an hour or two at most.

I then proceeded by subway to the offices of the China Aid Council in the Bowery where I met with the two other members of the expedition—a Dr. Charles H. Parsons and Miss Jean Ewen, an excellent nurse, I had heard, and fluent in Chinese, who had served in Shantung for two years before the Japanese invasion began. Our meeting lasted three hours, focusing on the many details yet to be seen to. It was an optimistic meeting, I recall. I spoke of the importance of this mission, as a good unto itself and as the first wave of the internationalism we'd seen in Spain. We would be the first of many hundreds of medical teams to go over, providing the necessary inspiration. We will put China on the map over here, I said. This war will not go unaided.

Just before nine o'clock, after the meeting was dissolved, I found a telephone and dialled Pitcairn's hotel. I asked the clerk at the desk to put me through to his room, but he didn't pick up his telephone. I wrote him a note explaining the nature of the China expedition, our itinerary, departure times, members' names, et cetera, hoping he might present this to the editors of his newspaper back in London, then jumped in a cab to the Bentley. I planned to leave the note at the front desk, but I saw Pitcairn sitting in the hotel bar, hidden away in a dark corner. His face registered surprise.

I said, "I'd have mistaken you for some sort of spy, sitting over here in the shadows."

"Jesus Christ, old man," he said, standing up. He hesitated in offering his hand, and anyone watching might have thought I'd stolen his wife. "It's good to see you," he said, and in a moment he reassembled himself, but only just. It was as if he was unsure of me.

"Got you at a bad moment?" I said.

"Sit," he said. "Not at all."

The following Tuesday I boarded a train with Jean Ewen and Charles Parsons, bound for Seattle. From there we would cross the border up to Vancouver, where we'd depart for Hong Kong on a steamer. Charles chatted away with the other drinkers in the bar car and Jean managed to busy herself reading. I'd brought along a journalist's account of life with the Chinese Communists called *China's Red Army Marches* but found it difficult going. So distracted that concentration was very near impossible, I instead ended up watching a good bit of Indiana and Illinois roll past my window.

Three days later we arrived in Vancouver, a city hunched and brooding under a gloomy January rain. Like a vain woman, I remember thinking, it was as blessed by its natural wonders as it was cursed by its temperamental moods. The damp and the early dark cast a great pall, and the melancholy that had seized me since New York did not lighten but only increased when I found Pitcairn's telegram waiting for me at the Hotel Vancouver. I tucked it into my breast pocket and made dinner arrangements with Charles and Jean, then retired to my room, where I tore open the envelope. *Norman, the editors have rejected the China idea. Bad luck. You're on your own. Frank.*

The following morning the three of us gathered in the hotel lobby and took a cab to the port. Our luggage had gone off earlier that morning to the baggage master. I remember feeling a rush of excitement when the three great stacks of the *Empress of Asia* came into view. Gulls circled in and out of the clouds, dipping curiously like chaperones eager to glimpse the passengers they would accompany out to sea. In the excitement of the moment, the pure childlike thrill of standing before such an impressive vessel, I forgot the telegram and the succinct phrasing that so cleverly, so accurately, had let me know precisely what Pitcairn thought of me. *You're on your own.*

* * *

Midnight brings a faint thunder of fighting from the east. There is a cool dampness in the air. November in Chang Yu, Hopei Province. I am carried up from a shallow sleep. Just now I rose from my cot and saw dull flashes of light illuminating the far-off hills. Someone is taking it in the teeth. We won't know more for another day, maybe two. I believe my thoughts might have awakened me, if the fighting hadn't.

There is some pleasure as well, but mostly it is mystery and hard work that goes into the remaking of a man's life. I am finding that now. What I mean is that nothing I can say in these pages amounts to half or even a quarter of the truth as I knew it then. I'm talking about the actual experience of life. About the sound of crickets in summer and the peace and wonder that fills your heart when you sit back and begin to accept the enormity of the world as it is presented to you when August comes and you feel the day and nature calling out to you. There is a full-on glory to this witnessing that only the greatest artists are able to capture. I will always believe I have seen the peasants working the great wheat harvests of Russia because I've read *Anna Karenina,* but I remind myself that Tolstoy is a once-in-a-century artist. I suppose what I'm trying to say is that the writing of a man's life at least gives you an idea of just how special it all was to him the first time around.

I recall standing on the deck of that magnificent ship, the *Empress of Asia,* and feeling the reality of what I was doing. I was leaving you. The full force of my decision came to me that morning as an almost physical pain. Much as I tried, I was unable to shake it off. But I also remember, as if possessed of two hearts, the serene joy of watching a flock of gulls darting among the ship's three funnels high above the promenade deck and thinking I had now found my freedom. More gulls fluttered just off the stern, picking heels of bread from a girl's hand. I imagined she was someone else, perhaps you, as you might appear at the age of eight or ten. She wore a blue wool coat and bonnet, and had beautiful blond curls. As she fed the birds, the woman I assumed was her mother held her by her free hand, careful not to let go as the girl leaned forward over the railing.

The child's delight was palpable. She shrieked with joy every time a gull took a piece of bread and lifted in the wind. The sun shone for most of the morning and this, too, raised my spirits somewhat. As the noon hour approached, clouds crossed over the ship, the last of the gulls folded their wings east, and it was then that remarkable columns of sunlight descended from above. This I took as a blessing upon us all, and every visible passenger seemed inspired by the spectacle of light spinning down through the clouds into the dark ocean, and by the thrill of having such a great steamer as the *Empress* underfoot, so solidly bearing us forth.

After the girl in blue waved goodbye to the last of her gulls, my colleagues and I decided to take lunch at the promenade deck's veranda café, situated at the ship's stern. We ordered a generous plate of assorted sandwiches, and Dr. Parsons, himself a surgeon, thought it a grand idea to toast the commencement of our journey with a whiskey and soda. It being quite early, Miss Ewen and I shared a small pitcher of Pimm's with lemon and cucumber. We watched the wide fan of the engine's turbines bubble and spread far below us, and before two hours had passed we'd cleared the Juan de Fuca Strait. Vancouver Island faded in the distance and then the continent itself began to slip away—her coastline, her mountains—and finally we were ringed by what seemed an eternity of water. Our conversation that afternoon was generally enjoyable and full of optimism, but inwardly I was troubled by the weight of my leaving.

I close my eyes now and recall the riches of that passage, the food, the cleanliness, the small troubles which from here seem so unimportant. What I remember is the gleam of silver tea sets, the potted palms and lilies that dotted the passageways, the pleasant light entering the

tall, arched windows of the café where I took my breakfast most
mornings. Now, cruelly, the aromas of the ship's kitchens appear from
nowhere, waking me with the false promise of braised lamb, fresh
cheese, roasted garlic. The *Empress* boasted a luxury that seems happily ludicrous. She ran more quietly than my dreams are ever able to
promise, prowled as they are by the groans of dying men and mortar
fire.

That first day, as we ate our lunch, I suggested to my colleagues that
we indulge ourselves as best we could because the present conditions
were sure not to last. The crossing to Hong Kong would take nineteen
days. After that, I said, nothing was guaranteed. We should conserve
our strength for the coming rigours. I planned to stay occupied during
the crossing, intending to push certain gloomy thoughts aside while
devoting myself to the preparations still pending. I would descend to
the hold to check on our cargo, consisting of a fully equipped field
hospital, complete the last of the background study I'd carried on
board regarding matters of Chinese geography and politics, and send
a number of telegrams ahead to Hong Kong and back to the China
Aid Council in New York concerning various administrative points of
interest. I also intended to seek confirmation that our man in Hong
Kong would indeed meet us at the Ambassador Hotel, where we
planned to stay briefly before our journey north to the mainland. As I
outlined my itinerary, I noticed that Parsons had begun fidgeting. His
eyes wandered. His glass was empty. He began tapping his fingers
lightly on the tabletop, then raised his hand to call for the waitress.

I had calculated that my tasks might consume only a fraction of
my time on board, as I had set out with a more immediate interest at
hand. I had intended to sit at this typewriter (much newer then) and
collect my thoughts for you, if one day you should care to read them.
But the sea air failed to prove a sufficient inspiration for this first
attempt, sincere though it was, for my heart felt on the point of bursting. Perhaps the sad reality of my departure tormented me more than
I was aware. More than once I began this history, still unsure as to my
deepest motives, for the truth comes—if at all—at its own stubborn

pace. Stymied, I had no idea how to begin or what a man might say in circumstances such as mine. Where he might find the words.

What did I discover? That I was as dishonest to myself at sea as I had always been on land. Troubled, I strolled the winter decks, consumed by misgiving.

In my wandering I learned the ship's plan, a welcome distraction. Her many sections and decks were connected by a vast series of passageways, stairs and promenades, but some of these—rectilinear as any ship's plan is—were as narrow and confining as the medieval streets of a small European village. In certain sections she was quite cramped and claustrophobic, but those very same cramped passageways then opened suddenly to an airy lounge or plush dining hall or spacious reading room or bar every bit as ornate and charming as a town square in Seville or Siena. I carried my thoughts into each of these rooms and, in a state of introspection, watched the great ocean pass below. I circled her four continuous decks—shelter, upper, main and lower—all of which extended the full length of the ship, some 590 feet. I visited her cafés, restaurants and bars, her dining, reading and smoking rooms. I stood at the bow and wondered what I was headed into. At the stern I gazed back at what I'd left behind.

It is pleasurable even now to recall the luxuries of first-class passage. Delicious memories for a starved body. O the bounty we take for granted! I slept on a firm mattress smelling of cleanliness and not red clay and manure. My body ached with excess, not starvation. My cabin was a nest of pleasures situated on the upper deck, beneath the second and third funnels. I heard nothing of the ship's great engines and might as well have been camped on the shores of a remote northern lake. The cabin boasted a cherry-wood sideboard and dresser, two cavernous armchairs, a claw-foot coffee table positioned between them and an oak writing desk and chair of a type you might find in the stateliest manor in England. Unimaginable luxury compared to the cold mud, stone walls and dirt floors of these huts I now call home, with their broken windows and poorly thatched roofs.

The ship was redolent with delicious flavours. Roast beef on upper deck. Cuban cigars on shelter deck. Perfumes in the ballroom. My cabin was scented by lilies refreshed on a daily basis by a pretty Chinese lady named Mrs. Qimeia. She spoke English quite well, as did most of the Chinese stewards and stewardesses. One morning early in the voyage I introduced myself when she knocked at my door. She was modest, courteous, self-contained and efficient. As she tidied up I offered my gratitude for her fine attention to detail.

"Does this flower have a name?" I said.

"They are called stargazers, sir, a species of lily," she said. "We have a florist on board if you would like to send some."

"Perhaps I will," I said.

The lady blushed, of course. I asked if she might furnish my bed with a third pillow—a detail I dearly miss here, with not a single pillow—and wished her a good morning, then left the room in her capable hands.

I spent many hours in the lounge beneath the first and second funnels, reading and making notes on the coming expedition. It was there I tried again to begin this document, but looming demands pulled me away, or so I let myself believe. I worked as well on articles—political commentary, a paper on thoracic medicine, my specialty, another on triage procedures—and wrote letters to friends and associates. Delicate tables and chairs in the French neo-classical style gave the room a wonderful opulence. On clear days the great domed skylight overhead admitted a full warming sun.

Here I claimed a comfortable sofa facing a wide fireplace and, after a period of writing, started in on one of the books I'd carried on board. Passengers generally gathered in the lounge between eleven o'clock and noon, three and five, and then on into the evening after the dining halls emptied. Outside those hours it was a relaxing place for reading and study. The carpet was a warm russet, like the sofas, the lamp shades and curtains framing the rectangular port-facing windows.

When the lounge became too busy, I transplanted myself to the writing room, which was always quiet and ideal for study, though not so for those of us who compose on clumsy machines like this. Here I found the studious passengers, the chronic letter-writers, the poets, introverts, insomniacs and melancholics. In this room we hardly made eye contact with one another. We each stared down some far-off face, summoned a disembodied voice—a friend or lover waiting on the other side, perhaps even a daughter. The sea, we seemed convinced, spoke her own language: secret, coded only for the finest ear. Maybe in that room we stood a better chance of making some sense of what was to be found in its silence.

I spent many hours attempting to begin this story, but when I could bear it no longer I returned to the safety of administrative matters. Again I had failed. I concentrated on the China Aid Council, and on a certain crisis that was developing between myself and Parsons. Early on I was still hopeful—certain, even—that our expedition would reap great rewards. We were dedicated to the cause. But for the sake of complete honesty I must admit that there were signs of trouble only a few days into the voyage. Not unwelcome difficulties, at that. I was pleased to have something to distract me from the story I was struggling and failing to tell.

Charles Parsons was only slightly older, perhaps in his mid-fifties. At one time an excellent surgeon, he had in recent years been severely reduced by alcohol and by this time was well descended from the height of his powers. I don't know why he drank, exactly, but I do recall my astonishment at noticing, on our first day at sea, not the slightest pang of conscience or even *awareness* on his part when he suggested we avail ourselves of the funds we'd been entrusted with to pay for our drinks and plate of sandwiches. Quite surprised, I folded the bills back into his hand and asked the server to put the lunch on my meal chit, telling Parsons it was my pleasure. It was then that I began to harbour some doubt regarding his commitment. If left unchecked, I feared he would make a significant dent in our resources, and I resolved to keep an eye on him, though I had no intention of creeping around the ship like some sort of spy.

Of my other associate, the Canadian nurse Jean Ewen, I knew very little aside from the fact that her father was a prominent Communist back home, a highly regarded man I'd met on a number of occasions in Montreal and Winnipeg. While I saw quickly that his daughter took after him, she refused to call herself a dyed-in-the-wool Communist. She told me at our first meeting in New York that she'd never put much stock in labels, political, philosophical or otherwise. Perhaps she might call herself a pragmatist, I suggested. She lifted her eyebrows and smiled, indicating that even this might obscure the truth. She was quite young, in her late twenties, I would guess, and still quite collegial, despite her two years in China. That first day out from Vancouver she wore a black Lilly Daché cap and cape and looked set for a Sunday afternoon football game or ride through Central Park. Her dark brown eyes roamed upward to the funnels. "It's impossible to imagine that civilization can build a ship as glorious as this and still possess the mentality to wage war!" Her dark hair was cut short, just below the ear. She looked every bit the youthful adventurer that she was. Her neck, quite thin, was pale and delicate. I offered her my scarf, which she refused with a smile. She seemed nothing but a slip of a girl to me, pretty, almost dainty. "I see," I said, "you will stand up to the cold, then?" I couldn't help but wonder how she would fare under the pressures of war, and thought she might well surprise me.

I remember strolling above deck early on a splendid morning, three or four days in. I took great pleasure in filling my lungs with cold sea air as I watched the light reach up from below the horizon, as if some magical far-off land of fire and dragons were eager to catch my attention. On one level at least, I had already begun preparing myself mentally for this war on the other side of the world, bracing myself for its terrors, and that lovely thin strip of orange and yellow hovering over the sea brought a sense of calm I knew I couldn't trust. Out there the war raged; on board a different sort had just begun, and the gloomy thoughts of my leaving still turned in the back of my mind. As I walked and full morning light finally filled the sky, I saw that little girl in blue who had so caught my attention our first morning out.

Today she wasn't feeding the gulls but standing alone at the railing, beside a life raft, watching the sea below. It seemed unsafe to me, a child alone at the precipice. The woman I'd taken to be her mother sat reading on a nearby bench, dressed in a red overcoat and white shawl, and taking no notice. She wore thick, black-framed sunglasses. I stopped and watched nervously as out from under her bonnet the girl's strawberry-blond hair spilled and danced about the circle of her face. She placed a foot on the bottom rung of the rail and lifted her other foot.

"Wait there," I called.

I suppose my urgent tone startled the girl. She stepped down, as if caught out, and turned with a guilty look on her face. The woman looked up from her book.

Somewhat embarrassed, I tipped my hat and stepped forward. "I'm sorry," I said. "She was climbing up. I'm not sure if you were aware of that."

"Oh, the dear thing knows no limits," she said. "I've told her a dozen times."

"Well, then."

"I suppose I'm not as fond of looking after children as I am of reading these silly poems." Vaguely she waved the book between us.

"What poems are those?"

"Do you know Wallace Stevens?" she said.

It turned out the woman was not the child's mother but her young aunt and as her temporary guardian was returning her to Hong Kong, where the girl's father held some post in the British Consulate. I presented my card, and we were soon immersed in a conversation about Stevens's poems. Her name was Gwendolyn Chambers. Two years into her doctoral thesis on eighteenth-century poetics, she'd recently fallen madly in love with the Modern Poets and was now reconsidering her studies. She was young, articulate and, not least of all, wonderfully selfless, I told her, in that she should journey such a long distance to deliver the child to her mother.

She laughed and said, "I'm not half as selfless as you might think."

As we spoke, the girl gravitated back to the life raft to look down at the water, but she did not step up onto the railing again.

I've been thinking about the possibility of my never finding you, an impossible thought that wakes me up at four in the morning. It is as if our bodies are programmed to wake up then so we can take our worries out for a stroll and exercise our darkest fears. We are at our weakest then, as if all we think we know is put aside at that hour and replaced by everything that's fearsome and terrifying. It is an intolerable thought, a full life without you, and that is why it haunts me. I could not stand that life, I promise you.

The weather was unchanged six or seven days into the Pacific crossing: cool, constant, predictable. By then I had modelled myself after it to a degree and established a daily ritual designed mostly, I believe, to prolong my self-deception. Mornings began with a brisk stroll up top, followed by a light breakfast at the veranda café. There I took a coffee and eggs with toast, juice and fruit. A fraternal atmosphere among the diners was pleasantly distracting. I sat among families, businessmen and adventurers, people who knew nothing of me or my plans for joining the Communist struggle against Japan. Most mornings I greeted the girl and her aunt, the engaging Miss Chambers, and soon we began breakfasting together. With Gwendolyn I spoke of poetry and art. I had over the years written a few poems myself—of course, none as good as Stevens's—and so had a number of ideas on the subject. I shared with her my belief that only through art could the truth of a non-shared experience be transmitted.

"Yes," she said, "I believe you're right."

"Poetry—good poetry, at least, like Stevens's—must evolve as the natural product of the subconscious mind. But here, you see, I have a bit of a problem. I believe art must be useful. It must teach us. What I'm asking for is the moral superiority of the artist. Yet if it comes from the unconscious mind, and if it must serve or educate in some positive fashion, well, then I'm asking quite a lot of the poor sod, aren't I?"

"Doesn't beauty count, Doctor?" she said. "What's to be said for beauty?"

"Beauty is an attribute of great art, I think, not the driving purpose behind it."

Later, after a pause in our weighty conversation, I turned to the niece and spoke of ornithology—she'd been enthralled by those seagulls—as well as doctoring and Vancouver's Stanley Park, where I'd been told she often played with her little friends. By then I knew the child, Alicia, was as engaging, precocious and bright as her aunt. She spoke with great excitement about seeing her parents in Hong Kong, and asked many questions about what it was like "to make someone better again." I told her it was a splendid feeling, that there was really nothing quite like it.

"I should like to become ill while on board, then," she said, "so you can cure me."

Alicia told me her father had once been gravely ill in Hong Kong, and a wonderful doctor had "cut him open" and "removed some things." I was pleased, naturally, by her regard for the profession.

It was on a windless morning of making my rounds that my suspicions regarding Parsons were confirmed. I had, the day before, met the ship's mascot, Baltazar, a blue and gold macaw. He was a constant fixture in the games room on the promenade deck, over which he regally presided, taking great joy in distracting serious gentlemen from their billiards with a well-timed squawk. I believe he was trying to say "bankshot" or "big shot," but "Bangkok" is also a distinct possibility. In any case he was an entertaining and intelligent bird. I watched him scramble various "parrot puzzles" with his claws. His principal keeper, a man named Mr. Wisniowski, administered the games room.

Baltazar was thirty-four years old and had made the *Empress* his home for the past fifteen years. He'd been rescued from a house of ill-repute in Manila, so the story went, when the police raided the premises and hauled his caretakers away, leaving the poor bird alone and destitute. There was a whiff of nostalgia about him, and this seemed even more pronounced when he welcomed the occasional female visitor with a nasally triumphant *"Bienvenida guapa!"* His head was a deep blue with an emerald-green crown. His neck, which Mr. Wisniowski called his "beard," though it looked nothing like it to me, was black, like his beak, and offered a striking contrast to his saffron-yellow underbelly. His primary feathers were a dark blue, his tail a somewhat softer blue. His rough cheeks looked as though he'd just endured a rather inexpert shave, though I was informed all macaws have only a thin striping of feathers there. His ice-blue eyes I found most penetrating.

His primary enjoyments seemed to be swinging on his ropes, heckling or complimenting the room's visitors, gnawing away at wooden chew toys and, of course, working on his puzzles, which Mr. Wisniowski had made, and I was invited to add to or improve if so inclined. He was remarkably agile with his sharp grey claws. He could remove the cork from a re-corked bottle in less than eight seconds, and delicately empty and refill a pack of cigarettes without shredding a single one. As if in encore he stripped a key chain of its owner's keys while hanging upside-down. He was a talented fellow, that Baltazar. Likely he had learned many of his skills from the working ladies of Manila, and no doubt they miss the old bird now, wherever they are. Despite his raucous ways—he sometimes could be quite loud—he was a treasure to visit on my rounds of the ship, and a very welcome diversion.

The day after meeting Baltazar I entered the games room only to find Parsons sitting on a bar stool in front of a snifter of brandy. "Will you have one with me, Doctor?" he asked. "Wet your whistle?" I told him it was a little early, though perhaps we could meet for a drink in a few hours' time? I thought this perfectly reasonable. I wanted to voice my concern indirectly, and thereby keep things civil between us.

"I'd be happy to invite you," I said. "Anyway, we could go down to the Steerage Bar. This one's a bit dear, I think."

"Not to worry," he answered, touching his front pocket. "Courtesy of the CAC."

I said, "Of course, you're aware that's not your money to spend."

"Now, now, one or two won't hurt, I'm sure."

"Doctor, I don't care what you do on your own time," I said, "but I'll tell you this only once: that is not your money to spend."

I had met people like Parsons over the years. In Montreal. In Madrid. I knew his sort well enough, the selfish addiction, the lying. He was the wicked and lazy servant in the Parable of the Talents who'd buried his talents in a bottle of rye.

Later, I found Jean on the promenade deck just outside the veranda café, bundled up and leaning against the railing watching the ocean. When I told her what I'd discovered, she clasped her hands over the railing and seemed justifiably concerned. I spoke in an even, hushed tone. We were shoulder to shoulder, close enough that I noticed the scent of her perfume, light, almost sweet, that came and went with the swirling wind. I suggested we come to an easy agreement as to our course of action regarding Charles, and to that end I recommended cabling New York with the demand that he be forced to provide an accounting of every last dime spent on board the *Empress of Asia*. This would definitely cut off his access to the remaining funds he carried.

Waiting for her consent, I watched the water far below us swirl and lap up against the bow like a live animal. It was deep blue, almost black.

"No," she said at last, "I will not join you in this coup."

"Please, don't let's overdramatize," I said. "This is merely a pragmatic reassignment of duties."

I went on to explain that only a directive from the China Aid Council would knock some sense into his sodden head, as he would never listen to us, certainly not to me. A strong scent of perfume came off her face then, or her neck.

"No," she said again, her answer as flat-out as it was incomprehensible. She would do no such thing. Needless to say I was taken aback. It was for the good of the cause, I insisted, keeping my voice level. I pushed her, still quietly, but with greater insistence.

"No, I will not," she said. She would give me no reason.

I wondered if her youth and inexperience prevented her from "tattling" on a colleague—an inexcusably adolescent way of looking at things, the least offensive reason available. Worse still would be a lack of commitment to the cause we were sailing into. Maybe she suffered from a fear of her own subordination, or simply an inferiority complex. Knowing Miss Ewen as I did, not well, surely, but well enough, I couldn't believe she would be so limited, so meek. I hoped above all that she'd taken this stand out of some misguided sense of compassion for a sick man. I was not afraid of ruffling feathers, I told her. Achieving our goals was of vastly greater importance than one man's suffering.

She said, still staring out to the ocean, "I know your reputation well enough, Doctor."

"Then you know I'm right," I said. To this she said nothing. "By the time we get to Hong Kong there'll be nothing left. You must reconsider. You know as well as I do how Parsons sits at that bar all day long. Good Lord, brandy for breakfast! I've seen it myself. It's astonishing. I swear I'll throw him overboard before he depletes our funds entirely. With or without your help."

This caused her to turn her head. She stared at me with those big dark young eyes of hers. She really was quite lovely, I realized then. "You will be throwing no one overboard, Doctor Bethune, today or any other day during this crossing. Not while I'm on board."

* * *

The evening after I confronted Jean began no differently from any other. On finishing with my writing, I was surprised to discover that it was nearing midnight. I'd been writing a paper for a medical journal, and with the intention of returning to it in the morning I set my notes aside and sought out a quiet stretch of deck up top. The ocean was calm and the air cold, a rich dampness that happily reminded me of my youth on the great Georgian Bay. I leaned against the rail and attempted to clear my thoughts. It was a wondrous thing to scatter the anxieties of the day over the ocean's wide expanse, and that is what I intended to do before retiring for the night. A glowing light was just barely visible in the west, a remnant of someone else's day, and a universe of stars sparkled overhead. I breathed deeply and conjured an image of you, my daughter, as you might be, warm, tiny, sleeping in your mother's arms.

Along the length of the deck, solemn, bundled figures leaned over the rail, caught in their own silent reveries. One of these figures, the closest to me, thirty or forty paces off, tossed a cigarette over the rail, hunched his shoulders and started for the nearest hatch, then stopped as if reconsidering. A cold wind was picking up. To me it was bracing, but for this man it might have been too much. I held my image of you a moment longer, wondering what at that precise time you were doing, when a voice interrupted my thoughts. It was Parsons. He was standing beside me.

"It's a long way down, Bethune," he said.

"Taking a break from the bar, are we?"

"Not too long a break, don't worry. Just off to the bank." He jangled the key to his cabin.

"You're a disgrace, Parsons."

"I suppose you wish we could all be a bit more like you." It was a stupid reversal. He was looking for a confrontation and past talking to, guaranteed more drunk than sober by this time of night. "You consider this your own personal cause, don't you. You think my bar tab will give the Japanese the advantage in China? That Fascism will overrun all of Asia because of a few drinks?"

"I think it best you pay your own way, Parsons," I told him, "nothing more than that. How you choose to deal with your problems is no concern of mine."

"Nor is it any concern of mine how you deal with yours. A thing like that—Madrid—stays with you, doesn't it."

I was silent, looking into his eyes.

"Yes," he said. "Madrid will be with you forever." He smiled, waiting for a fitting riposte. "Nothing to add? No righteous words from the great Bethune? Good, then I'll leave you to think this one through." And he turned casually, owning the moment, and walked away.

Clearly he thought he had something on me, but I'd been unable to ask what that might be, exactly. I suppose the violence of his emotion had silenced me. I will never argue with a drunk, not if I can help it, though I was eager to put the matter to rest.

The following morning, I planned to contact the CAC without Miss Ewen's help, even though I understood full well that only one name on the wire would be less persuasive. The telegraph room was situated just off the Captain's nest, and I was greeted there by a bright-looking young man. For a moment I was taken by the commanding perspective: below sat the entirety of the ship, bow to stern, port to starboard, while all around us the ocean stretched, peerless and indifferent. The young lad smiled and nodded. After commenting on the fine view, I explained the urgency of my telegram and directed him to send it off at the earliest convenience, and to inform me the moment my answer was received. Then I tipped my hat and left him to his work.

After a slow game of billiards with a fellow passenger I drank a lemonade in the lounge then retired to my cabin to look over some of my notes. It was a pleasant morning, unrushed yet quietly productive. I had sublimated my gloomy thoughts, and the possibility that Charles Parsons knew something more than he should have became a distant bother, not overly concerning. I caught up on some reading and later strolled the decks, learning the ship's plan more thoroughly. I enjoyed the views and, half past noon, snacked on a salmon omelette with jam and coffee at the café with a distinguished-looking Englishman who had some business with the Empress lines. As we talked, the ship's Captain greeted my companion, who then introduced us. Captain Aldridge Lawson seemed very interested in my work, as he had trained in medicine at Cambridge for a brief time before the Great War. He told me if I was free that evening he would be honoured by my presence at his table. I said he should count on it.

Later that day, as I was preparing for dinner, the knock I'd been waiting for sounded at my door. The lad from the telegraph office handed me a small envelope, barely the size of a personal calling card. I gave him a few coins and closed the door. It was not the news I'd been expecting. After reading the message, I slipped the telegram in my pocket. I have carried it with me to this day as a memento of the idiocy of bureaucrats everywhere.

DR H N BETHUNE
EMPRESS OF ASIA

COMMITTEE HAS COMPLETE FAITH IN ALL MEMBERS
OF EXPEDITION STOP WILL REQUIRE NO CHANGE OF
ACCOUNTING PRACTICES BEST OF LUCK

Despite this setback, I managed to pass a pleasant evening at dinner. Topics of discussion were as wide ranging as oceanic navigation, politics, medicine and, finally, over cognac and a cigar, the Great War. As a young man, our Captain had sailed on board HMS *Excelsior* as a petty officer with the Royal Navy. Also at the Captain's table was a terribly sententious missionary named Billingsley, out of Union College in Missouri, who showed a great interest in our expedition. He too was a fighting man, he said, but in God's army. "Bibles, not guns," he added. It turned out he was a Seventh Day Adventist. When I welcomed him to the struggle on behalf of the armed atheists and Communists of the world, he looked at me with an expression of true horror, as if he had never before laid eyes on a dirty Communist. His eyes seemed to ask how someone of obvious intelligence could support such a despicable social fantasy. Heads turned, and the other conversations at our table fell silent. The Reverend Mr. Billingsley regained his composure enough to say, "You're not *really* a Communist! Surely you see there is no future in Communism."

"On the contrary," I said, "that is precisely the future I hope will prevail. We have seen the avarice of Capitalism. Capitalism cannot care for the sick and needy. Capitalism can only enrich those still hungry for riches despite their obscene wealth."

He reached for his glass, sipped his wine and returned the glass to its place, then he folded his hands on the table and looked directly into my eyes. "We are bringing the word of God to those who hunger for it. Nothing less than the word of Jesus Christ. Spiritual hunger is what's bringing us, Doctor, and there's nothing faddish about that. Spiritual hunger is in many ways more devastating than the hunger for bread."

"My father might have said the same thing," I told him.

"Oh?" he said.

"He enjoyed a lofty career in the Presbyterian Church."

"Well, there you see. Perhaps he and I would see eye to eye."

"Perhaps you would have," I said. "He passed away some years ago."

He said, "I'm sorry to hear it."

"He had the Devil on the run his whole life."

"Isn't that what we all aspire to, Doctor Bethune, such an urgency of purpose? In one sense or another? To combat injustice, disease, war? The Devil has many names." As the white-gloved waiters appeared with a kingly looking roast of beef, I told Billingsley the story of how my family had moved from town to town in the service of the Church, and how in the end it was revealed that a pursuit of the Devil had rather little to do with it.

"Perhaps your father knew something you did not," he said. "Allow me to say that a son should not be so quick to dismiss his father's ideas."

I refrained from rolling my eyes. I only smiled, tilted my wineglass, drank and waited for an opportunity to shift the direction of our conversation. I feared that Billingsley might attempt to hatch some moral out of any story I might tell, or draw an unlikely parallel between me and my father and his desire to rout out evil wherever he should find it. For once I was not up to a heated discussion, and I didn't bother telling him that it was the people of those small Ontario towns, at first invigorated but soon threatened and finally wearied by my father's overbearing righteousness, who had sent us packing again and again.

The following morning Jean appeared at the entrance of the veranda café, wearing again the cap and cape she'd worn our first day out. I was sitting at my usual table, to port, beside a large window. It was not so uncommon, her stopping for breakfast there. We'd shared coffee and toast a number of times. I decided to cut to the point.

"Doctor Parsons is a thief *and* an outrageous drunk. I don't know for what you owe him your allegiance, but he cornered me the other night. He was talking nonsense. You wouldn't believe what he was going on about."

"Oh?" she said.

"What he said really isn't important. What's important is the quality of the man, not the nature of his lies. It is the fact of his lies that matters."

"He's willing to travel thousands of miles—"

"Look at the reality. It is the trusting nature of your youth that hopes for the best even when that's clearly unattainable."

"I think you underestimate—"

"My dear," I interrupted, "you're prone to *over*estimation. There is no alternative but to send that telegram. You will grant me that, I'm sure." I waited a moment to ensure my point had been made. She was silent. Believing all was settled, I got back to work.

Determined study has always been for me an effective tonic in the face of struggles. After taking my morning walk, I settled down quietly in the deep silence of the lounge. I felt the tension and bother of dealing with such a nuisance as Parsons fall away from me and was pleased to regain my focus. Around noon I decided, as a favour to myself, to stop off at the bar on the upper deck to take something before proceeding to the café for a light meal. I felt I owed myself a treat. I'd been under a fair bit of strain and had, I thought, held up rather well. A familiar optimism was returning to me.

Just as I rounded a tall bookshelf, a man brushed against me. I was carrying a journalistic account of the China situation called *Far Eastern Front*. This young man, about thirty or thirty-five, nodded politely, glimpsed the title and said, "Snow, hell of a writer," then introduced himself. When I gave him my name, Eli Ansell said, "Ah, yes, Doctor Bethune, I was told you were on board. What a great honour."

"You're off to the war, then," I said, "or just an interested Sinologist?"

"Both," he said. "As a journalist, actually."

It took me some minutes to realize that I'd read a number of his pieces in *Voice of Action*, a Seattle-based newspaper, including an explosive article five or so years before about an innocent Negro accused of murdering a white man. The newspaper's coverage had obliged the authorities to admit the truth: that their case was racially biased and the accused totally innocent. I told him I'd followed all this as closely as I could, living at the time in Detroit. A member of the American Newspaper Guild, he was off to cover the same war I was headed into. Slim and elegant with a pencil-thin moustache, narrow fingers and a sharp, dimpled chin, he had a strong nose, thick black hair, and—I saw as our crossing continued—he was forever scribbling in a small notebook he carried with him everywhere. I asked what he expected to find in China.

"I hope to get to Nanking," he said. "What's happening there is fascinating. I understand that Tang Shengzhi's ordered a retreat to the other side of the Yangtze. The city's fallen to the Japanese. There are rumours of a street purge. I have a name to focus on—a Kraut, a Nazi, actually, called John Rabe. He's there with the Siemens China Corporation. Now he's head of the International Committee that's trying to protect whoever they can. They're setting up safety zones and getting embassies to open their doors to refugees. It's a powerful irony, a Nazi sticking his neck out like that given what they've been up to in Europe. It's a compelling story, and news is just starting to trickle out. Incredible stuff, really. The numbers are astonishing if you happen to believe them."

"The only war people care about these days," I said, "is in Spain."

"Causes don't interest me so much as stories. Characters, Doctor. Without heroes and villains a war doesn't sell papers. The man makes the story. Speaking as a journalist, that is."

"Quite the opposite in my case," I said.

"How's that?"

I thought of Spain, and then of what awaited us in China. "People don't interest me as much as the cause they fight for."

Earlier this evening I asked Ho to sit for me. He was uncharacteristically still, quietly reading a thin, well-thumbed book. I walked back to my hut to fetch pad and pencil. He regarded me with some curiosity, then simply resumed reading. When I finished drawing I showed him my work. I think I rather like it, but I can't tell from his reaction if he's pleased or not. I'll call it *Chinese Boy Reading*.

Well, the truth is, I needed to know what Parsons knew about Madrid. What did he think might frighten me? I had nothing to hide, so what blackmail could he have up his sleeve? Perhaps my conversation with Ansell about Nanking had inspired me to take matters into my own hands. Or maybe it was simply frustration. Whatever the reason, I resolved to meet Parsons head-on, since the tomfoolery between us had become time-consuming. I decided to confront him as early in the morning as possible, before the first drink touched his lips. He would, I hoped, be forthcoming, if asked directly what rumours he'd heard, from whom. Then we could have it out. For the first time in days I felt buoyant.

That morning I knocked at cabin C37 and silently stood, waiting. After a moment I knocked again. "Parsons?" I called out. "Listen, open up, it's Bethune."

There was no answer, so I tried the door and found it unlocked, then pushed it open and looked inside. The bed was unmade, with clothing strewn about, and on the ledge by the porthole sat an empty liquor bottle, beside it an overflowing ashtray. I stepped across the threshold and again called, "Parsons?" I could hear the shower running in the bathroom.

Surveying the cabin, I noticed a stack of envelopes tied with string on the dresser to the right of the bathroom door. Scattered there were a number of folders, a set of keys, a wallet, a loosely knotted necktie and an unframed photograph, curling up at the edges, of a young woman. When I turned it over and read the inscription, I felt a moment of mercy for him. Nothing in it made me think that the pretty young woman on the reverse was dead, but it was somehow obvious enough. Exhibit 1. Parsons's entire world was contained within that picture of the young woman of seventeen or eighteen—an only child, I imagined, I don't know why.

I stepped forward and examined the pile of envelopes. The third from the top, bearing the seal of the China Aid Council, contained the money in question. Minus a week's worth of drinking, it was all there. I tucked the envelope into my breast pocket and silently closed the door behind me.

Up on the promenade deck a few moments later, I found it was a chilly, bright and refreshing morning. As I rounded the bow from port to starboard, I spotted Alicia with her Aunt Gwendolyn and thought perhaps this might be an opportune time to engage them in conversation. They were taking the sun, sitting side by side in a pair of rented lounge chairs. "I wonder," I said, approaching them, "if I might make a request?"

"Anything at all, Doctor Bethune," Gwendolyn said.

I'd been mulling something over for a number of days, in fact ever since seeing Alicia feeding the seagulls that first morning. "I'm looking to make a portrait, and I'd be greatly honoured if Alicia would agree to sit for me. She is such a lovely child, as of course you know."

"Oh, yes," Alicia replied. "Please, I've never had my picture painted! Do say yes, Gwen!"

Gwendolyn smiled and said she had no objections, though I suspected she might herself have wanted a painter to fuss over her.

"You say you've never had your portrait painted?" I was still standing, slightly hunched, cupping my knees with my hands. "Well, then, what about it?"

Only slightly chilled under the weak winter sun, we met every morning on the promenade deck. She was always there, waiting for me, as prompt and energetic as she was young and pretty, and pleased to have an adult taking her so seriously. After a casual greeting and friendly chitchat, she sat perfectly still and without complaint, wrapped in a heavy sweater, for long stretches at a time: with eyes staring out to sea; sitting, standing; lying back on her deck chair; sometimes curling a lock of hair between her fingers. Her aunt was always in the next chair, quietly reading one of her poetry books.

One morning Gwendolyn straightened her back and said, "Will you just listen to this one? It's so lovely it makes me want to throw myself into the ocean and die!"

After that day she started reading to us while I worked. Her niece listened quietly. I wondered what an eight-year-old thinks when an adult says something about throwing herself into the ocean, but it wasn't long before I saw that she understood her aunt's flights of fancy and extravagant speech. Often, when Alicia began to fidget, usually after half an hour, I recommended a break of ten or fifteen minutes. She skipped rope while Gwendolyn and I spoke about the civil war in China and the subsequent Japanese invasion, and about her interests as a student of poetry. She read the "new poetry," as she called it, because it was real and unfettered by convention or tradition. Smiling, she admitted she could only ever be an observer of genius. Perhaps, I said, but an astute observer, I'm sure. As I painted in the pale winter sunlight, chilled but comfortable enough, she read Eliot for us and Pound and William Carlos Williams and Wallace Stevens. The Pacific stretched as far as the eye could see.

We were, by then, well away from where we'd started, yet still many days from where we were headed. The colours of the ocean were muted, but it was always calm, flat and soothing, with browns and greys. Sometimes, if the light touched the surface just so, I could see a shine as of liquid mercury at the forward edge of a soft rise in the water. I painted the young girl sitting, standing, or lying while, hidden in the inner breast pocket of my light green Abercrombie & Fitch jacket, I carried the stolen money.

Time spent with Alicia and Gwendolyn was a welcome respite. I began to enjoy the company of this child and her poetry-loving aunt for their own sake, as well as for the entertainment and diversion they promised. I was appreciative of their indulgence of my painterly musings. I was not as gifted as I may have made myself out to be, though I had dabbled for many years, principally in the portraits of various friends and intimate acquaintances. Yet despite the hours spent painting Alicia, and the calming presence of the smooth ocean, the crossing was by then proving tedious.

At the end of my fourth day at the easel, I turned to glimpse an unusually dark cloud on the far eastern horizon and saw the Captain walking purposefully toward me. Could there finally be a storm on the way? I wondered. The cloud, it turned out, immense though it was, was not in our path. The Captain greeted me and, with some curiosity, regarded my painting for a moment without speaking. "You are a surprising man, indeed," he said at last.

"How so?" I asked. I didn't turn from the canvas.

"Do you play Bach and Mozart too, Doctor?"

"I have far less art in me than you think, Captain. I only entertain myself. It helps fill the time."

"I wonder if you might have heard," he said, "the news from Doctor Parsons?"

"What news is that?"

"He didn't tell you? It seems we have a thief on board."

"A thief?"

"Oh, the doctor was terribly upset. Rightly so, I should say. A fair bit of money's gone missing." He quoted the amount in question, the precise amount hidden in my inner breast pocket. "This isn't common knowledge, of course," he said.

"Of course. But you've got established methods on board, I imagine. A protocol for this sort of situation?"

"Oh, yes, we'll get our man, Doctor Bethune. Not to worry. There are certain tricks we have for bringing a man like this forward."

"Yes, I'm sure you have," I said.

I walked a tightrope. I kept busy, all the while willing the ship to make land. Most mornings I met with the girl and her aunt and painted while listening to the poems of Wallace Stevens.

Complacencies of the peignoir, and late
Coffee and oranges in a sunny chair,
And the green freedom of a cockatoo
Upon a rug mingle to dissipate
The holy hush of ancient sacrifice.

When she finished reading the poem, I said, "Did you know we have a macaw on board? An intelligent creature. I will take you both one morning to see him."

Little by little, the endless expanse of the Pacific began to shape my imagination. The ocean became a vast desert and we a minute organism crawling over its back. I immersed myself in the details of the painting as the words fell from Gwendolyn's lips. The green freedom of a cockatoo. The oranges. The light. The peignoir. When the light faded, however, I yet again set out to begin this story, and yet again failed. I was two men. Busy, engaging and visible by day. But alone in my cabin at night, solemn and introspective, my dreams troubled. The mornings were most productive. Dabbling. Listening. Dreaming as I painted portraits that gave me no end of relief.

Of course, there were options. I considered sneaking back with the money, slipping it under Parsons's door or between that stack of envelopes where I'd found it. But that brought me back to the problem of keeping Parsons sober, and long enough to hold his tongue. Plus he'd polish off another good chunk of money that would certainly have better uses in less than a month's time. One morning, as I touched my brush to a lovely daub of fresh-face pink I'd just created, the Captain rounded the corner. Had I been found out?

"Doctor," he said with a wide grin. "Good morning. I wonder if you would consider a proposition." He stopped to consider the painting. "Why, this is coming along nicely."

"A proposition?"

"I would be honoured if you would deliver an address for us. Something very informal. Unofficial. Something personal, perhaps. I understand you were quite active about Madrid, speaking to audiences on the radio and so on, and back in Canada before joining us. I've talked to a number of passengers who remember you from the wireless."

I asked him what he had in mind.

"Nothing political, of course," he said. "That wouldn't do. We shan't get into that on board here. Not quite appropriate, you understand. But something . . . more personal, I wonder? Anything, really. People are interested, Doctor. You've led an interesting life. Made a name for yourself. We have a good many important passengers on board, and I've asked a number of them. Sort of an onboard lecture series. Keeps the mind busy."

"Indeed," I said.

"Think about it, will you?"

"But I have no idea what to talk about beyond my interest in politics and medicine. This is very flattering, Captain, but personal stories? I'm not so good at that."

"Well, think about it, anyway."

Yet I was obliged to admit to myself that the idea had intrigued me. In fact I couldn't stop thinking about the offer, for a number of reasons. Was I flattered? Yes, I was. But I smelled an opportunity here, too, to advance the cause of justice in China.

Am feeling buoyed today, despite the cold. General Nieh has promised to secure a dynamo and a small gas engine to run it. Every bit counts, and this is more than a bit. A dynamo-electric machine is as good as gold out here. I have also requested a Chinese dictionary. My language skills are well below what they should be. Mr. Tung helps immeasurably with that, but how I would like to go the extra mile for these fine people here. They bend over backwards to make me as comfortable as possible and all I seem to do is show my impatience with them. Patience never was my strong suit, as I'm sure you've gathered, and this war's fearsome horrors are taking a toll on what little stock I started with. Every morning I remind myself that my medical staff were tilling the fields and tending livestock only nine months ago, never even having heard of such basic materials as a catheter or cotton gauze. The work is drearily repetitive and sad—so many dead and wounded, in cold relentless enough to break a healthy man—but emotionally I'm feeling better these days. Some small signs of hope, starting with the dynamo. Given all the supplies needed and twenty or thirty trained medical staff, I would be the happiest man on earth.

* * *

One morning on board, after a difficult night, I was stepping out to meet Alicia and her aunt for another sitting. When I opened my cabin door I was surprised to find Miss Ewen standing there. We startled one another.

"You've surprised me," she said, regaining her composure.

"You've not come calling for me?"

"I'm just walking," she said. "Learning the ship."

"I'm on my way up top. I'll walk with you." She was dressed in a cream-coloured dress and jacket suit. She was very pretty that day, I remember, with a light grey handkerchief over her hair. "I suppose it's blowing out there a bit," I said.

"Yes," she said, "it is."

As we walked the length of the corridor she asked about the supplies I carried under my arm. I told her about the portrait I was painting.

"You've fortified yourself against this monotony," she said. "Good for you. On board one has so much time to think. Perhaps a little too much."

"The mind can go in circles," I said.

We turned a corner and ascended a flight of stairs.

"I *was* coming to call, actually," she said. "You caught me in the midst of reconsidering."

"Reconsidering?"

"Yes, I'm ashamed to say. I wanted to talk to you about Charles."

"You've reconsidered my proposal?"

"I think he invented his story about someone stealing the money."

"Why do you say that?" I said. "Do you know something?"

"There is no evidence that anyone entered his quarters. I've spoken to the Captain on this matter. There's nothing to go on but his word. We already know of his drinking. That's the only thing we really do know."

"What do you suggest, then?" I asked.

"It's a terrible mess. It's all unravelling, isn't it."

We came upon a hatch leading out to the promenade deck. I pushed it open for her and touched her elbow ever so slightly as she stepped over the small rise and out into the morning sunshine. "I feel so traitorous. Villainous. The fact is, I just don't know."

"You may feel as you must, Miss Ewen, but you must also feel right about sending the telegram. I will not force you. This has to be your decision."

"It is," she said.

It was clear that Jean found it unkind and perhaps even dishonourable to go behind Parsons's back as we eventually did, and that she felt she might have crushed something in herself in turning on this "kind and helpless man." I assured her we had no other choice. She knew, finally, what she had to do. The telegram went out that same afternoon, signed by the both of us, requesting that the CAC relieve Parsons of his financial responsibilities. We stayed together a short time after that, walking slowly. I assured her that we had pursued the correct course of action. She seemed needful of assurance, so I told her that when replacement funds were eventually wired to Hong Kong, as surely they would be, every last dime would be used for the purpose intended. In that we could be proud.

What about Parsons, then, now that Jean and I had sent the telegram?

I was careful about reintroducing the money into the coffers of the expedition. It couldn't simply reappear, just like that, without raising suspicion. What I did was this: I accepted the Captain's offer to speak, on the condition that following my address, donations might be made in a discreet manner to a non-political, non-partisan humanitarian effort to benefit victims of the war in China. The Captain was delighted to comply.

When we received a telegram in response to ours two days later—which happened to be the day of my lecture—it officially discharged

Parsons of all financial duties and "effected a transfer to Dr. Bethune." He might not have known before then that I'd actively set about undermining him, but he would know it now, just as I knew surely enough that not much time would pass before he came to take my measure.

During the increasing turbulence of those days I quite miraculously cobbled together some thoughts for the talk I'd promised to give. So it was, after a torturously long dinner on Friday evening, that our Captain rose, tapping his wineglass with a slender silver fork, and called the hall's attention to where I sat at the head table. Billingsley, Parsons, Jean and Gwendolyn, with pretty Alicia, were all seated about the room. The Captain cleared his throat with great force and said, "Ladies and gentlemen, tonight we have the honour . . ." and so on, and after his humbling introduction I rose, bowed as graciously as possible, and walked to the podium, which stood at the front of the hall, where a small team of busboys had assembled it as we ate. The first face I saw, of course, was that of my chief adversary.

Parsons smiled at me, and in that moment I was convinced that he'd put the Captain up to this. Invite Bethune, by all means, he would have said, he won't be able to resist. The man's vanity is unsurpassed. I returned his smile. Perhaps for a moment my mind went blank with fear. The diners were silent now. I might have blinked uncontrollably and fidgeted with my hands. Yet I remember thinking, quite clearly, too, that this was what it must feel like to stand before your accuser— your victim, in a sense—while observed by a jury of your peers, your every tic observed, registered, every pause, every garbled word, every drop of pitiable sweat as you made your case. My case, indeed. And so I began:

"Ladies and gentlemen." My eyes roamed over the audience. I was by then a practised public speaker. I'd taken my film about the mobile unit in Spain to over fifty cities in Canada and the United States, and had lectured in a great many teaching hospitals. I tried to regulate my breathing. "It is an honour to share with you some thoughts I have compiled here on the . . ."

He was waiting. Well, let him wait.

" . . . on the nature of . . . truth."

Could I be as audacious as this? I hope you will forgive me.

"The entire world," I continued, "indeed, humanity itself, craves the basic foundation of truth, the bedrock of our existence. Political truth. Moral truth. Social truth. Aesthetic truth."

My notes, I noticed then, were still folded in my hand. I'd not had the presence of mind to follow what I had prepared.

"Humanity. The man to your left. The woman to your right. We, all of us. Choose whatever avenue you care to look down, and on a clear day you'll see what we all want in this life, no matter where you live or whom you love. And that thing is truth. The fundamental truth of the ages, equality, purity, brotherhood. The most profound question of existence, the question of *why*, can only be answered thus, with an appeal to truth. That each man bears within his soul the dignity and value of a thousand men, and each of that thousand, each within his soul, likewise possesses the dignity and value of that one man. Are we not here, I wonder, on board this ship, on this earth, to seek and to find the truth as it resides within each of us, in whatever form we may carry it? We must all have this basis, this foundation, for the lives we lead, for without it we are lost, loveless and bereft. Life's handiwork—our deeds—shall mark us all, individually, as seekers of truth, and it is by these markers that we know if we succeed or fail in this life.

"None of us is perfect. No science or religion or church can make that claim. But it is the perfection of our dreams that may deliver us through that great searching; and those dreams—of how the world should be, might be one day, shall be one day—fuel our hope and the fire in our breasts that we might leave this place a little better than we found it.

"This evening I stand here before you, at the invitation of our Captain and in so great a room as this, aboard such a proud vessel, to share my thoughts on the essence of *man*. For it is the men of character who enact the necessary changes that lead us, as a society, from one momentous change to the next.

"We are at just such a juncture here, at a moment of change. And it is up to us. We are the privileged generation on whom falls this greatest of responsibilities."

I sipped from my water glass and waited, but he did not rise.

"We are, most of us, strangers aboard this ship. Yet even still we are a community, a whole society of shared stories, ideals and aspirations. And it is from our experience, our shared history, that we derive these ideals and aspirations. When I think back to my own father, most certainly a wise man, to be sure, but also headstrong, prone to outburst and deeply set in his ways, I can recall mostly conflict, yes, the common conflicts of father and son, but also conflicts of a more profound nature. Yet without his example and the subsequent differences that rose between us, I would have been unable to help change my small corner of the world—and I hope my work shall continue. Why this reflection on my good father? Simply to say that there are conflicts between good men. Honest men. And when injury is sustained, let the weaker man understand that the fight was one of ideals, not personalities. Principle, not spite. My father was such a man, and though our principles clashed, our respect sustained us. Let that be true of all men as we struggle to make our way in the world."

His head was turned down. He'd picked up a spoon and was cleaning out the last of the Devonshire cream from his strawberry torte.

"I would not at this moment find myself in your midst, sailing to Asia, toward that struggle presently underway in China, without the battle that ensued between myself and my father, this clash of wills that did so much to remind me of my limitations, but also of my potential. I would urge you all to seek out the nobility that each of us holds within and to give forgiveness when it is offered, even silently, and when a man stands exposed before you to rise above your limitations, to find that fundamental truth we all share, that need for purity and justice for the one man and the thousand men. For our life and times rest in the hands of the many millions of individuals like yourselves in this world who will be brave enough to conquer first the injustice within our own hearts, and then the injustice of others."

The applause from the audience rose before me. I bowed modestly. "Thank you," I said. I smiled, bowed again, then sat down.

ENVELOPE FOUR

A lovely day, finally, here in the First Sub-District of Yang Chia Chuang. It is early December. We for weeks have been having rotten weather, but yesterday the cold cloud cover broke to reveal a razor-sharp, ice-blue sky. I managed a walk up the hill just north of camp and enjoyed the sound of virgin snow crunching under my boots. It is a youthful sound, and I hope you come to know it. I was able to clear my head, if only for a moment, and inhale the perfect day. Very invigorating. The respite didn't last long, of course. But it was a much-needed reminder that such moments are still possible in this mad rush to kill one another.

Perhaps it's still early enough in this story to admit to you without fear of stating the obvious that the people in my life—those who surround me now, who crowd my past—are and always have been my fuel, my inspiration, my *tabula rasa*. I cut my teeth upon their sores and injuries, illnesses and deaths. This life you hold before you is built upon the broken lives of thousands. In these dark moments I seem no more than an assemblage of their parts. In this I do not condemn myself, but there is a sadness there. Any truthful man of medicine, indeed science, will tell you the same.

But will he truly understand it, how indebted we are to misfortune, upheaval and disaster? That is another question. How, for example, an engineer benefits from the collapse of a bridge spanning the Thames, the Seine, the Ganges. Among the dead sadly bobbing in the waters below he is able to locate the structural flaw triggered by the final, unsupportable sixty-three pounds that was the nine-year-old boy accompanying his mother to school. The final straw in mangled clothes. This is the pursuit of science: the mastery and manipulation of facts revealed to us through tragedy and misfortune. Yes, mastery and manipulation. It is all but carrion for the vultures of progress such as myself. And though the test of Parsons was hardly scientific, that evening's manipulation of words aboard the *Empress* stands as an example of the dedicated scientist's will to survive to see another day.

Though I have successfully approximated the words I spoke that evening, I must confess that at the time I hardly knew what I was saying. For a time Parsons's silence was equally confusing. He said not a word. He had me as good as naked before the crowd and simply smiled. In fact he politely applauded. Of course, it is not unusual that the words of a duplicitous man be honoured. We see it everywhere with our politicians, bishops and bankers. But Parsons turned the other cheek. Could he be as big as that? Was he, with that silence, demonstrating his superiority or intellectual indifference? To these words, a shallow invention of the moment, he turned his cheek.

There's nothing like deprivation to get you thinking about who you are and what you're made of. And when you do, it registers as something of a shock that there is no easy answer. What comes instead of answers is a deep morass of images, doubts and contradictions. They applauded my words! My strength of spirit and selflessness were heralded. Perhaps we all have such shameful episodes.

So it seemed my gamble had paid off. All donations received that day went into the CAC's coffers, with an additional amount in the form of the money I'd rescued. With his reduced responsibilities and total absence of funds, Charles Parsons was silenced. An alcoholic without his comfort is like a bear without claws—at least this one was. What I didn't know was whether he'd chosen silence or it had been chosen for him. During the four days we remained on board, he seemed unable to bear the confines of his own skin. I don't know if he suffered hallucinations, but his withdrawal was a terrible thing to watch. How I admired Miss Ewen then—and strangely envied Parsons. She visited his cabin often and, I imagine, provided him with the moral support of a kind and patient soul. Did they ever talk of me or the conspiracy I'd engineered? I couldn't say. But I'm certain she felt partly responsible for his condition, though of course she hadn't separated him from the treasury that had enabled his good humour and tacit dominance over me. He no longer attended meals but ate, if at all, alone in his cabin.

On the nineteenth day of our crossing, the edge of Asia came into view just as a storm appeared on the western horizon. Charles, leaning over the rail, vomited, having just a moment before attempted a bit of porridge at breakfast. It was his first visit to the café since my talk. When I looked up and saw land in a thin, incandescent shimmer of blue light between sea and sky, I said, with great relief, "There it is, Charles. Have you ever seen anything like it? And those storm clouds to whip up the sea in our wake like a dragon snapping at our heels!"

He turned his head up, watched for a moment and was sick again. I left him to his misery, returning to my cabin to prepare the portmanteau in which I carried my most personal possessions, including a number of paints, brushes and small canvases. I then made arrangements with the head porter regarding the field hospital, having determined the day before that this should be sent directly to the proper holding facility once we docked. I found Mrs. Qimei, shook her hand and told her to look for a little something under the third pillow she'd provided me with our first day out. Finally, I sought out Miss Ewen to inquire if she could use a hand. Around noon I returned to the forward deck. The storm was behind us, closer still. Mile-high thunderheads cast a shadow over the ship, but we were outside its immediate influence, and Hong Kong was clearly visible ahead, sparkling in bright sunlight. It looked, from the bow, even from the distance of a hundred miles, perhaps, a busy and optimistic town. It was a sign of hope, a beacon pulling us in. We would beat the storm and complete the crossing without seasickness. As I stood admiring the view, the Captain approached.

"The case will stay open, naturally," he said, after I inquired. "There are still procedures. Lines of inquiry."

"Could this be a crime with no criminal? Is that possible?"

"We have beaten the weather by only a few hours," he said. "Our man may think he's gotten away with something too, I suspect." We shook. "Perhaps we will meet again," he said.

"I should like that."

Mid-afternoon, after walking about the ship to bid farewell to passengers, such as the journalist Ansell, with whom I'd shared a drink and conversation, we entered Victoria Harbour. We disembarked with great excitement, and after passing through Customs and collecting our things from the baggage master we entered a waiting throng. Gwendolyn and the girl were greeted by a young woman— Alicia's mother, no doubt—and I decided not to interrupt their happy reunion.

I was just then thinking that our adventure was now truly begun, when Parsons turned to me, quite recovered from his sickness that morning. In fact he was defiant.

"What is it?" I said.

He put his finger in my face. "Bethune, you're a son of a bitch."

"Let's just get on with it, shall we?" I said. "We've got bigger fish to fry, don't you think?"

His face turned red. He looked as if he were about to explode. "You're a manipulative scheming son of a bitch. And you," he said, turning to Jean, "you were part of this. But I'll give you some advice. He found you useful. No more than that. How much longer before he sticks a knife in your back? He's not here for the reasons he says. Ask him about Madrid. Go on, ask him."

"Charles," she said.

"Jesus Christ, woman!"

The poor girl simply shook her head, flummoxed.

He cursed, turned and pushed through the crowd. When I lost sight of him I said, "Should we follow him?"

"He has every right to detest us for what we've done," she said.

The rest of that first day in Hong Kong she wouldn't speak to me. For a time that afternoon I believed I'd soon be on my own. Without a word, she cut through the crowd to begin arranging our transportation to the hotel. Rather foolishly, like an imp of a husband suffering the vile moods of a temperamental wife, I meekly soldiered on. But before long, I shook off this constricting fantasy by quickly running through the facts as they stood. If she didn't grasp the basic assumptions of war, sacrifice and adaptability, well, she would have to learn.

Our cabs were rickshaws piloted by coolies, whom we found among a large group of labourers gathered at the port's entrance. Our man loaded our luggage in the small compartment at the back of the contraption, helped Jean up and off we went. We rode in silence but for the quick breaths of the fellow ahead of us, his rapid pedalling and the general buzz of the city. It was a refreshing tour in that it provided much diversion. After the sombre blues and greys of the winter-bleak Pacific, we saw here a wild feast of smells and sounds and colours. Kabob and fruit vendors filled the air with their delicious offerings. Even now, I recall the joyful clatter of the busy streets, the racket the coolies made calling after one another in their flat nasal tongue, the local merchants rubbing elbows with the fashionably dressed Brits shuffling between appointments. It was a land where nationalities and races met, I saw immediately, and nothing like Europe. There was too much to absorb and too much at stake for the petty concerns of a young nurse to interfere. It was already passing as I watched this glorious city unfold before my eyes. I had made it. And if the topic of Madrid happened to surface between us, well, that would be dismissed as the raving of a detoxifying alcoholic.

We were delivered to the Ambassador Hotel, in the Wan Chai district of shops and restaurants, but found no communication waiting from our contact or any indication that he might make himself known. By now it was quite clear that Jean would spend the rest of the afternoon digesting the fact of Parsons's defection. I would use the time to ponder alternative plans. "What do you say we meet down here in the morning?"

She agreed without a word, just a nod, and left me. After unpacking in my room I sat and considered our circumstances. First, she was only sulking. Second, I must compose a note to our contact, which I left at the front desk in a sealed envelope. In it I indicated that we'd arrived and were eager to commence the next leg of our journey to the mainland.

I used the remainder of the afternoon to go over the final edit of my paper for *The Journal of Thoracic Medicine*. I typed out a clean copy and left it at the front desk to be posted. It was by now past six o'clock. I decided a brisk walk to stretch my legs was in order, then asked the concierge for the most recent English-language newspapers. He produced a three-day-old edition of the *South China Morning Post* and a *Manchester Guardian* dated January 8. I thanked the man, tucked the papers under my arm and set out to find a well-lit bar and catch up on what was happening in the world. The evening sky was clear and cold. It was dark now. I wandered through the neighbourhood for close to half an hour before dipping into a small pub named The Goose's Lantern. You might have thought you were in Soho or Piccadilly. I found a quiet corner, ordered a double brandy and flipped through the *Guardian* first. I wasn't merely surprised by what I found, I was overjoyed. After reading the article through twice, I tore it out and put it in my pocket.

Madrid

The rebel military commander at Teruel, Colonel Rey Dancourt, has surrendered with 1,500 men, it is claimed. The

Colonel is reported to have said that only a small group of rebels, with whom he had been out of touch, remained in the Convent of Santa Clara. His surrender would seem to indicate that no more than a handful of rebels are now putting up resistance there.

Outside the city, however, the battle still continues with unabated fury. The rebels are daily massing new troops in order to recapture Teruel. These troops are being withdrawn from other fronts.

The Republican Command declares that the rebels today employed the famous Italian "Black Arrows" for the first time on this front.

Yesterday, which saw the fiercest fighting since the rebel counter-offensive began, they made repeated attacks from Concud, the village to the northwest. Preceded by intense artillery and aviation bombardments, these attacks were supported by tanks and armoured cars. The Republican infantry, it is claimed, not only maintained their positions but forced the attackers to retire with heavy losses.

In the Muela de Teruel sector the Republicans took the offensive and occupied several positions, which they held under fire, on the Villastar–Teruel road.

The rebel army is considered here a spent and weary force. During the last eight days it has suffered several setbacks and enormous casualties. It is felt that the rebels' determination to recover Teruel is dictated by the knowledge that its presence in the hands of the Government must completely upset plans for any offensive on other fronts.

It was a major victory, as you can see. Delighted, I ordered another drink. After savouring this news a moment longer I turned to the *Post* and found nothing about the war in Spain, only a small article about the situation in Nanking, where Ansell was heading to look for his good Nazi. This wasn't such a joyous bit of news. The story itself concerned not the fall of the city but an article published only a few days before in an Osaka newspaper. The *Mainichi Shinbun* reportage had been about morale-boosting among the troops, and two officers said to have engaged in a "killing competition" on December 24, tallying over a hundred Chinese civilians each; final score, it said, was 106 to 105. These murders had been sanctioned by Japanese command in order to provide inspiration for a patriotic song about their valiant warriors' shining swords of steel. Curiously, the *Post* presented this story without editorial comment, its blasé manner making an odd and terrible story even more disturbing. I'd seen men killed in Belgium, France and Spain. They'd always fallen on the battlefield. This type of systematic, barbaric slaughter had nothing to do with war. It was a new brand of Fascism, a nihilism even more absolute and hideous than what I'd witnessed in Spain.

I remember reading through both papers, and when finished I watched the street fill with nighttime revellers. I ordered another brandy, bought a package of cigarettes and smoked, pondering the recent developments near Madrid. Certainly they would reduce the likelihood of a renewed offensive against the capital, open the Madrid–Barcelona corridor and generally swing the war's momentum in favour of the Republic.

When I returned to the hotel, just before midnight, I found that our contact had not yet presented himself to the front desk. It now seemed he would not show, and that we would be denied the support promised by the Ba lu Jun, the anti-Japanese network based in Hong Kong that had organized the second leg of our journey. As the head of the unit, Parsons had likely been informed where to find them, but we had not. From this point on, we'd be responsible for arranging every-thing on our own. Annoyed and dismayed, I decided then and there to make alternative plans. With medical supplies that were urgently needed, I could not abide any avoidable delays.

The following afternoon, after meeting Jean for breakfast—at which we spoke politely, though she still seemed somewhat distant—I went out for a better look at the town, believing she only needed a bit more time to herself. I walked at a brisk pace but was often stopped in my tracks by the faces I encountered. Though temporarily trapped on this small island, already I felt the lure of a giant continent looming in the mist only forty miles to the west. Energy, excitement and mystery dripped from the air like the juices of a mango. Here were banks and streetcars, pharmacies, jewellers, groceries and fishmongers, pubs, currency exchangers, beggars and churches—all things I'd always known, but here angled differently, tinged in new and exciting colours that filled me with uncontained wonder. Everything that made a city modern. Yet I was also confronted by its historic self, shadows and myths shining in the eyes of a people, beautiful, diminutive and deferential. All around me I saw the undeniable hues of the ancient in the bony chests and wiry arms of the rickshaw coolies who plied these streets with the bountiful spirit of children, men who I now know might work a lifetime without ever owning the rickshaw they wheel about.

I awoke refreshed the next morning and breakfasted at the cafeteria on the ground floor. Jean joined me not long after I ordered, seemingly recovered from her mood. I told her I was glad this debacle was at last behind us. We spoke, finally, of the business at hand and decided we couldn't afford to wait on the caprice of an anonymous contact. Our man had failed us, so we resolved to take advantage of a contact of Jean's. She had, you'll remember, lived and worked in Shantung in the early 1930s. She had a number of connections, all foreign nationals, including the American journalist Agnes Smedley, whose book *China's Red Army Marches* I'd attempted to read on the train from New York to Seattle and finished on board the *Empress*. It offered a riveting account of Mao's famous Long March in 1935. Of course, I knew about this epic event before picking up the book. It was, without doubt, the most significant turning point to date in the Chinese civil war, as it had guaranteed the survival of the Communist Army. Mao Tse-tung had led tens of thousands of men from certain death at the hands of the Kuomintang, Chiang Kai-shek's Nationalist army, by breaking through their lines in southern China, at Kiangsi Province, and delivering them over a three-year, five-thousand-mile ordeal into the hard, desolate hills of Shensi Province, where they were able to reorganize and swell their fighting force by perhaps a hundredfold. Smedley grasped the enormity of this achievement perhaps better than any other journalist I was aware of. It would do well to make her acquaintance. Clearly she wasn't hampered by journalistic neutrality.

Jean got a cable off to Miss Smedley within the hour, and before noon we had received her reply, urging us to join her in Hankou, some seven hundred miles north, on the mainland.

Our arrangements with the China National Aviation Corporation were made that very day, and the following morning, close to nine o'clock, we climbed aboard our plane and bade farewell to Hong Kong. The DC-2 bounced around somewhat as she lifted into the air, and the noise of her twin engines rang through her thin silver plating with a vibrating scream that continued through the anxious length of the flight. The first hours over the mainland were spent seeking cloud cover, as all Chinese aviation, including civilian traffic, was considered legal prey by the Japanese fighters that regularly patrolled the skies west of the colony. One expected at any minute to see a pair of Ki-27s come racing out of the clouds, machine guns blazing, to send us to our deaths. I'll admit here feeling quite helpless, like a sitting duck, but Jean seemed perfectly calm. We touched down a few hours later on a grassy strip near Wuchow. Here our aircraft was refuelled as a dozen men, forming a human conveyor belt, passed hand to hand fifty or sixty five-gallon canisters of fuel, beginning at a small wood shed on the bank of the river and ending up in the fuselage of the plane, a process that took a good half hour. During this time all passengers—travellers of various nationalities and ethnicities—were invited to disembark and stretch their legs. This was also a safety precaution, as enemy fighters would find a fat, refuelling DC-2 an irresistible target for strafing or bombing.

I left Jean standing with the other passengers fifty yards upwind of the stench of gasoline, huddling together against the chill air, and wandered over to the river. My ears still ringing loudly from the noise of the engines, I passed over a dozen patches in the airstrip where bomb craters had been filled with sand and gravel—repairs so recent as to be soft under the heel. I bent down to leave my mark, put my handprint into the Chinese earth, and then continued on to the river. Finally, the flight attendant ushered us back aboard and the aircraft lifted off again. We inched northwest over the vast expanse of China toward Hankou, where Chiang Kai-shek had moved his government after the fall of Nanking.

As we flew farther west the threat of Japanese fighters diminished. They had by then taken only the coastal cities of Peking, Shanghai and, farther inland, Nanking, and had not come as far as this middle territory between the south and north. The Hupeh plains opened below us, a snowy vastness as mesmerizing as the Canadian prairies at mid-winter.

Finally, nearing five o'clock that afternoon, we began our final descent at Hankou, situated at the confluence of the great snow-fattened Han and Yangtze rivers. The city, a sprawling smudge of grey and black, rose from the banks, and half a mile north of the airfield a racetrack became visible—two specks on the face of that vast stretching landscape—as well as a number of small roadways, outbuildings and vehicles. Jean leaned into me to watch the scene open up below us, and the scent she wore brought to mind the first days of our crossing.

"A bit bumpy," I said.

"At least we didn't see the enemy."

"Soon enough."

The landing strip was slick with melted snow and, unlike the strip at Wuchow, paved. As we taxied in I noticed more recently filled in bomb craters, as if we'd flown out of reach of one arm of the enemy and directly into the other. We parked alongside four DC-2s belonging to the same airline and a lone biplane. Once we stopped on the tarmac, a ground attendant led us toward two rather antiquated buildings on the north end of the runway. A stiff wind was blowing. On the roofs of these two buildings three chimneys sticking up from among the red-and-white radio antennas billowed smoke. The attendant ushered us into the first building.

Here, as we waited for our luggage to appear, a western woman about my age entered through the main doors wearing a black velvet cloche hat, heavy cloth coat, thick dress and winter boots. She studied the newly arrived passengers and started in our direction. She was a remarkable-looking woman, beautiful in the extreme, I thought, with lustrous dark eyes and skin that brought to mind the Gypsies of southern Europe.

This, of course, was Agnes Smedley.

A life-long Socialist, by all accounts she was uniquely devoted to the advancement of women's and workers' rights. I knew she'd been charged in 1917 under something called the Espionage Act for speaking out against America's entry into the Great War. She had also spent time in prison for distributing educational literature on birth control.

When she saw Jean and me, in a Midwest accent she said, "I see you've brought a man this time!"

They embraced affectionately. I stood back for a moment, then introduced myself.

"Well, Doctor Bethune," she said, "you'll have to tell me all about Spain one day. I've heard about the work you were doing over there. Simply brilliant. I'd like to know more. But let's get something to eat now, shall we? I've arranged a little something for you."

Her face glowed with delight at the prospect of acting as our guide in this dreary, bleak waste. Then a high-pitched wailing erupted. My ears were still ringing from the noisy flight, and for a moment I didn't know what was happening, but the ground crew and guards and welcoming parties all seemed to recognize this as the wail of air-raid sirens. All at once the war was upon us—not inappropriately, I thought, as thus far we'd enjoyed too easy a time of it. Now the enemy was reminding us where we were.

"Blasted bloody Japs," Agnes Smedley said, "every time I'm here. Off they go with their damn bombs!"

She led us quickly out the door she'd just entered and across a field, opposite the airstrip, to an underground shelter that wasn't much more than a pit covered with timber and sandbags. The ground attendant rushed the remainder of the passengers and their receiving parties down into the hole, and the forty or fifty of us huddled together listening to the enemy come in low over the airfield.

She cocked an ear. "Mitsubishi two-seaters. Three of them."

"Where are they coming from?"

"Off Shanghai," she said. "They pay us regular visits every time I come out here, but they don't seem too interested in anything more than getting rid of their bombs. As if they just want to get back to where they started from. They hardly ever hit anything, just pester us. Mind you, they have a way of getting on your nerves."

"And can we count on any Chinese attack planes?"

"What planes would those be?" Miss Smedley said, dryly.

A male voice, the class clown most likely, called, "Welcome to Hankou," for which he got a few nervous twitters. Miss Smedley and I began chatting again, but every time the Japanese planes rounded and swooped low over the field a silent, collectively drawn breath was felt in the shelter. And when explosions were finally heard in the distance and the planes sped off, a palpable shared sigh issued before the chatter started up again. This happened five or six times, with at least one or two explosions on each pass, but the raid lasted no more than fifteen minutes.

When the all-clear siren sounded Jean and I decided to hang back in case we were needed. Two bombs had damaged the main building, and soldiers and the ground crew led us through the destruction, looking for casualties, with Agnes close behind offering rhetorical advice and direction. "Oh yes, move that beam. Yes, look under there. Well done." She was well-intentioned, at least.

The attack could have been much worse. Five other bombs had landed somewhere in the fields, far off their mark. But the acrid smell of cordite, a smell I knew so well, lingered in the air.

We found no casualties in the main building, and gathered our things together before proceeding to Miss Smedley's automobile, a green 1930-model Citroën. Then we heard a man calling as he ran toward us from the west. His clothes were lightly burned but he seemed none the worse for wear. When he caught up to us he spoke rapidly, not stopping to catch his breath, and kept pointing behind him. Naturally, I had no idea what he was saying. When Jean translated the gist of his message, we drove to the racetrack we'd flown over on our descent and found sixteen of his twenty horses had been killed outright by the Japanese bombs. He was their groomer. The stables had sustained a direct hit and the smell of burning horse flesh filled the air. Using an old pistol produced from Smedley's automobile, we euthanized the remaining four.

"Yes, welcome to Hankou," Smedley said bitterly, then walked out into the field and vomited.

Somewhat deflated, we climbed back in the car and drove for thirty minutes to a quiet, snowy street on the western edge of town, a few blocks up from the river. Here we found, behind clusters of poplars and birch, the modest home of Bishop Roots, an American Episcopalian convert to all things Chinese.

Opening his door to us, the Bishop gave a brief bow and boomed, "Well, the Japanese welcoming committee didn't put an end to you after all. You've survived your first day in Hankou. Well done. Please, enter," and waved us in.

As generous as he was bald, erudite and long-thinking, he and Agnes had organized a small reception of some twenty or twenty-five local VIPs. He'd been in China for over forty years, and knew everyone worth knowing. It was an impressive showing. Over the course of the evening we were presented to military officials mostly, but also journalists, artists, missionaries, professors and even a well-known actor from the Chinese stage, whose name escapes me now. The Bishop smiled broadly and nodded when introducing. His sense of destiny and assuredness reminded me of my father, in that he harboured no doubt whatsoever regarding the rightness of the struggle.

"Don't think of this war, Doctor Bethune, as you might of Spain, or any other," he said, leading me about by the elbow. "This is a Chinese war, and like all things Chinese it is unlike anything else. Imagine the struggle in Spain expanded a thousandfold, with a third prong, the full brunt of the Nazis, marching on Madrid. That third prong here, the Japanese, will fail, ultimately. But that will take time, in which the Communists will do most of the fighting. What's certain is that Chiang Kai-shek has already shown himself to be a coward. Only his kidnapping last year brought his Nationalists into the United Front in the first place. If the Communists hadn't turned him around, he'd still be a coward and an appeaser. Even his generals know this. They were behind his kidnapping, you know. Chang Hsue-liang and Yang Hu-ch'eng. This miraculous conversion. Suddenly he stopped talking about eradicating the Communists and turned his attention to the Japs. The lord of the house had permitted the infestation of rats in his basement, on the promise that they wouldn't raid the larder! Men like Chiang, you see, are very brave with the lives of others; with their own, the matter is quite different."

I asked the Bishop if he thought the United Front would hold.

"My daughter has just returned from Shensi Province, where Mao's forces are based. She reports wonderful things. An animated, galvanized people. This is more than a gathering movement. It's a revolution, and I believe it will hold long enough for the Maoists to defeat the Japanese in the north and extend their influence southward toward Nationalist territory. Their support spreads by the day. Chiang's willingness to tolerate the Japanese presence is mocked there on a daily basis by the common people. The United Front will last, but only as long as the Communists need it to."

He wasn't as interested in specifics, only the larger picture. He was impatient with talk of shifting front lines, supply routes and international aid—all subjects I was deeply interested in. He was perfectly avuncular, though, and in so being could not have been less condescending or superior. His contempt for Generalissimo Chiang, the Chinese Franco, was refreshing.

"Of course," he said, "the important thing is that the Japanese be repelled. A most barbarous enemy, I believe. There is talk of rape houses they call Consolation Houses. No, we'll accept the meagre Nationalist support until we drive these devils out. And if Chiang can stomach the alliance long enough, we'll use his resources. Land for time, that is what they're saying these days. China has enough terrain to kill an enemy twice or three times as powerful as the Japanese."

"Land for time?" asked Jean.

"Ceding land so the Chinese forces can regroup—buying time, as it were, acre by acre, in order to put something of a resistance together and establish factories in the west of the country."

"The farther away from the ports," I said, "the harder it is for the Japanese."

"The Japs have a superior air force, but yes, you're right. The existing industries are on the coast. The farther they have to extend themselves, the better for Mao."

"High-stakes poker," I said. "How much do you give? How long do you wait?"

"It's the only game the Communists can win at this point. You've seen what the enemy is capable of doing. Peking, Shanghai, Nanking, all cities within a hundred miles of the coast. They can control city blocks and government buildings in Shanghai, but let's see if they can control the Chinese countryside, five million square miles."

The Bishop introduced us to a Dr. R. K. S. Lim, head of the Chinese Red Cross. The small man bowed politely before me, expertly balancing a cup of tea as he did so. I bowed in return, and the Bishop acted as our interpreter. Lim, noting that my reputation preceded me, said he was eager to have me and my assistant join his organization. "They're in the thick of things, really," said the Bishop, "but since the Red Cross is a non-aligned organization, your safety is quite assured. But then, anything can happen."

"Please tell the doctor that we are not concerned for ourselves but for the men offering their lives in the fight against Fascism."

"May I wish you all the best," Dr. Lim said, and withdrew.

We were next introduced to Lieutenant Chin Po-ku, the Coordinator of Medical Supplies for the Communist Eighth Route Army, presently engaging the Japanese, and under the military command of General Chu Teh.

"It is an honour, sir, to meet the great war surgeon Bethune," he said. His hair was parted down the middle, Western style. "The Chinese people have observed your struggle against European Fascism."

"As we take inspiration from this nation's fighting will."

"An exceedingly polite race, really," said the Bishop, smiling. "You'll find that."

"Tell him I'm eager to put into practice here what we learned in Spain. Tell him that with the right supplies and support, I'll establish units like the one established in that country, where our survival rate on the front lines was close to 90 per cent. Tell him the new medical techniques I bring to the guerrilla war in China will be a shining example to the world, and that I'm eager to get to the front as soon as possible. Please tell him that the first order of business is to arrange for our transport to the Eighth Route Army's base."

The Bishop obliged, yet despite my expertise and enthusiasm, I was told that issuing a pass ensuring transit north would take some time, since the Nationalist government held that swath of territory. Meanwhile Hankou, as the de facto capital since the fall of Nanking, was sure to provide a stimulating sojourn. It was, the Lieutenant added, full of entertainments and internationals, including spies, British naval officers, black-marketeers and prostitutes.

"And sometimes they're not so easy to tell apart," said the Bishop, smiling.

Growing impatient, I said, "Tell him I'm here to work. And the sooner the better. I don't care to socialize with expats. Ask him how long we might expect to be delayed."

"Impossible to say," said the Lieutenant.

"Days?" I asked.

The Bishop smiled yet again and didn't bother translating the question. "You would do well, Doctor Bethune, to think of this war as an old mule labouring up a mountain trail. Nothing about it moves very swiftly. Nor should it, my good man. History such as this must be savoured." And with that he took my arm, and Jean's, and delivered us to a small table set with tea and cakes, where we found Agnes Smedley, bottle of gin in hand, holding court with a Finnish industrialist and a short, unshaven Italian journalist.

It has occurred to me that I have not spoken much about your mother's family, but sadly I know little of her life before we met. I wish I could tell you some things about her childhood and your maternal grandparents, but the simple fact is I cannot. I know only what she told me. I suppose your mother left me with so little in that regard because we never really understood how precious the time we had together truly was. That it would be taken so quickly. We believed Spain was only the beginning, I suppose. What she told me was that her carpenter father had gone to America in search of work at the age of twenty-eight, never to return. As so many men did in his day, he crossed the Atlantic to find a new life and prepare the way for the rest of the family. After three months he would send for them. With a pack on his back, he climbed aboard the SS *Numidian,* sailing from Stockholm. He promptly found a steady job at a lumberyard in Chicago, on the north side of the river, but also what he hadn't bargained for and couldn't possibly fight against. Enraptured by the dream of new beginnings, he found a life there before his family was able to join him. A fresh start, he heard everyone saying, is the meaning of America.

So he fell in love with the pretty German maid who worked at his rooming house in the Swedish neighbourhood of Armour Square. He believed a young German wife was what young America had intended for him. "So there, you see," your mother told me, "we were left behind, Mother and I. But I always thought of him. I always wondered. Always prayed that the letter telling us to come would arrive the next day, or the next. I still live like that, always expecting something to change in my life. But it never does. Maybe that's why I came here. War changes everything."

"It changes a person," I said.

"But I'm still waiting for something."

"Then I'll take you to America. That will change you. It turns you into something you can't know. There you can never rest, never appreciate. You only aspire. It's like a war."

"I don't know how we managed," she said, "to live without a man in the house. I think my mother forgave him, but his absence was always painful. Then one day a solicitor came to say he was sorry to inform us that my father had died. It was a great loss, he said."

"What happened then?" I asked.

"He'd left money behind, enough that my mother didn't have to work any longer. We moved to the seaside, and when his body didn't come home we had our own services there. My mother prayed that I would have the strength to forgive my father, and I prayed as well. We stood in the sea and prayed and then went up to our cabin and prepared a meal together." She paused. "When I got older I began to see what my mother had been forced into when we had nothing. I saw that it was not our failure but the failure and shame of living without the protection of a man in a man's world. I began to understand my mother's degradation." She looked at me. "Does that shock you?"

"I'm sorry," I said, feeling embarrassed. It is a shameful thing to say. Sometimes we're embarrassed by our silences, if not by our inability to care about things we should have known all along. "This is what brought you here?"

She said, "Prostitution is a form of nihilism, wouldn't you say?"

It is easy to judge those you don't know, but often difficult to accept the ways of those whom you do.

I have wrestled with this thought now for some time. I wish I'd had the chance to meet your grandmother, to stand in the sea and listen to that prayer.

It became clear soon enough that the Bishop knew all too well what he was talking about. The transit passes proved a major stumbling block that held us back no less than three weeks. But I decided that I would not spend this time idly, as a tourist samples the local foods and takes in the sights. Everywhere I looked those first days in Hankou, on all the faces I encountered, I saw tales of the greater struggle waiting just beyond our reach. The Bishop was again correct. As the seat of the Nationalist government, the city was lively, bristling with military attachés, British officers, and American privateers (the Flying Tigers were making something of a name for themselves there), diplomats and businessmen, as well as the artistic and society types, the "war tourists," as your mother called them, that feed off the glamorous danger of a besieged and transitional capital. I was told, I think by Smedley, that the British authors Auden and Isherwood had passed through Hankou only days before, looking for their next book. I knew they'd been in Spain, with the Republicans, and wished them well, but also hoped they were truly interested in the cause.

China was now the only story. Here one saw the many refugees flowing down from the north, the simple villagers and farmers mercilessly ripped from their land and now hapless in a city unprepared for their arrival. But they were not a story. They were a fact. Meanwhile, the international problem was growing. Mixed in with the Tartars, Manchus and Mongols, I discovered around this time the small but very noticeable community of white Russians, blurry-eyed and violent, that favoured certain teahouses and bars in the seedier neighbourhoods. Their daytime melancholy often rose to a peak of drunken violence by nightfall. Early on during my stay, I saw a group of them walking unsteadily down the wet, snowy street, clearly drunk. It was a cold Tuesday evening. One man produced a bottle from his heavy coat—Russian vodka, probably—took a long drink and unceremoniously broke it over a companion's head. That man fell to the ground, stunned, and for a moment remained on all fours, like a beaten dog, blood emerging from his long shaggy hair. I was about to intervene when suddenly he rose and lunged at his friend. They set upon one another in a rage, then just as quickly, and without a word, collapsed into each other's arms in hilarity.

War tourism, so agreeable to some, was obviously not for me. I could not stand by, simply observing. After three days, and at my insistence, Jean and I were given a temporary assignment at the Presbyterian Mission Hospital in Han-yang, a quarter of an hour west of Hankou, until such time as we would be provided with our transit papers north.

We found the hospital in a sadly primitive state, barely limping into the twentieth century. It was in desperate need of supplies and equipment, overrun with TB and typhus, its staff undertrained and overworked. Temporary though we might be, its management would certainly benefit from the expertise of two experienced staff. The director, an ebullient Englishman named Morrissey who enjoyed drinking rice wine and telling stories of his youth in Manchester, was a good doctor, an island of iron will and professional conduct in a country torn apart by internal conflict and a foreign invader. He simply could do no more. Grateful for our help, on more than one occasion he very nearly begged us to reconsider our plans for heading north.

Morrissey, having been in China some twenty years, turned out to be a great and prolific gossip. He knew all the latest, it seemed. He spoke with great relish of an odd romantic entanglement between a Portuguese consular official and a German general's wife; he was very good with a German accent and, for some reason, quite ruthless toward the Portuguese. I think gossiping, along with the rice wine, was his preferred method of saving himself from overpowering anxieties. Occasionally we dined together, Jean sometimes joining us. He seemed to long for English-speaking company and took every opportunity to take me aside for a chat. He had a pretty wife from Hankou and a grown child now studying in England. He was very obviously homesick, despite his deep roots here, and quite despondent when finally our transit passes were issued.

During the almost daily bombing sorties over the city, our orderly descent into the cellars beneath the hospital was uneventful and routine. We treated a variety of wounds, primarily lower-body trauma, as most wounds above the waist prove fatal within twenty-four hours. We moved those patients we could, others remained in their wards. One day, preparing a leg for amputation, I was thinking how grateful I was to be back at work after close to two months away from it, when the sirens sounded. I looked up, and Jean was waiting for my order. This poor man, like so many others, had been subjected to unimaginable horrors over his long journey to my table—on average, over ninety hours—from the nearest front. I walked quickly to the window and watched the Japanese planes on their approach. By then I knew my aircraft. The three planes coming in were the Ki-15 Mitsubishi, a light attack bomber. I turned back to the man, who was still conscious. Just before the sirens started up, he'd attempted to thank me with a salute for doing him the service of cutting off his leg. When I turned to face him from the window, he smiled and mustered what strength he had left to raise his right hand and shoo me away to the basement shelter.

"You go," I told Jean. "I'll stay with this man."

As I said, there had been raids almost every day, but the bombs usually fell miles away, toward the middle of the city or harmlessly into the river. In lighter moments we'd even begun calling the bombs "fish killers." What Smedley had said was true, for the most part: the

Japanese pilots seemed eager to get rid of their bombs as quickly as they could, before coming into range of the feeble air defences. People died in Hankou and Han-yang, yes, but more often as a result of bad luck than precise bombing.

In a moment, however, we heard the radial engines screaming toward us. These pilots, for whatever reason, were not of the jittery type we'd grown used to. The anti-aircraft guns started up, but the planes didn't veer off and they came in low over the city. Then came the sound of a bomb whistling through the air, and another, and another, followed by a series of explosions. I laid my body over the patient, a slow, deliberate act, almost as if I were covering him with a blanket. Jean ducked close in to the exterior wall and hugged her knees as the entire hospital shook with the force of an earthquake. The window just above her was blown out, filling the room with shards of glass. A powerful fist of air filled the room and turned our guts and shook loose plaster and debris, raising a cloud of dust so thick that I could see nothing before me but a dull haze.

I lay atop the man for many minutes, protecting his wound. When the sound of the planes began to recede, the rescue teams began to fill the yard and hallways, the dust began to clear and the all-clear sirens sounded, I pulled myself up to find the man grinning from ear to ear. Jean got back up onto her feet, unhurt, and dusted herself off as if she'd just slid in to home base. She smiled.

"Jesus Christ," I said, "show a little fear at least."

The patient said something to me.

"What's he saying?" I asked her.

"He says his ancestors are grateful and he's thanking you."

It was here, in Hankou and Han-yang, and with Dr. Morrissey's help, that my introduction to the Chinese way of being and thinking began. Every day I was surprised by something I learned. He answered an endless number of questions and was very helpful on the most basic issues of manners, custom and diet. He shared his ideas and provided me with volumes of reading, which unfortunately I was only able to skim, for my time, as you can imagine, was stretched quite thin. Where it was our natural tendency to treat the world as an entity distinct from ourselves and our interests, he said, the Chinese held that the individual was intricately connected to a greater, older, wider world and could not exist without it. There was a certain indebtedness and responsibility that they were always aware of. He described the Chinese spirit as hierarchical, based on age and wisdom, and much more reverent of the past than the Western mind. This brought to mind the selflessness of the man who'd bidden me to retreat to the air-raid shelter at the expense of his own safety, and his unusual gratitude when I had chosen not to.

"He thanked me on behalf of his ancestors," I said. "It was an unusual sort of thank-you."

Morrissey leaned in and said, "Norman, that's it, right there. You've got it. If you want to understand the Chinese, remember that moment." We were sitting in his cramped office overlooking a lovely park, its cherry trees covered with a light dusting of snow.

"Have I?"

"Well, you see, it's faith for us in the West, isn't it? Faith in God. Faith in a cause. Whatever you believe in, it's faith, this self-imposed engine that, rightly or wrongly, permits us to hold on to our beliefs. Are you a religious man, Doctor?"

"No," I said. Not like my father, I thought.

"I didn't suspect so. For the Chinese, faith is nothing. What they have in place of it is duty. You see it in the real religion here. Buddhism? Confucianism? That's horses——t. This civilization's been around for thousands of years, and those ideas only for a few hundred. The real religion here is ancestor worship. In every house, every cave, every room you'll find a shrine, a candle, something that represents the dearly departed, and not just granny or your favourite dead aunt. And any people whose principal religion is situated in a pure devotion to duty," he said, leaning back in his chair and crossing his hands over his lap, "will never, not in a thousand years, lose a war."

It was during one of our conversations that Morrissey began to ask questions about Spain. He was cut off here and desperate for news. I told him what I could, attempting to provide an overview of the political realities there and a frank assessment of our chances for victory. I mentioned the victory at Teruel, the one I'd read about in the *Guardian,* but didn't have any news more recent than that. I described in some detail the mobile blood-transfusion unit and the documentary Karpathi and Kline had made. He listened with great attention, and pursued a line of questioning consistent with a medical man's interests. After we had exhausted the topic, he suggested I might be interested in visiting Hankou's Changchun Studios, the most famous of the film studios in the country, where the Hungarian Robert Capa was spending a couple of days, preparing some groundwork for a documentary.

I asked him if he knew Capa. Though I'd never met him while in Spain, I knew his most famous pictures, particularly the "moment of death" photograph that had garnered him, and the Spanish War, such attention. Morrissey told me that he did not, but had been informed of his arrival in Hankou—from Spain via London and Hong Kong— only two or three days before. He knew everything that happened in Hankou, this Morrissey, especially if it involved well-known foreigners.

You know what I thought the other day? In this Godless army I imagined myself a chaplain administering last rites. Can you imagine? At least playing tricks with myself gives me an occasional chuckle.

I have just now recalled something. I wrote recently that your mother had talked to me only of her father's journey to America and the difficult times that resulted. Well, I have remembered something else that you might be interested in hearing about. She told me that her favourite place on earth was her mother's kitchen. She didn't even have to think about it. We were playing a silly game to help pass the time, waiting for Kajsa's blood to fill the bottle sitting next to her. We both added to the blood supply as often as we could, usually after hours when the clinic was closed to the donating public. "Where would you be if you could be any place on earth?" I said, and she said, "In your arms," and I said, "Seriously," and she said, "Sitting on the counter in my mother's kitchen waiting for the apple-nut strip to come out of the oven." I said, "That sounds perfect," and slipped the cannula from the vein. When I applied the gauze and told her to bend her arm she said, "Light as a feather. Can I go now, Doctor?"

The following Saturday in Hankou, stealing a moment away from the hospital, we hired a rickshaw to deliver us to the studio, located in an industrial corner of the city, with the Yangtze at its eastern edge. The lot covered twelve acres and was a busy hive of men and women, all eagerly serving the war effort. My first five minutes there I was obliged to remind myself that the wounded I saw walking about laughing, with their heads bandaged, bleeding from gaping wounds, were in fact actors in costume. The set we visited was a perfect replica of the interior of a city apartment, with its walls blown out and windows smashed. The resources were vastly superior to those we'd had at our disposal in Madrid. We did not find Capa but spent an interesting hour watching them shoot a propaganda film that would be completed and ready for the screen within two months.

Two days later, another rickshaw brought me to the offices of Chiang Kai-shek's confidant and publicity chief, Hollington Tong. He was a severe-looking man with square shoulders and a hard, impatient gaze. Every afternoon he stared down a gathering of jaundiced American and British correspondents who, unimpressed, slouched in their chairs, doodling, daydreaming or otherwise waiting for the true story to come their way. At the conclusion of each press conference, these men reconvened at The Blond Dutchman, a bar frequented by white Russians and voyeuristic Americans, where they caught up on the real news from the front. This, at least, according to Agnes Smedley. I was very eager for the latest word on the war, both official and unofficial, and this, she told me, was where you could hear it. At the press conference, the government told you what it wanted you to know; for everything else you went to the Dutchman.

I arrived early, under a cold grey sky, and was ushered into a small room by an unassuming clerk. Uncomfortable wooden stools had been placed before a large oak desk, from which I presumed the daily press release would be read. Posters on the walls declared the rightness of the Generalissimo and Madam Chiang's New Life Movement. This was Chiang's thinly disguised attempt to fill the vacuum left in the hearts and lives of people who have been denied the inspiration of Communism. In place of a true social ethic, Chiang's movement calls for a ban on spitting, smoking in public places, and the fraternization of men and women in the street. There is even said to exist on file the proper length of sleeve of a chaste woman's frock—one inch longer or shorter and her virtue will be questioned. In its highly rigid code of conduct, you find nothing directed to the inspiration of the spirit, only a schoolmarm's list of rules.

Other posters consisted of colourful drawings of a group of Chinese tanks, a squadron of I-15bis fighter planes and troops rolling forward to the Sea of Japan. There was no mention here of the Red Army or Mao's heroic trek north to Shensi or the tens of millions of peasants who'd taken up arms in his name. This was the sanitized face of two Chinas, united for the time being against the Japanese. I sat at the back of the office and was wondering if I'd come to the right place when Eli Ansell, the journalist I'd met on board the *Empress of Asia,* stepped inside and smiled. "Good to see you again, Doctor Bethune," he said. "They told me you were in town. Have you met this degenerate? We've been looking everywhere for you."

The degenerate to Ansell's left was in fact a very handsome man with a wide grin. I recognized him immediately as Robert Capa, his likeness having accompanied some of his magazine work. His dark wavy hair was slicked back, Valentino-like. The man deserved a harem. You might be forgiven for imagining you were in the presence of a motion-picture celebrity or high-living Continental but for his reputation as a recklessly brave and superbly talented photographer. He was barely in his mid-twenties, I think. After we were introduced he asked what had drawn me from Madrid.

"Wouldn't it be the rightness of it?"

"Convincing enough answer," he said. "Madrid was right, too, though, wouldn't you say?"

"What about you, Ansell, did you get to Nanking?" I asked. "Did you meet your good Nazi? What was the name?"

"Yes. I tracked him down. John Rabe. I found him at the German Consulate smoking a large cigar. He's saved more lives than a whole fleet of surgeons. Incredible, really. But still a loathsome sort. A wonderful study in contrasts."

"I trust you'll do something with it," I said.

"Likely. But I've got this degenerate on my hands, and all he wants to do is take pictures of beautiful girls and get drunk."

"I prefer the Spanish face," Capa said.

"Isn't that scandalous? You've no shame, do you, Capa? You should be congratulated for your candour, then shot for your vanity."

Soon three other correspondents arrived to complete our small gathering, two Brits and an American. We chatted briefly, then sat down on our uncomfortable little stools. Mr. Tong entered the room, followed by a small man wearing glasses. This second man was Mr. T. T. Li. Mr. Tong began the press conference by rapping his knuckles on the surface of the table where he sat, clearing his throat and welcoming us to Hankou on behalf of General Chiang. His presentation lasted perhaps three minutes. He spoke in unadorned English of the United Front's triumphs, studiously avoiding any mention of its setbacks. He received no questions from the gallery, whereupon he vacated his seat for Mr. Li, who then read the day's official press release. Afterwards, we all made for the Dutchman.

"I saw you in Kline's documentary," Capa said. "I'm here to make one myself."

He explained that he wanted to find a mobile unit of the Eighth Route Army and follow a child soldier around to see if that could be turned into a documentary. "You know, a child's face in war."

"There are lots of those," I said.

The Dutchman was underground, cavern-like, with arched brick ceilings and deep recesses like the vestibules I'd seen under Madrid. We sat at a wooden table in one of these recesses. The bar was loud. A man at the far end of the room was playing a piano, his long, scrawny back hunched over the keys, swaying slightly. The air was thick with tobacco smoke. I saw no Chinese.

"Your friend here believes you should be shot," I said.

"The Hungarian is to be shot at dawn," Capa said. "Do you know what Capa means, Doctor? It is not my real name. My old name is Friedmann, you know. But Capa—*capa*, that's 'shark' in Hungarian. Shark. Do you know who Robert Capa is? He is my invention. It's true. I am an invention. He who sits before you is an invention. At this precise moment a drunken invention. If I cease what I'm doing I no longer exist. I know I will die soon."

"That's lovely," I said.

"But you are not an invention, I can see that. You are a serious man, Doctor. You are a scientist. A pragmatist and a realist."

"I think the Shark is drunk," I said, turning to Ansell.

"Have you ever brought a dead man back to life, Doctor?"

"I suppose *you* have?" I said.

"You think I'm drunk but I have. More than once. My falling soldier's alive, you see. He is alive. He lives on in *VU* magazine, September 23, 1936. And *LIFE* magazine, July 12, 1937. I have given him life. He is resurrected. This is the power of art. Such a man didn't have a fighting chance before he died, if you see what I mean. Perhaps he was a noble fellow. Perhaps he loved his wife. Perhaps he had children and a glass of wine after work. But now he is immortalized."

Ansell was sitting in the corner, his back against the brick wall. "We need more to drink," he said. "I think the Shark's falling asleep."

Capa said, with his eyes closed, "I think I'll go find the war tomorrow."

It occurred to me yesterday that this landscape in northern China is a tremendous demonstration of God's great will and design. Isn't that a funny thing to admit? Or something my father might have said? How pleased he would be to know that, but in truth I'm almost inclined to agree with him on this point. It is really quite stunning out here, these hills so perfectly formed. Can nature be so geometrical, so studied? They say the Russian steppe is quite similar. But beyond this mathematical precision, what befalls you here is a sense of tranquility. Is this only my yearning for some order among all this raging chaos? Could this be the same reason my father aspired to his God? The irony is not lost on me that this landscape is busy with death. But let us remember, it is not this good earth's fault that so many murderous armies should prowl over her fine skin!

I would not wish upon my worst enemy a journey as difficult and circuitous as ours was to reach the Eighth Route Army in Shensi Province. Thousands of uprooted peasants swelled the railcars, and the lines we travelled on and the various towns and villages we passed through repeatedly fell under attack. It was an ordeal I would like to forget. Rivers ran swollen, slowing our progress. We stopped often to treat the wounded, and this too slowed our progress. The Eighth Route Army was in retreat, and eventually we were forced to fall into retreat with them. At Tung-kuan, our first stop, a Canadian Red Cross worker advised us to turn back. It was advice we decided to ignore, instead waiting a number of days until we were finally able to find a train heading north to Linfen. Upon our arrival, the city was in a frenzy of motor vehicles, horse-drawn wagons and civilians on foot, carrying with them what few personal belongings they had, streaming south to Tung-kuan, where we'd just come from. The state of confusion was so great that we weren't able to report to the local military commander, for whom we might have done some good. After painful deliberation we decided we had no option but to return to Tung-kuan.

We found room in a railcar loaded with an irreplaceable cargo of government-issue rice, perhaps four hundred bags in all, stacked right to the ceiling. Approximately three hours into our journey, however, in the middle of the night, I was awakened by an all-encompassing silence. We were no longer moving. Wondering if the track had been sabotaged or blockaded, or if at any moment we'd fall under attack, I leaned my head out the window into the darkness. Crickets were all I could hear. I looked ahead and saw that the locomotive had left us behind on the siding of some backwater station, in a village called Goasi, if I was to believe the sign posted on the wall. Ours was the only car left behind.

I woke Jean up and said, "It's time we made some new plans." After I explained our situation, we stepped down from the railcar.

"How far behind do you think the Japanese are?" she asked.

"Far enough not to worry. I'll find the quartermaster."

It was a clear night, the stars shining overhead. It seemed all of China was asleep. The quartermaster, the major who'd granted us permission to ride back to Tung-kuan, was already off the train and organizing the nearby villages for the evacuation of his precious rice.

By first light the following day he had arranged, in the name of the United Front, for the purchase of every mule in the village, totalling forty-two, along with a cart for each beast onto which volunteers would transfer the load. After three or four hours of lifting, sometime near mid-morning, I discovered that almost all my personal possessions, trunk and portmanteau, were gone. I was down to the old Remington and my kitbag, as was Jean down to hers, though she didn't seem the least bit concerned.

It was near noon by the time we'd transferred the last of the rice sacks. The quartermaster informed us that instead of going on to Tung-kuan, he and his guard, approximately fifty men and boys carrying only five rifles among them, would make the three-hundred-mile trek to Yan'an, back in the direction we'd just travelled. We were left with no alternative but to accompany them, for otherwise, with no transportation whatever, we'd have been abandoned in that village.

The first ten miles, despite the circumstances, made for an almost pleasant outing. The air was clear and the sun shining. Over my shoulder was slung only my kitbag, to the outside of which I'd securely lashed the Remington. My boots were still in a decent state of repair. I was not yet skin and bone. It seemed this leg of the journey might provide some temporary respite from the chaos we'd witnessed at Tung-kuan. I might even have smiled out there on that dusty track, for the peace that descended over me, moving as we did at our snail's pace over that seemingly endless expanse, might almost have been described as "trance-like."

A few miles on, however, the reality of the war returned to me. In quick succession we encountered three walled villages whose inhabitants had fled or were unwilling to show themselves. The terror that was sweeping the land could not have been made more clear. Or so I thought, until my melancholy was replaced with fear by the sound of approaching aircraft. Two Japanese bombers appeared on the horizon as two missiles. Their drone grew louder, and then ferocious as they screamed overhead. We scattered, leaving the mules and cargo helplessly exposed. As the two aircraft roared past, the lead bomber dipped its wings to and fro to indicate to the second plane the decision to attack. Cutting a wide arc against the blue sky, they came around again to begin the hunt. The animals waiting below were easy prey, still locked to their carts.

What followed was a vicious display.

When the planes retreated Jean and I tended to the four wounded men, none of them critical, and then helped to clear the mule carcasses, which we heaped at the side of the road like mounds of red and grey sacking.

It was a miserable night of walking. Our spirits were battered by the attack, and matters were made worse by the damp cold that stung to the bone. We walked in silence. The night sky beckoned; the hard dirt road battered the feet.

Before first light we reached the Fen River, where we rested at an inn while waiting for an opportunity to cross over to Chiang-chou. As the barges that were finally provided for our animals and cargo were loaded, I studied the river and the far bank and the profile of Chiang-chou as it sat upon a low hill. I pulled my coat collar up against a biting wind. The Fen was swift and dangerous-looking, and when, mid-morning, I finally stepped onto the far bank and entered the town, newly chilled but grateful we'd made it that far, I discovered that it was largely abandoned, like those walled villages behind us. The Japanese cavalry was said to be only a half day's ride to the east. Mostly the old and the infirm remained. We treated as many of them as we could through the day and into the night before nodding off in a small room of the rectory provided for us by the two Dutch Franciscan priests who presided over this dying town.

Shortly after the noon hour on the following day we resumed our journey. A cold wind rushed at our backs and whipped up the tails of the animals before us. Our immediate objective being Ho-chin, some thirty miles distant and set on the banks of the Fen, we followed the river's southwest flow. We encountered dozens of wounded, all of whom we tended to with our ever-diminishing cache of supplies. As we walked, our ranks were joined by hundreds of refugees: desperate, lost souls who seemed much relieved to fall in with our ragged column. We were a river swollen by many dozens of human tributaries, and on March 3, still barely twelve hours ahead of the Japanese, we entered Ho-chin.

That grim town had fallen into a riot of misrule. Officers had lost the trust and discipline of their retreating soldiers. There was no organization among them. Desperate men roamed the neighbourhoods kicking at the black, long-eared pigs that snorted through the refuse piles heaped and stinking at every turn. Our numbers dispersed into the muddy streets for the night, and the following morning, anxious to leave that place, we made for the promise of the Yellow River. On the other side lay Shensi Province, our sanctuary. We would put the river between us and the enemy.

We collected in a deep gorge on the banks of the Yellow River, our party and many thousands of pitiful refugees and armed fighters, a full day's march from Ho-chin. It was an interminable night we passed on that cold, rough ground. The river pulsed and splashed out there in the dark, and in the dim light of the hundreds of campfires scattered along the riverbank crouched our expanse of miserable humanity. I walked among these people and offered what cursory medical attention I could. Infants, toddlers, young mothers. The aged. As I tended to the wounded and the infirm I read the fear of the unknown in their faces. How much had the enemy gained on us? Would we even survive the night?

In the morning Jean and I were among the first to cross, along with many wounded and precious supplies. Snow fell heavily from a charcoal sky to further engorge the river, which was, I now saw in the dim light, treacherous with jagged ice floes. There were only four junks in service at this crossing point, each with a capacity of approximately one hundred passengers. It would be slow going to clear the east bank, I remember thinking, and easy hunting for the enemy should the evacuation stall.

The first night on the other side, we set up a makeshift triage unit in a nearby village, which we then transferred to a cave closer to the river when the Japanese artillery barrage began the following afternoon. There in that cave, some forty feet underground, Jean performed with a consummate and unwavering professionalism. If she felt fear during the attack, I couldn't see it in her eyes or her actions.

Committed to caring for the wounded, she showed no thought for her personal safety and repeatedly forswore the security of the cave to greet the stretcher-bearers, without regard for the constant shelling.

She also proved to be a useful interpreter of language and customs. On the second day of the bombardment I remember a wounded boy was delivered to me. The barge that had carried him across the river had received a direct hit. Dozens of women and children had been killed outright or drowned. This boy's mother, a woman of no more than twenty, had survived the attack and somehow managed to pull him to shore. Wet and shivering, she stood before us and begged us to save her son. Jean told her that we would do all we could, and then an orderly led her out. Not much later we heard a strange, primitive howl echoing down into the depths of the cave.

When asked what was happening, Jean said, "The boy's mother is calling his soul back. She thinks it's lost out there, wandering in the hills."

It took four days to evacuate the east shore of the Yellow River. On the morning of our departure the day broke sunny and clear. As we emerged from that cave for the last time I wondered about the many souls that would be left behind there, including that boy's, trapped between the steep walls of that valley.

I asked Jean if she believed any of that business about scattered souls. A contemplative mood had seized me. She shrugged and looked down across the river into occupied China and said, "I don't know what I believe any more."

At Han-ch'eng, after a full day's walk, we slept in a village house, provided for us by the military council of the region, on beds of wood and straw that were at least dry if not warm and comfortable. Sheets of stiff white paper served as windowpanes. Our only source of light was a single candle propped up in a wine bottle. The label, though mostly obscured by wax, looked impressive.

"Where would you find a bottle of wine like that in the middle of this war?" I said, wishing it were still waiting to be drunk. "It's French."

"It's probably been empty for twenty years," Jean said.

Some minutes of silence passed between us.

"You're still young," I said. "You have something to look forward to when you get back."

"That seems very far off."

A light wind rattled the paper window.

"Yes, it does," I said. "What will you do when you get home?"

"Who says I'm going home?"

Outside there was no noise to indicate fighting in the area, only the sounds of the nighttime village. Doors closing. Distant calling. A dog.

I said, "You like it here that much?"

"I think I do," she said.

"Tell me something about Shantung. Why there? Why not somewhere else?"

"Where would you have me go?"

"That's up to you," I said.

She looked at me, her eyes glowing in the candlelight. "I've been thinking about what Charles said that day."

"What was that?" I asked.

"Something about Madrid."

"Parsons wasn't *in* Madrid," I said. "Madrid is long gone."

Here I am, Christmas in China. Not a soul around here has heard of it. It came and went yesterday without a peep, and truthfully I wasn't bothered. It was possibly the most peaceful Christmas I have ever experienced, though likely the coldest one, too. Some things are best kept to oneself out here. That's what I decided. I sat with my memories for as long as I could stay awake, watching my small fire, and that was enough. Maybe I'm getting used to it out here. Perish the thought!

We were stalled in Han-ch'eng for a week, waiting for transport to be sent down from Sian. The two-hundred-mile journey took another two days, and when we arrived we were presented to Chu Teh, Commander-in-Chief of the Eighth Route Army. It was a great relief to see with our own eyes the capable intelligence of this man after so many days of chaos and retreat. My confidence in the ultimate success of this struggle had not been dashed, but it had been severely tested under those trying conditions. Here was a man who inspired those around him.

At the conclusion of our meeting, the Commander promised to augment the field hospital that I thought was still waiting for us back in Hong Kong with any supplies presently at his disposal. When I told him of my concern for our field hospital, and how it would be safely transferred over that great distance, he informed me that it was already on its way under military escort.

Weary but excited as we set out, I pondered the vast fields of wheat that reached to the horizon, up some inches already, and their graceful dance beneath the endless sky. We were nearing the end of our journey; it was already late March 1938. We were among a caravan of supply trucks moving north to Yan'an that would reach that city after three days of slow, steady driving. When we passed over the loess plateau of Chin-kang K'u, where pale-yellow silt, like fine gold dust, collected along ridges to form terraces of astonishing geometrical precision, I imagined a painter's delight in the face of such beauty, and remembered the paleness of your mother's skin, and my failed attempts at capturing her likeness. It seemed already that a lifetime had passed.

We were greeted in Yan'an by a group of children who crowded up singing a happy greeting I was unable to understand. I embraced the smallest of them, who seemed no more than twelve or thirteen years old, and he held on to me as a son would a father. The frozen town had heard of our impending arrival. There was excitement afoot. It was known a man had crossed an ocean in his efforts to join them. But my journey had spawned rumours. This man had been killed—not native here, he was sadly untested on the treacherous footing—first by rock slide, then machine-gun fire, mortar barrage, dysentery and diphtheria. They said, too, that he'd died of starvation, his leg pinned beneath a shifting boulder.

So it was as if a ghost or a minor god appeared before these people on that cold March afternoon sixteen months ago, bearing what supplies a small fleet of trucks—guarded by fifty soldiers—could carry. At my side was Jean Ewen, by then more exhausted from our journey and my relentless ideals than I was able to tell. My brave Florence Nightingale. Many of these children had never seen white people with their own eyes, apart from an American doctor named George Hatem who'd lived among them for more than a year. Here he was known as Ma Hai-te, and he now stepped through the gathering crowd.

"You've made it, Doctor, wonderful," he said.

We eagerly shook hands. "The excellent nurse, Miss Jean Ewen," I said.

"I'm honoured," he said.

"This is a wonderful welcoming party," Jean said. "Thank you."

"Entirely spontaneous, believe me. It's not every day we get visitors from the outside. You coming up here is a real morale-booster. It's a sign that the world is listening."

"I wish it were true," I said, "but we shall change that, the three of us."

As Dr. Hatem led us around the centre of the town, the crowd of children followed, sniggering and laughing whenever we spoke. When we turned our attention to them, rubbing heads and embracing them, they swarmed even closer, as if eager to be touched by the mysterious foreigners. It was a wonderful moment for us, our grand arrival. But it was also a sad reminder of the war surrounding us. Despite their high spirits, we saw immediately the malnourishment in their eyes and skin. It was a starving population. When I touched one boy's head, he took my hand and held it tightly, then began pulling me. It was, it seemed, an offer to lead me around town. We laughed. "You've found your guide," Dr. Hatem said. "Hang on to him, you'll need a boy."

He was a delicate child, his face terribly thin. I wondered whether he would even survive the last of the winter snows. But his smile was radiant.

"Ask him his name," I said.

"Ho Tzu-hsin," Dr. Hatem told me.

"And how old is he?"

He and Jean spoke with the boy, and then Jean said, "He's sixteen. He says he has no one left. His parents were killed at the start of the war."

I was surprised that he was as old as that. To my eyes he looked only twelve or thirteen. He could not have weighed a hundred pounds. I placed my fur cap on his head and put my arm around him.

"All right," I said, "tell the boy he's hired."

The good doctor did so, and directed him to deliver our things to the Yan'an Guest House. This is where all visitors stayed their first days here. We walked ahead, through the narrow winding streets, and found our lodging at the base of a small hill on the edge of town. It was an ancient wooden building in what looked to be the signature architecture of ancient China.

"The Han Dynasty," our host corrected me.

Its soffits ran sloping off its clay roof like a curling moustache. Its doors were heavy as trees and painted a bright red. In the reception room, small carved dragons licked out at passersby from the door frames. Near the end of the tour, we were shown our rooms, and the boy appeared to await my instruction. I gestured for him to enter, and to place my bags on the floor. After he did, I thanked him in Chinese. He nodded and smiled, then withdrew.

Yan'an is a dry, dusty city; it is completely treeless, in fact, and so you might imagine it as a rather hard, cheerless place. Nothing could be further from the truth. What it lacks on the one hand is more than compensated for by the revolutionary hopes of all those who flock there. It is a city whose inspiration and ideals are not for a moment contained by the ancient walls that run around its perimeter.

It was there that Mao Tse-tung's Long March ended in triumph only three years ago, and there the Great Leader still resides. It claims its own university and military college and functions as the operational centre of the war against Japan. In those three short years its population has swollen from less than ten thousand to perhaps three hundred thousand, due to the influx of Chinese and internationalists, workers and intellectuals, eager to take up the anti-Fascist struggle. As a protection against aerial bombardment, student collectives dig their own dwellings into the gritty loam of the hills that surround this town, and there they live and study, wholly devoted to the improvement of self and society. There is not an idle hand to be seen there. Not once did I witness the inhumane degradation of beggar or vagrant, for all are swept up in the greater cause.

After a very brief tour of the hospital, Dr. Hatem took us to a co-operative noodle house busy with diners, women and men alike dressed in bulky uniforms of grey cotton that looked very warm and well suited to the harsh conditions of rural life. They all seemed exceptionally lively, despite appalling dietary realities. Over our meal of wheat noodles, Dr. Hatem explained that each man in Yan'an was provided with four cents a day for basic foodstuffs, and students or soldiers double that. As five hundred grams of meat cost forty cents, one's daily intake was dangerously lacking in certain proteins and fat-soluble vitamins. Added to these concerns, the extreme cold and overcrowding in the caves produced ideal conditions for TB. He had already treated dozens of cases this month.

After dinner the doctor showed us the cave in which he lived. It had the dimensions of a large living room, going back into the hill some twenty-five or thirty feet, with rounded ceilings that, like the walls, were painted white. It was heated by a charcoal-burning stove. By the light of a kerosene lamp he prepared coffee captured, he explained, along with a Japanese officer. We took our cups and sat on low wooden benches. Outside the temperature was no higher than minus ten degrees centigrade, but inside it was considerably warmer. Even before the war, Dr. Hatem told us, people preferred these caves to the houses in the town, which often were much more difficult to heat. He then said he'd heard that our team included three medical personnel, or had he heard wrong?

"No, you didn't," Jean said. "We started as three."

"What happened?"

"There was some trouble during the crossing. The man was an alcoholic. A sad case, really. He drank and, to continue his drinking, stole money. The money he was holding for us. I put an end to it."

Jean looked up at me sharply when I said that.

"Good for you, Doctor," he said. "Shameless S.O.B., it sounds like."

"Shameless enough, yes," I said. "We turned him around at Hong Kong. We won't be hearing from him any more."

We were walking back to the guest house, just the two of us, when Jean said, "You weren't talking about the telegram, were you, when you said that about putting an end to it? You took the money, didn't you."

I didn't deny it.

"Of course you did," she said. "I don't know why I didn't see that right away."

"You knew just as well as I did that someone had to get that money back. I wasn't going to wait two weeks for a telegram."

"And you led me to believe—"

"I led you to believe nothing you didn't already choose to believe. I only wish I'd taken it sooner."

"And Charles? You cared nothing for him. You helped him believe he was a criminal. I think he actually believed you in the end."

"Was I supposed to care for him?" I asked. "He believed what his conscience told him to believe. At least he had that, a conscience. I myself didn't make him believe anything." We were standing face to face.

"Forget about that. It's over. Look where we are now. Look there," I said, pointing to the hundreds of cave dwellings. Each door, painted white, shone like a pearl against the dark cliff. It was a beautiful, cold night, and our breath was steam at our mouths. "Behind each of those doors up there, do you know what you have? You have the heart of the revolution waiting for our help. This is the centre of it all. Don't waste the opportunity with pointless moralizing over Charles."

"At any expense?" she said.

"Expense? I committed no crime at all. Don't you understand that? It wasn't his money. It belonged to these people here, and it's because of me they'll have access to it now. I can save dozens of lives with the money I retrieved."

She turned and strode angrily up the hill to the guest house. I followed along, but I was in no rush. If my point hadn't been clearly made here, once and for all, it never would be. There was nothing more to say. I was relieved to be turning in for the night, and relieved to be rid of her. Her temperament was beginning to wear on me. Naturally, she was troubled by the business with the money. But did she now believe she couldn't trust me? It seemed some kernel of doubt would never go away. She was tender, even immature. I wondered if perhaps I'd misjudged her preparedness for what was to come, because what we'd seen and done to this point was scarcely the tip of the iceberg. She had, thus far, been very brave indeed, but in a short time we would see hardships much greater than these brief clashes and occasional aerial bombings.

The day had been exhausting, and perhaps the long journey had exacerbated her reaction upon finding out what had really happened on board the *Empress*. In any case there was not much I could do now. Once in my room, I stripped down and rolled into bed. But then, too excited to sleep, I got up and stood at the window, looking at the surrounding caves and hills and the ancient pagoda bathed in moonlight under the great dark sky of China.

I have arrived, I thought. I am finally here.

I must have just dozed off when a knock sounded at my door. For a moment I supposed it was Jean, though I could think of no reason why she'd be calling so late. And when I opened the door, a slight young man was standing before me. He spoke softly, and while understanding nothing of what he said I could guess from his manner that he was sorry for the late disruption. He indicated that I should follow him, waving me forward. I dressed quickly, stepped across the hall and knocked on Jean's door. "We are being summoned," I said. It took her only a few moments to ready herself. I could hear her moving about in her room, and when she joined me it was without a word.

The man led us to a cave on the north cliff. It was a steep climb. He didn't speak. Naturally, I presumed we were being called to a medical emergency and hoped all the supplies we might need would already be there, wherever we were going. He knocked once at a white door that bore no marking or insignia. No guards were stationed there, nothing out of the ordinary. As we waited I watched the town below, in its mountain cup of darkness. A ringed moon seemed only moments away from dipping behind the walls of the ancient city. I turned when the door was opened, and we were ushered in. Halfway toward the back of the cave I saw a tall man standing in the light of a single candle. He turned to us casually, as if surprised by our presence, his face still shrouded in shadow. He was dressed in a blue uniform no different from any other I'd seen in the village. He was, though, unusually tall.

The man stepped toward us out of the darkness. His high, pronounced cheekbones lengthened an already gaunt face. His thick head of hair, parted down the middle, was unkempt and much longer than you usually saw on men in this country. His appearance was rumpled and dishevelled, his large bright eyes were radiant in the half-light. It was immediately clear that we stood in a commanding presence. All these things I noticed as he stepped closer and gripped my two hands. He grinned widely as the interpreter, who'd just then emerged from the shadows, translated his first words to me. "A compote?" he asked.

I will never be able to transmit to you fully the mixture of confusion and pride I felt that night as I sat in the cave of the Chairman of the Central Soviet Government, Mao Tse-tung. But had he brought me there in the middle of the night to share his dessert? Mao was already a legend, as he surely is as you read this, perhaps decades from now—a man whose tactical brilliance had engineered the salvation of thirty thousand men and women from the Generalissimo Chiang's noose in Kiangsi; a man whose vision, expressed through the "Rules of Discipline and Points of Attention," acknowledged that a people's revolution would earn their respect and support through education, not terror; a man whose will was a force to be used for the people, not against them. How, then, could this inspired revolutionary be summoning us to his cave after midnight for *dessert*?

"He's saying he'd like to share his compote with us," Jean told me.

"Please tell the Chairman I do not understand."

Through his interpreter, he said, "There is no mistake, Doctor. We have lovely local sour plums."

Still not convinced, I merely nodded. The translator walked to the back of the cave and returned a moment later with a small tray.

"He's offering plums," Jean said.

His aide placed the dessert on a small table set against the rock wall to my right and said, "Please, sit." Mao Tse-tung gestured with his hand, as if bidding us to begin.

I dipped a wooden spoon into the bowl of plums before me, nodded and tasted the fruit. I smiled. "Yes. Tell him it's very good. It's lovely, thank you."

The interpreter spoke. Mao listened, then smiled. I had imagined, were I ever to meet such a great man as this, weighty pronouncements on political economics, dialectical materialism and the social sciences. Yet what I saw here was a simple man, generous, almost light-hearted. We ate in silence for a few minutes, and he cleaned his bowl with the thorough attention of a thirsty cat at its milk dish. He dipped his head with quiet enthusiasm, indicating his satisfaction, and said through his interpreter, "Well, Doctor Bethune. Welcome."

"It's an honour," I said. "My companion has travelled with me from America. She is an excellent nurse. Miss Jean Ewen."

He welcomed us both, and when she said something in Chinese, his face lit up. Delighted, he slapped the table with his palm. After a short exchange he turned to me again.

"There is medical work here for you," he said. "Our doctors will learn from you. This, and not the lovely plums," he said, smiling, "is the reason you have been brought to me in the middle of the night."

"We would like to begin immediately," I said.

"There is time. Tomorrow you may begin. Tonight we will discuss your ideas on improving medical care at the front. You will have your perspective. I know something about your work in Spain. You will have ideas. It is not every day a celebrated battle surgeon comes to us from the West." He nodded. *Begin,* he seemed to say.

"My ideas are simple," I said. "Their implementation is not."

"What are these simple ideas?"

"Front-line medical care. A mobile blood-transfusion unit."

As I outlined the logistics of getting the idea off the ground—training staff, procuring equipment and funding—a different side of the man began to emerge. He was an eager student, a brilliant strategist who asked many questions. Cool and analytical in his thinking, he sometimes paused for long moments to consider something that had been said. I watched his mind working, his dark eyes moving between me and Jean and the depths of the cave. His questions were the very ones I'd asked myself when first setting up the unit in Spain, and even some I had not. His hands, folded before him on the table, remained perfectly still. "We must take cultural realities into consideration," he said, "when talking of blood donations." His head nodded slowly. "Such a thing is a very foreign concept for people here. Perhaps not so for Europeans. Here it is bordering on witchery."

"Your army will follow your instructions," I said, then I quoted from his First Rule of Discipline. " 'A soldier must without hesitation carry out all orders issued to him.' "

Again, he nodded. "Very good, but he must first understand the necessity of the order. He must be educated."

Our interview lasted long into the night. Jean helped greatly with the interpreting and added much to the conversation. Mao listened respectfully, nodding, and thanked her for her thoughts each time she finished speaking.

He said, "And who now leads the people in Spain? I have heard of a man named Durruti."

I reported that he'd been dead for two years. There was no true representative, I said. It was a weakness for the Spanish people. There was suspicion and ill will among the parties. I told him of Largo Caballero, leader of the Popular Front. They called him the Spanish Lenin. I said, "He has united the Communists and Socialists and the Republican Union Party. But the anarchists are outside this union."

Near the end of our meeting I informed Mao Tse-tung of the supplies we had brought with us from America, and the additional supplies that had been promised by Chu Teh, Commander-in-Chief of the Eighth Route Army. Our field hospital would pass through Nationalist-held territory on its journey here from the south. It was my argument that the Yan'an Border Region Hospital, consisting of nothing more than a vast series of cold damp caves, would be the safest destination. Of primary concern was the fact that the Nationalists had stipulated that our supplies, in order to pass through their territory, must be utilized only on the civilian population, not the Communist Army. The danger of the Nationalists closing their territory to future shipments was indeed high, I insisted, and that would doom any mobile blood unit in Shensi Province to failure.

"Chiang Kai-shek," said Mao, "will manufacture other reasons to close the supply routes when he learns of our successes." He rose then and crossed the narrow room to a desk on which sat a candle and writing paper and pens, returning with two small booklets. "You may find time for this. Perhaps the lady will translate this for you, Doctor Bethune. Do you read Chinese characters, *mademoiselle*? Your Chinese is very good."

"Not many," she said.

They shared a brief exchange in Chinese, and then the Chairman said, through his assistant, "Well, then, Doctor, you will have to find another translator for these writings."

I saluted. Chairman Mao extended his hand to us and said, "Your day has now begun. Welcome to Yan'an."

We accepted his gift, shook his hand, saluted and were then led out by the assistant. When the cave door opened, fresh, cold morning air rushed over us and the bright sunlight startled our eyes. Blinking, and refreshed by the sharp air in our lungs, we started down the narrow rocky path toward the guest house.

"What was that last bit about?" I said.

"He said if I weren't such a talented nurse, I might be used as a translator. It's a rarity, foreign Chinese-speakers."

"We all have a part in this," I said, "whichever role you choose to play."

As we walked down the pebbled hill a curious sense of freedom enveloped me, and I felt more purposeful than I'd ever been. It was as if on this glorious morning of hope I had been absolved of all frailty and self-interest. I would devote myself exclusively to the fight ahead. It was a duty now, purer than religion or blood. Seeing only a Chinese future, I yearned to immerse myself in the conflict that surrounded us. The great man's passion had taken hold of me.

ENVELOPE FIVE

We are at the front near Ho Chien, Hopei Province, with the 120th. No sleep tonight. Just listening to the silence. I've always loved that, generally. I would love to share a silent night like this with you, sitting on some front step somewhere, or in a garden, just listening. How I loved hearing spring rain splashing against the new leaves. Do you know that sound? The guns will start again, soon enough. Can I put them out of mind, if only for an evening?

You will suspect by now that there must be a reason, apart from the war itself, that in my fiftieth year, I find life here so essential. Naturally I'm not referring to the abundant lilies and the wild beauty of this landscape. Certainly I refer to neither the food, so inadequate and unvaried, nor the conversations, for I stand alone, isolated in this language but for the help of my interpreter, the good Mr. Tung. What, then, could the attraction be, other than the denial and sacrifice that surround me? I can almost fool myself into believing the rumbling of my stomach is a soft purr of contentment, not the cry of hunger. Or that the pain in my head and the deafness in my left ear are the welcome reminders of greater agonies I have eluded. This is not a question of half empty or half full. The world here, to arrest any misconception, is almost entirely used up, broken, lost. There is no joy. No pleasure. Nonetheless, I cannot help but feel that beyond all the obvious destruction, something else is off kilter, that something—perhaps disguised in the noble drapery of self-sacrifice, yet there in my own deepest reaches—is in full downward spiral. My beliefs, I assure you, are sound. What's troublesome, as Parsons was so eager to point out, are my motivations.

I do have my work, and isn't that enough? If not loved by the daughter I've never met, at least I have a place where I'm necessary—and, more than most, I know the importance of belonging. My life has never seemed so crucial. To date I have performed more than seven hundred operations and examined well over a thousand who were sick, injured or wounded. I have written three textbooks to be used for medical training. Last year in these rough lands I travelled some three thousand miles, every step of which heightened my commitment and quickened my blood. But still I regret the bias and greed of this world, its blind eyes, its false pretenses, its first and second and third conditions layered one atop the other like a teetering Pisa of compromised ideals. I resent the deceptions of Madrid—or, to be clear, the lies—that have reduced this country to little more than the second, desperate chance of an embattled man.

I have been thinking to ask Mr. Tung to deliver these pages to George Hatem in case anything happens to me. I believe he'd prove a reliable courier. What a great and useless abstraction all this typing would be if chucked in the incinerator with some dead doctor's bloody smock!

In Yan'an last year, I lay awake at night, turning, those weeks we spent waiting for our travel status to be clarified. We worked sixteen hours a day but made little progress. The war seemed eager to demonstrate that it would not so quickly recognize my efforts, or even my presence. Its appetites were astonishing. And the conditions of the cave hospital were like nothing I had ever seen. April rains muddied the world around us, reminding me of the nightmare of Belgium. Anxieties only worsened when word came that our supplies had been stalled in Sian. After a few days I decided Jean should return there in order to speed their safe delivery to Yan'an. With her command of the language, she was the obvious and logical choice. She departed on April 25.

You are correct. She did not return.

Three days later, the supplies arrived. It was a great surprise when Ho appeared and began tugging at my sleeve. He kept injecting my arm with a make-believe needle and holding his head in his hands. After the confusion—followed by handshakes and back-slaps—I sent word to Jean that she was to return immediately. Twenty-four hours passed with no word of confirmation, so perhaps she was already en route. I waited another day and sent a second telegram, gruffly worded, perhaps. I wonder if she ever did get it.

On the fourth day I set out for the front without her.

Some small part of me was still hopeful, though. My desire to see her again perhaps had to do with the fact that I felt I needed to berate her for a failure of conscience, or soft ideals. A doctor finds his students' weaknesses and turns them into strengths, and a delicate stomach should be trained to tolerate all manner of bile. Of course, I wondered where she'd gone, and why. Somehow appalled by me, or still moping about Parsons, or caught up in a situation more demanding than she'd expected?

In early May I completed the final stage of my long journey to the Border Regions with Richard Brown, an Anglican doctor I'd met in Sian. We were just six miles west of the Yellow River, some seventy miles south of the Great Wall. Dr. Brown had arrived in Yan'an sometime mid-April, on loan from the Mission Hospital in Sian. I'd found him a quiet and patient man, admirably handy and self-reliant. Such was his dedication to the cause that he had decided to devote his two months' leave to our work in Shensi Province. I imagined his colleagues bemoaning his absence hourly. We didn't speak of Jean, though I suspected he felt my mood. I was surly, agitated, short. Neither did I let him know of my admiration for him, but it was refreshing to watch his talents and abilities display themselves as our journey continued. When a lorry broke down, he tended to it. He would walk fifty yards off the road, disappear for ten minutes, then return with a hare in each hand. He read the stars for directions, spoke the language and commanded the respect of our escorts on a personal level that seemed unimaginable to me. That he showed no interest in my moods seemed even more impressive.

I began to suspect he knew what had happened, for it was no secret that I'd been travelling with a nurse who'd failed to return to duty as instructed. Could this be of a personal nature? A lovers' spat? It would do no good that a pretty young nurse had affected the great doctor so thoroughly, causing him to behave so unprofessionally.

One night we encamped on the pebbled bank of a small stream. Our escort of twelve fighters, two guides, two orderlies and a cook were already pulling out their woollen sleeping bags. Dr. Brown and I stayed by the fire. As the stream crackled and splashed in the dark, I said, "If she showed up now I'd have her shot as a deserter." He looked at me but said nothing.

The following day's drive was slow, impeded by rain and mud. The roads of Spain were racetracks compared to these of packed dirt, ungraded and often washed out and treacherous. We followed the Yen River upstream before our road veered off into the Loess Hills. We crossed tributaries of the Yen at three points, and each time the wheels of the big trucks spun wildly in the silt as if suspended in mid-air. The first night we spent in a hamlet not far off the road and gratefully accepted the offerings of what little food the locals possessed. Before departing in the early morning we treated a case of pneumonia, a leg wound, a bloody abscess and two influenzas. The second night, after a full day of slow driving, we reached an isolated village of perhaps a thousand souls, many of whom hadn't tasted meat in months. A diet so lacking in protein had left its mark on this small population— gaunt, pale, some of them suffering from advanced malnutrition. I wondered for the first time, driving into the heart of the war, how a people so generally undernourished, so weakened by famine and these incredibly harsh surroundings, could defeat an adversary as efficient and ruthless as the Japanese.

It was there, that very evening, this puzzle was solved. Dr. Brown and I were told about a young child who'd been trapped in a collapsed building, far above ground level, pinned by rubble too precarious and heavy for anyone to help her.

"How long has she been up there?" I asked.

"Twelve days."

The woman led us to her daughter, whose head was clearly visible beneath a large rock five times her size. She was unconscious. The village had studied the problem, we were told, and after a week had determined, mercilessly, that the girl would die there. Early on a crowd had gathered every morning, but no onlookers remained. Retreating out of guilt and helplessness, people had returned to their own misery. Alone, the mother had used brick and wood planking harvested from the fallen building to fashion a platform rising to the height of her daughter's ordeal. She now lived with her up there, twenty feet above the village. All night she spoke and sang to the girl, caressing her hair and promising her she'd be freed from that prison, and during the day she brought her water and whatever herbal medicines she could scrounge that might help her sleep.

She led us through a narrow dirt lane to the building, whose north side was collapsed but for a single exterior wall. I saw the girl halfway up, pinned by an enormous slab of rock and mortar. Only the top of her head was visible. Her mother wasn't crying. She was concentrating as she called out to her that, as Dr. Brown translated, the foreign doctors had come. Foreign doctors. Imagine. Special men from the West.

There was no response. I believed the girl was unconscious.

There was only enough room on the platform for one person. First the mother climbed up, held her daughter's head for a moment and whispered in her ear. When she came down she spoke with Dr. Brown, who then went up and examined the child as best he could. When he came down he told me her breathing was shallow. He saw no trauma to the head but could tell nothing of her internal injuries, and there was likely severe damage to the body. She might last another few days in there, no more, nor was there any way of extracting her.

The mother said something I couldn't understand, and Dr. Brown told me, "She's saying we have to help her."

The woman didn't speak after he explained there was nothing we could do. She stopped insisting and bowed deeply. Then she climbed back up onto her platform and sat quietly with the child. It was heartbreaking.

The moon was full when I returned to the building later that night, unable to sleep. It was well past midnight, and a silence surrounded the village. The girl's mother stirred and looked down as I climbed up the rickety ladder. There wasn't enough room for both of us, so I sat on a large stone in the broken wall. The girl's head was perhaps two feet below me, facing down. In the bright moonlight I could see the individual strands of dark hair, lovingly brushed. She wasn't moving. Once I was up there, her mother paid me no more attention. It was as if she again were alone with her daughter. I opened my coat pocket and offered her the syringe I'd prepared. She clearly understood its purpose, but would not take it. I sat with her a while longer, then climbed down and walked unhappily back to my bed.

Next morning, we continued north through terrain empty of tree or bush. We crossed eight rivers in one day without seeing a single bridge. The next five nights we stayed in villages and treated the ill and dying before sleeping in borrowed rooms on mud floors, but never again did I see anything as terrible as that child trapped in the building. Her image haunted me as I lay staring up at some dark ceiling while Ho slept the sleep of the innocent and untroubled.

Conditions at the Eighth Route Army Base Hospital in Ho-chia Chuang were even more horrifying than those at Yan'an. Hungry cats were permitted to sit unmolested upon windowsills and under chairs waiting for discarded bandages to be dropped to the soiled floor, while men were starved of medicine and care. The entire hospital smelled of death and decay. The doctors and nurses were visibly exhausted, scandalously undertrained and thoroughly demoralized. After we treated the most urgent cases (which took five full days), the sorry staff was assembled before me. "This will not stand," I said. "Mr. Tung? Tell them, in the strongest terms possible, that I have had the dishonour of teaching undergraduate medical students with a more solid foundation in medicine and anatomy." I was, perhaps, overly harsh. But is that even relevant? This is not the real world here, after all, if by that one means a world interested in the delicate egos and moods of the faint-hearted. This is no hospital ward where we punch a clock and entertain notions of seniority, union dues and advancement. This is an alternate world, an unreal world. It is a world of man's blackest construction.

Shall I tell you what was in that syringe I left for the mother? You will know. It was enough. That is all I can say. I held it to my arm to demonstrate the procedure. I pretended to stick myself, then indicated where the thumb compresses the pump. I did it again, holding it out and miming the steps. She watched, silently. Then I handed it to her and climbed down the ladder.

The mother might have left it there, or thrown it into the rubble below, or sold the unused needle in the local black market. Or perhaps she slipped it into her daughter's arm, then into her own.

Please do not judge me. The world cannot be cleaved into two convenient halves of right and wrong. War and peace, black and white. Lovely notions, but terribly flawed. I hope you will understand that these words and actions stand only for my own thoughts and deeds and are meant to represent no one else and no other place or thing. I saw a situation and acted as best I knew how. I claim no privileged domain over right and wrong, not as it applies to individual behaviour. I have seen too much of the world to trick myself into believing that. You will have your own sense of how things should be, and that is as it should be.

* * *

Ho sits on an upturned trunk beside the window, looking through my recent drawings. What does he learn from them? Perhaps he's not a poet after all but an artist or surgeon intent on overtaking the great Bethune at his own game. How pleased I should be! Perhaps he will be my student one day. I have put tea on for us. When it's ready, I will flip open the Chinese dictionary and ask if he takes sugar. I might see him smile.

It was at Ho-chia Chuang, a border town of perhaps ten thousand situated between Shansi and Shensi provinces, that I cemented my reputation as a feared presence. Eyes turned down at my approach. I was a feared officer by then, a man of legendary temper. How I shudder now at the thought. People shrank from my presence. Conversations ceased, and in silence they gave the open-palmed salute to the forehead. I understood the dead, so the living and their small concerns did not interest me. It was as though I saved my compassion for the dying. For anyone else I had no patience, and this I regret. The near-dead, curled and silent or clawing the air in their pathetic contortions, were my only concern. So what if my students, those would-be doctors, nurses, orderlies and aides, could not stomach the arrogance of a stranger, even if he happened to be the pinnacle of their aspirations? Well, then, they were dressed down, shamed for their selfishness and told to leave.

Upon my arrival I made myself available for queries and then, when no one spoke, their eyes downcast, I ordered each man and woman to formulate a question. "Make it a good one," I said. I demanded that they learn, and fast. "Those of you with strength and character will change the direction of this war, and will stay on here. The others will find postings elsewhere," I said. "Nothing matters here at all except the comfort and dignity of our patients." With each question posed, if I sensed weakness I'd remind the speaker of his profound ignorance; when he returned the next day, I'd heap praise upon him. Nothing but exactitude, dedication and order would suffice. I told them it was my duty to rid the hospital of anyone whose natural inclination was to drop bloody gauze on the floor, ignore the pain of his patients or dream about the end of his shift before it had scarcely begun. That person was useless to us. At times now I cringe when recalling my tone, but I made a hospital out of that chaos. That is our triumph, and it must be remembered.

After those few days it became clear enough that no one but I could achieve a similar success throughout the entire Border Region. I was the most experienced and most capable. For the Director of Medical Services of the Eighth Route Army, Dr. Chiang Chi-tsien, I prepared a written report concentrating on the lack of sanitary conditions and proper medical training, the frequently incorrect use of medicines and an overall and alarming absence of supplies and discipline. I conducted a thorough investigation, interviewed the entire staff, ran through all the procedures. This facility had failed utterly, and I had no reason to believe it was different from any other in the region. The underlying problem, I concluded, was the Eighth Army's woeful lack of adequate training. I had begun to remedy this situation, I said, and detailed my preliminary efforts.

After I spoke with Dr. Chiang, it was decided that I would prepare a manual outlining basic measures regarding sanitation, wound cleaning and dressing that could be printed as a booklet and distributed to clinics and field hospitals throughout the province and beyond.

In order to continue this work I departed on a tour of the front near the end of May. I was accompanied by Mr. Tung and Ho, my boy, two student surgeons, a Mr. Ping and a Mr. Sun, a nurse and an armed escort of three soldiers. For over six weeks we travelled from village to village like a Gypsy caravan. Instead of bottled herbs and ancient recipes we carried as much spotty evidence of the twentieth century as could be loaded onto our sweaty, half-starved, overworked animals, as if we aimed to deliver the healing powers of modern medicine and technique over the limitless reaches of an undiscovered empire.

We were still without a permanent base we could return to. By mid-July Dr. Brown was obliged to return to the Mission Hospital from which he'd been given leave. Now I was alone for the first time since meeting Jean in New York fifteen months before, and the only trained doctor in over 100,000 square miles. As a distraction from the reality of these overwhelming odds, I threw myself into my work with even greater vigour and spent my days reorganizing all medical procedures at Sung-yen K'ou. Of course, there was nothing so grand as a hospital there, only a series of huts and shacks that had been appropriated from the villagers, a breeding ground for untold infection, in which wounded men lay, largely unattended in their filth, stretched out on their hard mattresses with not so much as a blanket or change of clothes.

In order to begin the process of correcting the lamentable conditions there, I saw to the construction of an operating room, a sterilizer, one hundred leg and arm splints, standardized dressing trays, urinals, bedpans, stretcher racks and an incinerator.

To instill routine and improve procedure, I drew up operational checklists defining nursing responsibilities, began holding one-hour tutorials on basic aspects of anatomy and physiology, making much use of a blackboard, and convened a weekly conference at which questions and concerns might be raised. I was aided in this respect by the indefatigable interpreter, Mr. Tung, who had proven himself more than useful in getting across not only my words but also my displeasure, disgust and rage at the frequent incompetence.

It was here at Sung-yen K'ou, in sight of the Great Wall some ten miles distant, that we built our hospital in the shell of an abandoned Buddhist temple. Beside this structure, I was provided an office in a small house that had belonged to a large farming family who had perished in the war. Given seed money of two thousand dollars over a period of two months, carpenters and stonemasons transformed the temple into the Demonstration Hospital, whose thirty beds would serve as a training centre for all medical matters. Every morning, sometimes as early as six, I was awakened by the sound of hammers, saws and axes. It was with the pride and humility of a beneficent ruler that I walked among the rising walls of this great cathedral, encouraging the workers with a cheer or double handshake, bowing deeply under the hot sun to praise their efforts.

My hospital opened three months later, on September 15, 1938. It was indeed a proud day, and one that I wish I had been able to share with your dear mother. How her face would have glowed with joy. But I did not stay long to bask in the glory, the Japanese made sure of that. We struck out for Hopei Province, where there were new reports of a gathering threat. Throughout the remainder of that month and well into October we travelled by horse and by foot, with three tethered mules bearing the burden of our equipment and supplies, visiting one village after another. Ho and Mr. Tung were always at my side; the latter now, in addition to bridging the linguistic divide between me and the world, served as my anaesthetist. We moved from skirmish to skirmish operating and, when time permitted, instructing those men and women who were able to learn.

One night, shortly after the evening meal, a young man approached me and Mr. Tung. When he saluted me, I rose.

"What is it?" I asked.

His face was visibly upset. Not unlike Ho, he was very young.

Mr. Tung listened to him and then turned to me. "There has been an attack," he said, "on Sung-yen K'ou. The Japanese have overrun the town. Nothing is left."

"The hospital?" I said.

"Destroyed," he said.

Ho appeared then. He had not yet heard the news. He leaned

across the table. I suppose now he was going to remove my plate. Perhaps it was the expression I wore on my face, the rage he saw there, but before he was able to withdraw his hand, I grabbed his wrist and raised it to my face, examining it as if for some abrasion or proof of . . . I don't know what. I knew I had terrified him, though, and I had no business doing that. From the corner of my eye I could see the fear on his face as he glanced at Mr. Tung. His limp hand offered no resistance. I threw it down in disgust and walked out into the dark.

I walked through the village and out into the country. I don't know precisely where. But there are hours I cannot account for. The Japanese knew perfectly well how to strike at the morale of the Eighth, how to cut its heart out perfectly. I had been warned that the hospital might prove an irresistible target, yet my persuasiveness and vanity had won that argument. And as if to shame myself further still I had assaulted the person as loyal to me as if he were my own son. Children are the heritage of the Lord, I heard myself say.

The following morning I awoke in my tent. My limbs ached. My stomach was empty. I dressed and slipped out from under the tent flap. Light was just breaking over the hills. Ho sat alone by the cooking fire. He rose and saluted, still afraid of me. When I motioned with a hand to my mouth, he turned to the fire and began preparing my meal. Watching him, I wondered: Had I become my father?

I have been thinking a fair bit about mortality lately. You might suppose I've always done this, but you would be wrong. You might lose your shirt on that one. I have spent a lifetime in the presence of death. I have watched it, touched it, regretted it, bereaved it and done my best to dodge it for these last forty-nine years, but it strikes me as odd that I have not really pondered it. I am not one to duck philosophical issues, nor am I easily frightened. Could there be in the inner reaches of my heart some residual Christian belief that I draw upon in moments of need? It surprises me even to think this.

It has been a difficult stretch, lately. We are all worn out. I'm often too tired to write and yet find myself wandering in thought more than is usual, even for the dreamer I am. I've been recalling the surgery I underwent to collapse my tubercular lung so many years ago, in October of 1927. Why should this occur to me now? I remember walking lost among the great dark trees along the shores at Saranac Lake the day before the procedure, in my mind running through the operation I'd chosen to subject myself to, when I saw my old mother quietly standing beside a large pine, watching me. I hadn't known she was coming. I had informed her as to the state of my health, of course, and the date of my surgery. Even so, her presence there surprised me. It was as if she'd felt her own life's blood at the edge of extinction.

We walked together quietly. A light breeze drifted over the lake. It was an odd reversal, I thought, the mother walking slowly for the son, who in turn resembled an old man shuffling off to his own funeral.

"I know what I'm saying," she told me. "I know you'll be fine. There is still much in this world for you to do, Norman."

"The world needs a fair bit of correcting, I'll grant you that, but I'm not so sure I am the one to do it."

She took my hand in hers. "You are a special man. You're on this earth for a reason. The Lord will see that you understand that reason."

I said, "That I can offer myself as a guinea pig?"

She said, sternly, "Don't mock His ways."

"What, then, is this great plan of His? The Kaiser? Sixteen million dead of the bloody Spanish influenza? Is that His great plan? Forgive me if I don't drop down on my knees."

"Will you pray with me?"

I looked at her. "You know I almost killed a man? Only three weeks ago. Frances's lover. Did the war do that to me—the faithless, jealous husband?"

She didn't say anything. We were stopped, standing on a pebbled shore. Out before us the lake was a sheet of unbroken glass, reflecting the sky. Here was all Heaven and Earth spread before us and I could think only of mocking the beliefs that had formed me and defined the one woman who had always loved me, unconditionally, perfectly.

I said, "What do you think of God's plan now, Mother? A murderer if I'd shown half the bravery I like to think I have."

She turned and walked back up the shore. I'd hurt her gravely, saying that. I thought I'd driven her away for good. To my shame, I was glad to have her gone.

That night we ate in silence. She had reserved a guest cabin. We sat on her porch, our chairs positioned to face the lake.

"I want to apologize," I said. "I haven't been thinking straight."

"I know. A mother knows."

I said, "He couldn't come?"

"Your father gave it a fair bit of considering. He fears his congregation would be lost without him. I told him it was the other way around. 'You should think about that,' I said. He didn't appreciate my saying that and went upstairs for the rest of the night. At breakfast he gave me a letter. He went out without touching a thing."

She got up and went into the cabin. The screen door slammed. The sound carried over the lake. She returned a moment later and placed the sealed envelope before me. I didn't move to pick it up.

"He's a good man, Norman," she said.

"I'll read it later."

That letter remained unopened, tucked into the pages of a medical text, for the rest of my stay at the sanatorium. When I left, the book was packed among others and shipped, after the house where Frances and I had lived in Detroit was closed down, to Montreal, where it remained sealed, forgotten, until Father died in 1932. The evening I learned of his death, I opened the letter.

I poured myself a strong brandy, sat at the kitchen table of my small apartment and inserted a knife into a slit at the corner of the envelope, pulling the blade along the crease. I took the page out and read it, then folded and returned it to its envelope.

I found it again on an October morning, four years later, as I packed up my things for Spain. It was a poignant reminder of the end of things, a good life frustrated by silence and shame. Without thinking much about it, I slipped the letter into one of the books I'd set aside for the journey and resumed my packing. But I have kept it with me ever since, and want you to read it now.

Toronto
Oct 22, 1927

Dear Norman,

You have by now spoken with Mother, and perhaps she is at this very moment sitting before you, watching you read this letter from your absent father. Perhaps you are alone in that little cabin you have written to us about, I hope in swift and complete recovery following your operation. Either way I regret the fact that I have been unable to visit with you at Saranac Lake. I am told by a congregant—James McGovern, Jacob's son, do you remember him?—that it is a lovely place of trees and hills and peaceful dark lakes. Much like Muskoka, he says, where you spent your early years. In any case, I am hopeful that this peace James referred to fills your heart now at this trying time.

As a father getting on in years I see that my life's regrets are not few. Principal among them is the reality that for many years now I have been somewhat estranged from you, my son, and yet not in any absolute sense, for our relations are commonly respectful, as you will likely agree. But it is clear enough that there has remained between us an enmity the root of which I cannot but fail to explain or grasp. We are, it often seems at familial gatherings, reserved and suspicious strangers obliged to share a taxicab during a spot of summer rain. A mean characterization, but do you agree? It has been this way for as long as I can remember, and it is a terrible thing to admit, as I write this, so late (though God will show us that it is never too late) on the eve of this serious medical predicament you now face. Perhaps I have been too hard, too distant, too demanding a father? I am willing to assume what guilt I must in order that we together root out this hardness that you harbour toward me, for in my heart I feel much pride and love for you, as any father could toward his son. It is my great and sincere wish that you soften your thoughts toward your aging father, and that from this medical treatment you will emerge healthy and strong.

You must know you are not alone at this time. "After these things the word of the LORD came unto Abram in a vision, saying, 'Fear not, Abram: I am thy shield, and thy exceeding great reward.' " Genesis 15:1

Please remember these words, Norman.

Your brother, Malcolm, and sister, Janet, send their love, as your dear Mother will have told you.

Your Father

I am proud to say I have pulled together a regular unit to accompany me on some short inspection tours throughout northern Shansi and Hopei. It is a good group, consisting of the two surgical students, Mr. Pin and Mr. Sun, as well as Ho and Mr. Tung. We are usually accompanied by a military escort of between two and twelve men, depending on the distance and area we are to cover. Behind enemy lines we usually take only two, as a larger group is more easily detected.

Recently we went up to Chia Kuan, a small grey town serving as a temporary base for soldiers of the 359th Brigade, and overrun with lice, chickens and more coughing black pigs. There we were greeted by Dr. Ku, Chief of Sanitary Service, and a Mr. Yuan, Political Commissar, both of that same brigade. It might once have been a picturesque village, Chia Kuan, whose mud streets were then dusted like Christmas brownies by dancing snow, but it had been transformed into a wasteland of sickly poultry eagerly pecking at one another's startled eyes. Among the wounded men of the 359th, gangrene and the insidious bubbling abscesses caused by indifferent medical attention were chief among our concerns. In one day we treated seventeen patients, operating on five, one of whom, only eighteen or nineteen years of age, had lost the lower half of his face. What was so remarkable in this boy was that his eyes, only a breath above his disfigurement, had retained a soulful, almost angelic innocence. He seemed to watch patiently as I went about my work. That is not possible, I know, but those eyes led me to believe that in his mind—his mouth having vanished—he was, perhaps for an instant, smiling at me. Still a child not long absent from his mother's arms, despite this mortal wound he was capable of hope. His eyes had not lost their belief that this world he knew, so harsh and uncaring, might yet yield goodness. They were the beautiful eyes of youth, and then, two hours later, he was dead.

We continued west to Chuan Lin Kiou, where we established another base for treating men from the 359th. Thirty-five more were delivered to us from Lia Yuan, a three-day trek over unforgiving road. The day after arriving there I was presented to Brigade Commander Wang Chen. He was tall for a Chinese, elegant and very serious, with the hands of a musician and the fine features of a leading man in the cinema. He received me in a large stone house at the edge of the village that had been given over to Company Command, its walls festooned with maps. He rose from his desk, saluted and welcomed me to Chuan Lin Kiou, then asked my opinion of the medical conditions in the military district. Again, Mr. Tung translated.

"They are very poor," I told him.

"And here in Chuan Lin Kiou?"

"Also very poor," I said. "The care your men have received is bordering on outright neglect."

He tilted his head back and stared at me, as raven-eyed and fearsome as a wronged protagonist in some Cantonese opera who was poised to take the head off an old adversary. He rose and leaned over his desk on his clenched fists. I believed at the very least that Mr. Tung and I were about to be ejected.

A half minute passed, but I didn't once remove my eyes from his. "Tell him again, Mr. Tung, that his men are dying needlessly."

"Do you think this is Hong Kong?" was his response, after my words were translated. "Do you suppose the world is at your disposal? We are surrounded by the enemy and bound by hundreds of thousands of square miles with few roads and no rail line. Paris does not care about us, Doctor. London does not care. Nor does Washington. Surely you know this. We have nothing here but our will to defeat the enemy."

"The world is coming," I told him. "I am an example of that."

"And when they bring us supplies you shall have all you ask for. But not until then."

"I ask only to know in advance when your troops will next attack."

He looked amused. "What will this achieve?"

"Beyond saving lives? Is there more?"

"Yes, you can prepare their graves in advance." With a rueful smile he sat down.

The high mortality rate of the 359th, I explained, was due to infection and gangrene, and this might be severely reduced if a mobile medical unit were deployed within two miles of combat. Such a unit would require notification of an impending action in order to establish an aid station and administer treatment within five or ten hours instead of the usual forty or more. If wounds were treated faster, infection rates would fall. "That is what is killing your men now. Infection. Sepsis."

He thanked me, then rose and saluted.

I believed my appeal had fallen on deaf ears. The fact that I was a foreign national, I thought, had not gone in my favour. I'd met many such men here, angered by the world's indifference to their suffering, and I could hardly say I blamed him. But that evening I saw Commander Chen enter our operating theatre like a man retaking the stage to reconsider his conscience. He stood at the front of the room and said nothing as my two students performed an amputation. He stood silently while I searched inside a man's abdomen for fragments of the bayonet shattered inside him. Small bubbles of gas escaping from his crusted wound told me the infection was deep, and I withdrew the shards of hard metal and dropped them into the tin cup at my side.

He stayed with us through the night and the following day, observing us at our work. In the afternoon I was summoned again to the room lined with maps and informed that my mobile unit should be readied to operate behind any future engagements with the Japanese.

Three days later, on the evening of the 26th, I was summoned from my tent and informed that three regiments of the Eighth Route Army were preparing an assault on a Japanese line north of Lin Chu, some forty miles northwest. The logistics were detailed in the extreme. Delighted to begin preparations, I instructed Ho to gather my non-medical essentials—cold weather clothing, sleeping gear and so forth—before nightfall. We arrived at our base, Tsai Chia Yu, in the early morning. There we were provided a guide to deliver us to Hei Ssu, a village of perhaps two dozen homes set beside a narrow mountain stream. I was pleased to see that a small aid station had been prepared in advance, even though it was housed in a primitive stone dwelling whose four rough walls were covered only by flat shale laid atop heavy branches. Only one glassless window looked west over a breathtaking landscape of wind-blown scrub rising gently to the world's snowy heights. We had over seven hours before the Eighth Regiment's wounded began arriving late that afternoon. I rested for an hour. Retrieving a notebook from my pack, I recorded some observations for my monthly report and then took the booklet Mao had given me and studied its mysterious characters, imagining what wisdom they held, before closing my eyes and waiting for the casualties to arrive.

* * *

I'm thinking about your mother now more than ever. The farther I move away in time, the more often she returns to me, and it sometimes feels to me that we're two pencil points in a slowly closing circle. One day we will touch hands and the circle will be closed, I'm almost sure.

It's dark now, and quiet, which makes remembering an easy thing.

Today my memory is of a walk in the hills we took together. Earlier that day I'd told her about the blue, shimmering sea, and watching helplessly as the planes came in over a harbour in the south of the country. I'd seen a boy of five or six years stare up in awe, with a child's absolute wonder, as they swooped in low, as if he expected the pilot to wave to him from that sleek, speeding airship. Even when the crowd began to scatter, he stood fixed in place, enraptured, as the bomb was released. It wobbled awkwardly like a stick swinging through the air, and exploded far enough away that the concussive force didn't knock him over. But an eye-blink later, his head jerked suddenly back, his knees gave and he collapsed, and died as the harbour rose up in horror and flames.

I told your mother this two weeks after she'd taken those photographs of the tank column heading for the Guadalajara front.

A Catalan surgeon named Frederick Duran Jordá asked me to talk to his team in the sierra north of Madrid about my transfusion unit. He was hoping to start up something similar in Barcelona. I had returned from the southeast only three days before, and the news of the attack on the Almería–Málaga road had beaten me back to Madrid.

That evening in the sierra, in a large stone house on the edge of a village, I came to discover that the conference wasn't what I had been led to believe. A car had come down to Madrid for us and, an hour later, dropped us at the gate of a large walled property. Here we were met by two men dressed in green and brown corduroy coats and pants. They wore berets and well-worn mountain boots and each carried a rifle. One of them accompanied us through a garden, past an empty swimming pool and into the house, where we were introduced to Captain Weber, from Syracuse, New York, a Spanish captain named Aroca and El Viti, the leader of a partisan group based near Segovia, a large, fit man who didn't smile and continually bit the inside of his mouth. The American asked if Kajsa would please wait outside.

"This is my assistant," I said, which by then was my custom.

"That's fine," he said. "Would your assistant mind waiting outside?"

I walked her out to the garden. When I returned Weber explained that a man of my expertise was needed in the hills near Segovia. My specific knowledge was required, he said. He was not able to go into detail.

"Once you have arrived," he said, "you will be told what you're needed for. Not before then." He nodded at the partisan. "This man will guide you, El Viti. He knows only where he's to take you." Aroca listened carefully, his eyes moving back and forth between the two foreigners.

"I can be ready in twenty-four hours," I said.

"Tonight," Weber said. "It must be tonight."

"Can I see your orders?"

From his breast pocket, the Spaniard withdrew a document. It was stamped and signed by General José Miaja.

"You're opening another front at Segovia?"

He ignored the question. "This man will take you. It must be tonight."

"The girl?"

"No," he said.

In the late afternoon, as I waited for nightfall, your mother and I walked over the rocky fields at the edge of the town. We were just under an hour north of Madrid, and another hour from Segovia. I didn't know where this man with dark emotionless eyes was taking me, but it couldn't be as bad as Almería. The hills rose up into low mountains in the distance, and all around us grassy tussocks seemed like small islands among paths carved by generations of wandering goats.

We climbed over a stone wall covered in bramble and black raspberry. I was distracted. My thoughts had been in Almería and the small boy I'd seen fold over on his knees, but now my imagination was up in the hills, over the Guadarrama Pass. Their coming up into this territory meant that they were planning on opening a new front at Segovia, and this entailed medical reconnaissance. I wondered when the assault would commence.

Kajsa was unusually quiet, and I supposed she was troubled by the incident at the house.

"Do you ever want to have children?" she said after a while.

"Not after what I saw down south."

A driver and I had taken a new Renault down to Málaga, which was already emptying itself out, a whole city of refugees heading east on the coastal road to Almería. A hundred thousand people glutted this thin artery running parallel to the sea. We drove headlong into a catastrophe of women and children, twenty miles of sick and broken people and animals dying at the side of the road. Occasionally, without hurry, a Heinkel dipped from the clouds for a strafing. We began ferrying whoever we could the seventy miles to Almería. And then the bombers came. We saved hundreds from the jaws of death only to deliver them into the belly of the beast.

Walking, we came to a shallow gully. I stepped over, then leaned back to offer my hand. She took it, and stepped across.

"Not even eventually?" she said. "After all this?"

"I can't imagine a time when all this is over."

We walked along the gravel road to the village.

The village sat on a hill looking down over a greening valley studded with grey stone fencing, goat trails and, far below, the road and rail leading back to Madrid. We walked along the high street, where most of the shops were closed and soon only the bars would be open. We wandered the smaller streets that reached up the hillside and ended at rock walls or abandoned buildings looking for somewhere smaller and quieter to have a drink, but nothing was open up there.

We went back down to the bar beside the fruit-seller, who was just then pulling the steel grate down over his storefront. He didn't look at us as we walked by him into the bar, which was crowded with men and their families. It was the hour of the aperitif, close to eight o'clock. The air was thick with black tobacco smoke and loud talk.

An empty table at the back of the bar overlooked the valley, where the evening sun cast a low golden light that left a lake of shadow below us but turned the eastern slope of the valley a resplendent, fiery green. We sat down with our drinks and watched two men playing chess at the table next to ours. One of them, much older, was being beaten badly and had only a few pieces left. The other man, who I realized was his son, was showing no mercy as he took one piece after another. Both father and son had short, stubby fingers. They were both labourers. The father didn't look up as his son brusquely knocked pawns, knights and rooks off the board with his own pieces.

I gazed down at the road. "Madrid's only thirty or forty miles away, full of terrified mothers."

"It doesn't look as if there's a war on from here. From here it just looks like Spain."

I said, "I don't know what Spain looks like without a war going on."

I turned to the chess game. The son was smiling widely, pleased that his old father was two or three moves away from losing his king. He called the waiter over, ordered another anis and lit a cigarette. He smoked *Ideales,* the labourer's brand. Apparently, his elderly opponent didn't merit another anis.

"Where is that American captain taking you?"

"Up into the hills."

"What's happening there?"

"I don't know," I said.

The son was now standing over his father. The old man's king was on the floor by their feet, and he sat without moving, his hands resting on his thighs. His head bobbed slightly, then was still. His son was talking to him, but he didn't answer. Puzzled, he laid a hand on his father's shoulder.

I stood and stepped over, touched the old man's hand and neck, then turned to your mother.

"Tell him his father is dead."

We returned to the villa, both of us quite unsettled, and two guards led us down a series of winding streets to a small plaza on the other side of the village with a cathedral on one side and a small bar on the other. The partisan was standing there smoking a cigarette. He snorted, smiled and spat.

"A drink before we leave," he told us.

We followed him into the bar, whose ceiling was something to behold. Legs of ham hung from the beams, each with a small cup piercing the bottom to catch the drippings of grease. Kajsa had been quiet for a long time.

"The girl?" said El Viti.

"My assistant comes with me."

He shrugged.

When the barman began mopping the floor, we carried our drinks and a white plate of olives out to the sidewalk and enjoyed the last of the day's sun on our faces. He began spitting again, slowly and delicately, turning his back to us. I mentioned that I'd been told that from the Guadarrama Mountains, over the hill from this village, you could see all the way to Old Castile. He said the view toward the north was of strategic importance, and for this reason small outposts and pillboxes had been constructed along this range and staffed by men from the villages on the south side. I gazed up at the cathedral, opposite us, crowned with empty storks' nests.

"Those old monuments are good for something at least." He snorted and spat.

"The observation posts on the mountain?" I asked.

He speared an olive, ate it and threw his toothpick to the sidewalk.

"No," he said, "I mean this *puta* church and the old *puta* buzzards up there sh——ting on the priest's head all through the day. Everyone s——ts on the priests these days, even the *puta* storks. I s——t on the milk. It is not so pleasant to be a priest now, my son," he said, smiling.

I suspected he was in favour of shooting every last priest in Spain. We'd all heard stories of summary executions.

"It's a lovely birdhouse," I said.

He smiled again, then said to Kajsa, "The men up there—they haven't seen a woman in weeks. They'll tear you to pieces with their eyes. Going up there is not something you want to do."

"I go with the Doctor," she said.

"How far are we going?" I said.

"We shall arrive in the morning, at first light," he said. "How are your legs?"

"My legs are fine," I said.

"And the lady?"

"The lady's legs are fine," she said.

He told his barkeep friend to leave his mop and prepare food for us. We drank another vermouth while talking about the war. Kajsa was sipping a brandy.

"What about those bunkers?" I said. "How often do those men come down here?"

"Whenever they feel like it. Everyone here is for the Republic. On this side of the mountain there is no trouble." A whistle sounded from inside the bar. He went inside and returned with a large rucksack.

"Food?" I said.

"Ours and the lunches of the others. We do not go up empty-handed."

We finished our drinks and I went inside to pay, but the man waved me away with his big hand. "*Viva la República*," he said. I answered in kind, thanked him, and the three of us set off along cool narrow streets where old ladies stood in their doorways and rabbits and *botas* hung in shop windows. Beside the town post box we met up with the two guards and another man, all carrying carbines. They did not speak.

We took the dirt road leading out to the main highway, also dirt, and walked for a quarter of an hour until we turned on a secondary road and followed it into the foothills where a yellow gate marked the trail that would lead us up to the old partisans who sat watching, day and night, for movement in the valley below. I wondered if there was a man of importance up there whose wounds needed tending, a man who couldn't be moved. That wasn't likely, though I no longer cared to ask. El Viti would say nothing. His English was good, but we spoke little as we walked. He cleared his throat of phlegm and set a steady pace up a dry streambed gouged deep into the rock. Large boulders that had been washed loose and fallen fir and pine trees slowed our progress considerably. Through the trees I could see horses on the side of the mountain. Branches overhead obscured the last of the day's light, and the air was cold. The three men accompanying us did not speak.

Occasionally we discovered small pools of water, and I asked if there were any fish.

"Farther down," the guide said, "below the town. If they've not all been blown up. You know, Doctor, that a Spaniard has no sport. He uses a stick of dynamite."

One of the other men said something, and he translated. "He says if we used our ordnance on the enemy and not on the trout we might kill more Fascists."

One of the men quietly began to sing, and a moment later the others joined him. It was a song I'd heard before, but in the dark it sounded remorseful.

Nearing midnight we approached an observation post at the ridge overlooking the northern slope. We came from the west and stopped two hundred yards off, and one of the men disappeared into the darkness. Fifteen minutes later he returned and led us to the clearing where the sentry stood waiting, his carbine over his shoulder. Wisps of snow blew over his boots, and a bright moon lit his gaunt, grey face. An old man, he tried to smile but looked tired, as if he'd just been woken up or this war had been going on his entire life.

"It is quiet here," he said. "What have you brought me to eat?"

He talked with the others while El Viti showed me the stone building the man occupied. Constructed of native stone and thus invisible as a man-made structure, it wasn't much more than a cave with a firepit and viewing window and a log for a bench, but it was positioned so that everything below was visible for fifty miles. That sparkle of lights was Segovia, and, our guide said, you could see dust or flashing glass or metal from any convoy of more than three trucks at a distance of twenty miles.

We left the man his food and a bottle of wine, and continuing west along the ridge we met more such men, all over sixty. Each time, one of our guards went forward to warn the sentry of our approach. The fingers of the last man were clawed with rheumatism, and the snow there covered the path. I wondered how he managed so high up. After giving him the food and wine, we walked on.

Over his shoulder, El Viti said, "We shall eat something when we get to the top, higher up along the ridge. *Señora,* how are these old men, are they as bad as I said?"

"They're happier to see the wine than they are to see a woman," she said. "And it's '*señorita.*' I belong to no one."

He looked at me, then at her, and smiled.

I saw him wondering what the correction implied. *I am with no one.* To a mountain man like this, it meant, *Even if I am with the doctor, he has no claim over me.* We continued up the path. It was very cold now, and the footing on snow-covered rocks was treacherous. Yet the men carrying the guns moved easily, their breathing untroubled, whereas my lungs burned. Perhaps they knew these trails from boyhood. The path soon disappeared, dropping into a bend. One of the men walked ahead. Then me, then Kajsa. I followed it down a slight incline and then up and up until I could see the end of the treeline. It would be light in a few hours.

I assumed the men somehow knew what had transpired. I felt their superior grins. An important doctor who can't keep a rein on his woman, they would be thinking. Perhaps this is how foreigners are, with all their grand talk, nothing more than cuckolds. I loosened the straps of my rucksack and continued on, wanting to send them all to the devil.

Then I heard your mother cry out, a short shriek that filled the night air completely. I ran back along the trail and found her buckled over on her knees and holding her stomach. She looked up and she dropped her hands to the ground.

"I am all right," she said. "Keep those men away."

"You have to rest."

"I'll be fine," she said. "Just keep those men away."

Before long, she regained her strength and we took her back down to the last observation post. I left her there with the old man with the clawed fingers, then started off again up the mountain.

Five days later, back in Madrid, I met her at the Crystal Palace in the Retiro Park, where we'd emerged from the tunnels into daylight almost two months before.

"I'm sorry about all that," she said.

Her cheeks were flushed. In fact she looked as healthy as I'd ever seen her, as though she carried a light within her, and I told her so. She turned and watched the ducks nibbling the underwater weed of the pond. The sun shone. It was late April.

"I have something for you," I said. The perfume was wrapped in brown paper, and the small envelope held a card on which I'd written a poem. She read it, and then I asked, "Do you have time tonight? You could wear this."

"I'm not sure I want to," she said.

On the opposite shore the towering statue of Alfonso XII, over-dressed in his cautious suit of sandbags, looked south over the city.

We walked up to the boating lake and sat at the busy outdoor café and drank coffees with anis. It was a nice break from the war, I remember thinking.

I regret the delay in getting on with this narrative, but I have come to Yang Chia Chuang to begin work on establishing a training school. I have little time for anything other than this important project. There is still much work to be done, Lord knows, but the first hurdle, and perhaps the highest, has been cleared: I have persuaded Dr. Chiang Chi-tsien, Director of Medical Services for the Eighth Route Army, and a number of his fellow colleagues, that within months such a school will begin to ease the chronic shortage of medical care at the front, and that I'm the only person available to make the school a reality. It is my hope that in the first six months we will prepare hundreds of mobile medical units. My efforts on the ground have not been enough, as I cannot win this war fracture by fracture, heart by heart. I understand, now, that my time is best spent educating a new generation of doctors and nurses.

I have completed the medical text I began some months ago. Despite overwork and exhaustion this has been a time of great energy and optimism. I envision each regiment of the Red Army equipped with its own field unit, and with this school, and possibly others, we might achieve that goal. I might spend a day in the operating theatre and save perhaps ten lives. What a wonderful day that is. But now, with this program, I might save a thousand.

What is the qualitative difference between the deed done for its own sake and one accomplished for purely selfish reasons, though resulting in the same benefit? Is there one? Does it matter? I was unable to consider this question during those months in Madrid. But now that I am asking it of myself here in the thin air of this mountain night, I am forced to pause and look about me.

What do these people do but give every ounce of sweat to the labours of survival and an improved lot for the future? Not a single man or woman, not even a child, Ho would assure me, places himself or herself above this cause. And can I say the same? I wonder how much of my life has become a drama in which I daily costume myself in gown and mask. How much of my life has taken its own course, in spite of me? I will give of myself to the last breath, of that I have no doubt. But has the actor been outwitted by the grand tragedy he serves?

Shortly after the New Year, thirty qualified candidates chosen from all corners of the Border Regions arrived to Yang Chia Chuang to immerse themselves in the three-week course I had prepared. There they would learn the essentials of front-line medical care. By then I was under no illusion. I was not teaching the art of surgery, but my students were learning the basic skills so vitally required and so often lacking at aid stations throughout the territories. Graduates would return to their precincts with that vital knowledge and continue the process of education. It was a far cry from the actual surgical training truly required, but it met an urgent need.

Within four weeks I was confident that the school was capable of operating without my stewardship. I was eager to return to the field. It was an unhappy addiction, these frequent forays, but of pre-eminent importance. Through that hard winter and into the spring my eighteen-member team sought out field hospitals, medical units and guerrilla fighters. We were strafed, bombed and sniped, pursued by the Japanese, and we very nearly froze to death almost every night before March brought its first thaw. Always we came upon wounded who were holed up, entrenched, and dying all manners of death—from trauma, sepsis, starvation, TB. Great numbers or simply one man, abandoned to his fate. We were received as angels of mercy. So far gone were the hopes of the men we encountered that any help at all, even if only to help them die faster, was welcomed. Under enemy fire we cut and stitched, stabilizing peasants and partisans and regular soldiers so they might be delivered out of harm's way.

For some time I had been riding a horse captured from the Japanese. One day, while returning from an inspection tour, I got to wondering what might have become of its previous owner. Lost in thought, I rode on, only slightly behind our lead guide. Perhaps I'd been partially hypnotized by the slow clomp of the beast beneath me, exhausted as I was, and by the thin air of that mountain altitude. Where was he? I wondered. Who had he been? Perhaps not so unlike me. Was he somewhere behind us, like so many of his comrades, eyeless, their dirt-filled mouths crying out mutely for a solemn return to the homeland? Yes, your horse is alive, I wanted to say, alive, if miserable in its new calling, and you are not. The beast outlives its master.

I wondered if perhaps it would be appropriate to shoot it once I arrived at the Base Hospital, as if in respect for its fallen owner, but it had proven too useful for that. Spurring it on, I pondered if it was better to be a beast of burden or, say, a little monk nibbling away at time as a mouse does cheese? A horse has a use, at least, and a quiet dignity in its labours. A monk is utterly useless and without consequence. I forgave the animal its origins and urged it to climb higher. It was early morning. The light was faint, almost blue, the sun not fully over the ridge to the west.

Near midday we came across a man alone and left for dead. The Japanese hadn't done such a thorough job on him. Perhaps they'd left him like this for a reason, or else had become bored with their torture, impatient to move on to better things. I asked Mr. Tung to come forward. The other men kept away. I dismounted and with Mr. Tung walked over to the man. The landscape was barren. The wind, carrying small flakes now, prowled in upward dancing surges. Snow snaked between the rocks as if scurrying from itself.

He was lying there, watching as we approached. He made no gesture, no movement, but his eyes were full of life and terror. His severed hands lay beside him, gripped in comradely greeting. When I kneeled down, his gaze shifted to his hands and made a strange face. It was as if he were trying to make them respond. His legs were broken and splayed out, bent and distorted from beneath him, his knees snapped backwards. He would be dead in a matter of minutes.

There was a wound in his chest I could fit my hand into, and his lungs were filling. There was no use for Mr. Tung since the man couldn't talk. He tried to smile at me, it was an apologetic smile, then he looked at his hands again. They were just out of reach. He seemed more aware than I had ever been in my entire life. Of all the eternity of moments that had been lived and were yet to be lived, this one in this timeless place, and with us as bystanders, had been fully dedicated to this simple man. This was the centre-point of his life. This was the fire, the flame moving underground. It was perhaps all he would amount to. Whether the precious facts of his life were in any respect complete or significant, it didn't matter now. This was the most important moment in his life, the exact moment of consciousness he'd wondered about while sleeping in caves and on the rocks of this mountain, freezing, sweating, eating gruel and starving, listening to his friends' stories of home, he himself dreaming of his life and always trying to imagine what death would be like when it came. And now, as I'd seen hundreds of times before in the faces of other men, he was sitting patiently, resignedly, staring down over the retreating landscape.

He sat before his entire life and waited to die as I sat beside him. Perhaps he'd raised his hands in supplication to his murderers, beseeching them, and then the *katana,* in a swift arc of reply, had cut through the air.

After he died, I crossed his arms over his chest and placed his hands there, curled, still clasped. Then we mounted our animals and started off once more.

Ho has joined me now. I do not usually write during daylight hours. There's never enough time. But today I have completed my rounds and performed three surgeries and managed to eat a bite and still there's light in the sky. I sat down and was just about to begin when Ho came to my door. Seeing my typewriter he retreated deferentially, but I got up and pulled him inside and asked him to sit. So here he sits, watching and waiting.

Last night I dreamed you came to me here. You were a child. "Go," I said. "The war will be over soon, and I will come for you." You looked at me and your smile revealed you were missing two teeth. You knew nothing of the horrors of this world, only its perfect beauty. I took you in my arms and carried you outside to a pasture with a stream and a bright light falling from the blue heavens and majestic oaks thrumming in the breeze. I set you down in the grass and went back inside.

Ho is a patient lad to sit here like this. Why do I invite him in here? Is it that I, too, am alone?

To keep him occupied I handed him a sheaf of pencil drawings I've been working on, with no words but the title. The most recent is "Burn Injury of the Left Arm with Surgical Amputation." He nods enthusiastically.

I've been thinking lately about matrimony—mine, to be precise. A strange preoccupation in the middle of a war. I have been thinking about you finding happiness with a good and patient man. Does that mark me as sentimental? Well, so be it. Perhaps he's leaning over your shoulder as you read this. I find that thought comforting. No union in life is as dear as marriage, and though I may have been more susceptible than most to the frailties of the heart, I still believe it. None of us is so different in that regard. We all harbour an abiding belief that even after failure there can be hope for the future. That is our greatest resource, I think, eternal hope. Some basic truths bear repeating, and this is one of them. I can tell you that the mystery of our loves is the deepest mystery we have, the most beautiful and ennobling, too, and the most deserving of our ceaseless energies and wonder. I imagine you will know by the time you read this that a first love is not often successful. I discovered this when I was younger, that one failure might strengthen you for another. The name of the woman who helped me to become that better man your mother fell in love with was Frances Penney. She became my wife, and two times I left her, walking back into my lonely life.

The Great War had ended and I had begun writing and painting again. I had found employment at number 23 Great Ormond Street, London, working with children. One evening, in the fall of 1920, I met with an Australian friend, Clifford Ellington, at a pub in Soho. We were talking over a number of my poems and having a glass of beer when a group of four young women entered the pub. One was glamorous-looking, very beautiful. Her large eyes darted around the bar, and she produced a cigarette from her purse. She made much of this simple act. It was very much worthy of the pictures, I remember thinking.

Her dark hair was cut short, bobbed, as all the girls were wearing it then. She crossed her legs under her chair, then leaned into the middle of the table and remarked upon something that made her friends laugh. The four of them looked inelegantly in our direction as they did so. "A flock of parakeets mocking the baboons," Ellington said. The server spoke with the young ladies and returned behind the bar, where we were standing. She busied herself with polishing a glass while the barman prepared their drinks. My left elbow was damp from leaning on the bar where someone had spilt a beer. My heart thumping, I asked the server, "Would you please mop this up for me?"

We returned to our discussion, Ellington arguing that I should refrain from sending my poems out. He held the sheaf of poems in his hand, waving them as he spoke. They were, he said, childish and morbid, vain and self-important. Very nearly offended, I suggested he didn't have an ounce of creative or critical blood in his veins. "Bethune, this is not poetry," he said, or something along those lines. He was an intelligent man and a very good doctor, and I enjoyed his company immensely. But I found it difficult to take his criticism seriously, though foolishly I'd asked for it. I never really liked his poems, greatly inspired by a fashionable Australian poet of the day who for good reason had yet to be discovered anywhere else in the English-speaking world.

"Norman, you're a charming drunk and a gifted doctor," Ellington said, "but I would advise you to hold off with these. They make you seem a bit pathetic, really."

I was pleased to change the subject. "For the sake of keeping the peace, let's concentrate on the parakeets over there."

"I don't know why you wouldn't write about that. You know women almost as well as you understand the lower intestine."

"You are vaguely pathetic yourself, aren't you."

"After you," he said.

"No, after you," I said, but we didn't move.

"I suppose we'll be bachelors the rest of our lives," Ellington concluded.

Well, those girls took the initiative and soon we were shaking hands all around, drinking and having a grand time. Later, after we'd visited a number of pubs, I stopped dead in my tracks. I had left the sheaf of poems somewhere. Perhaps Ellington was right about them being a bit vain, for I was less a gifted poet than a confessional one. They served as a journal, a diary in verse, so to speak, and without them I was lost. Abruptly I excused myself and left the party. Ellington saluted drunkenly, not the least bit concerned. Why would he be? I retraced our footsteps and in each locale my mood grew darker. I was stricken. I'd neglected to make carbons of the pages, and they were such long poems that I'd committed only a few of them to memory.

I was perhaps even more despondent the next day. On my way home from the hospital I stopped in at the Pig & Clover, where Ellington and I had started the previous evening. The pub was filling up but I was in no mood for socializing. I noticed a pretty young woman reading at the other end of the bar, a half-pint of Guinness before her. I couldn't help but smile when she glanced up. I saw something romantic about a pretty woman reading alone in a bar. I was not so different from her, I thought, craving solitude and seeking company in a book. This spoke of the sort of quiet desperation I often felt, and which most others chose to conceal.

When she turned the page I saw what she was reading was held in a sheaf. I rose quickly. "Excuse me," I said, "that belongs to me."

"You wrote these?"

I closed the booklet.

"I'm sorry. I thought it was a menu. I saw it here," she said, pointing, "wedged up against the wall. I think they're quite beautiful." She glanced at the cover. "H. Norman Bethune?"

"Yes."

"Frances Penney," she said, offering her hand. "Will you publish these?"

"One day, I'm hoping."

"I liked the one about the British Museum. It was very sad, somehow. You won't mind my asking who Agnes is?"

"I made her up."

"May I?" she said, reaching for the sheaf. I eased off my hand. She flipped through and found the page. She read the poem aloud.

I have carried it with me in memory all this time.

Nurse Agnes of Cambridge Visits the British
Museum with Limping Soldier

He had never considered the souls
buried within the clay and gold,
the distant stone and iron brow
that held their long gaze
found so properly housed
in the greatest museums of the age;

They were just masks, he'd thought,
pretty things set out for display

on any afternoon of
any given day.

What are they though, she said that
afternoon, but reminders that you shall see
that same look of death looking
back at thee?

In a future exhibit entitled Post
Post Byzantium of the Long Lost Apocalypse
entry 5 shillings
the one expression we least of all deserved
will represent our age
and all its men
forever preserved.

Save your money, sir, and take a walk instead;
any good nurse will tell you more
about Nephthys of Egypt
than the old curators of the dead.

Her soft Scottish voice stayed quietly between us. Frances was, I decided right then, a remarkable beauty. When she finished reading she did not lift her eyes. She stayed like that, leaning slightly forward into the page. She might have been reading through the poem again, looking for some key to slip into a lock I had fashioned without any conscious intention. She might have been stalling, searching for kind things to say. I was ready to pounce on any interpretation she might offer, as I'd been the night before when Ellington had offered his thoughts. At most I'd thank her for recovering my poems, then leave. I waited, growing more uncomfortable by the second. She seemed so entirely lost in the page and unaware of me that I was free, nervous though I was, to let my eyes roam over her. She wore her striking dark hair cut short and parted on the left side, the tips of it curling in to her face just below her ear. Her eyes gleamed as they moved back and forth in the dirty half-light of the pub.

"But did you love her?" she finally asked, looking up at me.

The question came as a surprise. "It's make-believe," I said.

"But you can't invent emotions."

"Not if they're genuine, I suppose."

"Did the young man love her, then?"

"I'm not sure," I said.

I saw her again the following week. That is when she first called me her Poet-Doctor. I didn't mind. In fact I was thrilled. She brought me books of poetry: Donne, Shelley, Byron. While I had read most of them, I happily accepted these gifts inscribed with lovely notes. We nosed about the old bookshops on Charing Cross Road, and naturally I took her to the British Museum. I introduced her to Ellington, as she did me to her girlfriends, Norma, a pretty secretary at one of the larger law firms in the city, and Eunice, a student at Chelsea College. At the time I was a solitary creature, riddled by my own romantic impulses and irked by crowds. In solitude I was safe, but not happy. Frances cured that in me.

As a young doctor I was used to sharing myself with the sick and the dying, perhaps because their solitude and complete dependence on me made it all but impossible that I might be slighted or denied. There is comfort to be taken in the fact that a brash young doctor is never pushed away, for he brings hope in times when it is most precious. Young love is a different matter entirely. At first what I felt for Frances was confusing, often painful and always difficult. As I said, I was solitary by nature, and no single individual could change that. Frances, of course, devoured the company of others. She encouraged me to share my dreams and emotions. I painted portraits of my young love and praised her in my poems. Though cautious, I was an idealist,

I can see that now, for those oblique paintings and colourless poems were at least a young man's attempt to understand and glorify this new world he'd recently entered. But soon enough those efforts revealed my deficiencies. We didn't talk about the war. We shared our food and friends. With me she shared her money, for she'd been left a fair bit by her wealthy father, and with her I shared my ambition and hunger for the world.

I will admit to being a bit of a dandy in those days. You would probably laugh if you could see how I went about town wearing a wing collar, black tie, gloves and homburg, smoking a Dunhill pipe with an aristocratic French-turned bowl and carrying in my right hand a silver-tipped cane. I must have looked ridiculous, though it was all in keeping with the finer tastes and fashions of the day. I recall with some amusement now that I was asked to attend a number of dinners and parties at the great houses of many famous people, to whom I was introduced as one of London's most promising medical men. Some of these individuals were recognized as pioneers in their chosen fields—whether fellow physicians, business tycoons or professors—while others were famous only for the company they kept. I was not easily swayed or impressed by these social functions, though they were, as I say, an entertaining and pleasant diversion from the demands of establishing one's practice. In October 1923 I became the house surgeon at Great Ormond Street and gave myself over completely to my duties at the hospital. I withdrew almost entirely from the exciting if shallow demands of "society." Of course, Frances and I were in greater demand as a result of my heightened prospects, but I was happily consumed by my work at the hospital and Frances herself had little time for socializing.

We were a pair to behold in those days. We shared our money with the old antique dealers of Portobello, the young painters of Soho and whoever else sparked our appetites, from the bohemians of Marble Arch and Brick Lane to the fine restaurateurs of Covent Garden and Piccadilly. In the hospital at Great Ormond Street I didn't think much about Frances, but once returned to our parallel world, I shared with her a grand opulence in our decision to marry, and then with the men who drove our horse cabs through Paris and Rome on our honeymoon we continued to share what money we carried, and with the waiters and barmen in Vienna, too. We shared first-class cabins with American tourists and stopped with them in somnolent French villages and at the boisterous Italian seasides. We amused ourselves with these travelling strangers until it was time to resume our own journey, always with names and addresses scribbled into dime-store novels and on train-ticket envelopes. This wealth and freedom provided us with a world of friends that soon, as in all romantic comedies they must, trickled to nothing when shortly after our return, our inheritance and optimism fell flat. Once the old man's money was used up we waited in London for a change for the better. Surely it would come.

We sojourned on Sunday mornings and drank champagne, trying in vain to recapture that sense of effortless motion, and the following year we made the decision so many were making then. North America was heaped before us like an unclaimed ante, and we would avail ourselves of it.

On the ship over, we took a modest cabin. We were a handsome couple, still finely dressed in cashmere and silk, now relegated to steerage. Much of the crossing we spent reading and playing cards. I might have written a poem or two. In the windowless cafeteria that served our class, we supped on bread and lentils, watched the old men at their dominoes, and waited.

The winter snows were heavy on the ground when we made port at Montreal. From there we journeyed to the small town of Stratford, Ontario, a sad forgery of the inspired original, where my sister had lived since marrying. We did not linger there. After a dreary car ride into Quebec scuppered the idea of settling in that small European outpost, we felt stranded in a wilderness bigger than France itself, and it became clear that the marriage would not last in this Precambrian waste.

We drove southwest and crossed the border into Michigan. We found an apartment at 411 Seldon Street, near the ravenous centre of Detroit. There, where I believed I would earn my fortune, I gained my first true understanding of the underclass—Southern Negroes, Hungarians, Italians, Yugoslavs, Poles, Russians, migrant workers from Mexico, all second-class citizens lured there by the promise of opportunity, as I had been, so few of whom would ever rise out of their impoverished and diseased neighbourhoods. What did I do? Still bewitched by the dream, I opened my practice to the richest of that city, determined to make my name and become rich myself. But it was to the needs of the poor that my heart began to be pulled.

On the fringes of this wealthy city lived people whose only means of survival was luck, guile, criminality or some combination of the three. Detroit soon seemed to me a petri dish for the doomed experiment of Capitalism. I remember well the night I spent at the railyard, working to save a Mexican labourer's baby. The families gathered outside the boxcar in the dark waiting for word about the mother and her newborn. The small fires they'd built along the edge of the tracks glowed and flickered. The men slowly passed a bottle among themselves. I told the husband to close the boxcar door, and then he knelt again beside his wife and began muttering his prayers. I knew this man, who cleaned the office building across from the Seldon Street apartment. The baby was in the breech position. When I delicately attempted to turn the baby around, the mother fainted from the pain. Her husband kept praying. *"Dios,"* he said again and again. Perhaps he was praying for the American Dream to shine down on his family and rescue their child, or maybe for enough money so his wife could deliver his child in a regular hospital, like the white people whose offices he cleaned. Filled with sleeping bags, utensils, paper bags and backpacks, the boxcar was home to the families waiting outside in the switching yard. He spoke some English, and I told him, "Do not watch this." I removed a blade from my bag. "Do not watch this." I cut the woman's abdomen, down through the skin and fat and muscle and into the membrane of the uterus, then scooped their baby boy out of his mother's suffocating womb like a blind blue fawn.

Today is my birthday. March 4. Somehow Ho found out about it and attempted to make something special. Well, his resources are limited, as you know. At the evening meal he produced a rice cake with a small candle stuck into it. He sprinkled a half-spoonful of sugar over it and presented me with it while Mr. Tung and a number of others gathered round and attempted an uneven if not unrecognizable rendition of "Happy Birthday." It was the best present I could have asked for. After a bit of light-hearted banter we got back to work.

Now I am alone, thinking through the day. It's past midnight.

I have been thinking about how there's a point in your life when a birthday becomes a sad marker of time passed rather than a pleasant survey of times to come. Do you know what I mean? We get closer to death with each passing year, and it affects people. But not me. I'm glad Ho found that silly candle and helped celebrate the day. I suppose I'm still amazed by the rapturous wonder of being alive. I hope you will understand the gift that being alive is, even in the hardest times.

There are so many moments in your life I have missed already. Your first tooth. Your first step. I never even got to hold you. But I'm thinking about that now, and I want you to know that I understand what I have missed in your life, and in mine. This is something I regret very deeply. I have delivered a number of babies in my day and birth has always seemed a miracle beyond any sane man's comprehension, but I don't think I ever truly understood the pure ecstatic wonder of birth simply because those beautiful babies I helped into the world were not mine.

Now I close my eyes and think of you running through swells of field grass whooping and hollering with all the power of your young lungs, muscular and celestial. Though you are yet an infant, as I write this I see you moving through the fields—an image that gives me great joy. And tonight I will sleep with you in my arms.

* * *

We were quarrelling over money. How clearly I recall it! We quarrelled over every aspect of our life together, over the tilt of my hat and the shine on my shoes. Something had to give, I suppose. Now, in retrospect, I'm glad it did. Frances went off to Nova Scotia to visit a girlfriend from Scotland, and from there she journeyed to California to conspire with her brother, or so I thought, in the land of sunshine and freedom.

How I envied her! It was an extended holiday away from her husband, and from grim, desolate Detroit. While she was away I wrote artful letters of contrition, blame, compromise and reconciliation. I wrote what I thought love was, what it was that bound us together. I sent only the graceful ones. I have no doubt she was sincere in her original premise—simply some time away, nothing more. What spouse doesn't dream of such escapes? Perhaps you will know this yourself one day, and realize that longings don't necessarily foreshadow the end of love but perhaps invite a new beginning for a tired and hurt love. But by then she'd felt entitled to call me overbearing more than once. Perhaps time away was not a sufficient cure. I was not an easy man. We hoped to close this chapter of our life and resume our love affair, as a reader returns to a difficult book after a restful sleep, refreshed and eager to see its hero through to the end. I wrote often. I needed her, I said, but also needed some time alone before I could love her again. My letters, you see, were an elegant batch of contradictions.

I remember one evening, not long after she returned, sitting at the kitchen table working over some lecture notes. Frances was sitting in a deep chair by the living room window. I'd heard her turning the pages of a novel. After working for quite some time, I rose to stretch my legs. When I entered the living room she looked up. I remember her closing the book, slowly, over her finger, and smiling. In her I saw a woman who just then, as if in a moment of revelation, had given herself over to her husband, completely and absolutely.

"Do you have something to tell me?" I said.

"Silly man. Like what?"

What she wanted was to live as a good wife should. The metamorphosis was startling. It was as if she'd been seized by the American Dream. This is what I always wanted, she seemed to say, and with the man I always wanted. To be together, here, in this place, or any place. There was in this emotional embrace all I feared and hated in the world. Instead of a loving wife content to live in the misery of this grey existence, I saw a total, unabashed surrender. I saw pity, falsehood, the embrace of second best. And eventually I came to see a spirited woman willing, finally, to submit to me. How had I destroyed her? That restlessness that burned within her—and within both of us—along with a refusal to submit was suddenly replaced by a smiling, pathetic contentment.

"But I'm so happy," she said, "with what we have. I realize that now."

I stood frozen. Here, in the squalor of our life, in one of the few truly benign and peaceful moments she'd ever offered me, I had the desire to obliterate her from my sinful heart. I would have preferred saucers and plates shattering against the dingy wallpaper to her coquettish smile. But there she sat, her face framed by a dark-paned window, smiling that lovely smile. I thought her more beautiful than ever. She leaned slightly back into her chair, then stood, and I strode across the room to take her in my arms. I didn't know if this was love or a selfish act that was a kind of revenge. Afterwards, I realized how desperately I did not want her in my life. The invented domesticity of home-life suddenly sickened me. The entire world awaited me: that was one truth I was sure of. She spoke to me softly, questioningly, while I watched the ceiling of our bedroom, and soon I returned to my lecture notes.

Was that the evening our life changed? Was it then, as my fingers touched her, that she saw the hard, distant man she'd married? The brilliant facade crumbles as eventually it must. I had used my gifts against her—I know this now—as an adversary might, to deceive a woman who was willing to believe in me.

The next morning, as she prepared breakfast, I said, "I didn't tell you last night." I was sitting at the table.

"That you love me? I noticed."

"I've been feeling poorly," I said. I shifted in my seat. "Fatigued. I had it checked while you were away."

"Why didn't you tell me sooner? What? What is it?"

"There is tuberculosis in my left lung."

She sat in a chair across from me and took my hand.

"We might be able to do something about it."

"How advanced is it? How long—?"

"A man at the College, a Doctor Amberson, speaks highly of a sanatorium in the Adirondacks. I might be able to get a place there. There's a chance."

"You see? Yes, a few months of bedrest," she said, caressing my face. "That's all you'll need."

"Please don't cry."

"You've been working too hard," she said.

"Yes."

"A few months and you'll come back better."

"Yes," I said.

"And then there'll be babies and everything will be all right."

"Please don't cry," I said again.

I didn't know how long I had to live. It might have been six months. The TB spiders, as I thought of them, had already firmly housed themselves in my left lung. It was likely they would take up residence in the right one, too, if I weren't admitted somewhere quickly.

The Trudeau Sanatorium had been founded in 1884 by a doctor from New York named Edward Livingstone Trudeau and quickly recognized as one of the best of its kind. Trudeau had been drawn from New York to the Adirondacks by the promise of clear air and untouched forests. These, he thought, were the ideal climatic conditions to help heal the afflicted lungs of a TB patient. In October I went there alone to place my name on the wait list, then headed north over the border to pass my days at the Calydor Sanatorium in Gravenhurst, Ontario. At the time I was unable to sidestep the grim irony of returning to the sawdust town of my birth with the distinct possibility of dying there. My life, book-ended by the narrow prospects of that sleepy, insular place, would prove deadeningly, pathetically inconsequential. I lay there confined to a bed, writing letters to Frances while waiting for a space to open at the Trudeau, never sure that I would go out into the world again. It was a misery, but the pained romantic and brooding poet in me relished the solitude.

The time spent away from Frances acted as a balm. Remembering only the happiness we'd shared, I grew optimistic. When I recovered, that sad chapter in our lives would close and we could return to our love affair. I needed her, I wrote, but in order for me to love her again, as she deserved to be loved, some part of me first had to die, and it would die here in the place of my birth. This return to my hometown was, of course, heavy with symbolic meanings not lost on me. I hoped for a rebirth, if you'll permit the poetic licence. I wrote poems and confessional letters. I bared my soul. There were, I wrote, certain things about myself that could stand second consideration. I was contrite. But here was an opportunity. I was committed to returning as a new man, I said, in body and in spirit. I would look afresh into my heart, and find in this dreary isolation a new optimism.

Not long after I returned to Frances, only a month later, our marriage stumbled again. We were both back into the thick of it. The optimistic words about our future had meant nothing. It was as if we'd never been apart. We finally agreed upon an official separation. Then, in the middle of December, the wait list for the Trudeau cleared.

Deep in the heart of the Adirondacks, I bunked with a young physician named John Barnwell and was restricted to bedrest. It was customary to be given passes to leave the grounds just three times a month, but I resisted all attempts to constrain me. Anxiety over Frances, and the financial status of my practice now floundering back in Detroit, only added to my desperation. Sick as I was, I was also deeply resistant to the idea of someone exerting control over my life after I'd already given up what little freedom it offered. I was restless and eager to declare myself however I could.

As a remedy for the monotony, Barnwell and I soon took to visiting Brook's Tavern, a small establishment on the road leading into the town of Saranac, its walls covered with fishing and hunting memorabilia, stuffed trout and deer and wolf heads and antique hunting rifles and colourful pheasants and photographs of proud men standing beside poles sagging under the weight of snow hares, wild turkeys and grouse. The log building contained a bar and a small dining room, . with an outfitters' shack butted up against the west end where you might purchase hunting and fishing gear, camping supplies, tobacco, stamps, magazines and newspapers. Pickerel, trout, perch, whitefish and venison were offered on the menu, though we never arrived before the kitchen had closed. It was only at night we came here, after the sanatorium had closed down for the evening. As patients we were not permitted to drink or smoke, and so as a consequence of this most reasonable policy our little establishment became a welcome oasis of liquor and tobacco in an abstemious sea of lake, rock and pine. The owner came to know us well. He was a sympathetic New Yorker who'd lost his leg at the Battle of Manila Bay in the Philippines. He limped around behind the bar on his prosthesis, pulling draft beers and pouring single-ounce shots for the foresters, travellers and locals who collected there after everything else had shut.

During the day I recall reading widely, making full use of the sanatorium's library. I also delivered a series of lectures on human anatomy to the nursing students at the school connected with the sanatorium. In order to further distract myself I laid out a scheme to establish a university on the grounds, since I'd noticed how many highly specialized patients, myself included, had been attracted there. To provide much needed status, and to fill out faculty requirements, I decided my new university should be affiliated with NYU and McGill University in Montreal. It was a wonder no one had thought before of a highly specialized teaching hospital at the foot of the Adirondacks. I took my plans to the Trudeau board and explained in the greatest detail the need for just such an institution, but my hopes were dashed by a table of wooden, conservative men who saw little value and no practicality in this enterprise. That night, in my familiar oasis, I listened to stories of the Battle of Manila Bay.

Around this time, I arranged for the sale of my private practice, then sinking into a morass of unpaid bills and shrinking patient lists. These negotiations briefly kept me busy and lifted the tedium off my shoulders. A young doctor by the name of Wruble paid me $5,000, a small triumph that did little to assuage my financial anxieties. Toward that end I returned to Detroit and resumed my teaching at the Detroit College of Medicine and Surgery.

Things between me and Frances had not improved, and on a grey Sunday afternoon in April, I said the inevitable words: "I want you to do me a favour, Frances. I want you to divorce me. It will do you a world of good to get away from me. You're miserable, you must admit that. We've tried long enough. You want to go home. You want to be happy. You want a family. I can give you none of those things."

She stared at me silently, expressionless. And so, without another word, after only three short years of marriage, that was that.

My health took a turn for the worse shortly afterward. I checked into the Trudeau again in June of that year, 1927, but my return was cloaked in dread. It was now clear to me that my TB was no less than a death sentence. My friend Barnwell had died over the winter, and I would surely die there too. The odds were highly stacked against me. The slightest physical task was now practically unendurable, and walking fifty paces soon became intolerable. At my insistence, Frances had retained a lawyer, and our separation would become legally binding by the end of the summer. I was alone, as I'd wanted to be, though I know now this solitude stemmed not from purely selfless motives, as I'd led Frances to believe, but from a selfish and destructive anger.

I can tell you now that I did very little in those days to be proud of. Ill health is a terrible thing, however you choose to look at it. But for some people the thought of death is a first step toward redemption. To getting his affairs in order. To setting things right between himself and those he may have wronged. After a last hushed conversation and a handshake, he makes his peace. There is a beauty there that I marvel at whenever I see it.

It shames me to admit that I sought neither peace nor redemption. Instead, my anger and frustration grew to the point that I decided to take my own life. I stared up at the ceiling of my cabin, the pressure and pain in my chest increasing by the hour, running through the most efficient manners of suicide. For days I lay motionless in my bed, summoning the courage.

It is not easy for me to tell you this. I have always wished, if and when the time ever came, that I would be able to offer my life up to you as a shining example of the wisdom and the glories that accrue as you grow old. But I was simply ungrateful, consumed with resentment for the hand I'd been dealt. I know now that each single day is a wonder and privilege to behold, yet during those difficult months, held in the grip of that illness, the opposite thought became stronger as my body grew weaker. The lake was only a hundred yards away, no more, and in the mornings I'd walk there slowly, resting when necessary, to stand on the shore and imagine sinking into the water.

In the infirmary I slipped the first 50 cc ampoule of morphine into my pocket. As a doctor, I knew what was needed. At night, sleepless, I imagined myself floating out onto Saranac Lake under a ringed moon, wearied, heavy with that diseased lung, yet warmed by the late hour's peacefulness and the soft summer breeze shifting the water's glassy surface. These last few moments alone in a rowboat would prove to be the focus of my life, the narrow end of a funnel that had collected and directed all experience to this one last perfect moment of distillation. Somehow the night would know this and show both gratitude and a proper respect. It was there in the ringed moon, in the dirge of the loons crying for the end of me, in the moonlight on the water, in the harmony of midnight. I knew a man could never know a greater solitude than the one he sees as he peers into his soul and prepares for his death. Having seen it in other men, I now saw it in myself.

Yet as I lay on my bed on those nights, I remembered all the damage I had done to others. None of my triumphs sparkled there, only my failures and the sentence of death that was the heaviness in my lung. I imagined the warmth of the drug streaming through my veins, the euphoria that would rise up within me as I disappeared into the lake.

I needed only one last ampoule. One sunny morning I sat quietly on the front step of the infirmary, gaunt, frail and grey, yet filled with resolve. I knew this trial would soon be over. As I gathered my strength to continue on, a young woman from the main desk approached to tell me that Mrs. Bethune was calling on the telephone. She then helped me inside, my elbow in her tender grasp as if I were an eighty-year-old pensioner, to where the receiver of the telephone sat on a handsome edition of *Walden Pond*. I picked it up and heard Frances's voice. She was in tears.

"Please, Norman, promise me only this."

I waited.

"Promise you'll do nothing," she said. "It was my fault. I was foolish."

"What happened?" I said. I'd heard of her new companion, a pioneer in children's speech therapy at Johns Hopkins who was, according to a letter she'd sent some weeks before, a kind and elegant man.

She'd spent the weekend with him in Pittsburgh, she said, where he'd gone for a conference. She'd humiliated herself, following him around like a puppy until he sent her away.

I imagined their time together, the humiliation. It was a reflection of my own callousness. "Did he do anything else?" I said. "Did he touch you?" I was overwhelmed by jealousy and rage.

This is a shameful episode in my life that pains me now to recount, especially to you. I was not the man I am today, please understand that. I was seized by an insanity I'd never known before and have not known since. But this abject, perverse insanity shaped me for the better, which is why I include the episode here. Through adversity we reach the stars, I've always enjoyed that thought. Since then I've attempted to live up to it in my own way, by pursuing the work I do. Back then it directed me away from the darkness of self-destruction and allowed me to see what awaited me.

What did I do? I dragged myself across two states with a mind to wreak revenge on a man I'd never met. The man who'd taken my place at my wife's side. Through the window of my train compartment I watched the flickering lights of sleeping villages and desolate whistle-stops. The world was indifferent to my passage and the murderous hate I carried.

It was early morning when my train pulled in at Pennsylvania Station. Commuters ran for their connections; young boys waved newspapers in the air that tomorrow would feature the face of the murderer I would become. Weakened further by my journey, I was jostled and bumped as I made my way out onto Liberty Avenue and hailed a cab. Frances had named the hotel where the man I was looking for could be found. It was a respectable establishment only four blocks from the station. I took a room there, rested for the balance of the morning, then journeyed down into the street. I purchased a pistol, left a note for the speech therapist at the front desk and waited for evening.

I held the pistol in my right hand. A surgeon's hand. I sat in wait by the window of my room, watching the street, listening for footsteps just beyond my door. My fingers felt every bit as dead as that cold steel. Was it my destiny to be the first Bethune to kill not in war but in a last, defiant act of love? Could this be so wrong? Would I not be vindicated? I knew the man hadn't touched her, but he had abused her nonetheless. He had led her to believe that he could replace me and had failed to do so. He had dashed her hopes, as I had so often done.

The pistol grew slippery with my nerves. I paced. I was sick to my stomach. The afternoon and evening wore on. I stared at the gun, barely able to believe that I was there, about to commit this crime, but also convinced that this was, in some bleak narrative, a merciful end to my story. I was no more than an embodiment of gloom: not a dime to my name, my wife gone, my health destroyed. I had seen death so often that another would make little difference either way.

When the knock came I raised my eyes from the pistol to the door, more fearful than I'd ever been. Trembling, I rose and placed the gun under the bed pillow, then walked over and opened the door. Standing before me was a short man, already undone by life, it seemed, around forty years old. He wore a grey suit and shoes of tired leather.

He tipped his hat. "Doctor Bethune?"

When he entered, I closed the door and crossed the floor to stand by the window. "Drink?" I said.

"No," he said.

I stared at him.

"You've come all this way to speak with me?" he asked. "I understand you're ill."

"It's none of your concern how far I've come."

He stood awkwardly, hat in both hands.

I picked up my glass. "I've lost my wife to you, so there probably isn't much left to say. Should I talk to you? Should I ask how things are going between you? Should I express an interest in your affair?"

"No," he said.

"We agree on at least one thing, then," I said.

He was standing in front of the closed door. I poured a glass of whiskey, then turned and walked it over to him. My hand brushed against his when he took the drink. He didn't raise the glass, just stood there watching me.

"I understand you are separating, legally separating," he said. "I would not come between a man and his wife."

"What about a dying man and his wife?" I said, reaching under the pillow. "What about that?" Then I hit him across the face with the butt-end of the pistol. "Would you come between them?"

His head jerked back again and again as I kept hitting him. A wound opened on the left side of his face. I didn't stop until he fell to the floor.

It was then that I looked into his eyes. Then I knelt beside him and wept, begging his forgiveness.

I tended to his wounds and sat with him in silence. When he was able to walk I delivered him to the hospital, then rode the train back to the Adirondacks and strode firmly, as morning broke across the hills, into my second life.

I hope Ho will do me the kindness of never writing a poem about me. He would find only confusion and contradiction. He might even imagine horns sprouting out of my head. I would tell him as much, if I could. But if he chose to look, to really look, what would he discover in a man like me? Ho is an observant fellow, after all, and just might, one day, take after the Chinese poet whose work he has committed to memory. His eyes hang a moment longer than they would otherwise, collecting a last glimpse, a delicate wrinkle. Isn't this the modus operandi of the poet? He is one for details unobserved by others. He notices habits, tics, hidden joys and fears. Who knows? When I am here, watching, he is so deferential as to be almost invisible. He glances at a certain cherished likeness set here, to my right, angled just so to catch the light. It has not moved in weeks, despite the fact that he often takes it up in his hand and looks for my likeness in the soft features. It is a painting. But no, the portrait isn't what it seems, I want to tell him. Despite the likeness. It is not who I would like it to be. Despite the thrill of possibility, despite this deepest wish.

Ho has learned the peculiarities of a stranger. No doubt he thinks this need for pure undeniable order is common to all foreigners, strange incomprehensible devils that we are. But he cannot always be right, perceptive though he is. He will tell his friends that I devote all my writing efforts to medical and administrative matters, offering this as another example of my commitment to this cause. He would not be far off in thinking that. I have devoted a great deal of time of late to the last of my three textbooks, as well as the ongoing struggle to keep up with the monthly medical reports I'm responsible for. The light in my window signals the sleeplessness of a devoted man. But he knows nothing of this secret text, yours and mine. Here you have the re-imagining of a life in all its crepuscular beauty. Perhaps he would, if he knew, revere the efforts of this exploration. But despite his poet's soul these words would make as much sense to him as a Shakespearean sonnet or a Catholic mass. You see, I have been here long enough that he cannot imagine me having a past anywhere else. And can I blame him? As far as he's concerned I have stepped out from the clouds. I'm only as good as his best poem, perfectly internalized and subjective. Not entirely real, in any case, and conjured from the mists. Any life outside these mountainous walls, though richly imagined, can be no more real than the promise of Belgian chocolate or American tobacco.

I see him out in the night, a small dark figure set against the tower-ing rock of the Jui Li San Mountain and hear him talking with the other boys as they smoke their local tobacco. The rancid plumes dis-appear in a laugh. Quiet talk of the war, girls, food, the things boys like to talk about—but certainly also about the man at the edge of the vil-lage hunched obsessively over his trusty Remington. The mad white doctor, they might say, the bloody terror, the saviour, the half-deaf surgeon who fell from the sky. The man who in a rage yells and throws dull scalpels at terrified nurses. What must they think of me? What sort of poem do you shape in the image of a stick of a man who moves like a machine between patients without rest for three and four days at a time? In the absence of sleep I dunk my head in buckets of freezing water. My raging is easily enough explained away. It might even be understandable. In any case, they do not judge, and bless them for that.

Another clear evening. I have been studying the moon from my win-dow. Do you know the Shelley poem?

Art thou pale for weariness
Of climbing heaven and gazing on the earth
Wandering companionless
Among the stars that have a different birth.

It is my honour to share Shelley's moon with you tonight.

Last night Ho came to strip off the ribbon as he usually does. I lay still, too anxious and distracted to sleep. He worked silently, first rewinding, then releasing the small wheel from its housing. His hunched silhouette at my desk, a young, slight Bethune, I thought. He rose, then slipped out the door.

Man's absurdity survives like diamonds in this peasant land, and we are reminded of this with depressing regularity. I recall not too long ago we were lacking blood of a certain type, namely B positive. There was nothing unusual in this, since blood supply is as constantly uncertain as the air is thin up here. Countless times I have used my own veins to demonstrate the donor procedure to these peasants, but an infuriating mystery and fear still surrounds this basic operation. One afternoon, a dying man was admitted to my care. We checked all the patients' charts and found that we had a compatible donor only a few beds down. I called on him and, through an interpreter, informed him of the situation. Perhaps the expression on my face registered my disbelief and disgust when he refused. He shook his head from side to side like a child standing at the edge of a lake, afraid to take his first swimming lesson. He put his hands over his eyes.

I said, "Tell him he is a brave man."

My interpreter did so.

I said, "Tell him he kills the Fascists to save his comrades-in-arms."

My interpreter did so.

I said, "Tell him it is strange that he is willing to die for his brothers, yet refuses to give them his blood."

My interpreter did so.

I said, "Tell him this is a feather tickling your arm compared to a bullet."

My interpreter did so.

I offered to demonstrate the procedure myself. The man shook his head in terror. I held the cannula for him to see. I said, "This is not a bullet. This is a pinprick."

He pushed my hand away.

He smelled of the mountains he'd spent the last two years fighting in. Even after several days with us he carried the scent of the soil and horses and the ragged clothes he'd worn for months and of the men he'd killed and seen killed. These smells had soaked into his skin. He was fearful not of the small prick in his arm but of the modern wonder of science. It didn't involve pain or sacrifice or death, only the elementary truths of his world. I might have remembered that, but I didn't care to.

I ordered him restrained, and he whimpered as the cannula entered his arm. I both hated and pitied him. After his blood was introduced to the patient, I stood in the cool sunlight and watched the distant peaks shining in the north, at the edge of Mongolia.

Tonight the lilies in their clay pot outside this window look as though they've turned to charcoal. It is as if my staring at them all week has bled the lustre from their stems and leaves. The failed light has robbed them of their colours. Maybe I likewise have been robbed of my own certainty.

But isn't that the point? A certain man is a lazy man. Here I am, committed as never before, yet robed in doubt. If only my father had known the feeling.

I never looked at that man again. It shames me to say I passed in front of his bed half a dozen times afterwards and didn't once even glance at him.

*   *   *

Another month gone. We are with the Third Regiment Sanitary Service at Shin Pei, West Hopei. A warm glorious spring rain spilled over the countryside this afternoon. Now I see moonlight sparkling in the puddles outside my window. The moon insists that we take note, all of us, even those too timid to look up.

ENVELOPE SIX

I left Madrid in springtime, gathered my few things together and retreated. I told my associates my work was done, that I was needed elsewhere. They pretended to be sorry. Was there not enough work here? What could be so urgent as to force me to abandon Madrid?

The documentary was finished, I explained, and I would take it to America to raise money for the Republic. I would report stories of our progress here to the outside world. Your mother understood. I told her the night I finished her portrait.

"Go," she said. "I'll be all right."

Months later I was sitting at a table at the Bentley Park Hotel in New York struggling with that feeling of unease I was telling you about. The feeling I described to you of thinking Pitcairn was hiding something from me. Do you remember me telling you that?

It was not him hiding the truth. Months ago, when I recalled that conversation for you, I was not strong enough to relive it truthfully. Now, perhaps, I am.

"You're a slippery fish tonight," I said.

"Nerves, I suppose."

"Let's have a drink, then," I said, summoning the waitress.

I remember thinking that he was trying to rediscover the camaraderie we'd shared in Madrid not that long ago, eight or nine months.

Certainly not long enough to explain his discomfort. Men generally are changed by too much living, I thought, too much adventure, too much ducking into bomb shelters. I saw it in myself. Perhaps this was why he'd come to America.

Hoping to put him at ease, I said, "Isn't it true that when you're out there, all you want is to come home? You're sitting in some dingy cellar wondering why the hell you're there, wishing it all away. Then, poof— you're suddenly home and safe in your comfortable bed and you still can't help thinking: why am I here?" I said, "People like us, Frank, with the *choice* to come or go, we're the difficult ones, aren't we."

He didn't say anything.

"War's a bloody beautiful sport," I said, "until you see what it's done to you. Sometimes I think it's a lot safer not to leave it at all."

He said, "I'm not even sure you know about it."

"What would you have me know that I don't know already?" Of course, I took this as a knock against me. I looked him in the eye, ready for a more serious challenge.

I realized then that he wanted to talk about your mother.

Was he going to tell me that she'd gone back to Sweden, or come to America in search of her father's legacy? Or was he going to tell me she was up in Chicago retracing his footsteps, that she'd simply quit the war and wasn't the person I'd thought her to be?

The drinks came, and he took a long swallow.

"Well, why the face?" I said. "You look like you're going to be sick on me."

"They took her in a second time, right after you left. I don't know if you heard that. Madrid was full of cutthroats and informers. You know how it was. Calebras was a f——ing jingoistic fraud. You know as well as I do."

"Yes."

"Kajsa was convinced he'd teamed up with Sorensen and Sise. They wanted to humiliate you. They each had their own reasons. But that didn't matter. Calebras wanted the mobile unit under his name. They wanted the glory to go to the Spanish. The others just wanted to get you out. They thought you were cracking up. Sise thought you had a death wish. He always said you were a reckless son of a bitch. Sorensen didn't like your grandstanding, your chasing after reporters all the time. He said your claim that it was all for the good of the unit was horses——t. Your fundraising, too. It was all about your vanity, he said. You were more important than the wounded, the cause, the war."

He shook his head. "I met with Kajsa once a couple of months after you left. She said it was Sorensen who'd alerted the authorities about all the foreigners coming around to the clinic. And the maps, the photographs. If he believed it, I don't know. But it worked. He got their attention. You saw how they swooped down. That was the first real strike against you."

"They drummed me out," I said. "You think I don't know that? I'm glad I had the film to fall on. Better than a sword."

"The next step was to bring her into it. She was the perfect humiliation. She worked with the Mujeres Libres, a branch of the anarchist FAI. The anarchists scared the s——t out of the Popular Front alliance. You know how it went in Madrid. If they wanted to take you out of the picture, discredit you completely, the easiest way was to set Kajsa up as an anarchist, even a spy."

"That's absurd," I said.

"I know it is."

"Where is she now?"

"After you left she told me she was worried about getting taken in again. She said you were the only person who could protect her. I told her it was dangerous even talking. I'd never seen her like that. 'Just get out,' I said. 'Get up to France.' "

He picked up his glass and swished the liquid, but didn't drink.

"Where is she now?" I said.

I was greeted by three men at the entrance to the clinic the morning after meeting your mother at the Retiro Park. I recognized one of them from that encounter my first morning in Madrid the previous November, when I was detained on account of my suit and moustache. I couldn't tell if he recognized me. It was just luck, and bad luck at that, for our paths to cross again. He and his two colleagues were accompanied by four armed guards, two down below in the street, the other two standing beside the lift on the third floor. My assistant, who hurried to the door when I appeared, was told firmly to return to her business. We by then had a staff of no less than twenty-five, and in full view I was led into my office. The door was closed behind us. The leader, whom I'd never seen before, motioned to a man carrying a briefcase to flip it open, and he produced the bottle of perfume and the card I'd given Kajsa the day before. In English he said, "Please sit down." He paused, as if considering something from a number of different angles. "Yes, you see, this is interesting. Here I see you have written some words about love. You are a man of many talents, Doctor." He held up the card. "These are your words?"

"What is this?" I asked.

"What is this? You will tell me now." His English was clear but heavily accented. "I can ask the same. What am I looking at?"

"Perfume," I said. "A gift. A token."

"And this?" he said, holding up a series of photographs.

"Where did you get them?"

"Of course you know where," he said.

"Pictures. Bridges and roads."

"And tank columns. A doctor interested in tanks?"

"That photograph is incidental."

"And to whom do you pass these photographs? Only the Swede?"

"They are for our purposes. They are for study. To minimize travel time."

"Whose travel time?"

"The travel time of this unit."

"We know this work you do, Doctor. The Spanish people thank you. Yes. But it is something else to distribute these photographs, considering this company the Doctor keeps." He lifted his eyebrows. "What can we think of this situation?"

He pointed at the perfume and card, which he'd set on the desk. "It's a wonderful thing to be loved. To have a woman. But we do things for women, too often stupid things. We cheat for them, we lie for them, we commit criminal, illegal acts for them. We betray our friends for them. For what? Only to be with the Swede? Two times more. Ten times more." He repeated this in Spanish for the benefit of his colleagues, and I recognized a vulgar word. "When you have so many nice Spanish girls to go with, you go with the Swede, and then you talk to her about bridges and tanks?"

The village is quiet. Nighttime in Shin Pei.

They are shooting dogs up in the high villages and eating them with what little rice and millet the peasants left behind, spilled from pockets and hastily packed bags. At least the enemy is starving too, that is our one consolation. When it is known they are near, the last of the peasants move off into the night toward the next village, some fifteen or twenty miles away. Then, when that village falls a day later, those who looked upon the fleeing souls with pity now scoop up what can be carried and join the exodus, and so grows the wave of refugees washing down from the mountain villages of north China. Soon Wu-t'ai and all of Shensi and Hopei provinces will be empty but for the partisans and remaining dogs and the invading Japanese. The lucky peasants will find the Peiping–Hankou rail line, eighty miles to the east, and travel down along it to wait out the war in the south, in Sian and Louyang.

To the west and east it is no different. It is rumoured that the southern corridor that connects us to the rest of China will close by late summer. The war is all around us. It is a noose. But here, in the quiet of this mud-brick house, I am in an untouched oasis. When I'm not leaning over a casualty in one of our makeshift surgical huts, I can close my eyes and wonder what the air would taste like if unspoiled by the smell of suppurative wounds and camphor and cordite. What would this world be like if I were with you back in Spain or Montreal, or wherever they took you?

First, imagine a mountain stream at first light, carrying with it one living man and one dead. The living man is your father; the other, his guide. I hear the stream that we rode down the mountain on only four days ago. Its splashing still echoes in my head. I hear it through the night, in the still air. How impossible the war seems on nights like these. It is as quiet as a conversation with the dead.

We'd been waiting for our guide at an assigned meeting point for less than an hour when he stepped out of the dark like some ragged phantom, a thin wisp of a boy, very near starving. He didn't look relieved to see us, only troubled. We welcomed him and gave him tea and rice. The medical unit consisted of Ho, Mr. Tung, two student surgeons and two armed escorts. We watched the boy eat and drink and waited for the night to deepen. Clouds crossed over a bright moon. It was prudent to travel in this part of the country only after dark. The boy was troubled because he knew well enough that it was much more difficult to lead a troop of seven up into the mountains than it was to come down alone from there. He finished his meal, and when he sat back, one of the student surgeons offered him some tobacco and he rolled a cigarette in his thin fingers and smoked it until the ember died. We waited another twenty minutes until the darkness was almost complete. The boy spoke to Mr. Tung, who then asked me if I was ready, and we set out in single file, the guide and an armed escort first, then me, then Ho and Mr. Tung, then the two student surgeons, each member of my team leading an animal, and finally the second escort. Up we started into the Wu-t'ai Mountains.

We walked at a steady pace for two hours without stopping to rest, pausing only when the boy slipped into the darkness ahead to make certain that the area was clear for us. Ten minutes later he would reappear and indicate the way and off again we would walk, a silent column of men and beasts moving into the deepening darkness of the mountains. The night was warm. There was very little breeze and the air was comfortable and smelled of sage and wild mint. The boy held us up with only a single word to Tung, who would look at me, and the rest of the column would halt as the boy slipped out again and left us waiting there. This occurred seven times. On the eighth, the boy did not return. It was past midnight.

"Mr. Tung?" I whispered.

"I don't know," he said.

"Ten more minutes. Then you will lead the others back to where we started. I'll wait here for the boy."

After half an hour I told Tung to go, instructing him to remain at the camp below until daylight and then return to Chin-kang K'u.

"And you?" he said.

"I will find you in the morning."

I watched their faces as Tung translated my orders. Ho would not show his face to me, as he expected I'd think less of him if I saw terror or tears or both in his eyes. I handed him the reins to my animal and he walked the horse back down the trail.

After they left I sat quietly in the dark and watched the moon move through the high clouds. When they parted there was light enough to see by. The guide would know where to find me if he was still alive and he hadn't abandoned us. It was now past two o'clock. I believed I was the last man fighting this war. The last man in China. So immense was the quiet and solitude that I might as well have been the last man on earth. The enormity of the sky felt larger than the vastness of all oceans and all memory. The stars were infinite, and below them the silence was suddenly broken by a sound that might have been the boy returning from his reconnaissance. I didn't move, just sat looking up into the infinite sky and listened and waited for a sign. I waited ten minutes. My heart raced. The sound did not come again. I waited another half hour and the boy did not appear.

I dozed off and it was nearly morning when I awoke. I stood up and moved about. It felt good to stretch my legs. With my pack I moved slowly outward in the direction the boy had gone. I heard another sound. This time it was closer, and it wasn't the sound of a footfall or a dull thud but the human sound of a sob or groan. I moved toward it, despite telling myself this was a baited trap, remembering the night I'd carried Robert Pearce on my back. But as I moved forward now the sound came again with more clarity, and I stopped in order to place it. I walked another fifty yards into the darkness, low to the ground, and there I found it. I practically stepped on it.

This boy was no older than our guide. His Japanese uniform was in rags. He was sitting up against a rock, his right hand pressed against his neck, eyes bulging with pain and dehydration. The stab wound was just above the collarbone. Blood dripped onto his chest and pooled in his lap. He watched me approach without making a sound. He was unarmed. Then I saw the body of our guide, lying not far from the soldier. The bayonet had pierced his chest, and it seemed incredible that he'd been able to turn and slash the man who'd stabbed him before he died. The rifle and bayonet lay on the ground beside him. I positioned the boy face up, crossed his hands over his chest and rolled his eyes shut, then returned to the Japanese and examined the wound. He did not resist as I pulled open his shirt.

"You will die very soon," I said, "like the boy you killed. I know you don't understand me." I pointed to the boy lying beside the rifle and bayonet. "Like him."

It seemed his slight nod was meant to offer acknowledgment or agreement or resignation. He didn't say a word.

I sat beside him while he died. It took only a few minutes. He whispered softly, and I touched his face and said, "There you go."

I hoisted our guide over my shoulder and started down the hill. It was easy going at first. He was so slight that I barely noticed him. Returning to the stream where we'd begun our expedition the evening before, I walked over the hard, uneven ground, and soon began to feel his weight in my knees, then as a pain in my shoulders. I laid the boy on the ground and sat down for a minute, breathing heavily. I didn't know how much farther I had to go before I would find Tung and the others in my party. I was wondering about the odds of my survival, alone and unarmed, with very little food and water, when again I thought of that nighttime journey through the mud-fields of Belgium a full lifetime ago. Was it my turn to die now? Why had I survived these extra twenty years when others had been in the ground all this time? Why, in my third war, was I still alive?

I pulled the boy back up onto my opposite shoulder and started walking again, as fast as I could, no longer certain that I wasn't moving deeper into the occupied north. The dead boy's head was bumping against my midsection, legs kicking against my back. The rhythmical bouncing of his knees and feet began to play on me and I started hearing his voice echoing up through my body. He didn't like being held upside-down for such a long period of time, he said. I should stop so we both could rest. I did not listen to him. I kept on, and he kept asking to be put down. I said my first words to the boy. "Shut up," I said. "You're no longer living and have no right to speak. Just stay as you are, and I'll get you back so they can do what must be done. But just stop talking so much, someone's going to hear us."

He fell silent for a time. I tried to walk with less of a bounce to keep him quiet. But the path grew difficult and again his feet pounded into me and his voice rang into my gut and up into my inner ear.

"No," I said, "I believe I have every right to be here. No, I shouldn't have died twenty years ago. No, it's not just that others died and I lived. Of course not. There's no plan out there. There is no fairness. You step into a roomful of Spanish flu and come out with not so much as a cough. Some people get out without a scratch. It's not about being deserving or skillful or even lucky because luck implies something too. It's only about random chance. It's a roulette wheel, this world."

He didn't answer, and I just kept walking. I came to what I believed was the stream where we'd met this boy the night before. I didn't know if he was still talking. I'd stopped listening. I stood on the bank, wondering if my remaining strength would allow me to ford the stream. I stepped in and began the crossing. The stream was rocky and swift but not deep. In the middle I stopped, exhausted, and sat down in the water. I leaned back on the boy to end his talking for good. His mouth filled with water, and then I fell asleep, my face turned up to the sky.

In the morning I dug his grave beside the stream with the five members of his band who'd discovered me bobbing in the shallow water, still hoisted up on his body. They shook my hand to thank me for returning their comrade to them. They knew of me, the White One Who Comes. It was their camp we'd been destined for, fifteen miles west of where they found me. I examined each of the men after we put the boy in the ground. They suffered from malnutrition, two of them from abscesses in the teeth, one from an improperly dressed flesh wound on the hand. I administered what care I could with the few supplies I carried. Then we sat and fed ourselves, not far from the fresh grave. I kept looking over at it, wondering if he was listening to his friends' conversation. In the daylight it all seemed ludicrous, and I dismissed the night as an eventful hallucination. I had been close to an exhausted collapse for two weeks. The partisans took me to Chin-kang K'u, eight miles downstream, transferred me to the care of a medical team I'd recently inspected there and bade me farewell.

I have not thought of that boy's words until now, tonight. The dead do not have words. I know that. Only the dying have words, and those who are still to come.

No sleep again tonight. It is past two in the morning. Today I operated for seventeen hours. How strange it is that the mind controls the body so, even when the body can barely hold itself upright. But I am thinking, of course, always thinking.

I can see your mother now as she would have awoken on the morning of my interrogation. The thugs were coming.

She sat up when the door was thrown open. The men occupied the room with a borrowed authority. The questions began immediately, from a bespectacled, leather-coated man who bobbed on his toes as he waited for the preferred response. He leaned into her face, smiling and threatening as he looked into the eyes of a woman who, before the war, he would have approached—if he'd dared to at all—like a timorous boy. Who would have caused him more fear than outrage. The war is a lucky place for some, as he might have known, a field of opportunity. What delightful turns of fortune we find in these times. A woman alone in her room.

His associate, a shorter, uglier man, sifted through her possessions. Her clothing, books and toiletries came alive most pleasurably in his hands. When he picked up Kajsa's hairbrush from beside a half-full glass of water, he noticed on the pale pine desk by the bathroom door a book that held the envelope containing the photographs.

I have been thinking much about how value is ascribed to one's life after the act of living is done. Not deeds or accomplishments. What I mean is that a part of me will live on in you even though I will not have had the privilege and responsibility of being part of your life, at least not fully. Even if I live to meet you there will always be this gulf, which is why I need to write this history for you. That is a failure of the first order. You see, there are so many things I will miss telling you, as a father would, through the years as you grow into adulthood. The small and inconsequential things and moments that make up the great quilt of your existence. What would we have learned from each other had we shared but one walk through an August rainstorm? What infinitesimal yet lasting truth would you have taken with you and remembered over my grave had we tossed a baseball back and forth on a Sunday afternoon? Well, what do you have now? You have none of that. Only the dry touch of these pages.

*   *   *

I found out about your mother at the hotel bar in New York. I've been trying to think of a better way of telling you about this, but have not been able to, and I'm sorry that I have to tell you now. I think I've been trying to protect you. Though you have every right to know the circumstances, it seems I have only been picking away at subtleties, stalling, hoping to wake up and find all of this nothing more than a terrible dream. It is proper and respectful, then, at this point, to be as forthright as possible. All my life revolves in a mysterious circle. At the beginning and the end and in the centre is the story that begins now.

I recall distinctly how my arms and fingers began to tingle and the room shifted slightly forward when I learned of your mother's death. As a boy I used to love walking through grass tall enough to reach over my head. It was the sensation of being hidden from the world, yet so thoroughly immersed in it. No one for miles around could see me, even from a high point on a hill or rooftop, so connected was I to the earth and its elements. That's something like the sensation of losing someone. You are never in your life so alive, and so aware of being alive, yet so isolated and abandoned, as when a loved one is taken from you. The planet will move right through you like wind through stalks of grass.

There are so many unexplored shadows.

In New York, Pitcairn leaned into the table and said, "Get in touch with the FAI, with the Mujeres Libres, Norman. The war won't go on forever. Wait till the war is over, then go back there. Go to the orphanage where Kajsa got work for those street girls." He paused. "They waited."

I said, "For what?"

"They waited until your daughter was born."

Today I remembered Genesis. I stood in the footprints of Abraham and understood the brutality of the world. It is man's first and last state. "And he looked toward Sodom and Gomorrah, and toward all the land of the plain, and beheld, and lo, the smoke of the country went up as the smoke of a furnace." Say what you will, they knew what they were talking about. I marvel sometimes at how spot-on the Good Book really is. The only instinct that rivals our urge to scour this planet with its own blood is this urge to weep.

We, too, are eating dog now. I suppose enemies in all the wars of all the ages have shared one another's basic miseries. It tastes the same in my mouth as it does in theirs. Certainly more binds us together than separates us, isn't that the point? Isn't it a fact that it's only the strength of ideas that wrenches us worlds apart? Yet how strange it is that we're willing to kill for ideas. In peacetime an idea can be bought and sold with money, argument, dismissal. It can be ignored outright and no one bats an eye. Not in war. How undervalued life becomes out here, and how precious the idea.

Ho has just now presented himself and sits on the upturned trunk, waiting. I have pulled out a couple of new drawings. He seems impressed.

You know, I think he's beginning to learn something from these drawings. This pleases me.

I am pleased, too, when the peasant farmer turned training nurse learns quickly and asks intelligent questions. Such are my accomplishments now. I am pleased when Ho sits with me, watching me write or flipping through these drawings of mine. I am pleased when only one arm and not two must be amputated, when there are only three deaths and not sixteen. Beyond my most basic needs, I enjoy little physical comfort. I don't mind this so much, though I am lonely. It seems I have been in training for this life for a long time.

It strikes me with brutal force that I don't know myself nearly as well as a man my age should, especially considering how close I am to death on any given day. I'm forty-nine years old. Isn't that old enough? How long is a man supposed to wait before he knows for certain that no ray of light will shine from above, that no eternal rest or emptiness will come, that his life was well spent or wasted?

I can say with confidence that my life here is spent well. At least I know that. But on balance? What about everything that preceded my work here? Can one good year make up for so much lost time? I am happy. Is that good enough? I am happy and lonely and not convinced either that I will return to you or that I will not.

Will I have the strength to see that you receive this story?

My physical presence has been diminished somewhat. If you'd known the before and after versions of your father you would be quite shocked, I am sure. I'm very near skeletal and half-deaf and always chilled. These clothes I have brought from home, I noticed just this morning, are now baggy beyond recognition. My teeth ache, my energy's low and I've been battling a deep, persistent cough. Yet on occasion I feel a sense of destiny waiting for me here, though I cannot account for it. If I have time in the mornings I go walking. I enjoy watching the sun come up, and when its orange and yellow light touches the mountains I feel as blessed with purpose as this planet is with beauty. Make some good use of your life, I was told. Well, here I am. In these moments I'm confident that this is what I was born to do, to stand here at the edge of existence in the light of a new day and heal with these hands those who can be healed and commit to the unknown those who cannot. It is as if it's no longer up to me. My mother, in the end, was probably right. These talents of mine are only on loan.

I think you know Spain was my great disappointment, the death of my idealism and of part of me. But I can assure you there will be no second failure. I have learned my lesson. There are rumours that things again are teetering on the edge in Europe. Will there soon be a time when only the dead enjoy their peace, when one war will follow another, with another after that, and so on, with no end in sight? War might be for your generation as it was for mine, but I certainly hope that is not the case.

Please do not misunderstand. Does it sound as if I've given up? I have not. Remember what I said: We do not go down without a fight, we Bethunes. What I see here gives me reason to hope. I am not planning on dying a martyr's death in China or anywhere else. I'm deeply committed to this struggle, nothing more. I would give my life for it, and might end up doing just that, but I will take no joy in it. I am, I think, too in love with all this Creation out here.

Despite the lice and hunger and the ignorance and poverty and withering solitude, I confess to a devotion stronger than anything I've ever known. I even feel privileged for it. I hope you understand what I'm trying to say. Perhaps you think less of me for this life I have taken on. Surely you will feel some resentment. But you can see the good in it, too, can't you? There isn't a bone of common sense left unbroken in my body; you'd be right on the money about that, if it's crossed your mind. But do you remember what I said to your mother that day, that common sense and ideals don't often go hand in hand? Well, I think that just about sums up my life.

This morning Ho came to me with my favourite breakfast. He has finally perfected the boiled egg! The poor boy, how I ride him. How he wants to please me! And the abuse I dole out in return! I made such a fuss when I saw that egg. I suppose I was trying to make it up to him. He was very proud. After a hundred attempts here it was. For six months he has, when in possession of an egg, slaughtered it, so to speak, with his overzealous ways. Perhaps he is a poet, after all. Hapless in the domestic arena, prone to episodes of daydream, lost in those hot-water bubbles.

We commemorated the occasion with a photograph. Before the doorway of my mud-brick house we set up a small knee-high table and my straw-backed chair. I sat and leaned into my egg like a king over his banquet. Ho stood to my left, holding a magazine that had been sitting on the chair I now occupied. Why he picked up a year-old English-language magazine I cannot say. Perhaps this was some small bridge into my life. Perhaps there was more relief on his face than pride.

"This is a memento," I said. "There, translate. Please tell him this is a perfect egg." The man with the camera, Mr. Tung, addressed the boy holding the magazine.

I said, "Tell him I'm leaving. Tell him I'm leaving but that I'll be back. I'll be back in six months."

"Will he go with you?" he said.

"He will not," I said. "He stays. Let him go back to his village if he likes."

September. I have taken some time off from writing. You will forgive me, I hope. Over the last month we have toured the aid stations in the surrounding villages and instructed the local staff. We travelled by horse and mule, and there was a fair bit of walking, too. My old Japanese animal came in handy, though his torn and battered hooves have seen better days. The poor beast isn't quite cut out for this terrain of mountain trail and rock slides, and I almost think a lowly burro might be better suited for my purposes.

Yes, of late I have been occupied, mind, spirit and body. There is no rest to be had here. Along with my travels I have also just completed the final draft of a book that will not, alas, provoke literary controversy. It's called *Organization and Technique for Division Field Hospitals in Guerrilla Warfare,* and the good Mr. Tung is now working on the translation full bore. When he's finished it will be printed and widely distributed in under a month by the Regional Government. So you see, busy in body and mind. There simply hasn't been time. My writing, my surgeries, my teaching at the hospital that was once, not so long ago, the Buddhist temple of this polite and desecrated village, threatened to consume me entirely. (We have displaced a large number of hapless monks, by the way—obsequious, soft and annoying men who are certainly not lacking in time, a remarkably aimless lot.)

But now there is at least a break in my routine, and I can return to these pages. Here I sit in this small grey mud-and-brick town of Shin Pei, so similar to the other villages I've occupied over these last twelve or fourteen months, again back at this account of life, war and memory. Patience, please. But the war, the deprivation, the heat, these are factors that send my imagination in all directions. I would be a different man strolling along the Champs-Elysées, with bowler hat and cane. Or bathing at Sunnyside Beach in Toronto. Or boating on that small lake in the Retiro Park. Perhaps one day you will jump into the great Lake Ontario from your father's shoulders. You, a pink little thing, shrieking with all the world's delight. How my heart explodes at the thought! The month is September, somewhere around the sixteenth or seventeenth, I think. With the completion of that witless textbook, basic illustrations included, a space now opens before me at this typewriter, a space I may now fill with thoughts of you, and all I can think about is going home, of meeting you, holding your wiggling body up to the sun.

What is happening back there? I am desperate for news. All I see are San Francisco papers and magazines, a year or two old, used by merchants as wrapping for sugar, tea and cakes. And not even political pages but reviews of Frances Farmer and Cary Grant in *The Toast of New York* and the new Terraplane Coupe automobile. Perhaps one day we shall have such an automobile, you and I, and I shall spirit you about grandly, blowing the horn to the wind.

Tonight the world is consumed by these ravenous mountains. So many are waiting to die. The Japanese noose tightens. Colours drain from the courtyard, from these flowers in their clay pots. The night in her mercy erases all evidence of men. Only voices carry through the dark, but now, hushed, they seem more animal than human. Staring at this page, lost in thought, it's as if I'm looking through my one last window to the world.

Last night, Mr. Tung appeared at my door and said, "If you release the boy from your service he will die."

I stood. "Why do you think that?"

"If he returns to his village, he will die there. Do you know what a House of Consolation is?"

"No," I said. "Not precisely."

"One of these places was set up in his town after the Japanese came. The rest of his family was captured, his mother and two sisters. He lived in the hills outside his town for months, waiting for the Japanese to leave, but sneaked back in at night. He knew it well. It was not so difficult. The Japanese soldiers were easy to fool. He knew enough not to venture out under a moonlit sky. By then the enemy believed they owned the town and had grown complacent. Often the boy went to his house. His father was dead, taken away by the Nationalists years before. He never saw any sign that his mother and sisters had been there looking for him, as he was looking for them, but he left notes in case they came, saying that he was safe and not to worry.

"One night he slipped past a store where an old man had sold goods from faraway cities like Shanghai and Sian. Teas and herbs and medicines. But the storefront had been altered. It had been taken over by the Japanese, like everything else in the village. He did not know its purpose. The sign, in Chinese, said: HALL FOR JAPAN–CHINA FRIEND-SHIP. He told me he looked in the window. It was very late at night, almost morning, in fact. But if the hall required guards, none were stationed here. He imagined it could not be such an important place. And why would a Friendship Hall require guards? He climbed through a window.

"At first he heard nothing. Then the sound of weeping drew him through two rooms to a large warehouse without windows where the old man was said to have stored a car, but the boy had never seen it. It was very dark in the warehouse and he waited for his eyes to adjust. Before long he could see many women tied to their beds, simple boards covered in straw. The women stretched out on them were of different ages, but mostly young, some younger than the boy. There were twenty-two women in all. The boy's mother and two sisters occupied the last three beds to the right. He ran to them and kneeled at his mother's bedside. 'I am here, I can take you away,' he said, 'all of you.' His mother kissed him and began to weep. She told her son to leave. 'They will come soon, at first light,' she said. 'Any minute now. Go quickly.' The men would come with red ticket stubs, she told her son, checked for each visit, allowing them to enter here and choose any one of them. 'Go, please. You cannot see this.' "

Mr. Tung paused.

"He tried to free her. He struggled with the ropes lashing her wrists, but it was no use. He was too frightened and so young. He was fifteen years old. His younger sister began to cry. His mother shushed her. The other women were quiet. They were straining their heads, watching to see what the boy would do. His mother said, 'Listen to me. Go now. Go as far away from this war as you can. Do not return for us. They will capture you. They will think nothing of killing you. Go away from this place.'

"He heard the first men enter the front room of the old man's store. Everyone's head turned. Their loud boots stomped against the wooden floor. Their two voices were businesslike and unrushed. These were the military keepers of the Friendship Hall preparing for a new day. Soon after the morning meal the soldiers bearing their red tickets would stroll over and strip down to their loincloths and wait patiently for the administrators to take their tickets, check the small box that indicated another visit had been made and then admit them through the last door into the warehouse of women.

"The boy begged his mother to let him help her and his sisters, but she said, 'You cannot help us. We are already dead.'

"The sound of soldiers walking and talking began to fill the streets.

The occupied town was awake now. The loud voices of the men approached. As the door to the warehouse opened, the boy slipped under his mother's bed and the men began their selection. He remained frozen under his mother's bed until night fell."

We sat quietly for some time. Afterward, I let Mr. Tung out the door, then lay down on my cot and stared out into the night.

I will come to you. You shall see.

ENVELOPE SEVEN

I have just now been studying my hands, which scarcely resemble the ones I started this journey with. They are more skilled, yes, and as steady as they have always been. Determined, yes. But even if they've aged into the claws of a monster, how could they send this boy back to certain death?

I am exhausted. Sick. My teeth rotten. My eyesight blurred and uncertain. I'm skin and bone, my ribs showing through as clearly as if in an anatomical drawing. If the left ear isn't ringing with the sound of distant artillery, it is completely silent.

I have been thinking about the boy.

Why am I going back? To find out what is happening. To investigate the dithering and procrastinating ways of spineless bureaucrats in New York and Toronto. To rip off some heads, if I must. I was promised funding that is nowhere to be seen. I have received no word from the China Aid Council or the American League for Peace and Democracy. Resolutely, I am off to whip up some trouble and give them a piece of my mind. Despite my bony chest I am ready for a fight. In response to my repeated requests for updates on the absent funding I have received not a word, not a postcard, not a kiss blown to the wind. So I mean to go and find out myself. I shall cross to the other side of Shensi and go down on foot to Yan'an, some five hundred miles. I estimate it will take six weeks; then I'll go on to Chungking and Yunan by way of French Indochina, jump a boat for Hong Kong and buy my way onto a freighter laden with tea and rice bound for Hawaii, the land of my father's timid embrace. Two weeks later, sometime in late February 1940, I will make landfall in San Francisco. A triumphant return. A walk along the beach, perhaps, a bottle and a pretty girl. All innocent, nothing untoward. That is the least they can afford me, an hour or two to gaze back over the bay at sunset. Perhaps I'll become drunk on champagne and sleep till noon in clean sheets up to my chin, smothered by a harem of pillows, and enjoy a three o'clock luncheon at the bar in the near presence of beautiful women and their enterprising young men.

I have already made preparations. I am leaving within two to three weeks. Of course, it will be difficult to abandon this place. And to abandon him, my faithful servant. I am his best hope for surviving this war. I know it and he knows it. But his vulnerability cannot dictate the arc of history. Without me they will likely put a rifle in his hands. The partisans will take him; he'll go of his own accord. A hundred-pound soldier off to protect the Motherland. Last month we celebrated his eighteenth birthday. He is a man now. You wouldn't know it to look at him, but his voice cracked long ago and is oddly deep, even in this nasal language—and so much more incongruous issued from that weak chest. He puffed himself up and recited a poem composed for the occasion. I clapped when everyone else did, then Mr. Tung whispered into my ear, "It tells of the Great Bethune's struggle."

Clever boy, I thought. But which struggle? What would he think of the Great Bethune if he knew of my excitement about returning to America, and without him? Am I allowed such thoughts? Since making my decision I am rejuvenated, helium-inflated, drunk with joy. But is this joy purely for the good work I shall do there? My aim is to raise for this war effort $1,000 per month in gold, and yet the promise of clean sheets, hot roast beef and French wine crowd my heart. What do you think of that, poor Ho? Have I deceived you? What he does not know of me! Yes, a starved man must replenish himself. But there is more. Of course there is. More than anything else, what awaits is you. And it is to you I shall pass this irregular, green-typed stack of petroleum- and lavender-scented archaeology, so that you will have the truth in your hands, come what may. This is my great optimism. This is the calm silence that now greets these eager peasants as I attempt to impart to them the basic laws and practice of sanitation, physiology and biology. This is the joy that fills me as I walk silently to my brick-and-mud shack after sixteen hours of surgery, rest my aching elbows on this desk and roll another sheet into the machine— the first clack, the ringing imprint upon the refreshed ribbon, like a small stinging bullet. Is life so good that I am to be provided a second chance? Will I find you? Will you love me as a child loves her father? Can I love you, an unknown existence so close to my own? Does a family await, after all? I must finish this story before I can know.

But now, you ask, am I too happy dreaming of a homecoming and champagne to remember the festering wounds and lice and horror of this place? Am I too enamoured of thunderous, admiring applause to step back into the lion's jaws? No. With my joy comes renewed energies. I step back into it. You see, you power my heart. You enliven me. By now, what is it I have left to prove?

We returned to the front, at Hua Ta, on the banks of the T'ang River, and there set up shop, our workhouse of small miracles, in an old farmhouse that had been cleared out and prepared for our arrival on the orders of an intellectual-looking regimental commander by the name of Jao. He was a small man who wore a pair of round black-rimmed glasses on his small nose and walked with an untidy rolling limp in his left leg, making it seem as if he'd been caught in an invisible surge of water that pulled forever to the left. When I received word of an impending attack I decided that this would be the last of my daredevil overland crossings before setting out for the other side of Shensi and Yunan and my glorious homecoming.

When our team arrived, poor Ho by then dragging his feet, I conducted an inspection of the building and surrounding facilities, then presented myself to the hobbled commander to pass along a list of our requirements. He read through the list, the good man, and handed it to his assistant with instructions that I be provided with all we needed. He then informed me to expect casualties within six hours. I returned to the farmhouse–aid station to oversee the preparations and quickly ate a bowl of rice provided by Ho, along with a pot of tea. On the stone wall of the house, sitting over my emptied plate, I studied the formal portrait of the family that had once lived here, or so I supposed. They were a hungry-looking lot, a mother and father and three small children smiling with rehearsed conviction and dressed in their Sunday village best. I wondered what foods they could have put in their mouths for the price of that professional photograph and those crisply pleated fabrics. They were, unfortunately, nowhere to be seen in the village. Like so many others they had been pushed from their home and now, very likely, were more skeletal than ever.

When the wounded began to arrive I believed the flow might never stop. It was a large assault consisting of three regiments. For three days we did not rest, the wounded coming in a steady torrent. We ate standing as the next casualty was laid before us. The sharp autumn air, this high up, tingled on my fingertips. My nose, ever active, always alert to the morbid fecal smells of a nicked bowel, rejoiced in the mountain breeze that lifted the curtain of that refugee family's home. We worked. We ate. We slept in ten-minute intervals. As time moved forward it began, too, to move backward. I stumbled. I began to dream. In these waking dreams I imagined this family. When I saw a small girl's head encased in the stone wall, unconscious though smiling, a syringe held like a rose in her teeth, I put my own head in a bucket of ice water.

On the second day, treating a badly broken leg, I was using a chisel that had been taken from a farmhouse near Chi Huei two or three months back. Imagine the creator of, among other instruments, the

Bethune Rib Shears humbling himself with a lowly carpenter's chisel. But I—always adapting, innovating—had discovered certain properties in its construction that proved beneficial for my work. It was nicely weighted and its hardwood handle could withstand long and frequent bouts of boiling, for disinfecting. Primarily, though, it was the tempered steel, forged in Belgium, that made it so useful in cutting through and shaving off bone. How this tool had travelled so far I couldn't say, but I am glad it did. When I get out of this war you will not find it in my black bag of doctor's instruments, yet it has proved highly useful over the months. On that particular day, however, this chisel that had sat so comfortably in my hand for so long jumped off the splintered femur of the unconscious man beneath me and dug into the middle finger of my left hand.

One of the nurses quickly disinfected and wrapped the cut. Hindered, but not grievously so, I tidied up the amputation, put my head in a refreshed bucket of cold water and then, an hour later, had a second nurse re-dress the wound. As she did so I sent Ho for a candle and had him melt it down. He presented the melted wax to me in a rice bowl which, oddly enough, bore a small illustration of a flamingo, and I bathed the wrapped finger in the wax so as to seal it against infection. Another inspiration, really. Luxury of luxuries. This was as close as I'd come to wearing rubber gloves in longer than I could remember. Bandaged like a lollipop, the waxed finger was awkward and heavy, and for the rest of the day I might as well have worked with only the right hand. The following day, after three hours' rest, when I examined my wound, the cut looked fine. But halfway through the morning I decided I couldn't continue like this. I peeled the wax off the finger and got back to work.

This morning I awoke from a dream. It was of the morning the *Empress* set sail. From the height of the promenade deck, Jean and Charles had been enjoying the view of the dockyards and the city beyond, leaning over the rails, I suppose pretending they had their own send-off party down there, smiling and waving. I attempted to push myself forward into the excitement of the moment but I felt a weight on my chest. After a minute or two I excused myself and went below decks to find my cabin. But when I inserted my key and pushed the door open, the room was occupied.

Your mother, in the form of the painting I'd made of her at the Santander, was sitting on the bed. In it her shoulders were covered by a blanket, and she smiled.

I touched my hand to the painting. When I did, her face began to disappear, the paint coming off like dust under my hand until only the canvas remained.

When I awoke in the pre-dawn morning of the fourth day, only two days ago, Ho looked at me with concern. My body was trembling from lack of sleep. He himself looked unwell in the struggling light of the small stove-fire he'd set in the far corner of that one-room house to warm my tea. Then Mr. Tung stepped inside.

"What news have you heard?" I asked. Ho handed me my tea. I sat sipping, both hands shaking.

"Only that they're near," Mr. Tung said.

"How near?" The tea spilled. "Another cup, Ho."

"They will be here soon," Mr. Tung said. "Before midday. We are falling back."

The limp-footed regimental commander summoned me to his quarters and said the line had collapsed. He praised our work, thanking me personally, and then ordered our return to the Base Hospital at Yang Chia Chuang. He saluted, turned and parted, that leftward tide pulling at his body more strongly than ever. Straight-backed, I returned along the dirt path to the farmhouse–aid station. As the rose-coloured sunlight began to warm the western face of the distant Mo-t'ien Mountains, I felt an unusual buoyancy take hold. I felt almost euphoric. Then, entering the building I again saw, and for the last time, the strange face of that dead child framed by the perfect construction of fallen stone that contained her. I stopped to study her. She made a lovely picture. But now she was dead. What Capa might have done with her! I thought. What lasting images he could have produced, those hardened veins reanimated with silver nitrate and mercury, bathed in his alchemist's bath and introduced to the world as another anthemic tribute to the horror of war. Yes, he was a famous man. Relentless. Driven by the beauty of conviction. "You," I said. "Yes, you."

The dead girl opened her eyes. "Me?" she said.

Visions of children bricked into standing walls notwithstanding, I am well. Do you doubt my sanity? These spells shall pass. It is overwork, my dear. Physical exhaustion, nothing more. So what do I do in the meantime, as I wait out these small hallucinations? They are no more than a dizzy inconvenience. What do I do? I wonder about you. I wonder what might have been. I wonder what you will make of this history. Will you permit me the idea, the fantasy, that one day, as an older woman perhaps, you will turn these pages with forgiving sighs? The very name, the Border Regions, for all its portent, for all its distant mystery, connotes ambiguity, possibility, breadth. Will I benefit in this undeclared realm? Where certainty fades can there be rejuvenation? Does forgiveness live here in this unknowable terrain? Yet this wide landscape is really only the one small chair that holds me, this one small house. This could be anywhere. Can you see the bejewelled monster that crawls into my dreams as I sleep? Do you share the same monsters? Mornings aboard the *Empress,* those distant brief mornings with small Alicia, that lovely child, and the poems her aunt read to us while I painted return to me often:

Among twenty snowy mountains,
The only moving thing
Was the eye of the blackbird.

I wonder now if there could be a more desolate poem, or a quieter life, than that of a poet who brings silence down so absolutely upon an entire mountain range with fourteen simple words. Perhaps this is why I find it comforting, this illusion of company that writing to you now affords me. These words, though hacked and banged out on this old machine, though so crude compared to those of an artist, bring you here to these Border Regions, where I no longer own my past but instead offer it to you. You see, these words mark you as present. With them I can place, see and touch you. You are whole. And in some ways, as I write this I, too, am whole. I find wonder and warmth, and if this world I now occupy lacks anything it is those two dreams of wonder and warmth. You are my last opportunity; you are the moving eye of the blackbird.

Will I place this package in your young hand and say, "Wait till you are older"?

The question is this: When will you be old enough to understand me, yet still young enough to forgive?

The war exists. It is a raven hanging in the clouds over Tu Ping Ti and over the whole of this magnificent land. It picks at holes in the stomach and strips of unclaimed flesh. Tired, I ask myself what difference one man can make. On a beautiful autumn night. I wonder how I ever got it into my head that I might hold down every man who refuses to offer his blood. Can I teach the world how things should be done? Can I change the ways of these people, so backward and noble? Yet those questions pose another: Could I bear to be away from this place? The answer is no. Of course not. But that isn't good enough. There is no real answer.

I pick at the truth like some weakened bird of prey.

With each page I can't help but think I reduce myself yet another degree in your estimation. Why? Perhaps I can't stop myself now. Will you hang on long enough? Have I nothing left to recommend me? Perhaps I know in my heart of hearts that you will never lay eyes on your father's words. Has this solitude led me so wide from my original path that I'm afraid to say what I set out to do? Which was what—to sway you? Elicit forgiveness? Embolden myself? Record the facts? Now none of this matters. The enemy encircles us, bearing down from the north, east, south and west. Their hungry machines eat away at this small oasis with each passing day. The noose closes.

Yet here I am. More important is my desire to surround myself with the thick blanket of these memories. Only that. I wait for these hours of escape. It warms me, this simple act of memory and reconstruction. I am sustained. I have a voice in this silent land. I return to this darkened house chilled and hungry but almost peaceful. Every night it's the same. A lonely man's imagined dialogue with the portraits of you and your mother. On occasions when the war becomes everything, I can hear myself and the anger in my voice, the exhausted frustration. Then I stop writing, alarmed that I'm talking only to myself. Is the great Bethune talking to himself? Is this what I have become? Does Ho listen? Does he scurry off to find Mr. Tung to aid in his eavesdropping? I go days without uttering anything but barked commands and threats of discipline. I send people from my sight like an enraged schoolmaster. Even my own voice sounds strange to me now, as do the things that bring me pleasure. Steamed potatoes mixed with eggs and sugar, for example. This is Ho's current specialty, which he brings to me wearing the proud face of a master chef. He really is something. This morning, though, I thought I detected a smirk of recognition not very well camouflaged by a smile. The nerve! I think. The little bastard. The servant poisons his king. Is that what these dizzy spells amount to? What secret does he throw into this hash?

I imagined the terror that would have plagued your mother as she bore down upon that struggling mass within her, knowing that once her body had completed its birthing she would be wheeled out and placed against a wall, or shot there in her bed, still with the warmth of your exit burning on her flesh. It was unimaginable. I could imagine nothing else. It possessed my thoughts. I stood at my hotel window and watched New York City below, wandering in my mind through the maze of possibilities. It was a world of indifference I saw below me, both to the death of your mother and to the war that claimed her. It was one and the same, a tragic absurdity that these people simply didn't matter. If the death was not in your house, you didn't bother with it; if death was busy elsewhere, all the better. I could not tolerate these images flooding over me. I imagined the agony of your birth, which your mother knew would signal her own death.

I know now how unjust were my first thoughts toward you, the result of a madness that took hold of my vile heart.

How can I even write them now? Only with the belief that you will never see this. Only with the comforting thought that I will fail in this task and my secrets will remain.

When a child is born we offer expressions of joy, hearty handshakes, even the odd cigar. Here is evidence of nature's generosity, this simple miracle providing an opportunity to live one's life over again and to correct one's errors and to embrace what one failed to cherish the first time around. These are thoughts a man might possess in normal times, but I felt only the terror of your mother's last days. For me, this was the embodiment of that betrayal of Spain.

I could not drive these thoughts away. For months they tormented me. From New York to Seattle, to Vancouver, then on board the *Empress* and finally into the vastness of this land, I was a man haunted by the terrible fact that I could feel rage against the innocent child whom I'd left behind.

I imagined it again and again. Your mother glancing over her shoulder as the door swung open. This at the Alemana, at our table. Were these the men who would take her away that last time while I carried my film between Montreal and Toronto?

Was I staring up at that documentary and thinking of your dear mother when they pulled you from her womb?

This is how I see it. The murderers released her after that first detention, allowing her back out into the world to lead her tormentors into a buzzing hive of plotters.

The Alemana tavern was busy by nine o'clock. The pale-yellow plaster walls were trimmed with dark oak and hung with cinema and bullfight posters. The zinc bar ran perpendicular to the street, with white dishes of cheese, sardines and olives, baskets of bread covered by a damp cloth.

By now the news of Bethune's ouster is old news. Pitcairn knows of the embarrassment. And he knows well enough, too, that his association with the woman sitting before him might facilitate his own speedy repatriation. Perhaps he'll go to New York, where his press credentials won't be revoked for talking with a Swedish national of dubious allegiances. I imagine his kind mouth twisting as he listens.

"I'm tired," she says, "I'm always tired now."

This perhaps is when she first mentions the tenacious pregnancy, the one believed at first to have been terminated as a consequence of a vigorous pace up a steep mountain trail.

His eyes narrow, the first question marked by the entrance of another trio of drinkers. "Does he know?"

"No. And he won't. He thinks the child—"

"I'm leaving for England next week. If I could get word to him—"

"He knows as much as he needs to know. If anything happens to me—"

"Nothing will happen. Go to France. Leave tonight."

"If anything happens—"

"Nothing will happen if you leave."

"If it does, take the baby. They won't hurt the baby."

She pushes her chair back. Its wooden paws drag loudly over the stone and sawdust floor. Heads turn. Beside them sits a young couple, infinitely less complicated, innocent as birds, really, silenced by this start. She rises and walks across the room. She might just be showing now, but hiding it cleverly under a loose sweater. Her friend, the newly appointed guardian, wonders if it could possibly come to that, a woman as formidable as this embarrassed by an unwelcome pregnancy.

Then, two months later, another round-up. Did she lead them to anyone? Those men, the same bunch who'd picked me up, by now would have grown bored. Were they surprised to see the growth in her belly? The little spy Bethune had left behind. The Communist's son or daughter. What negotiations would have ensued? We will spare your child, just tell us some names. Your child shall be looked after. Only some names for the sake of the child, no? We will wait for the child to come. Your child buys you three, maybe four weeks of life. The child of a miracle-worker, a good Communist. But you, we're not so sure of. Only a few names and perhaps it will see its father one day. Together they will remember you. Your legacy in exchange for a few names.

I knew nothing of this. I thought you'd died in the hills above Segovia. I knew only my anger. I'd been pushed out of Spain. I made do with what remained.

With that propaganda under my arm, I toured North America like some tweed-suited evangelist, eloquent, righteous, unforgiving—the very picture of my father. It was my rage that carried me. I didn't know what was happening back there. I had no contact with anyone. I had no idea where your mother had gone. The letters I wrote her in care of the Santander disappeared, swallowed by the war.

I presented that film in auditoriums, union halls, arenas, churches and theatres across Canada and America, and then, exhausted by my own righteousness, slipped back to brood quietly in the dark and watch how those scenes, so familiar, so devastating, played before the eyes of enraged Montreal, shocked Toronto, indignant New York, sympathetic Chicago. I was a huckster of ideals, nothing more, a travelling one-man circus, an itinerant used-car salesman. This was how I attempted to ease the anguish after my humiliating defeat. By working. By fighting harder.

Every night for four months I stared up at images of the opportunity that had been denied me, the place where I could do the most good, the war that so quickly became the symbol of my infamy, considering this black-and-white testimony the lasting document of my shame. And after the lights came up I would again rise to address the audience in the practised preacher's tones that could barely contain the anger mistaken every night for my seething hatred of Fascism and a passion for democracy.

Every day I arrived in or departed from a new town. Every presentation was as draining as if it were my last, me gasping as if I breathed with only one lung. I was a husk. I wrote nothing but pained letters to your mother. Painted nothing. I stayed half drunk. Thought of nothing but the treachery that had befallen me, of the Brutuses who'd slain me with their lies and conspiracies. I brooded, how I brooded. But was the focus of the hatred that had united Sise and Sorensen in cowardice to denounce me to the Party simply that they didn't like my methods? Imagine being surrounded by fallen neighbourhoods and screaming, dying children while your peers, these petty bureaucrats, are satisfied with nothing more than a gentle demeanour, a soft touch, the obsequiousness of an apprentice waiter. You will not find that here, I guarantee it, not in China!

There were occasions, I believed, when the audience sensed this moral panic, when, judging from the empty shine of the collection plates, I felt they'd seized upon my collapse—after the last drop of blood had been drained from my body, my lungs crushed with the effort and passion of my speech—by making donations that were nothing less than an insult to every man, woman and child in Spain and, above all, to me. And so here it was in Sudbury, northern Ontario, so close to the fields of my youth, that I was roundly snubbed, ignored and belittled by a crowd of seven hundred whose generosity totalled $22.40. $22.40! Did they know the true nature of my raging? Had the rumours already begun? I paced nervously back-stage as these blackguards mingled, surely sniggering at my public shame.

What does a man do in this circumstance? Or when he's trapped in the mud with a wounded comrade? He fights back. He lifts the man upon his shoulder and returns him to safety. He does not accept his fate. He argues for it. He fights. He walks stiffly back to the podium and berates the hundreds who remain for their petty selfishness, their adipose greed, their Fascist sympathies. Yes, this is what I did—that man I barely recognize now, whose breathless audacity shocks me still. He retakes centre stage and announces to the departing crowd's embarrassment that Spain is nothing if not the staging ground for the gathering war in Europe that shall consume the lives of our sons and daughters. The insult of $22.40 shall for-ever be connected to this miserable village! Spain is not simply a war of principle to suit your caprices, and it shall not be denigrated with the small change of a panhandler. This war is being waged deeply within each of us, and for each of us the enemy—in case you weren't listening the first time—is our darker nature, our selfishness, our comfortable denials. This is a struggle to restore man to his noble self! And on I went before that fearful, shocked crowd, rant-ing feverishly, and perhaps half drunk, I don't recall. But up the ante I did.

Ship. Plane. Automobile. Each journey was the same, yet each des-tination offered the slightest glimmer of hope. Would it be in Quebec, or the Maritimes, in Chicago, or in the towns and cities of California, on the Prairies, or in British Columbia that the film would speak in a new voice and transform itself into a kind of love story—to set the record straight and right the wrong? I waited and each time listened to the opening, always crushingly the same and, as I was myself, unable to be transformed into something more.

Your mother appears once in the documentary, a beautiful face caught for a moment, laughing in joyous union with the fighting men and women of Castile. Is it a party? A victory celebration? Was your mother giddy with love?

And then the painting, like a man on a stretcher, being evacuated from the Prado.

The delusional rage left me, for a time, in Toronto. Here I was the returning hero, a god fallen from the clouds but still god-like as he walks through the crowds and is lifted upon strong backs in triumphal celebration. How lovely it was, and how schizophrenic. Upon my arrival at Toronto's Union Station I was greeted by a sea of five thousand working men and women who waved me on as our car motored up Yonge Street to Queen's Park, where I mounted a makeshift stage and delivered my pronouncements from Europe. But a week later it was back to the same pleading anger, the same thinly disguised passions, the same pathetic wanderings.

And then, in January, I sat down in a hotel bar in New York with Pitcairn.

He told me of you and how I'd find you.

The evening casts magic over my village, this fairy-tale idyll of Asia—a spell of coppery light. The stream in the valley below rushes blindly on, its slashing music slipping up to the ears of the child soldiers who sit perched on the moist rock, its current cleansing the blood from these mountains.

Will the passage of time likewise wash the thought of you from my memories? Will the advancing months reduce these passions to shadows?

A surgeon in a theatre of war, I am accustomed to failure and the numbing effects of relentless slaughter. This cannot be overstated. Once upon a time, I walked through the night reciting favourite poems, in hopes of unburdening myself of a drudgery I could barely survive but which only hinted at the terror to come. Now I sit here content, polishing these fragments of memory in an attempt to make something of a life pitted by failure, abandonment and war. This is the one perfection remaining for me after a lifetime of compromise and fallen ideals. No, these musings shall not diminish that which is lost. You cannot fail in memory as you can, so horribly, in the operating theatre.

One hundred and four degrees at 6:45 a.m. I am with the Tenth Regiment. I don't know the name of this village but do not think it matters. The bustle of men is all around. Their calls to attention have awakened me, the cocking of rifles, the march of purposeful boots. We have been travelling for some time now, two or three days, I think, from village to village, with me largely unconscious, I am told, like a warm corpse upon its restless catafalque. Even when conscious I have been too ill to admire this vast kingdom. Perhaps I should let China take care of me for a change. A charming thought, being pampered. This is a situation I should learn from. It might help me become a better doctor. At least I can derive something from these wasted days. Illness is not anything I have ever been resigned to. Its pathetic, wheezing ways suit some, but not me.

How poorly I take instruction. I already knew that. It is not so comfortable here as it was at the Trudeau Sanatorium so many years ago, drinking and smoking and riding boats on the lake. Sickness as holiday—how good that seems now in the light of memory. We sat out on the porch gazing at the dark pines every night, remembering our freedom and health, if we weren't leaning against the bar at Brook's Tavern. I was tended to by admiring nurses. In my frailty, as the TB spiders nested in my lung, I organized lectures and prepared to take on the world. To think of that now. How sweet that sickness, how luxurious.

I am told five days have passed now since our return from that farmhouse–aid station. How I miss my typewriter. The ribbon's completely dry. Ho is unable to work his magic out here. We will have to wait for that. I miss the green letters and the scent of your mother's perfume. In the meantime, I hope you can make out this chicken-scratch. Ho has found me this stub of pencil and a small stack of writing paper, stolen from some functionary's desk, I suppose. Always scrounging, if not one thing then another. Now he stands at the entrance of the tent.

I have instructed the supervising medical officer to inform me if any abdominal or skull cases arrive. Even in this state, weakened but alert, I am the only one qualified. Perhaps I will drip this fever onto the hearts of my wounded comrades. The poetry is dire, I know, but there is something to it, you see, this suffering shared by comrades-at-arms. Blood and sweat. We shall rise again. This is not the first finger I have cut open during a surgery. I have sliced the heart out of the truth.

I am off soon to America with this badge of courage, and with my signed confession for you. If a lack of courage forces me to send this package in care of Frank Pitcairn, you will at least have it, long after I've retreated again from your life. I will defend myself no longer. The story speaks for itself. I already abandoned you once. And the first time is always the most difficult.

The absurd intrudes upon the absurd. Yes, acts of bravery there are. Every day for close to two years I have closed the eyes of men who performed such acts, perhaps despite themselves, and paid with their lives. I only wish my hands had been clean enough to leave unmarked the last touch of dignity on their faces, not smearing them with blood or worse. But no man is brave, not really. No sane or wise man. He is only running.

I did not tell you. When we returned from our latest tour I found the door to my house standing ajar. Sitting at my desk was the famous photographer Mr. Friedmann—Mr. Capa, otherwise known as the Shark. "Don't look so surprised," he said. "You're not that difficult to track down in this oversized country. How was it out there? It looks like you took a thrashing. The Japs get hold of you or something?"

"You've come to bring the dead back to life, have you?"

He said, "You look bloody awful. You'd better sit." He got up, but I didn't move. He shrugged, as if to put me at ease, and motioned to the half-finished portrait on my desk. "You're a bit of an artist, I see," he said. "Will wonders never cease?"

"What do you want?"

"We're not so different, really," he said.

"I'm not so sure that's true."

"You don't feel like a vulture sometimes?"

I said, "The death of high standards. You started with a good dose of it yourself. But neither of us is here for the reason you might expect. You can't really fight a war for the right reason. There never is a right reason. There's always something else—a lover, a death, revenge. Look at Ansell's man, the Nazi who saved five thousand Chinese. Life for life. A noble man, you'd think, right?"

I sat down on the floor.

"I'll come back. You look bloody awful, old man. But I'll bet you saved a dozen lives today." He helped me up and put me in my bed. "I inquired in Hankou," he said. "They say you're leaving."

"Soon."

"What is it?"

"I'll be better tomorrow," I said.

"Afterwards you won't need your boy, right?"

"He stays. When I go, he stays."

"I told you about my idea, didn't I?"

I said, "Ho Tzu-hsin is not a child soldier. He is a valet. A servant boy. He cooks and cleans."

"You know he'll become a soldier when you leave. I will follow him. My idea is complete in this way. An entire journey is a beautiful idea."

"I am not his father," I said. "He does as he likes."

"And that's why you can leave. He could live at least a while longer. Likely he'd already be dead if it weren't for you. You gave him a year, a year and a half. That's more than most of them get up here."

I said, "You will put your camera on him and wait for him to die."

"I'm filming this war. If that is the case, then I will film it."

"You're interested in watching a boy die. The instant of death, and then you go."

"He may survive. We can't be so certain."

"Go back to Spain, Capa."

He said, "That war is dead for me. Sooner or later all good causes die."

"At least we have that in common."

"Stay here, Bethune," he said, "for as long as you can. As long as something is left here for you."

"There is nothing."

"Isn't the boy something?"

"Take him," I said. "Make your film."

He walked to the door. "Maybe you should get some rest, old man."

Travelling these last days with the Third Regiment Sanitary Service on stretcher and mule-back, I'm bounced over this rocky Chinese land-scape like a bucket of snails.

This morning I again saw him, the boy studying one of my draw-ings. I was shivering in my cot, soaked by my feverish chills, and he, standing in the grey light, shining like some lucent dream-creature.

It shall be only days now before I am working again. I'm feeling better this morning, bright and alert. I have sent Ho off for another handful of Aspirin and a pot of coffee to help thin my blood. This should speed my recovery. Also he carries another message to the staff that I must be informed of any abdominal or skull cases. When I'm recovered I will catch up with Capa, wherever he's gone, snapping photographs to send out to the world, to tell him he cannot have the boy. The boy is mine. I have decided he will come with me to America. The face of Chinese youth. The innocence, the purity. He will be worth more to the cause there, in Bethune's Travelling Circus, than here. You shall meet the boy, my dear. You'll see what a noble youth he is. Perhaps he'll hold you in his arms. Perhaps he'll recite a poem for you. You will love him, surely. The abandoned children united. You see, we all have this in common. Behold this child, for you are he. Forgotten by all who loved him, then taken up in the great fraternal arms of this noble cause. How pleased the poster boy of the Chinese Revolution will be.

I have decided to talk with him. I will warn him that he must not be immortalized like one of his poems, by that photographer. I'll tell him to keep close to Mr. Tung until I'm well.

What could Capa do with little Ho? He prefers the Spanish face, after all, and I have never seen a more Chinese face! Under my arm and protection Ho will be an inspiration to future generations. Do you want to be worth more to the cause dead than alive? Your life's worth far more than that. You shall come to America! America awaits! The youth of the West shall learn from your example.

But not before I have an opportunity to ask some questions of him. Of course, my questions. I saw him studying my drawings again, last night after I finally blew out my lamp.

I must be informed of skull and abdominal cases.

I have been working on your portrait as I while away this sick time. I am inspired, electrified. How my energy has returned to me, for brief moments, at least. You are my tonic, my hope. Does that sound desperate? It is the truth. Now I shall go back in time and cross out all these odd ramblings that have escaped my feverish mind. I do not want to present a bad first impression. It seems I have been off my head these last few days. An elegant diagnosis, I know. But I am pleased to say I'm feeling better on this, the sixth day of this difficult stretch. The uncontrolled vomiting has left me weakened. But I am bright now, more than ever, and alert. The night was an improvement, and today the temperature, 102 degrees, is down somewhat.

This morning I asked after Capa. "Mr. Tung," I said, "where has he gone?" Mr. Tung was leaning over me, cooling my forehead with a wet towel. I waved him away. "Will you answer?"

At length, the delicate Mr. Tung said, "There is no photographer here, Doctor. We are alone."

"Has he taken the boy?"

Mr. Tung left my bedside. Without another word he left me.

When I awoke hours later I found this machine here, placed on a small stool beside the bed. I have been typing for some time now, perhaps hours, recounting what has transpired over these last few days. Did Mr. Tung bring it to me? Was this an apology for his rudeness? Or was it Ho, atoning for his strange behaviour? They will not answer my questions, but neither will they silence me. I shall not be silenced. Not here. Not in America. My ribbon is refreshed, though the ink is slightly off. Closer to blue than green now. You can see it. Yes, it must have been him. Blue is fine, I shall tell him. Don't be so cagey, boy!

I have rallied and I am sitting upright. Look, that wasn't so difficult. This thing sits comfortably on my skinny thighs. I feel the pop-pop of the keys resonate down into the femur. Writing on the bone. What a lovely metaphor to think about.

When I get to America I will show you my paintings and drawings, long after all this is done with. They are much better than these small doodles.

You know, I finished your mother's portrait the day I departed from Madrid. Did I tell you that? I wish you could have seen it. It was taken, along with my other belongings, from that stalled train in Goasi. Perhaps it will be returned to me one day, and you will see how beautiful she is. Of course, you can see that in my documentary, too. But film cannot capture the love of an artist. You will see how much I loved her.

How different it will be once we have won this war! I will show you more than the sketches buried under these green ramblings. Might something good come out of America after this? Has the war in Europe begun? Are you now safely growing to girlhood in a Stockholm neighbourhood? Or still in Madrid where Pitcairn told me I'd find you? Isn't that war finished?

I will have Ho help with my paintings and drawings. Where is he? He'll pack them up for me. And Mr. Tung, when he finishes with his translations. Perhaps I shall bring some along and leave them for you to look over when you are older, when Europe and America have come to help the war here. These mountains will only be a memory by then. I will know you. Perhaps I can visit you often. You'll be as beautiful as your mother. Wouldn't it be grand to see your mother and father together? We could walk along a riverbank holding hands. You'd enjoy that. *For if they fall, the one will lift up his fellow: but woe to him that is alone when he falleth; for he hath not another to help him up.* I have to leave my bed to find the boy, so will leave off here. Does he mean for the failing doctor to come crawling? Well, then, so be it. I will get up and march onwards. But I am tired. The doctor is tired. I will lie down here for a moment. I can get back to this soon enough. Perhaps I will tell Ho to soak this ribbon in the meantime. I see it's beginning to fade already. Where is he? Has he already started off to America? Those hills are too much for just one boy. I can take him on my shoulders. Are there any abdominal cases? I will stroll past the hospital for a look before we set off.

I hear the boy coming now. I know that lively step. I'll bet he's saying one of those old poems. A poem for you, perhaps.

How these hands tremble. There is still so much more to tell. As I write this I'm imperishable. I am completely here. Please know that. It pains me to leave these pages now. But I have to rest. How I am looking forward to completing this history. As you read this I'm radiant. We will be radiant together. Something tells me this can be a beautiful story after all. But first I will rest.

19 Dec 1939
Yan'an, Shensi Province

Comrade Mao Tse-tung
Chairman of the Central Soviet Government

Esteemed Chairman,

While the writings contained herein represent personal
histories that may be of interest to certain family members
of Doctor Bethune, this committee has found that they
cannot be used to serve the People in their struggle against
the Japanese Imperialist invaders or the Nationalist
Kuomintang Army. It must be stressed that, although the
Doctor's personal efforts in the Border Regions of Shensi
and Hopei provinces were exemplary and highly beneficial
to the Communist cause, it is also clear that certain of his
actions and beliefs can be viewed as less than exemplary of
and likely harmful to the Communist ideal, as it is so clearly
and inspiringly detailed in the Chairman's own political
writings. It is the considered opinion of this committee,
consisting of the undersigned, that Doctor Bethune's value
as a symbol of the rightness of this struggle would be
significantly reduced if these writings came to light. It is

recommended, therefore, that these seven envelopes remain untranslated from the original and sealed for the interim and that they be reopened and considered for translation only at the conclusion of a Communist victory, at such time as Doctor Bethune's importance as an international symbol of China's Marxist-Leninist Revolution is past and the historical and personal value of this memoir becomes its primary interest.

The various belongings of Doctor Bethune also recovered—including personal articles such as toiletries, the memoir herein recorded, and clothing, thirteen books and pamphlets, one painting of a girl (perhaps the seagull-child) and numerous drawings, one Remington 5 portable typewriter, seven maps (personally annotated) and various other medical and political pamphlets and treatises—may be examined by a separate committee regarding their propagandistic and/or historical value. It is recommended that if no appropriate committee can be formed at this time all articles be kept for a later date.

In conclusion, the committee finds that only with significant editing and rewriting will the Bethune memoir be suitable for translation and printing for wide-scale distribution. It is advisable that these documents remain sealed until that time. However, given the revolutionary and international importance of Doctor Bethune's life, a brief, more idealized biography or political eulogy of the subject might prove extremely beneficial to the present war effort, and find continuity in the larger canon of the Chairman's political and philosophical writings.

With comradely salutations,

Lu Ting-yi,
Director of the Propaganda Department of the
    Central Committee of the Chinese Communist
    Party, Yan'an

Major Szu Ping Ti,
translator, Propaganda Department, CCP

Lieutenant Tung Yueh-ch'ien,
interpreter for Dr. Bethune, Eighth Route Army

Zhou Erfu,
Lu Hsun Academy of Literature and Arts

Jean Ewen,
surgical nurse, Fung Yiu King Hospital,
    Hong Kong

ACKNOWLEDGEMENTS

While the central character in this novel is based on the Canadian doctor who served in Spain and China in the 1930s, the aesthetic concerns of storytelling often outweighed the more standard historical versions of the Bethune story. The same must be said of the other characters in this novel. They are based only loosely on actual characters who passed through Bethune's life or, in some cases, are completely imagined. The character of Kajsa von Rothman, however, is not my invention. Very little is known of her but for the suspicions that she inspired in Republican wartime Madrid. A 1937 government report makes it clear that von Rothman was officially suspect, and that her intimate relationship with Bethune, a high-profile Communist, was cause for concern. On January 4, 1937, all members of Bethune's staff at the Vergara Street address, including Bethune himself, were taken into custody for questioning. One of these men, an Austrian by the name of Harturg, is said to have been executed. Bethune and von Rothman were both released. Despite his great accomplishments in Spain, Bethune left that country under a dark cloud. Von Rothman's fate is not known.

In particular I am indebted to Larry Hannant's *The Politics of Passion: Norman Bethune's Writing and Art,* for bringing this history to my attention; Roderick Stewart's *Bethune,* for the outline of Bethune's life and the chronology of his travels in China; Mary Larratt Smith's *Prologue to Norman: The Canadian Bethunes,* for the family genealogy; Dave Love's *The Second Battle of Ypres, April 1915*; and W. H. Auden and Christopher Isherwood's *Journey to a War,* for their first-hand look at China at war.

I would also like to acknowledge the support of the Canada Council and the Ontario Arts Council, the staff at the Toronto Reference Library and the generosity of Beatrice Monti della Corte of the Santa Maddalena Foundation.

The newspaper clipping describing the re-taking of Teruel is as reported in *The Manchester Guardian,* January 8, 1938.

A NOTE ON THE TYPE

This book was set in Minion, a typeface produced by the Adobe Corporation specifically for the Macintosh personal computer, and released in 1990. Designed by Robert Slimbach, Minion combines the classic characteristics of old-style faces with the full compliment of weights required for modern typesetting.

Composed by Creative Graphics,
Allentown, Pennsylvania
Printed and bound by Berryville Graphics,
Berryville, Virginia